'Thea?' Daniel moved forward, then stopped himself. 'Thea, what's happened?'

Thea dropped her hands down and looked at him. 'Cora found out this morning that the CPS might have to drop the case and she took it really badly.'

Daniel glanced away for a moment. 'And?'

'She was in a terrible state!' Her voice broke and was thick with tears. 'Phil said she ran out of the office almost hysterical, he tried to go after her but . . .'

'Oh God, Thea, I'm so sorry.'

'You're sorry?' she cried. 'You do it just for the money, you destroy her and you're sorry?'

'Where is she?' Daniel asked. 'What's happened to her?'

'That's just it! We don't know!' She looked at him and he longed to touch her. 'Cora has disappeared,' Thea said, 'and the state she was in, God knows what might have happened to her.'

INDECENT ACT

Maria Barrett

WARNER BOOKS

A *Warner* Book

First published in Great Britain in 1999
by Little, Brown and Company
This edition published by Warner Books in 2000

Copyright © Maria Barrett, 1999

The moral right of the author has been asserted.

A CIP catalogue record for this book
is available from the British Library.

ISBN 0 7515 2478 6

Typeset by Palimpsest Book Production Limited,
Polmont, Stirlingshire
Printed and bound in Great Britain by
Clays Ltd, St Ives plc

Warner Books
A Division of
Little, Brown and Company (UK)
Brettenham House
Lancaster Place
London WC2E 7EN

For William, Lily and Edward,
with love

Acknowledgements

Thank you firstly to the team: to William who has garnished my reputation by telling his small friends that Mummy doesn't write children's books, she writes *adult* fiction; to Lily who provides the perfect research material for emotional complexity; and to Edward who has been a very good sleeper. My thanks to Emma who manages these three and me and much more. As always I am indebted to her for her kindness and love to the children, without which I couldn't work.

Thank you to my dear friend, Simon Waley, for all his legal help, working through the storyline, fine tuning my research and getting it right. Thank you also to Detective Sergeant Del Cuff of the Crawley Child Protection Team for his help with my research. I was impressed by his professionalism and sensitivity to the whole issue of rape and his hard work in changing the way that sex crimes are dealt with by the police. Any mistakes are mine. Thank you to Ellie Goodson for her knowledge and insight into the world of stripping; to Helen Anderson, a great job as always; to Barbara Boote for her continued support and enthusiasm for how and what I write; and to Mic Cheetham, my agent.

Finally, thank you to my Mum, who is always there for me, to June and Pat who do so much for all of us and as ever, especially to Jules. A happy year, thank God.

MB

Part One

Chapter One

Thea Marshall was conceived on a warm Indian summer's day in the middle of September, 1969. Her parents, Hedda and Jake, had just arrived back to 59, Park Road, Islington, after months touring the Asian continent in a VW combi van, and were rather taken with the notion of tantric sex. It was a miracle that she was conceived at all really, considering that Jake would spend up to six hours nurturing his erection, while Hedda lay prone on a bean bag waiting for an experience that was far more mental and spiritual than physical. But conceived she had been and then duly delivered, forty-two weeks later, into a pool of warm water amidst the wail of Indian sitars and a stream of shocked expletives from her mother.

'That was absolutely incredible,' Jake had said, stroking Hedda's brow and massaging a tiny amount of tiger balm into her temples. 'The most amazing experience of my—'

'Get off me!' Hedda had shouted. 'And take that disgusting stuff with you!' She looked up with tears in her eyes at the young GP who was about to stitch her. 'Amazing, eh? Incredible! Sew the whole bloody thing right up, all of it! Go on! Because I'm never ever going to do that again!'

*   *   *

And she hadn't. Thea was an only child in an intense, liberal, academic household where she often went unnoticed amongst the crowd of colleagues and students from the social sciences wing of the West Trant Polytechnic who commandeered the kitchen, smoking and drinking herb tea all hours of the day and night. She should have been precocious, noisy and difficult, perhaps even developed an eating disorder, and then she would have been entitled to her mother's attention, like all the other worthy causes Hedda Marshall was so involved with. But Thea was none of these things. She was an ordered, quiet and clever little girl, who shied away from attention and lost herself in fairy tales. She kept her room neat and tidy, loved needlework and produced small, detailed paintings of flowers and bowls of fruit in her art class.

She was nurtured intellectually, of course, was given the right toys at the right time, taken to the ballet and opera and told openly and plainly the facts of life at the age of eight. But she didn't really have a home, not the sort of home that she wanted, that the other children in her progressive left-wing state school had. She was never allowed fish fingers or tinned Heinz spaghetti, she had never had a birthday party with a proper tea and silly games. She had never snuggled up on the sofa with her parents to watch *The Sound of Music* on the TV or had to stay in for Sunday roast. She had been given a free rein, encouraged to experiment and shown the spirit of sisterhood. By the age of fifteen, however, Thea could cook a very nice chicken casserole, knew how to get value for money out of her weekly wash and had worked out an efficient house-cleaning rota that she could manage after school.

Hedda despaired. 'Where the hell does she get it from?' she repeatedly asked Jake, her friends and her colleagues. 'It's like some sort of generational throw-back. Here I am, in the thrust of feminism, with a good career, open marriage, HRT, personal pension plan, in fact everything I need to be my own person, and there she is, glued to the sodding soap powder commercials.' The unfairness of it rankled. Hedda had wanted a daughter who would identify with her, aspire to the same heroines and love tofu.

Then Thea met Hal.

It was in her first term at university – at least I did something right, said Hedda to Jake, on opening Thea's acceptance letter from New College, Oxford – he was a maths and physics scholar, with a flop of blond hair, a surfer's tan and a long wiry body encased in smooth downy-haired skin. He hailed from a big noisy family somewhere up in the north, a household full of women who adored him. He was the youngest of five, with four sisters, and was used to having the wrinkles ironed out of his life, which made him, amongst other things, easy, charming and very relaxed. Thea fell in love, a passionate, all-consuming and heartily sexual love, which was returned, albeit to a lesser degree, by Hal, and at last her parents understood something about her. Staying up late into the night, empty wine bottles left on the kitchen table, her bedroom door firmly locked and the constant creak and groan of the old-fashioned pine bed. This was youth, this was independence. And then, in June, halfway through the Trinity term, Thea came home one afternoon and told her parents that she was pregnant.

*   *   *

'What the hell do you mean, you're pregnant? For God's sake, Thea, I took you to the bloody doctor's for the pill at sixteen!'

Thea stood in the kitchen with her hands dug deep in the pockets of her coat while Hedda's colleague, Marian, from the Women's Refuge, sat at the table and stared at her with a mixture of pity and embarrassment.

'I just don't believe it,' Hedda went on. 'After all the things we've told you and done to ensure that you don't make exactly this sort of mistake!' Hedda reached for her cigarettes, lit up and perched on the edge of the table. She exchanged glances with Marian. 'I'm thoroughly disappointed, Thea, I really am! This is just so selfish of you, and particularly now, right in the middle of the rehousing project that Marian and I have worked so hard to set up! It's just one more thing that I have to deal with, one more added stress!' She stubbed her cigarette out, barely smoked, into a large, heavy glass ashtray that was already full to overflowing. A small scattering of ash fell on to the scrubbed pine and Thea itched to wipe it away with a damp cloth. 'We'll have to go through Mike,' Hedda said, referring to a local GP connected to the refuge. 'He'll be able to fix things up pretty quickly, I'd imagine. Perhaps I should give him a ring now, Marian, what d'you think? Is he in surgery at the moment?'

Marian looked at her watch, a neon pink and orange plastic affair, and nodded. 'He finishes at half past,' she answered. 'Ring and leave a message.'

'Right, I'll do that.' Hedda slid off the table and brushed past Thea out into the hall. She flicked through a huge

4

shabby brown leather organiser until she found what she wanted and picked up the phone. Dialling, she called over her shoulder to her daughter: 'How many weeks are you, Thea? Mike'll need to know.' Suddenly she put the receiver back. 'Oh Christ! You are only a few weeks gone, aren't you? You haven't been a complete prat and let it fester, have you?'

Thea stared open-mouthed at her mother. The hands inside her pockets were damp and slippery with sweat. 'I'm, erm . . .' She lost her voice and coughed. 'I'm, erm, erm, seven weeks, or eight, I think.'

Hedda rolled her eyes. 'Thank God for that! Right then, Thea, why don't you go upstairs and unpack your rucksack while I call Mike. Hopefully, we can get this thing sorted inside of a week.'

Thea struggled to find her voice again. 'Sorted?' she whispered. 'I . . .'

For the second time, Hedda replaced the receiver and turned to face her daughter. 'Let's get things absolutely clear before we go any further, shall we? I am assuming that you have no intention of ruining a good academic career, a bright future and a whole life ahead of you in order to lumber yourself with a baby. I am right, aren't I?'

'I, erm, I . . .' Thea willed herself to speak. She blinked rapidly several times and dug her fingers into a now wet palm. 'I, erm . . .' Again her voice trailed off and she stared down at the floor. Hedda picked up the receiver and started to dial.

'Good, that's settled.'

'No!' Thea suddenly blurted out. 'No. I mean, yes – I

mean no, no, you're not right, I do want to have the baby, I . . .'

Hedda gripped the hall table and stared tight-lipped at her daughter. 'Marian!' she called, her voice high and strangled. 'Marian! Can you come here right now?' Thea felt behind her for the support of the wall. Her mother glared at her. 'Marian, you'd better come,' Hedda cried, 'because if you don't, I really think I might hit her!'

Much later that day, Thea sat in her room, her hands on the still flat plane of her belly and listened to the rage of voices down in the kitchen. Jake was home, Mike the GP had been called and was sitting with Marian and Jude, another friend of Hedda's, while the arguments swelled back and forth on teenage pregnancy, abortion, help for single mothers and the rights of women to choose. Thea closed her eyes; she'd had it all afternoon. Still, they could rage all they liked, they could argue, row, swipe ideas across the room at each other, but nothing was going to make her change her mind. Thea knew what she wanted, or thought she did at least. She wanted the baby, she wanted the attention that having it produced, she wanted its love and affection and she wanted an idyllic family life. She could have those things too, she knew she could. She already had the attention, didn't she?

At nine-thirty, Jake served a vegetable chilli and called Thea downstairs for supper. He had laid the table around the people sitting at it and was ladling the dark red stew on to plates with a spoon of brown rice and bulgar wheat on the side. Thea walked across and stood by him. He smiled, handed her a plate and said, so quietly that she almost misheard him: 'Eat up, love, you and that baby need good wholesome food inside you.'

Thea held back the sudden overwhelming urge to cry and carried her plate across to the table. She sat, glanced briefly at the faces around her, then put her head down to eat. Hedda stood up and reached for another packet of cigarettes from the dresser. The air was already thick with smoke and Jake coughed. 'Hedda,' he said quietly, 'we're about to eat.'

'I can't eat!' Hedda announced. 'Not at a time like this!' She reached for her glass of wine, refilled it and swallowed a hefty mouthful. 'I'm surprised that you can, Jake, considering that our daughter is about to throw her life away on some romantic ideal of marriage and parenthood!'

'I didn't hear her say anything about marriage,' Jake countered. Hedda harrumphed and sat back down at the table.

'All right then, not marriage,' she said with restrained irritation. 'Parenthood. You have to agree with me, Jake, that it's not easy, in fact it's damn bloody hard work. Blood and sweat, lots of both, Thea, and no shortage of tears, I can tell you! It's not like the ads you see on telly with pristine babies smiling and bouncing around in soft snowy white towelling nappies! Tell her, Jake! Tell her what it's really like!'

Jake sighed. What could he tell Thea about being a parent? He remembered the exhaustion, the endless work, the fanatical sharing of responsibility that Hedda insisted upon, but he also remembered Thea's warmth and smell and endless love. For the only time in his life, for those few short years of her babyhood, Jake had been loved unconditionally and that was a memory he treasured. Placing the ladle back in the chilli, he turned and said, 'Hedda is right, Thea, it isn't easy having a baby, and it's something that I would hate to think of you doing on your own—'

'But I'm not on my own!' Thea interjected. 'I've got Hal!'

Hedda snorted derisively but Jake, kinder, said, 'I realise that, Thea, but he might not always be there. You're very young, both of you, and—'

'And one whiff of babies' sick and shit,' Hedda butted in, 'and he'll be off like a shot!'

Thea's bright face crumpled and she hung her head, big heavy tears dropping into her food.

'Hedda, that was unnecessary,' Jake said.

'Was it?' Hedda demanded. 'I don't think so. She thinks it's going to be like a Norman Rockwell painting! All golden heads bent over books by the firelight. But it isn't! It's hard work and compromise and never getting what you really want.'

Jake looked at his wife. Very carefully, he said, 'Is it, Hedda?'

She stared back at him and saw something like hurt in his eyes. She was embarrassed. 'It can be,' she finished.

Jake turned back to the food on the hob. 'Chilli, Marian?' His voice was calm; he had turned away from things again.

Marian, who was wheat intolerant, couldn't eat pulses or tomatoes and was allergic to spicy food, shook her head and poured herself more wine. She was already well on the way to an addled state of mind and body and was slumped on her elbows looking at no one and nothing in particular. Mike the GP stood up and crossed to Jake to collect his and Jude's plate. Jake spotted a couple of fiery red chillies and scooped them up into Jude's portion. He didn't like Jude; never had.

'You know you won't be able to manage, Thea, with a baby and a tough course at Oxford,' Hedda said, unable to leave the matter even for a few minutes while they ate. 'I don't know what anyone's told you about motherhood or subsidies for single parents but you can take it from me that it's no cheap ticket!'

Thea said nothing. Jake sat down with his own plate of food, glared at Hedda who had been about to light up and gently patted Thea on the leg under the table.

'God, I see hundreds of women like you, Thea, bright, able but struggling to be all things to all people and as a result unfulfilled.' Hedda had moved on from the West Trant Polytechnic a decade ago and into counselling. She ran a lucrative practice in Hampstead – which had paid the mortgage off on the house in Islington – and eased her social conscience by charity work at the refuge. 'And even if he does hang around, I don't know what use you think Hal is going to be! He's a nice enough boy but—'

Thea lifted her head. Having Jake next to her gave her the bit of courage that she needed. 'Hal has rented us a cottage out near Banbury.'

Hedda raised an eyebrow. 'A cottage? How perfect!'

Thea glanced at her mother, began a smile then picked up on Hedda's sarcasm and the smile faded. She swallowed down a mouthful of chilli, then said, 'I, erm, I wasn't planning to go back to college actually, Hedda.'

Hedda, with her glass raised halfway to her lips, froze.

'I don't like it. I, erm, I never have and I, erm, I think . . .' Thea looked at her father. He cleared his throat.

'She didn't actually want to go to New College,' he said. 'As far as I can remember, Hedda, I think' – he coughed again – 'I believe that you talked her into it. It's an incredible opportunity, I think you said, to be one of the academic élite, the country's *crème de la crème*.'

'Jake!' Jude put down her fork. 'I wouldn't have thought Hedda in the slightest bit capable of élitism! I'm sure that's not true, is it, Hedda?!'

Hedda gulped her wine. 'Not in so many words,' she said.

Jake turned to his daughter. 'What do you want to do, Thea darling? Hedda is right, you know, she's only thinking of you and your future, but the decision must be yours, we can't make it for you.'

'Why the hell not?' Hedda suddenly demanded. 'She's eighteen, Jake! What does she know about the rest of her life, for God's sake? What does she know about children? She's only just stopped being a child herself.'

'We've always taught her to think for herself, even as a child, Hedda.'

'Yes but . . .' Hedda threw up her hands, unable to finish. What she wanted to say was: But only if she thinks the right way, thinks the way we do, and she knew that wasn't fair. It couldn't be said. Thea had thought for herself and developed along an altogether different plane.

'Thea? You've decided that you want to have this baby,

but even after all that Hedda has said to you, even after listening to the arguments here today, do you still think this is the right thing to do?'

Thea lay her knife and fork down on her plate, neatly, side by side. 'Yes, Jake,' she said. She had never called either of them Mum and Dad, although she had longed to, many many times. 'It feels right, I can't even explain why, it just does. I want to be normal, that's all, a normal house, normal things, a partner, a baby. I just want an ordinary life.'

'And your degree?'

Hedda felt the urge to leap up and slap her daughter, or Jake or Jude for that matter, her best friend, whose smile barely covered the sneer behind it. Your degree, she wanted to cry, Oxford, the opportunity I never had, the chance of a lifetime. She clenched her teeth and waited for the answer. Thea looked across at her.

'I might finish it, but then I might not, I really don't know,' she said, and with that, Hedda burst into tears.

Chapter Two

Mason cottage, on the outskirts of a village called Duns Tew, near Banbury was dingy, small, isolated and cold but at least it wasn't damp, Thea told her father on the telephone that night. If it had been damp, she said, she didn't think she could have stood it. Not that Thea was complaining, of course, she'd had a good summer, living mostly outside during the continuous hot July and August days, cooking, keeping house, making a small herb garden and sewing endlessly for her baby, things that never quite turned out to look like the picture on the pattern. It had been lonely, of course, but that was only to be expected, so Thea told herself. Hal hadn't been there much, he'd had to go home to see his family, and then there was the trip to India, planned months ago that he just couldn't get out of, but she had kept herself busy, doing odd jobs, filling in the time as best she could and, even though it hadn't been quite what she'd expected, there was the prospect of the baby: that was enough to keep her going.

Once the autumn set in, though, Thea began to find it hard. The weather turned, suddenly, late in October and the cottage became icy cold at night. Hal had huge amounts of work and stayed in college during the week, the telephone had been cut off and only reconnected at Jake's insistence – and his payment of the bill – and Thea was big: large and dense and cumbersome. Every part of her seemed to swell, almost daily. Her breasts felt heavy and sore, her stomach was so fat that it altered her balance and gave her searing pains down the side of her thighs and the baby moved continuously, turning somersaults day and night, keeping her awake, kicking out its arms and legs so that she would see the shape of a foot stab out under the tightly stretched skin.

Some time before Christmas – a lonely one, spent in Islington with Jake and Hedda hardly speaking – Hal went off sex. He said that he didn't want to manhandle her in any way, upset her natural rhythm with the baby. But once, when she was nearly full term, Thea caught him looking at her as she stood naked, pulling a nightdress over her head, and his face had been rigid with shock, his mouth a small puckered line of disgust. After that he stayed in college at weekends as well and Thea found herself struggling through the days, making conversation with her unborn baby and taking the worn old magazines away from the doctor's surgery for want of something to read.

She spoke sometimes to Jake, but never to Hedda. There was none of the anticipated attention, just an isolated silence. Hedda had more or less come round to the situation, because she loved her daughter even though she didn't approve of or understand her, and she believed in tolerance. Sometimes Thea reversed the charges and chattered away for ages in a bright, dangerously high voice, and sometimes she hardly spoke at all. Jake worried about her, he worried incessantly, but that was something he would never confess to his wife.

'Of course it's terribly cold,' Thea went on that night. 'Terribly quiet and rural, but damp, damp is something I—'

'Thea?' Jake tried to interrupt her.

'Something I don't think would be at all good for the baby, or me for that matter, and it's impossible to get rid of, you have to—'

'Thea!' Jake raised his voice slightly and there was a small silence on the other end of the phone. 'Thea, are you all right? I mean it's bloody freezing and Hedda and I, well—' He broke off. He wasn't used to the interfering parent role. He and Hedda had agreed, right from the day Thea was born, that she would be allowed to live her own life, that they would only get involved if Thea asked them to. 'Well, we just sort of wondered,' he went on, 'if you were on your own or if Hal was there.'

'No, no I'm not alone,' Thea answered quickly, attempting to cover the ache of disappointment that seeped into everything she said and did. Hal wasn't there and she missed him terribly. 'I mean, well, I am at the moment, but – but Hal's coming back later.' The thing that Hedda and Jake had failed to realise was that Thea didn't know how to ask for their help. 'I'm fine,' she added in a small voice. 'Great actually.'

'Good.' Jake could see Hedda; she had come into the hall from the kitchen and was mouthing something at him. 'Thea, hang on a moment, I . . .' He saw that Hedda was asking if Thea was all right and he shrugged. 'Oh, right, of course. Yes, I'll let you go then. What time d'you expect Hal back?' He saw Hedda frown and shrugged again. 'OK,

Thea, yes, do that, any time. OK, 'bye now.' He hung up and turned away from Hedda. They had been together for over twenty years, had an open and equal partnership, talked about their affairs, holidayed separately, except with Thea, but now, since she had left, Jake couldn't help wondering if there was really any point to it. He couldn't help wondering if they'd lost something a long time ago and both of them were too busy and too selfish to bother with trying to find it. He couldn't help wondering if that thing was Thea.

'I'm going to the refuge tonight,' Hedda said, applying lipstick in front of the hall mirror. It amazed him that she never asked in detail about Thea. 'Shall we meet up for supper later, say around nine?'

'Is that a way of asking me to cook tonight?' Jake asked tersely.

Hedda stopped what she was doing and looked at him. 'No, not at all!' she answered equally as tersely. 'You know the house rules as well as I do, Jake. No one does anything in this house unless they want to.'

'No.' Maybe that was the problem. 'Of course not.' Maybe if Thea had had rules, maybe if they had been more hands on . . . He watched Hedda click the lid back on to her lipstick. 'I was going to do courgette bake, OK?'

Hedda smiled. It was a wide, deep, plum-coloured smile but there was no warmth in it. She couldn't talk about Thea, she had failed as a mother and she didn't know why Jake couldn't see it.

'I'll see you later then?'

'Yup.' Jake walked to the front door with her, reluctant to let her go, but unable to think of anything that would make her want to stay. 'Red or white?'

'Sorry?'

'Tonight? Red or white wine?'

'Oh God, anything.' she said with a hint of irritation. Jake closed the door after her and noticed for the first time ever that the house seemed to be in a perpetual state of silence.

Thea put the receiver down and stood with her back against the cold stone wall of the cottage. She'd had a dull ache in her lower back all afternoon, probably from clearing out that coal shed ready for the pram, she thought, wondering exactly when it was going to materialise. It was Hal's responsibility, he'd said he would get it organised but when or how wasn't really part of Hal's thinking process. Thea just hoped he hadn't forgotten, realised with a bite of disappointment that he probably had and moved slowly towards the kitchen to make herself a cup of tea. She lifted the heavy old iron kettle, took it to the sink, filled it and went to heave it on to the hot plate of the Rayburn. Just as she did so, her waters broke. With a tiny pop and a sudden great whoosh, her tights, her dress, her carpet slippers and a good portion of the floor were all suddenly awash with water. 'Oh shit!' she gasped, then bent double as a spasm of breath-taking pain seared through her uterus. Oh God, she thought, I think I'm going to have the baby! She stayed where she was, held her breath for a few moments trying to block out the pain, then miraculously remembered to pant. Inhaling and exhaling in short rhythmic bursts, she gripped the doorframe and somehow got through the contraction as her sodden tights, dress and slippers, now icy cold, clung to her body. As the pain receded, she looked up, took a deep breath and thinking more clearly and calmly than she had done for months, slowly climbed the small flight of stairs to her bedroom.

There, she found clean clothes, her hospital bag and her wash things. She splashed some cold water on to her face, changed as quickly as her bulky shape would allow, grabbed the bag and toiletries and went back downstairs. She picked up the phone, dialled the number of Hal's college and waited. Speaking to the porter, Thea was asked to wait, hung on for what seemed like hours and was finally told that Hal was not in his rooms. Not knowing what else to do, frightened and panicked that another bout of pain would come at any moment, Thea hung up without leaving a message. She crossed to the door, only conscious of the fact that she needed help but not thinking clearly enough to phone for an ambulance or call the hospital. She squeezed her feet into her wellies, pulled on a coat and left the cottage to walk to the farm up the road.

It took twenty minutes and by the time she arrived, she had had to stop twice, creased over with pain as two more contractions ripped through her. She knew what was happening, she had paid attention in her antenatal classes, but she had no idea that it could happen so fast. 'This is supposed to take hours,' she muttered through clenched teeth, as a third contraction took hold at the gate to Brandon Farm. She held on to the freezing metal and closed her eyes. She began to pant and count, all the time murmuring as much of Lear's 'The Owl and the Pussycat' as she could remember.

'Christ!' Thea felt a warm hand on her shoulder. 'Are you . . . ?' She let out a groan and gripped the metal bars of the gate even tighter, despite the fact that the cold burnt her skin. 'Yes, you are, hang on a minute.' The warm hand disappeared and Thea heard footsteps, then a few muffled shouts. She straightened with the receding pain as a middle-aged woman headed back towards her followed by the bright headlights of a car.

'Come on, lovey, looks like we need to get you to hospital.' The voice was strong and persuasive. 'We've got the car, just stand up as straight as you can while I open the gate and we'll get you inside and on the way to hospital in a jiffy. Are the labour pains coming fast, lovey?'

Thea felt her hands gently loosened off the metal gate. 'About every ten minutes or so.'

'Fine, plenty of time then, no need to worry.' Thea stumbled back a few paces as the car drove alongside her and the woman swung the gate open. She came back within seconds and eased Thea into the front passenger seat of the car. The car drove forward through the gate, the woman closed it and climbed into the back.

'Banbury General,' the woman said quietly to the man driving. 'We haven't got time to get to Oxford.' Thea closed her eyes, bent forward with another spasm of pain and silently began to cry.

'It's all right, dear, there's nothing to cry about. You're here now. Come on, up on to the trolley. Let's wheel you down to the delivery suite in style, shall we?'

Thea felt herself hoisted up on to a hard bed and looked behind her for the woman who'd brought her in. The bright overhead lights hurt her eyes and she felt sick. 'Where's . . .'

'Your mum, deary? She's gone down to the waiting room.'

Thea didn't have the strength to clarify the situation, she was muddled with pain. 'My bag!' she moaned. 'Where's my bag?' The trolley was being wheeled with precision and speed along a wide antiseptic-smelling corridor and Thea's nausea washed in great waves over her. 'My bag, I . . .'

'I've got your bag here, love, now don't you worry about your bag.' Thea tried to breathe as another contraction hit the pit of her uterus and she cried out. 'I'm . . . Oh God, I'm going to be . . .'

'Watch out, Mary!' the midwife shouted at her colleague. The trolley didn't stop as a slick of vomit hit first the midwife's clean starched blue uniform, then the shiny polished floor.

'That'll teach me not to put my plastic apron on, won't it?' she said across Thea's head. The other midwife smiled. She seemed to have produced a card bowl from out of thin air and Thea wondered if she was hallucinating. 'Try to be sick in here, deary,' she said. The trolley turned a corner, slammed through some double swing doors and into a darkened room.

'OK now, we're in the delivery suite, we've got everything here, no need to worry, erm . . . Theo? It is Theo?'

Thea shook her head. 'Thea,' she murmured, 'it's Thea.' The searing pain had given way to the most peculiar feeling, a sort of compressing of her uterus. 'I want to push,' she called out, 'I feel as if I want to push.'

One of the midwives stood by her head and gently wiped her brow. She took Thea's hand. 'You may feel as if you want to push, Thea, but you mustn't yet. All right, you've got to try and breathe through it. You mustn't push until you're fully dilated, until you're good and ready to deliver the baby. OK now, sweetheart?'

Thea gripped the midwife's hand. 'I want to push!' she cried, clenching her teeth. 'I think the baby's coming!'

'It's all right, Thea, calm down, this is a first baby, they rarely come this quick, just try and breathe, try and keep calm. Mary is going to examine you and we'll see how far on you are. Come on now, Thea, grip my hand and try to breathe, I'll count with you, come on, breathe in, one, two—'

'I can feel the baby's head!' Thea suddenly wailed. 'I've got to push!' The midwife dropped her hand and darted round to the end of the bed. 'Mary,' she shouted, then, under her breath: 'Here we go!' She glanced briefly over her shoulder and shouted again. 'Mary! We're about to deliver!'

She parted Thea's legs and looked up at her. Her face was completely calm, it was something Thea would always remember, for years afterwards, that in the midst of her own fear and panic, the midwife's face was completely calm.

'Well done, Thea, you were exactly right! The baby's on it's way! Come on now, you know how to push, you can feel what to do, it's completely natural. The head's right there and I need a good push to get it out, all right? Bear down now, all right? Push from your tummy. Come on now, good girl, push, push, PUSH! That's it! Good girl, that's fantastic! I've got the baby's head! I've got it, now we have to push the body out. It may take two or three goes but let's try and push really hard, OK? Take a deep breath, let it go and PUSH! Come on, Thea, PUSH!'

The other midwife had slipped into the room and taken Thea's hand without her even realising it. She held on to the woman's fingers, let out a long, harsh howl and pushed with all her might.

'That's it!' she heard. 'Come on, come on, I've got him, I've got your baby, Thea, he's out!' Thea felt her entire body flood with relief. 'Crikey, that was damn quick!' the midwife murmured. Thea glanced up as a scraggy, bloody, wrinkled baby was held out towards her, the midwife by her head opened her shirt and they laid him, Thomas Marshall, on to her breast. It was both the most exquisite joy and profound sadness she had ever experienced.

'Hello, Tom,' she said. 'I've been a long time waiting to love someone like you.'

Two hours after Tom had been born, Hal sat up in a girl named Lucy Cox's bed and stretched. She was a fellow mathematician, really very brilliant and not bad looking either, in an off-beat sort of way. He prodded her bare shoulder, she rolled over and he smiled.

'Shall we get dressed?'

Lucy yawned. There was a party on in town tonight and she had heard Hal promise earlier to go, but she wasn't sure she wanted to move. It was bitterly cold out and this was the warmest she'd been all week. The house she and three other students rented just off the Cowley Road was a pit: dirty, slug-infested and freezing. 'I don't think I fancy it,' she said. 'I don't mind if you go though, as long as you leave your electric heater here.'

Hal leant over and wound one of Lucy's long thin beaded

plaits of hair round his figner. 'Is that to ensure that I come back?'

Lucy moved away and pulled the covers up to her chin. 'No, it's because I'm bloody frozen in this hell hole and your heater is frankly the best thing about you.'

Hal laughed out loud. 'Bloody cheek!' He burrowed under the covers and pulled Lucy into a bear hug. Nothing ever offended Hal, insults hardly touched him, dislike just didn't enter his aura. He was very comfortable with himself, so why should it bother him if other people weren't? Having squeezed Lucy to the point of apology and both of them laughing, he disentangled himself and climbed out of bed. 'Right then,' he said, 'I'll go.' Reaching for his clothes, scattered randomly all over the floor, he pulled each item on as he found it, socks, shirt, sweater, boxers, then jeans and finally perched on the edge of the bed to lace up his boots. 'Can I borrow your phone before I go?' He finished lacing, straightened and dug in his pockets for some loose change. 'I want to call Thea and check she's all right.'

Lucy felt a stab of something she wasn't sure she could identify. Jealousy? Pity? 'Course,' she answered. 'When's the baby due?'

Hal shrugged. He wasn't just being evasive, he genuinely didn't know. 'She said she'll call me if anything happens.'

Lucy nodded. There was a brief silence, Lucy wondering if it was all an act and Hal thinking that he'd have to get a taxi in order to get to the party on time.

'I'll see you later then,' Hal said, standing.

'Yeah, sure.' Lucy propped herself up on her elbow, luxuriating in the unusual warmth of the room. 'Whenever.'

Hal smiled. 'No, not whenever, I want my heater back!' And, blowing her a kiss, he went downstairs.

Down in the kitchen of the house, Louise, Lucy's flatmate, was rushing about looking for her handbag. 'Oh hi, Hal! You haven't seen my bag, have you? I've got a taxi waiting and I can't find the blasted thing!'

Hal glanced around the room. 'You off to the party in Lanson Road, then?'

'Yes, if I ever get there! You couldn't be a real star and pop outside to let the bloke know I'm just coming, could you?'

Hal shrugged. It was a gesture he made often. Moving towards the front door, all thought of Thea gone, he spotted a satchel on the newel post under a pile of coats. 'Is your bag a brown leather satchel?' he called out.

Louise dashed into the hall. 'Yes! Have you found it?'

Hal rifled through the coats and tugged the bag free. 'Here!'

Louise grinned. 'Hal, you're a genius!' She reached forward and kissed him full on the lips. Then, grabbing her coat, she pulled it on and hurried over to the door. 'D'you need a lift anywhere?' She'd had a bit of a thing for Hal for ages, but had never really had the opportunity to get to know him.

'How about the party?'

Louise's face glowed. 'The party it is then!' she announced, opening the door. 'Come on, because this taxi's already cost me a fortune!'

Thea was in the first bed of an eight-bed ward, just near the door, supposedly screened off for privacy by a pair of faded old floral curtains but in reality party to every coming and going in the ward, every murmur, cry and movement. It was four a.m., Thomas had been in this world for seven hours and all he had done for most of them was howl. Thea was exhausted, she was hungry, dying for a cup of tea, sore and hormonal. Thomas needed comfort but she seemed unable to give him any. A stream of midwives – she'd seen five, all offering different advice – muttered bossily about latching on and colostrum, they squeezed her breasts and manipulated her nipples, trying to insert them into a tight rosebud mouth, pinched with shock and indignation at the light, cold and lack of womb. It didn't work; he wouldn't feed and he wouldn't sleep. Thea tried walking him up and down, letting him suck on her finger, rocking him; she tried the bedside lights on, the bedside lights off, talking to him, singing to him and finally, letting him lie on her breast, his face screwed up with anger, screaming while the tears slid silently down her face.

At six a.m., with the help of the ward sister, she finally managed to stuff a now chaffed and painful nipple into his mouth and he sucked. She lay back on the pillows, weak with relief and immediately fell asleep. At seven a.m., less than a full hour later, the ward lights went on and a trolley was wheeled in. It was the wake-up call, complete with a nice cup of tea.

Thea woke with a start, the start woke Thomas and he began to cry again. So did Thea. She wheeled him in his plastic trolley cot to the bathroom, let him wail while she took a lukewarm shower, still weeping, and dressed in some clean clothes, then wheeled him back to her bedside, took him out and started the struggle to feed. It took half an hour to latch him on to her nipple this time, but she managed it on her own, a small personal triumph that started her crying again and prompted the lady delivering her breakfast to sit on the side of the bed and put her arm round her. It was the first physical and emotional comfort she'd had and Thea gulped back noisy and uncontrollable sobs. 'Oh God,' she wept, 'it wasn't supposed to be like this! This isn't at all like I imagined it.'

'It rarely is,' the lady with the breakfast trolley said. She wanted to add that nothing much in life was, but it wasn't her business to say things like that. She handed Thea a tissue from the box on the side of the bed.

'Hal wasn't here,' Thea said, her sobs coming under control. 'He said he would be, he promised me and then when it came to it there wasn't time. He was out. I called but I didn't leave a message and he doesn't know . . .' Her voice broke and she blew her nose. Several minutes later, she said, 'No one knows.' Her voice was no more than a whisper. 'And I haven't got any money to ring.'

The trolley lady glanced at the stack of breakfasts getting cold and sighed heavily. She was a soft touch, she was, always had been and always would be. Taking Thea's hand, she patted it and said, 'Look, love, when you've finished feeding him and had yourself something to eat, why don't you come down to the kitchen and I'll lend you a quid to make some calls. You can pay me back when baby's dad arrives. All right?' Thea nodded but kept her gaze down. In the face of such kindness, she knew that if she looked at the woman she would cry again. 'Thank you,' she murmured.

'Not at all,' the lady said, getting to her arthritic feet. She touched Tom's head. 'He's a smashing baby. You're a lucky girl.' And with that, Thea burst into tears again.

Hal finally got the message about Thea mid-morning that day. He returned to college with his heater, was just lugging it up the stairs when the porter caught him.

'Your young lady called last night,' he said gruffly. He didn't like smooth young men and this one was so smooth as to be slippery. 'She rang last night, bout sevenish, and then again this morning, from Banbury General.'

Hal spun round on the narrow stairwell, banging the heater against the wall and overbalancing slightly. 'The hospital? Did she say anything, leave any message? Is she all right?'

'No, no message.' The porter frowned. 'And as for whether she's all right or not, that's not for me to say, is it? It's for you to find out, young man.'

'Oh yes! Shit, I mean – Right! Yes, thanks.' Hal went to smile but thought better of it and continued up the stairs to his rooms. Once inside, he dropped the heater with a crash, ran over to his cupboard, yanked out some clean clothes and changed into them without bothering to wash. He didn't have time to wash. Transferring his wallet, he grabbed his coat and rushed out again, racing down the stairs two at a time and just missing a collision in the hallway at the bottom. Ten minutes later, forgetting a present for either the baby or Thea, he was on his way to Banbury General Hospital.

Thea had also telephoned her parents. They too were

on their way to Banbury General, via their local high street for some flowers. Hedda was tense so she drove, preferring it that way, while Jake read the map. But she drove badly, not listening to instructions properly, taking wrong turns, forgetting to use fifth gear, and all the time talking about Thea as if now that the baby had been delivered everything could go back to exactly the way it had been before the pregnancy. Jake wondered if Hedda could recall how enormous the changes had been to their lives after Thea was born, then he remembered, gazing out at the changing landscape either side of the M40, that of course she wouldn't, she'd gone back to work after six weeks and he had been the one to stay at home to look after Thea that first year, taking a long and mythical sabbatical. He smiled and wondered if Tom would be as easy as Thea had been and then he realised for the first time in months that he was smiling because he was happy and not because he was supposed to be amused. It felt good. I think I'm going to like being a grandfather, he thought. Then he glanced across at his wife, her face set in grim concentration. That's if Hedda allows me to.

Hal was the first to arrive. He came just before they served lunch and the smell of macaroni cheese seemed to pervade the whole maternity unit. It made him uneasy, it was a nursery dish and one that he had never liked. As he walked into the ward, he walked right past Thea, her face ashen, her eyes pink and puffy from crying; he walked along to the end and had to turn around and scan the beds. He saw her at last, glanced at her stomach and rushed to the bed. 'You haven't had it!' he cried, taking her hands. 'I've got here in time, I'm so relieved, I thought . . .'

'Hal!' Thea pulled her hands away. 'Hal, I had a little boy, last night. He's there, in the cot.'

Hal's face was momentarily blank, he glanced at the cot, then at Thea's stomach. 'But I thought, I mean your tummy, I . . .'

Thea looked away. 'It takes days, sometimes weeks.' Fresh tears stung her eyes.

'Oh right, um, yes, I see.' Hal was embarrassed and a little shocked. There was a small silence. 'So you had it then!' he said.

'Yes,' Thea answered dully.

'Brilliant!'

Thea looked back at him. 'Really?'

Hal looked at her face. She'd been beautiful when he'd first seen her, just beautiful, tall and strong, radiant with health. He had loved her flesh, the firm roundness of it, her unstyled, thick hair, her strange out-of-place look. She was a contradiction, clever but unassuming about it, vulnerable with it. She had been clear-eyed and lovely; innocent. Now he could hardly recognise her and was filled with pity. Whether it was for himself or Thea, he didn't know. He touched her eyes with a cool fingertip and bent to kiss the top of her head. 'Yes, really,' he said, not at all sure that he meant it. He walked around the bed to the cot and peered in.

'I've never seen a newborn before,' he said. 'It's kind of weird-looking, isn't it?'

'He,' Thea said. 'And his name is Tom, Thomas Marshall.'

'Not Hal junior then?' He glanced up at Thea and finally she smiled.

'No,' she said. 'Most definitely not Hal junior.' And they both started to giggle.

Hedda and Jake hadn't expected laughter. Hedda wasn't sure what she had expected, but it hadn't been Hal, lolling in the chair next to the bed, with his feet up on it and the baby carelessly asleep on his lap. She hadn't expected Thea to look so exhausted, so pale and stranded, and she hadn't expected her own reaction, one of uncontrollable anger: anger towards Hal, for making her daughter pregnant, towards Thea for being such a damn fool and towards a tiny fifteen-hour-old baby for all the chaos and ruin he would engender.

As they stood by the bed and Jake looked down at his grandson with a tenderness that took him completely by surprise, Hedda remembered the presents and to try and relieve this sudden emotion, she pulled hers out of the bag and said, 'I've brought you something for yourself, Thea darling, because you'll get lots of things for the baby and you'll probably be sick of it all by the end of the month. Here.' She handed a package across, beautifully wrapped, as all Hedda's gifts were, and Thea took it, carefully removing the paper. Where, she was thinking, am I going to get loads of things for the baby from? She didn't even have a pram. Down to the tissue, Thea peeled it off and found a small Neals Yard box. 'Gosh,' she said nervously, and then on opening it: 'Gosh, how lovely.' It was an aromatherapy set, the burner and two starter oils.

'I chose lavender to keep you calm,' Hedda said, 'and

rosemary to stimulate concentration.' She smiled, thoroughly pleased with herself. 'But that goes with the other present. Go on, Thea, open the other one.'

Thea reached for the second gift, undoubtedly a book, and attempted a smile. She opened it and braced herself. It was Spenser's *The Faerie Queene*.

'I thought, knowing how much you love Milton, that you'd like this and, well, it's so important to the study of literature and if you ever thought about resuming your degree, well . . .' Hedda's voice faded and she shrugged.

Jake turned away. He could see that Thea was trying hard not to cry and Hal was looking at one of the nurses across the ward. Oh Hedda, he thought, why couldn't you leave well alone? Handing the huge John Lewis bag with his own gifts in to Thea, he said, 'Well, this isn't anything that might help you with your studies, I'm afraid.' He smiled as Thea took it. She looked inside. Nothing was wrapped and she saw two packs of white towelling babygrows, nappies, nappy cream, wipes, a packet of dummies, a pack of muslins. 'In case he chucks up all the time,' Jake said as she pulled it out. Next came a teddy, six pale blue vests, one smart outfit, in navy and white, two cotton blankets, two cot sheets, one wool blanket in blue and white check and a box of very expensive Belgian chocolates. 'Those are for you,' Jake said, 'I wouldn't suggest you try giving them to Tom, no matter how desperate you are to feed him.'

Thea smiled, then laughed, then began to cry again and said, 'Oh, Jake, thank you, thank you so much.'

Hal said, 'Blimey, what a lot of stuff! I had no idea he'd need any of that!'

'Of course not!' Hedda replied sarcastically. 'I'm sure there are many things that you have no idea about, Hal.'

'Hedda,' Jake warned.

'Oh really, Jake!' Hedda snapped. 'Look at all that clobber! It's ridiculous! It's not our responsibility.'

'No it isn't,' Thea said. 'But it's wonderful, I haven't got anything, it's just brilliant, Jake, it's—'

'It's cool, Jake,' Hal said.

They all turned to look at him.

'Cool?' Hedda demanded, her voice clipped and loud. 'Cool! Thea's father has to provide all the things that you should have provided and all you can say is it's cool!' She had lost her sense of reason. Perhaps it was seeing Thea, perhaps it was the fact that Jake had trumped her yet again with his gifts, perhaps it was just the realisation of her own inadequacy as a mother, buying a book instead of a teddy for her grandson, that fuelled her rage. But a rage it was and she wasn't able to hold it back. 'Look at you, sitting there – no, lounging there, without a care in the world! You don't care, do you? You don't give a damn about caring for Thea, looking after her and the baby!'

'Hedda,' Thea murmured. 'Please don't.'

'Whoa, hang on a minute!' Hal said. 'Are you asking me, or telling me? Anyway . . .' He was keeping his head. He could see Thea's stricken face and had no use for an argument. '. . . I didn't think that you believed in all that male/female role playing,' he said. He held his hands up in mock surrender to try and lighten the mood.

But Hedda couldn't be distracted. 'I don't!' she snarled. 'But I do believe in taking a bit of responsibility for one's actions and you clearly haven't done that at all!'

'Hedda!' Thea pleaded, her voice loud but tearful.

Hal was rarely roused from his casual charm but this had hit the spot. He stared at Hedda for a few moments, then said. 'This baby wasn't my idea, Hedda, so don't get all heavy with me about responsibility. I've never made any promises I can't keep. Have I, Thea?'

Thea looked down at the bed and shook her head as Hal stood up to hand Tom over to her. 'I didn't try to talk Thea into anything regarding this baby and, while we're at it, she damn well told me she was on the pill!'

'Hal!' Thea looked up aghast as the woman in the next bed, who was making no pretence about not listening in, shook her head and tutted loudly. Thea took Tom and cradled him, closing her eyes.

'Typical!' Hedda said. 'Bloody typical! Blame the whole thing on the woman! Let her handle it! God, you men make me sick!' She glared icily at Hal, who stood his ground and glared back.

Tom, who had woken on being moved, started to make small whining noises. Thea realised she had to feed him and flushed deeply.

'God, you've got a bloody cheek, young man!' Hedda announced. If there was one thing she had to have, it was the last word. 'That's all you're going to say about it, is it? That it wasn't your idea, so it's not your problem? Eh?'

She stared at Hal, who said rudely, 'Yeah, it is. So what do you intend to do about it?'

'I'm afraid . . .' Thea murmured, trying to interrupt.

'Do about it? Do about it!' Hedda's face and neck were flushed with anger. 'I'd bloody string you up by your balls, that's what I'd do about it if I had my own way!' she shouted.

'Hedda,' Jake snapped. 'That's enough!'

'No it isn't! It won't be enough until we find out what this insolent, irresponsible thug is going to do about Thea!'

'Hang me up by my balls, eh?' Hal sneered. 'Very liberal! Very PC!'

Thea was beginning to panic. 'I'm afraid,' she said, 'that I . . .' The whining noises turned to a small howl.

'I thought you'd always brought Thea up to live her own life.' Hal was into his stride now. He'd been brought up mostly by women, he was used to catcalling. 'Well, this is it! Her choice! I'm sorry that you don't like it, that it doesn't fit into your middle-class intellectual values. But that's hardly my bloody fault, is it?'

'Look, I'm sorry but I really have to . . .' Thea insisted, attempting to raise her voice to be heard. The howl turned to a scream. 'Oh for God's sake!' she suddenly cried in desperation. 'Why don't you all just go away and let me get on with it!' And to Hal's shock and horror, she released a blue-veined breast and for once latched Tom on without any struggle.

Thea was ready to leave the hospital, two days after Tom was born; they had been the longest two days of her life. She had signed the forms and now sat on the bed awaiting her discharge papers and a note for her GP. She sat alone, with Tom in her arms, Jake's carrier bag of presents by her side and Hedda's book in her overnight bag. Out in the small, shabby waiting room, Jake and Hedda sat waiting for her, locked in a tense, discordant silence. Hal had been in earlier that day, but had gone back to college on the bus, after a blazing row and Hedda's refusal either to allow him in the car or to lend him the money to get a taxi. So Thea was going home escorted by her parents but without the baby's father and Jake was seething, with Hedda for not giving way and with Hal for not standing his ground. Only it wasn't in Jake's nature to rant and rave as Hedda did, he was always non-confrontational, and thus he seethed in silence.

As the ward sister approached her bed, Thea glanced up. She stood for a moment with Thea's notes in a brown folder and her discharge letter ready, then pulled the curtains around the bed in one quick sharp movement and sat down next to Thea.

'You didn't know you could cry so much, did you?'

Thea shook her head, rubbed a hand over her swollen eyes and trailed it down to Tom's head, letting it rest there gently.

'It's not going to be easy, Thea, having a baby on your own.' The sister looked at her. 'You are pretty much on your own, is that right?'

Thea hesitated, on the point of lying, then realised that there was no point in pretending any more. She was on her own, had been really since she made the decision to have the baby. Hal had tried, in the beginning at least, over the summer when it all seemed idyllic, but not since October, not since the Michaelmas term began. Thea had been fooling herself that they were living together in the cottage, it was the only thing that had kept her going. 'Yes,' she said, 'I'm on my own.' She shrugged but it was an expression that belied the terrible anguish and pain that she felt. 'Pretty much.'

'Would you like me to contact social services for you? They can help, you know.'

Thea shook her head. She'd seen enough social workers and social work students in the kitchen of 59, Park Road, Islington over the years to make up her mind about them as a breed. 'No thanks,' she said. 'I've got my parents, they're coming home with me, and Hedda is a counsellor – I'm sure I can go to her if I need help.'

The ward sister wasn't familiar with Thea's family – why should she have been? – and so missed the irony of the comment. She nodded and said, 'You'll be visited by a midwife every day for the next eight days, so if you have any worries concerning the baby, you can discuss them with her. After that it's over to your health visitor; she's a trained midwife and can help with most postnatal problems.' She handed the file across to Thea. 'Our number here at the hospital is on the top of the file. Any emergencies and you can ring us. OK?' She went to stand. The girl was an odd one, she'd wept buckets over the past two days and had seemed at one point to go completely to pieces, and yet there was a resilience there, a toughness that was beginning to show through the vulnerability. Good luck to her, the ward sister thought, having heard most of the slanging match that had gone on at her bedside. I hope she is tough, because she's damn well going to need to be.

Chapter Three

It was her first full day on her own and as Thea finished wringing out the new white babygrow, took it through to the small front room to the clothes horse she had placed in front of the fire, she wondered if it was ever going to end. The babygrow joined the other two she'd had to wash earlier and, leaning forward to put another log on to the fire, she muttered: 'Three down, Tom my darling, three to go.' Tom lay on the floor on a blanket, still howling and Thea knelt to pick him up. The moment she did so he stopped. 'Ah ha. Cottoned on already, have you?' she said, nuzzling the soft skin of his cheek. She cradled him for a while in the crook of her arm, then gently moved him up on to her shoulder and went back to the kitchen.

One-handed, Thea filled the kettle with enough water to make a cup of tea, then put a couple of slices of bread into the toaster. She'd had no food when Hedda and Jake brought her home yesterday and Jake had gone up to the village shop to buy some basics. With the prospect of eggs, baked beans and toast, washed down with some strong PG Tips, Thea felt childishly elated. This hormone thing is bizarre, she thought, to be suddenly elated when I'm exhausted, it's freezing, I weep almost continuously, and despite pains in my stomach have to carry Tom around endlessly. She smiled, conscious of the fragility of her mood and got on with preparing her supper as best she could with only one arm.

With everything bubbling efficiently, she glanced down at Tom and saw that he'd fallen asleep at last. Carefully, Thea carried him back to the warm front room and placed him on a small mound of cushions, covered with a blanket. She went back to dish up her meal, but just as the kettle boiled, the phone rang.

'Blast!' she cursed, walking into the hall. The noise had woken Tom, who opened his mouth and wailed, the toast popped up and the beans started to simmer, hissing in the pan. Thea snatched up the receiver and said, 'Yes?'

'Hey! Thea, it's me!'

'Oh God, sorry, Hal. It's just that my supper's ready and I'm—'

'No worries, babe, I'll call later, I—'

'No! No, it's OK, it can wait.' She was delighted to hear from him, had been worrying that she might not. 'Are you all right? I mean, I'm sorry about Hedda yesterday, she—'

'She's a harridan! Christ, Thea, no wonder you wanted to get the hell out of there!'

'I didn't, I—'

'I think I'd have had a baby if it meant getting away from Hedda!' Hal laughed, in the easy way he had.

Thea flushed. 'It wasn't that, Hal, it was wanting to have someone to—'

'Sorry, babe? I missed that, I'm watching the footie over

the top of Lucy Cox's head and Chelsea just scored! Listen, I'll come over later, shall I?'

Thea thought about Tom, she wondered if he'd sleep at all. She thought about having to tidy up or maybe cook something for Hal and that depressed her, but she desperately wanted to see him so she said, 'Well, erm, yes, whatever you want.'

'Great. Look, I'll come about tenish. A few of the guys here want to buy me a drink to wet the baby's head.'

'I see,' Thea said quietly.

'So I'll come on after the pub. OK?'

She nodded. 'Yes, fine, I'll—' But she didn't finish her sentence; it seemed that Chelsea had scored again and Hal had hung up.

Thea put the phone down, dashed towards the piercing wail of her baby, picked him up and darted back into the kitchen. She was just in time. The beans were stuck to the bottom of the pan, the eggs were on the hard-boiled side and the toast had cooled but none of it was irretrievable. Placing Tom on the floor on his blanket for a moment, she assembled the food on a plate, buttered the toast and made a big mug of tea in less than sixty seconds. She heaped a large spoon of sugar into her tea, plonked everything on to a tray, along with the box of chocolates that Jake had given her and bent to pick up Tom again. With Tom over her shoulder and the tray in one hand, Thea went back to the front room, with something nearing fervid anticipation.

As she lay the tray on the floor and eased herself down next to it, still holding the baby, she breathed a huge sigh of relief and gently moved Tom up higher on to her shoulder so that she could eat more easily. She picked up a forkful of baked beans, heard the rumble of wind in Tom's tummy and just as she put the food into her mouth, the rumble worked its way up the tiny body and Tom was sick, right across her shoulder and all down her back.

Hal downed the last of his pint and smiled, not focusing on the small group gathered at the table. He'd drunk too much, on top of a joint, and sat mellow and unthinking in the warm smoky atmosphere of the pub.

'Hal, it's ten-fifteen, shouldn't you think about getting a cab out to the cottage?'

One of his mates nudged him, hard, and brought him back into touch with reality. He blinked and sighed. 'Oh, um, yeah, yeah, I've gotta get out to see Thea. Can anyone lend me a fiver for the fare?'

Lucy Cox shook her head but still bent to find her bag and take out her purse. 'Here,' she said, handing a five-pound note across the table. 'I want it back though!'

'Yeah, sure.' Hal smiled and, tucking the note into his pocket, stood unsteadily and began to shuffle past his mates round the table to get out. Lucy stood up as well. 'I'd better walk you to the taxi rank,' she said. 'You might not make it on your own.' There was a chorus of catcalls and whistles to let her know that no one believed her and she frowned. 'He won't!' she insisted but everyone laughed.

Leaning on her for support, Hal waved at his friends and called out, 'See you tomorrow at the cottage, for tea, about four.' There was a general murmur of assent and, accompanied by Lucy, he left the pub. 'Shit,' he exclaimed, as the cold air hit him. 'I didn't think I was this pissed.'

He staggered for a few moments and put his hands up to his head.

Lucy took his arm. 'Come on,' she coaxed. 'You'll be fine once we've walked for a bit. It'll sober you up.'

'This is bloody good of you, Lucy,' Hal said, laying his head on her shoulder as they walked. 'I think you were right, I wouldn't have made it to the taxi on my own.' He slurred his words very slightly and Lucy put a hand up to stroke his hair. 'Hmmm,' he murmured, closing his eyes and suddenly missing his step.

'Oi!' she said sharply, elbowing him in the ribs. 'Don't go to sleep! You've got to get back to Duns Tew, remember?'

He opened his eyes again and sighed. 'Oh God, so I have.' He straightened, took a couple of deep breaths and pulled his sweater down. 'What time is it, Lucy?'

Lucy took his hand and pulled him along towards the taxi rank. 'Time to go and see your baby, Hal,' she said, denying herself the temptation to tell him to forget Duns Tew and come back with her. Lucy liked Hal, she liked him a lot, but she wasn't a romantic, she was a realist and in a small cottage in the Oxfordshire countryside Hal had a girlfriend and a baby. Lucy didn't want to get too involved.

'Here.' They reached the first taxi and Lucy leant towards the window. 'Near Banbury,' she said, then behind her to Hal: 'Address, Hal?'

'Duns Tew, Mason Cottage. I'll direct you once we get to the village, OK?'

'Right, mate.' The driver opened the back door of the cab and Hal turned to Lucy, reaching for her scarf and holding it in his hands.

'You coming to tea tomorrow?' She shrugged and Hal pulled her forward by her scarf to kiss her. 'Go on,' he said, 'I'd like you to.' She shrugged again and he pulled a face, kissed her again, then let her go.

'I'm not sure I should,' Lucy said.

'Why not?' Hal didn't really have any concept of morality. He was young and as far as he was concerned, had a whole life to live.

'I don't know,' Lucy answered, knowing exactly but not wanting to get into any discussion on Thea and commitment. 'I'll see how the day goes.'

Hal smiled. 'OK, whatever you want.' Things never mattered to him for very long; 'I'll see,' was a good enough answer, the sort he'd give himself. He climbed into the taxi and slumped back against the seat, letting Lucy slam the door shut after him. He waved as the car pulled off, saw Lucy turn back towards the pub, then without another thought for her, or Thea, he lay his head back, closed his eyes and passed out.

Thea had finally got Tom sleeping soundly and was just about to climb into bed herself when there was a knock on the door. She sighed, pulled a cardigan on over her nightdress and went to answer it. She knew it was Hal but what should have been a feeling of excitement was a dull ache inside her, not anger as such, more like habitual disappointment.

'Hal?' she called through the door.

'Yeah, hi! You haven't got any spare change have you, Thea? I owe this guy another quid.'

Thea pulled open the door and, without looking at Hal,

said, 'Yes, wait, I'll get it.' She returned with one of the precious pounds that Jake had given her to tide them over until her social security money came through and handed it to Hal.

'Where's your purse, babe?' he said. 'I ought to give the bloke a tip.'

Thea pulled her cardigan tight around her body. 'A pound is all I've got,' she said, tight-lipped. 'Sorry.'

'Shit,' Hal murmured, then: 'Oh well, never mind.' He gave the driver the extra coin, thanked him and shook his hand. Thea saw none of this, she had already gone inside.

'Thea?'

Thea was in the kitchen, filling the kettle. Hal stood in the doorway and watched her for a few moments. Her nightdress was thick cotton, a blue tartan, mid-calf length, and she wore an old navy cardigan over the top of it. On her feet were heavy wool socks and a pair of sheepskin slippers. As she shuffled about, finding the teapot, taking milk from the fridge, getting a mug down from the cupboard, Hal saw the shape of her breasts, large and heavy through the nightie, and felt himself harden.

'Don't bother with tea for me,' he said. Thea looked up. She was pale, faint blue shadows underlined her grey eyes and her face was pinched with exhaustion.

'You sure?'

'Yeah.' Hal moved across the kitchen to her and stood behind her, placing his arms around her, his hands on her breasts. 'Wow,' he murmured, kissing the back of her neck. He felt her tense and whispered, 'Come on, Thea, relax, baby.' She smelt odd, sweet and milky, but he found that even more of an excitement. 'These breasts are amazing, they—'

Suddenly Thea pulled away. 'Don't, Hal,' she said, turning to face him. 'I'm sorry, but I don't feel like it, I . . .'

Hal pushed a limp strand of hair off her face. 'Hey, no problem, babe, you're tired, I understand.' And he did too, it was part of the reason she loved him, he seemed to understand everything, there was never any pressure.

'Yes.' She softened towards him but could smell beer and cigarettes and after the smell of Tom it made her feel sick. Going back to the tea, she said, 'I think I'll have a cup.'

Hal stood back a pace. 'Yeah, sure.' He moved over to the fridge. 'There isn't anything to eat, is there? I've got the munchies.' Opening the fridge door, he peered inside. 'Oh wow! Chocolates!' And taking out the box that Jake had bought for Thea, he opened it and grabbed a handful of chocolates, stuffing them one after another into his mouth. 'Is there any bread for toast?' he mumbled, his mouth full.

Thea nodded, not trusting herself to speak. Why did it always have to go wrong? She took her mug of tea and moved aside to let him get to the toaster. 'I think I'll go to bed,' she said.

Hal glanced over his shoulder, then, as if suddenly sensing the situation, walked across to Thea and gently stroked her cheek. 'You get some sleep, babe,' he said. 'I'll be up to see you and Tom in a minute, OK?' He smiled at her and she nodded, feeling momentarily reassured. She looked up at him to smile, but he had already turned back to the toaster. 'You want some toast?' he asked.

'No, thanks.'

He didn't bother to look round again, although Thea waited for him to. She waited a minute or so, but he didn't. As far as he was concerned she was out of the room and out of his mind. She moved off towards the stairs, a deepening sense of resignation pressing down on her, like a dull, heavy weight. She had been warned, Hedda had told her it wouldn't be easy. Holding the tea in both hands to warm them, she said, 'Goodnight, Hal.'

Hal was digging in the fridge for the butter. He popped his head out. 'What?' He saw Thea by the door. 'Oh, yeah, right, 'night, babe.' Back in the fridge he pulled out the butter, then remembered something. 'Oh, Thea?'

Thea turned. 'Yes?'

'I asked a few people round for tea tomorrow, about four, four-thirty. You don't mind, do you?'

Thea held her breath for a moment, too frustrated to speak. After a pause, she said, 'Mind? Of course not.' Her voice was clipped. 'Why should I?'

But her irony was lost on Hal; he was too stoned to pick it up. He grinned. 'I knew you wouldn't,' he said, then: ''Night, babe.' And with that he went on buttering his toast.

At five a.m., in the pitch darkness of a winter morning, Thea swam up out of a drowning sleep and, suddenly feeling panicked, reached out for Tom. He was still there, nestled on her chest, the covers pulled up round his tiny body and his face pressed in close to her breast. Relief washed over her and she started to sink again, back down into sleep. He stirred, made a strange nasal sound, like a snort, then gave a small whimper. Thea opened her eyes, shifted slightly to ease the pressure on her body, then closed them again. She fell asleep almost immediately and woke with a start ten minutes later as Tom let out a howl.

Easing herself up a bit, she moved her head, first right, then left, trying to loosen the stiffness in her neck, and shook her arm, which had pins and needles. Last night was a blur. She couldn't distinguish sleep from waking and realised she had spent most of the night in a semi-upright position with Tom on her chest. He had fed on and off for much of the night and she thought that she had got up twice to change him, but couldn't quite remember. Beside her, flat on his back and snoring lightly, was Hal, in a deep, almost unconscious sleep.

Thea stayed where she was, registering the cold in the bedroom, then moved into a more comfortable position in order to let Tom feed. He latched on, seeming to have got the hang of it in the night, and she closed her eyes again. They stayed like that for twenty minutes, Tom feeding blissfully and Thea thirsty and irritated with the snoring beside her, wishing that Hal would wake up and offer to make her a cup of tea. He didn't.

When Tom had finished his feed, he fell asleep again and Thea lifted him gently into his basket. She looked at Hal, felt like poking him hard, but resisted, and went down to make herself a drink.

When Hal finally woke and rolled over in an empty bed, Thea had already been up for nearly eight hours. She had managed to bath, wash her hair and find clean, presentable clothes. Her stomach still had a puffed, baggy look to it, like a deflated balloon, and she was nowhere near wearing anything normal, but there were no stretch marks that she could find, which was a relief, and her breasts had lost their rock-solid, silicone feel and seemed to be more part of her than they had been yesterday. She had also fed Tom again, four times, bathed him, changed him twice and put him into a clean babygrow. She now lay on the shabby, hard, uncomfortable sofa, a rug over her and Tom, exhausted and unable to move.

On waking, she had expected to do a great deal more: tidy, iron, lay a fire, cook breakfast; the list went on. She had expected to be the shining example of motherhood, fresh and lovely, smelling of soap, a rosy-cheeked baby in her arms and the scent of cooking in the air. Instead, however, she found herself wondering aimlessly through the cottage, unthinking, despondent, drugged with exhaustion. She couldn't be bothered to wash up after Hal, let alone summon the energy and resources to cook for him. She felt bleak. Not depressed as such, nothing as tangible as that, just hopeless. She felt like a void, an empty space where Thea used to be.

'Thea?'

Looking up from the sofa, Thea saw Hal, in boxers and a sweater, dishevelled, his blond hair untidy, his face rough with first growth and felt the void get bigger. He smiled and she thought briefly that she hardly knew him; she loved him, but she hardly knew him.

'Hi,' he said gently, crossing to her and kneeling by her side. He bent across and kissed her, carefully and tenderly, on the mouth, then he traced the curve of Tom's cheek with his fingertip. 'Hello, little man,' he said. 'Any tea made?'

'No.' Thea watched his face and wondered if everything

came easy to Hal because nothing really touched him. She dismissed the thought; she was being negative. He was here, wasn't he?

'You OK, babe?' he asked.

Thea thought for a moment about telling him the truth, but it wasn't an honest question and she didn't think Hal really wanted to know the answer. 'Yes,' she said. 'A bit tired, but fine.'

He stood and stretched his long, still faintly tanned limbs. 'Good. Have you eaten?'

Thea shook her head.

'D'you fancy eggs and bacon?'

She hesitated, thinking for a moment that he was offering to cook, then he grinned and she remembered that Hal professed not to know how to cook. 'No, why?' she answered. 'Do you?'

'God, I'd absolutely love some!' Hal exclaimed. 'I spotted the bacon last night in the fridge and I've been dreaming about it ever since!'

Thea sighed. She swung her legs down on to the floor and sat up, holding the baby out to Hal. 'Here,' she said, 'Take Tom and I'll get something to eat.'

'Oh, um, right, yeah.' Hal took the baby with distinct unease, watched Thea walk towards the kitchen and said, 'He's asleep, I think I'll leave him here, on the sofa.'

'You can't,' Thea said. 'It's not safe.'

'No! Really?' Hal looked amazed and Thea bit back a sharp reply. 'What about the floor? We can leave him on the floor, can't we?'

'What? Like an old newspaper? Oh please, give him here if you don't want to hold him!' Thea suddenly snapped.

Hal looked injured. 'It was just a suggestion, babe, I don't know anything about babies, do I?'

Thea turned and glared at him. 'And I do?'

'Well, it was your idea,' Hal shot back.

'So you keep telling me!' Thea snarled. Her outburst woke Tom in her arms who opened his eyes, saw her and began to howl. 'Oh God!' she cried, 'I've only just fed him!'

Hal held up his hands in horror. 'Well, don't look at me, babe!'

'As if I would!' Thea suddenly shouted. 'When have you ever done anything useful?'

Hal raised an eyebrow. 'Nine months ago?' He smiled, meaning to lighten the situation, but it backfired.

'Oh, for God's sake!' Thea suddenly sobbed, unable to hold back the tears. 'Get out! Go on, go! I've had enough of you and your stupid sense of humour!'

Hal stood where he was and stared at her. He had the urge to take her at her word, pack the few belongings he kept here and leave, get the hell out of it, but that would involve making a decision, a big one, and he wasn't sure he could do that. He looked down at his hands for a few minutes, let Thea calm down, then said the most reasonable thing he could think of. 'I'll go to the pub for a while,' he offered. 'Let you cool off a bit. I'll be back in time for tea.'

For some reason he couldn't fathom, Thea turned her back on him and walked into the kitchen, slamming the door behind her.

Chapter Four

Things between Thea and Hal deteriorated. Hal had no real conception of what Thea was going through and found it easier to stay away. He was young and inexperienced, he knew nothing about responsibility and he had a degree to get, that was his priority.

Thea had known nothing about responsibility either, until she found herself with Tom, twenty-four hours a day, completely reliant on her for food, warmth and comfort. Then she knew the full meaning of the word, at just nineteen.

It wasn't easy; it wasn't anything like she had imagined. Of course, Hedda could have told her so, and would have done, if Jake had let her. But Jake kept Thea and Hedda apart, finding it better to travel up to Oxford straight after work on an evening that Hedda went to the refuge and see Thea on his own, with a car full of supplies from Sainsbury's and Boots.

Thea did, however, learn how to cope. She managed. She found a routine and she existed, in a sort of muddled, anxious state, moving from one day to the next without much joy. She loved Tom, but not in the way she had imagined she would love him, not in the all-consuming, rapturous way she'd read about. Perhaps, in amongst the daily grind and drudgery of domesticity that a baby in a cold cottage with no washing machine or dryer, no television and no money entailed, she didn't have time to think about love. She just had to get on with it. Perhaps, if she thought about love, she would have had to think about Hal and that was something she couldn't bear to do. So she carried on, caring for Tom and seeing Hal on the odd occasion that he made it out to the cottage, until the days began to lengthen and the earth warmed, sending bright yellow daffodils up through the grass to herald the spring. Then, just before the Easter vacation, Hal turned up out of the blue.

Thea was in the garden when he arrived. She was hanging out a basket full of babygrows to dry on the line in the weak spring sunshine and she carried Tom in a sling across her body. She wore the same clothes she had worn all winter, pregnancy leggings, a long-sleeved T-shirt with her navy cardigan over the top and thick wool socks with sheepskin slippers. Her shoulders were rounded with the weight of the baby, her thighs heavy and the fleshy bulge of her stomach was visible through the lycra that covered it.

Hal stood at the side gate to the garden and watched her for a few moments, not sure if he recognised this person, if he knew who or what Thea had become. He was even less sure of himself, of what he had to do with it all, so he did what he always did and put it from his mind. Walking into view, he called out, 'Thea?' and tried to smile when she spun round. 'Hi.'

Thea smiled back, but it was simply a movement of her mouth. 'Hello,' she answered. 'How are you?'

Hal shrugged. 'Fine, well, sort of.'

Thea nodded. 'I'll just finish these.'

'Yeah, sure, go ahead.' He didn't offer to help, but leant against the wall and took his sunglasses out of his pocket, slipping them on to his face. It took Thea some time, there was no energy in her movements, they were slow and robotic, but she finished eventually and joined Hal at the gate. He took the empty basket for her and led the way back round to the front of the house.

'It must be nice to have the windows open,' Hal said, walking inside.

'Yes.'

Thea went into the kitchen and filled the kettle. She placed it on the Rayburn and reached up to feel the clothes hanging on a drying rack above it.

'Is that new?' Hal asked.

'Yes, Jake put it up for me.'

'It's cool.'

Thea winced. Turning away from him, she busied herself with making tea.

'How's Tom?'

She glanced over her shoulder. 'He's fine.' There was a silence, interrupted only by the hiss of the kettle. 'D'you want tea?'

'No, no thanks, I can't stop, I've got a friend picking me up and I—' Hal broke off. Unused to doing anything that he didn't like, he was finding this almost impossible. There was another silence, Thea made herself tea in a mug, then Hal suddenly blurted out, 'Look, Thea, I've come to let you know that I'm leaving, leaving Oxford, in a week's time, at the end of term.'

Thea turned; her face had drained of all colour. 'Leaving?' She looked momentarily confused, then she nodded. 'Ah, for the Easter vac, right?'

Hal shuffled from foot to foot. 'No, not just for the Easter vac.' He stopped, took a breath and looked down. 'I mean for good. I'm changing courses, going to Newcastle University, to do pure maths. They don't think I'm going to pass my second year here, my tutor seems to think I haven't got the right attitude and, well, it's a case of jump before I'm pushed.'

Thea stood still. She held her tea, but her hand had begun to shake so she put it down, slopping some over the edge of the cup. She stared at Hal, at his downcast head. 'But what about me and Tom?' she murmured. Her heart hammered in her chest. 'What about us?'

Hal shrugged. 'Look, Thea, I don't know about us, I really don't. I mean, I can't help you with money because I don't have any and it's not as if I've been here, I mean, you won't even miss me, I'm never here.'

Thea began to cry. Everything he said was true but so was the fact that he was abandoning her.

Hal ran his hands through his hair. 'Oh shit,' he said. 'Thea, don't cry, please, I didn't want any of this to happen, honest I didn't. I didn't know it was all going to turn out like this!' He moved towards her but she edged back. 'I haven't given notice on the cottage, you can still rent it, we just have to change the lease. Look, I'm sorry, I . . .'

Thea blew her nose.

'Don't cry, Thea, please don't cry. It won't be that bad, honestly.'

She said nothing and the tears streamed unchecked down her face.

'God, Thea! It's not as if I've ever been any use to you!' Hal suddenly cried. 'I mean, I didn't know how to handle all this. It was all too much for me. Christ, I haven't even told my parents yet! I'm scared to death of telling them!' He sunk his head in his hands and stood there, helpless and ashamed.

Thea looked at him. She stared at the top of his head for some time and her sobs slowly receded. Hal was the same age as her and yet he seemed so young, so far removed from her that she wondered for a moment how he could ever have fathered her child. She wiped her face on the sleeve of her cardigan and said, 'I always wondered, you know, why they never came to see Tom, or rang even.'

Hal glanced up at her.

'Will you ever tell them?'

He thought for a moment, then shrugged.

'At least you're honest,' Thea said. She took a piece of kitchen paper off the roll on the work surface and blew her nose again, then she picked up her tea and swallowed down a mouthful.

'D'you want to go and get your things?'

Hal nodded.

'They're upstairs.'

He turned towards the door and looked back at her as if expecting more: more anger, more tears; but there was nothing. She was numb, empty and blank, and she was all cried out.

'Thea, I . . .'

Thea held her hand up and Hal stopped. 'Leave me your home address,' she said, 'and I'll keep in touch, let you know how Tom is.'

Hal nodded. He stood uneasily by the door, wondering if this was it.

'I think I'll take Tom out for a walk,' Thea went on. 'Can you lock the front door after you and leave the key round the back under the plant pot?'

'Yeah, sure.'

'Right.' Thea walked towards him and Hal moved aside to let her through. As she brushed past him, he felt the solid warm back of the baby and reached out to touch Tom. Thea stopped him.

'Don't,' she said sharply. 'Don't start something you don't wish to carry on.' Leaving his hand in mid air, she walked out of the house and away from Hal. It was the only way she could bear to do it.

For a long time after she returned to the house and saw that Hal had gone, Thea sat in the chilly front room with Tom in her arms and simply stared at the wall. She fed him, on and off, and got up to change him once, but that was all she did. It grew cold and dark but she made no fire and turned no lights on. She wrapped Tom in a blanket and lay him on the floor under the string hung with pieces of silver foil but she didn't talk to him or play with him at all.

Then, at seven, the phone rang; Thea ignored it. At eight, she stood, picked Tom up and took him up to the bathroom to wash and change him for bed. She touched his small, warm, silky-soft body with her rough, chapped hands, handling him with infinite tenderness, then carried him into her bedroom. It was cold in there; a room with three outside walls, it had a clammy chill to it that made her shiver. Switching on the electric blanket, she climbed into bed, still dressed and with her socks on, and put Tom to her breast. There, as he fed and slept through the night, Thea lay and stared out of the small cottage window at the inky black sky with a sense of drowning desperation.

It was ten-thirty. Jake stood in the hall with the receiver in his hand and let the phone ring on. This was his third call to Thea that evening and not one had been answered. He was worried. He told himself not to be, but he was. Thea never went out, she hadn't been out since Tom was born – another thing to worry about – so why wasn't she answering the phone? He hoped to God nothing had happened to her in that isolated place. Drumming his fingers on the hall table, he gave it another few rings and hung up. Just as he turned from the phone, Hedda came in.

'Hello. Been on the phone?'

'Yes, no answer.'

She took her coat off and draped it over the newel post along with her handbag, and dumped her briefcase on the floor. 'Good day?' she asked, as she did all this.

'Not bad.' Jake walked towards the kitchen.

'You all right, Jake?' Hedda stood in the doorway, untying her silk scarf.

Jake took an open bottle of red wine off the work surface and refilled his glass. 'Fine,' he answered. 'D'you want a glass?'

Hedda pulled a face, then said, 'Oh all right, go on.' He

poured and she accepted the glass. 'Come on, spit it out,' she said, taking her glass to the table and pulling out a chair. 'You're never this morose.'

'Thanks! That implies that I'm always morose but not usually this bad.'

Hedda raised an eyebrow. 'You said it.' She took a sip of wine. 'Oh come on, Jake, it was a joke.'

Jake walked across to the table and sat down opposite her. 'I was trying to ring Thea,' he said. Hedda tensed. 'I can't get any reply, I've rung three times tonight and there's no answer.'

'Perhaps she's out,' Hedda said sharply.

'No, Thea doesn't go out, Hedda, she hasn't been out since Tom was born.'

'You never told me that!'

'You never asked.'

She drank down a mouthful of wine, then said, 'But it's been weeks! She hasn't been out at all?'

Jake shook his head.

'Not to the supermarket or to a mothers' group? Not once?'

'She walks up to the village shop every three days or so for supplies, but apart from that no, I don't think so.'

'Jesus!' Hedda couldn't contain her shock. 'Why didn't you tell me this before? You should have said something, Jake, you should have told me. That isn't right, it isn't normal! She should have started making friends, seeing other mums, getting her life into order.'

'I know.'

There was a tense silence, then Hedda said reproachfully, 'You should have told me.'

Jake looked at her. '"I don't want to know", were your exact words, I think. "I don't want to hear endless chat about the baby and how wonderful it all is. She's throwing her life away and I don't want to have to listen to it." You did say that, didn't you, Hedda?'

Hedda didn't answer. She stood, went to her bag in the hall and found her cigarettes. She had been trying to cut down and left the packet in her bag with the idea that having to walk out to the hall to get them made it more difficult to smoke. Lighting up and returning the packet to her bag, she came into the kitchen and sat down again. 'Could the phone be out of order?' she asked.

'I don't know, that's the next step, I suppose. I'll ring the operator in a minute and get them to check the line.'

'And if it isn't? What then?'

Jake looked away from Hedda's penetrating gaze. There was a time when he would have taken her hand in his, held it for reassurance, but now he simply stared at the clock and did nothing. 'If there's still no reply in the morning,' he said, 'then I think I'll go down and see her.'

'You'll go? On your own?'

He looked back at her. 'Yes, as I have done all these past weeks.'

Hedda took the criticism without flinching. She knew about Jake's visits to Thea and she had chosen to ignore them. It was her way of dealing with the situation. 'But if it's all gone wrong, if she's unhappy, then she needs to be brought home, Jake, she needs help and, with all due respect, I think I'm the one to give it to her.'

'With all due respect, Hedda, I don't think Thea needs

anything until she asks for it. If she wants to come home then we bring her, but only if she wants to.'

Hedda snorted derisively and Jake felt his temper flare. He took a deep breath, held it and then let it out very slowly. Jake had once been so proud of the liberal, open marriage that he shared with Hedda, he'd once seen it as the way forward for a dying institution. Now he wondered if so many years of doing their own thing had simply served to separate them and that it wasn't a marriage at all, just a co-existence, two people living independent lives in the same house. He said, 'I think Thea might need some space, to sort her head out. That's what we need to give her, here, at home.'

Hedda, to his surprise, nodded. 'I think you're right,' she said, stubbing out her cigarette and drinking down the last of her wine. She stood up. 'And then we can get her back to university and get her life back on track.' She turned towards the door. 'Goodnight, Jake.' Without waiting for a reply, she went upstairs to bed.

Thea woke the following morning, having been up to feed Tom twice in the night and fallen asleep after the second feed, sitting upright, with Tom on the bed beside her. She opened her eyes, felt the habitual sinking in the pit of her stomach and closed them again. She had to get up, get washed, changed, go through the motions of living, of keeping herself together, but she couldn't be bothered. What was the point anyway? She never went anywhere or saw anyone. There was nothing to get up for. So she moved the pillows and eased herself down the bed, lying as still as she could so as not to wake Tom. And she stayed there, letting the phone ring unanswered downstairs, until Tom woke and she had to heave herself up and out of bed and lumber, unwashed and unchanged, through the dreary grind of the morning.

Jake parked his car up on the grass verge in front of the cottage, as much off the narrow country lane as he could manage, climbed out, locked up and headed towards the cottage. The curtains were still drawn, there were no lights on and he could hear no noise. 'Thea?' he suddenly called out, breaking into a run. 'Thea? Are you home?'

Thea was sitting alone in the dark. She had put Tom down for a sleep and, unable to summon enough energy to even make herself a drink, had slumped down on the floor in the front room with her head in her hands.

'Thea? Are you there?'

She started. She hadn't heard properly and wondered for a moment about getting up to see if someone was there, but changed her mind.

'Thea!'

She jumped as a sharp bang on the window made the glass rattle in the frame. 'Thea? If you're in there, open the bloody door!' Jake shouted. He was frightened now. 'Thea! Where the hell are you?'

It was Jake! Thea got to her feet, her limbs stiff from sitting so long in one position. She stumbled to the front door and, unlocking it, pulled it open, blinking at the sunlight. Jake appeared, she saw his face, saw him move to embrace her and without even knowing it, she started to cry. There was no wail, no sobbing, just silent, unstoppable tears.

'Oh Thea.' Jake held her, felt her fragility and stroked

her hair. 'It's OK,' he murmured, 'it's OK, I'm here now, there's no need to cry.'

Thea pulled back. She shook her head and stared at him, her face creased with pain. 'There is,' she whispered. 'Yes, there is. It's all gone wrong, all of it. Hal's left me and I don't know how to cope with it . . .' She broke off to wipe her face on the sleeve of her cardigan, which, from the look of it, she had done before.

'You'll manage,' Jake said. 'You'll get over him, Thea, I know you will—'

'No!' Thea suddenly cried, throwing her hands up. 'It's not him that I can't cope with, I don't care that he's gone, he was never here anyway, I . . . I . . .' She looked behind her as a piercing wail broke out. 'I can't cope with Tom, I don't how to do it, I . . .' The wail seemed to go on for ever, then there was a moment's pause, as Tom drew breath, and it started again. Thea put her hands up to her face and sobbed.

Jake stood where he was for a moment, then he made a split-second decision. This was as far as Thea would ever get in asking for help. He put his hands on Thea's shoulders and said, 'You stay here, don't move. I'm going to get Tom, throw your things in a bag and then we're going home. OK?' Thea didn't answer him but that didn't matter. He moved past her into the cottage, into the kitchen, where he went through the cupboards with great speed. He left the few odd bits of food and took only the unopened bottle of Calpol he found and a box of sterilising tablets. In the front room, he took the babygrows off the clothes horse, collected up a blanket off the floor and found a rattle on the sofa. Upstairs, he found Thea's holdall, zipped it open and literally threw everything he could find that belonged to her and Tom into it. When he'd finished, checking every drawer, the wardrobe and the bathroom cabinet, he was amazed that the bag wasn't even half full. He zipped it up, picked up Tom, still in his basket, and carried both downstairs.

'Does he need a feed?' he asked in the hall. Thea hadn't moved; she stood, still weeping, in the doorway and shook her head.

'I'll check his nappy then,' Jake said. Tom, who had momentarily shut up on being carried, set up wailing again and as Jake took him out and laid him on the floor he smiled at the baby. 'What a cross little face,' he said, lifting the edge of the disposable to peer at what might be inside. 'No, no dirty nappy, it's just bad temper then, is it?' He lifted Tom, held him for a few moments, then lay him back in the basket and went to Thea.

'Right, that's it then.' He held her baby out for her. 'Into the car. We'll stop in Oxford and buy him a car seat.'

She took Tom, glanced behind her at the cottage and walked out towards Jake's car. She said nothing and Jake wasn't sure if she really knew what was happening. He wasn't sure if she hadn't slipped so far under that she had lost her grasp on reality.

He followed her, slamming the door of the cottage behind him, and opened the rear passenger door for her. She hesitated and Jake thought she might change her mind, or ask what the hell was going on, but she didn't. She said, 'What shall I do with Tom?'

'Let's take him out of the basket. You strap yourself in

and then hold him on your lap. We'll sort him out properly as quickly as we can.'

Thea nodded, lifted Tom out and climbed into the car. Jake pulled the seatbelt between then. He put her things in the boot, then climbed in to the front and started the engine.

'You all right?' he asked, shifting into gear. But Thea didn't answer, she just cradled Tom on her lap and stared blankly out of the window. Jake didn't ask again. He moved the car off wondering what on earth they were going to do next.

Chapter Five

By the time they got to Islington, Jake had decided. He pulled up outside 59, Park Road, helped Thea out of the car and into the house, carried in Tom in his new car seat and then moved into action.

'Thea,' he said, 'why don't you go upstairs and have a really long, hot bath and I'll look after Tom.'

Thea glanced down at the baby, still asleep and looking very comfortable in his car seat. 'I haven't got any clean clothes,' she said. 'I've got nothing to change into.'

'Well, just put a towelling robe on then and I'll chuck a load in the washing machine.'

Still she hesitated; it was as if she was waiting for the catch.

'Go on,' Jake urged. 'There's gallons of hot water and if you want clean pants you can always borrow a pair of Hedda's.'

'A pair of Hedda's?'

'All right then, a pair of mine.'

At last Thea smiled. It was a tentative action but it was a start. She kissed the tip of her finger and placed it on Tom's forehead. 'I've never left him before,' she said, her foot on the first step. 'Not even to have a bath.'

'There's always a first time for everything,' Jake replied, and without waiting for Thea to hesitate further, he took Tom into the kitchen and put the kettle on for tea.

When he heard the water running, Jake got on the phone. First he called John Lewis and ordered a cot, some bedding, some new babygrows, vests, a changing mat, a bouncing chair and a musical mobile that played 'Hickory Dickory Dock', an item the sales lady insisted he couldn't do without. That done, he telephoned Hedda at work, left a message about Thea and asked his wife to call him back. Lastly he called the hairdresser that Hedda went to in Kensington and made an appointment for Thea the next day.

'She'll want a cut, treatments and a blow dry,' he said. 'Yes, with the top stylist please. Eleven-thirty? Yes, that sounds fine. Good, thanks.' He made a note of it and went to hang up. 'Oh, by the way, do you mind breast feeding in the salon?' There was a short, uncomfortable pause and he was told that they didn't. 'Good,' Jake said. 'We'll see you tomorrow then.' He rang off, went to fetch Tom and took him, miraculously still sound asleep in his car seat, upstairs to his study.

Jake had dismantled his desk by the time that Hedda arrived home. He was stacking the pieces neatly and putting the screws into a small jam jar as she came up the stairs.

'Jake?' She stood in the doorway frowning. 'Where's Thea and what on earth are you doing?'

'Thea is in the bath,' Jake replied, 'and I'm clearing my study, to make room for a cot. It's being delivered tomorrow.'

'A cot?'

He stopped what he was doing and turned to Hedda. 'Yes, a cot. Tom needs somewhere to sleep and that somewhere needs to be apart from Thea. I plan to slap some white emulsion on these walls tonight, once I've cleared the books, move a chest of drawers in here – that Victorian pine one we have on the landing to be precise, it's the right height for changing a baby on – and I'm going to bring the chaise in from the spare room, so there's somewhere for Thea to sit and feed in the night.' He dropped the last nut and bolt into the jam jar and screwed the top on.

Hedda leant against the doorframe. 'Jake, I think you've gone barmy,' she said coldly. 'I really do!'

He raised an eyebrow. 'Do you? I see.' Then he turned towards the window. 'I forgot to mention the blind. I thought I'd get one if those ready-made roller blinds from Homebase, bright red – or blue maybe – and put it up tomorrow. This Venetian slat thing is well past its sell-by date.'

'Jake!' Hedda snapped. 'What the hell is going on? You've brought Thea and the baby home because we think she's ill, has possibly got post-natal depression, and you think a spot of DIY is going to make everything all right?' She shook her head. 'I don't believe you! Thea needs proper help, counselling, she needs to be moved on in her life, she—'

'She needs some very basic things, Hedda!' Jake interjected, 'Like a cot for her baby, a room for him to sleep in so that she can have a bit of space for herself. She needs clothes for him, clothes for herself, she needs time, on her own and with Tom, she needs to boost her confidence, she needs practical, useful help.' He stared hard at Hedda but he didn't raise his voice. 'She does not need bloody counselling,' he said icily. 'Not now. Not yet.'

Hedda stared back. 'That's your opinion,' she said.

'Yes and that's the way it's going to be as well.' Jake bent and stacked the legs of the desk on top of the top and side pieces. He straightened. 'I won't argue about this, Hedda, and I won't give in either. I can help Thea, I'm already on sabbatical and my research paper can wait.'

Hedda snorted; they both knew what sabbatical meant. Jake had been made redundant from his post as senior lecturer in Sociological Studies at the West Trant Polytechnic when it was made into the North London University and so far, in nearly a year, he hadn't found another job. Hedda resented it, she privately thought him too ineffectual to get anything else and scoffed at his research paper.

'What about finding another job?' she demanded.

'That can wait too. We've got enough money, my redundancy package and you earn a considerable sum. We don't struggle—'

'You don't struggle!' Hedda snapped. Jake ignored her.

'Look, Thea needs help with Tom,' he went on, despite her glare. 'And I've racked my brains trying to think of how we can give it to her. I thought about nannies and au pairs and God knows what and the best I can come up with is me.'

'You?' Hedda walked into the room and closed the door behind her. 'Oh, very good! Now I know you've gone barmy!' she hissed, 'So all thought of our future has gone out of the window, has it?'

'No, it's just that—'

'That what? What on earth do you think you can contribute, Jake, at this stage in your life?'

'I can look after my grandson for a start!' Jake hissed back. 'It may have been some time ago but I have done it before, remember?'

'How could I forget,' Hedda said archly. 'Disgusting, stinking nappies all over the place, complete chaos, you too exhausted to even get it up at night!'

Jake kept his gaze on her face. 'Is that why you had an affair?' he asked. Hedda took a step back. Her face registered shock, then something like pain which she covered almost instantly. 'It was a long time ago, Jake,' she said, 'and anyway I thought we'd agreed not to be possessive.'

'You'd agreed.'

There was a silence and Hedda stared down at her hands, twisting her wedding ring round and round her finger. 'This doesn't concern Thea,' she said at last.

'No' Jake agreed. 'It doesn't.'

She knelt and looked at Tom, who was just stirring. 'He's very healthy looking,' she commented.

Jake knelt next to her. 'D'you want to hold him?'

'No, not yet,' she said quickly. 'Let him sleep.'

Jake unfastened the straps on the car seat and picked Tom out, holding him close. 'He's here to stay, Hedda, we can't change that. You may think he was a mistake, you may even be right, but he's entitled to a chance.' He looked at her over the top of Tom's head. 'Let's give it to him, eh?'

Hedda bit her lip, then she heard Thea come out of the bathroom and stood to open the door. 'Thea,' she called, 'we're in Jake's study.' As she turned away from Tom, Jake realised that she hadn't even replied.

Chapter Six

One night several weeks later, when Thea and Tom were well and truly settled in, Hedda came home earlier than expected. She had decided to give the refuge a miss; she was tired, the strain of having a baby in the house was far greater than she had imagined or remembered and the fact that Jake seemed to find it all a terrific idea was beginning to grate. She felt isolated in her own home; Jake had no time for her and she had little time for the baby. She had no one to talk to, which was bizarre really: she listened to other people's problems all day and every day and yet had nobody to discuss her own with.

She had friends, of course, Jude and Marian, but there was something about her friendships that had recently made Hedda feel uneasy. Although she would never admit it, Hedda had always felt superior to her friends; she had always been the giver, because she could well afford to give. But now she had problems, solid, unavoidable problems of her own, her superiority had slipped and that was hard to take. Despite all that she had done with her life, Hedda had not escaped the trials that befall lesser mortals. Her marriage was under enormous strain, the marriage that had once been the envy of all who met them; her daughter – who had never given her a day's worry in her life – had thrown up an illustrious academic career for single teenage motherhood; and to top it all, she was woken nightly and each morning at six a.m. by the whine of a small baby upon whose head fell the blame for everything that had gone wrong.

So, as she came in the door, hung her coat up and walked into the kitchen to pour herself a longed-for glass of chilled chardonnay, it was hardly surprising that she flipped at the sight of Jake in a red nose and green wig, playing peepo – a game she had always considered particularly mindless – with a cream silk scarf, covered in dribble and Tom, who was perched in his car seat on the pine table, a car seat that had left a deep ridged groove in the hand-polished wax finish of the table top.

'What the bloody hell is going on?' she cried, throwing her bag down on the floor. 'For God's sake, Jake! Look at the table! And look at my cushion!' She swiped it out of Jake's hand. 'Christ! Just look at it, will you? It's covered in crap!' Tom began to cry.

'It's only a cushion, Hedda,' Jake replied coldly, then, picking Tom up, said, 'You've made him cry.'

Hedda let out a long, pained growl. 'God give me strength!' she snapped. 'Where is the child's mother anyway?'

'The child's mother, as you so lovingly call her, is upstairs getting ready to go out.'

'Out? Go out?'

'Yes.'

'Oh great! Bloody great! So we're stuck with him again, are we? No supper to speak of, jiggling him about to keep him quiet, no peace at all, no music because it will wake him and certainly no sex, we haven't had sex since he arrived and he's not even our baby!'

Jake had soothed Tom back to smiles during Hedda's short outburst and now walked around with him facing outwards so that he could see all the action. 'Smile at Granny,' he cooed, at which Hedda's nostrils flared dangerously. Then he said, 'There's pizza, it's ready-made but I can just pop it in the oven when you're ready.'

'Pizza,' Hedda repeated, through clenched teeth. 'Jake,' she said, 'this has got to stop! I am going up to see Thea right now and tell her that you looking after Tom just isn't going to work.'

Jake didn't reply. He knew Hedda could say, declare, demand, shout, rant and even rave but he wasn't going to give up looking after Tom until Thea wanted him to.

'And while we're on the subject,' she went on, 'this child needs some constructive play, not pee-bloody-po with a tired middle-aged man trying to recreate his youth. He needs proper stimulation, learning toys, he needs to be stretched, shown his full potential, he needs—'

'Oh Hedda,' Jake sighed, 'please spare me. He's just learnt to smile and chuckle and he needs practice. He needs love and attention and laughter. There's plenty of time for learning.' He kissed Tom and placed him back in his car seat. 'Anyway,' he said, 'if I'd wanted to recreate my youth, I'd have bought a motorbike.' And picking Tom up, he took him into the sitting room to play uninterrupted there.

Hedda went upstairs. She heard the sound of the hair-dryer and knocked on Thea's bedroom door.

'Yup! Come in!'

Hedda opened the door. Thea was standing in front of the mirror trying to dry her hair. The new cut that Jake had initiated suited her, but she had no idea how to style it and consequently it flopped over one side of her face and had a strange kink in it on the other. Hedda sighed. It looked bizarre.

'Is that what you're wearing?' she asked.

Thea glanced down at her jeans, too tight and with an indelible stain on the thigh – probably nappy-rash cream – her shoes, two years old and hardly fashionable, and her sweater, Jake's V-necked M & S jersey in dull grey. 'Yes. I, erm . . .' She caught Hedda's disapproval and flushed. 'It's all I've got,' she said.

'I see.' Hedda chewed on her lip, all thought of chastisement vanishing at the sight of Thea's hopeless struggle to look nice. Her sympathies aroused, she said, 'Hang on, I think I've got a lipstick that would really suit you,' and, disappearing out of the room across the landing to her own bedroom, she returned a minute or so later with her make-up bag. She unzipped it, rummaged for a few moments and came up with a Chanel lipstick. 'Here,' she said. 'Try this.'

Thea took it, carefully applied it in front of her mirror and turned. 'OK?'

Hedda frowned momentarily; it wasn't OK, it was awful. 'Hmmm . . .' she murmured, rummaging again in the small bag. 'Not quite. Try this.' She produced another lipstick, handed it to Thea and waited for her to rub off the last effort with a tissue and try again.

'This better?'

Hedda stared, pulled a face, then shook her head. 'Wait,' she said. 'I think I've got the right colour downstairs in my handbag, I'll just go and fetch it.' She left the room; Thea heard her footsteps on the stairs and looked at herself in the mirror. She had dark brown hair, nothing spectacular, no auburn tints or chestnut gloss to it, along with pale skin, not the deep rose or olive complexion that usually goes with brunettes, just pale and easily burnt in the sun. She rubbed the lipstick off, leaving her mouth chaffed and sore looking and waited for Hedda to return. A minute or so later, Hedda came in with the lipstick, gave it to Thea and said, 'D'you want me to put it on for you?'

'No, no, it's fine, I think I can manage.' Thea turned to the mirror one last time and made a wide O with her mouth. She applied the lipstick and stood back, knowing that this was by far the worst colour.

'Oh dear,' Hedda said. 'I don't think that these deep colours suit you.'

'No,' Thea replied, 'they don't.' And without waiting for any other comment, rubbed hard at her lips and removed the horrible plum-coloured gloss. 'I'd better go,' she said. 'I'm running out of time.'

'Yes, yes of course.' Hedda was embarrassed at her futile attempt at help. 'Where are you off to?'

'The Royal Oak.' Thea almost shuddered as she said it. 'Just for a drink.'

'Right, I see.' She stood back to let Thea pass, then offered: 'We could go shopping sometime if you like, Thea, I mean, to get you a few new things. You could probably do with them and I could treat you, you know, help you out a bit.'

Thea stopped. She had never been shopping with Hedda, never. Her clothes had always been bought for her when she was little: a selection of what they used to call 'unisex' clothes, that were always in dark colours and always terribly practical; and then, when she was bigger, things from the teen department in Selfridges that Hedda was insistent she should wear. Thea had chosen items herself, of course, but that was with Jake, who never commented on what did or didn't look good and who was happy to let her find her own style.

'Gosh,' Thea said. 'Thanks, that would be great!' Then she caught the faintest glimmer of embarrassment in Hedda's eyes and realised the offer had been made out of pity. Her heart fell, and, avoiding looking at her mother, she made her way past her and down the stairs.

In the hall, she took a jacket out of the cupboard. It was a dark green anorak, an old one of Jake's that he used to go walking in, pulled it on and, to Hedda's horror, put the hood up. She called out to Jake, who came into the hall with Tom and kissed her, then held the baby up for his caress. Hedda watched this cosy domestic scene from the top of the stairs, unnoticed and unincluded. She watched Thea open the door and turn to glance up at her. ''Bye, Hedda,' Thea called, but as she held her hand up to wave, Hedda knew there was no warmth in her voice and wondered, again, just why she never seemed to get it right.

Thea rounded the corner of Park Road towards the pub, out of sight of the house, and stopped. She looked ahead at the Royal Oak, every window ablaze, its noise spilling out through the open doors on to the pavement outside and thought: I can't do it, I cannot go in there. She stood paralysed, rigid with embarrassment, her heart hammering in her chest and clutching her handbag in sweaty hands. It had been Jake's idea; she'd barely mentioned that the few people she'd met at the playgroup were meeting for a drink and, 'You'll want to go, Thea,' Jake had said, rounding on her and smiling. 'Surely? Now that you've got me to look after Tom.'

'Of course,' Thea had murmured and Jake, delighted that she seemed to have turned the corner at last, failed to hear the note of panic in her voice.

Now, Thea edged forward. She forced herself to cover the last few yards to just beyond the entrance to the saloon bar and stopped again. She ground her teeth. The noise was impossible: loud music, laughter, the roar of noisy conversation. 'I must go in,' she told herself. 'I must go in.'

And then suddenly, from what seemed like out of nowhere, she was knocked with such force that she was propelled bodily, shoulder first, into the brick wall of the pub. Another body fell on top of her; she screamed, or thought she did, but no sound came out of her mouth; then she fell heavily on to the pavement and cried out with pain.

'You fucking bastard!' a shrill high voice screamed in her ear. She was shoved down towards the cold, dirty concrete as the body on top of her struggled to get up. 'You dirty fucking bastard!' the scream went on. 'Don't you ever lay a finger on me again! You hear me?'

'Ah piss off, Cora! I've had it up to here with you. Go on, piss off!'

A door slammed, there was the faint echo of laughter, then: 'Bastard! I'll get you! You bastard!'

Thea lay very still. She had instinctively put her hands up to protect her head and now kept them there, terrified to get up. She heard a shuffle, a cough, then a small, sharp sob. Opening her eyes, Thea slid her hands away from her head and turned her face to the side. There was a body, in a pink nylon fake fur coat, slumped on the pavement. Thea rolled over. She raised herself up on one elbow, winced at the pain in her shoulder, then brought her knees up, rolling on to her side to sit up.

The pink nylon fur was a girl. Her head was bent forward and she was struggling to light a cigarette with a match between trembling fingers. Thea sat up.

'Bastard,' the girl whimpered. She lit the cigarette and glanced up. Her face had a swelling on one side, above her right eye, which, obviously freshly inflicted, was red and faintly shiny where her skin stretched over it.

'That looks sore,' Thea said.

The girl didn't answer. She dragged heavily on the cigarette and stared at the entrance to the public bar of the pub. Her face was wet with tears. 'Are you all right?' Thea ventured.

'Yeah, fuckin' fantastic!' the girl snapped. She looked at Thea, took her in at a glance, then said, 'You got any money to spare for a cup of tea?'

Thea nodded. 'Where can we get one?'

Incredulous, the girl shook her head. 'We?' she sneered and her face, with its swelling, looked peculiarly lopsided. 'I don't remember offering no invitations.'

Thea stood up. 'I think there's a place up by the tube station,' she said. 'I'll buy you a cup of tea and something to eat.'

The girl glanced up. She flicked a strand of brittle, platinum-blonde hair behind her ear and narrowed her eyes.

'You should get that seen to as well,' Thea said, rubbing her shoulder. 'The bastard obviously packs a mean punch.'

The girl smiled. Putting her cigarette in her mouth, she held it between pursed lips and offered a hand. Thea took it, pulling her to her feet. 'I'm Cora,' she said, brushing her legs and looking for tears in her tights. 'You?'

'Thea Marshall.'

'Thea? That's a bloody queer name!' She spotted a snag. 'Bugger!' she spat. 'He's fucked me bloody tights as well!'

'It's Greek for goddess.'

Cora took the fag out of her mouth. 'What is?' She took one last long drag on it and stamped it underfoot. Her shoes, pink and high-heeled with ankle straps, ground the cigarette until it disintegrated. 'Don't want no tramps smoking my fag ends,' Cora said. 'Come on, let's go before the bastard looks out to see if I'm still here and clocks me another one.' She shrugged the fake fur up over her shoulders and pulled it round her body.

'Your arm all right?' she asked as Thea fell into step with her. 'You took a hell of a bang.'

'Not sure,' Thea replied. 'Probably. Ask me again later and I'll tell you then.'

Cora glanced sidelong at her. 'You're a bit bloody posh, aren't you?'

Thea shrugged. 'I don't know. Am I?' They walked on in silence, Cora's heel tips tapping on the pavement, Thea's soft-soled shoes making no sound at all. Two streets down, they turned the corner towards the tube station where 'Lena's All Nite Café' was open.

'This the place?'

'Yes. Here.' Thea opened the door for Cora and stood aside to let her go through. Cora frowned, looked at her as if she'd just stepped off another planet and went in. Halfway through the door, she stopped and glanced over her shoulder. 'You're not a lesbo or anything, are you? Because I can tell you this now, I'm not into any of that stuff, OK?'

Thea blinked a couple of times, but that was the only indication she gave that she was shocked. She simply shook her head and said, 'No, I'm perfectly straight,' then walked in after Cora and found them both a table.

'D'you want something to eat?' she asked, pulling out a chair.

Cora, in the process of taking a ten-pack of cigarettes out of her pocket, looked up at the board, squinted, hesitated, then looked away. It was obvious she couldn't read. She said, 'Yeah, what is there?'

Thea caught her embarrassment, made no comment and read through the list on the board. Cora chose eggs, bacon, chips and beans. 'An' a cup of tea,' she called out, 'with two sugars.' Thea ordered, waited for the tea and came across to the table with it. She placed it on the Formica, stirred two sugars into both polystyrene cups and handed one across to Cora.

'Cora's an unusual name too,' she said, waiting for her tea to cool. Cora took a sip of hers, burnt her mouth and swore loudly.

'It's not my real name, I heard it on the telly once, years ago, and thought I'd have it.'

'It's nice. Pretty.'

Cora flushed. 'Yeah, well, it's all right.'

Thea said, 'Who's the bastard and why did he hit you?'

'What's this then, twenty questions?'

Thea shrugged. 'You don't have to tell me, I'm just curious, that's all.'

Cora looked inside her packet of cigarettes, saw that there was only one left and decided to save it until she'd eaten. She fiddled with the packet instead, tapping it on the Formica. 'The bastard's my bloke,' she said after a while, 'Ewert. He's sort of my bloke and sort of not. He—' She broke off, changed her mind about the cigarette and lit it. 'He don't mean it, this.' She stabbed a thumb in the direction of her swollen eye. 'He gets pissed off with me, that's all. I hang about a bit, get on his nerves. It's my own fault.'

Thea said nothing. She waited for Cora to go on but the woman behind the counter shouted her order, so she got up to fetch Cora a plate heaped with food.

Cora said, 'Why you doing this anyway?'

Again Thea shrugged. 'I don't know. I'm supposed to be out having a drink with friends, only they're not really friends and I'm not very good at all that kind of stuff – you know, socialising . . .'

'Socialising?' Cora stuffed a stacked forkful into her mouth. 'What's socialising?' she mumbled whilst chewing.

'What's what?'

Cora swallowed. 'Socia-thingy.'

'Socialising? It's, well, having a good time with friends, I suppose.'

'An' you don't like it?' Cora dunked a piece of fried bread into the runny yolk of her egg and licked the yolk off it.

'No, not really, not that much. But I said I'd go and I don't want to go home and admit that I didn't turn up.'

'Why not?'

Thea smiled. 'What's this? Twenty questions?'

Cora smiled back. She had strong, white, even teeth and her smile changed her face completely. 'Why don't you want to go home then?'

'Well . . .' Thea sighed. 'It's far too long and complicated to explain.'

'Yeah?' Cora, who had been shovelling food almost constantly into her mouth, stopped, put her knife and fork down on the plate and took a large swig of her tea. She swallowed, then flicked the ash off her cigarette still smoking in the ashtray and took a drag of it. 'I never liked home much either. Not after my mum got Gordon to move in.' She blew smoke out of the side of her mouth. 'Ran away so much they put me in care.' She smiled and rolled her eyes. 'That was far bloody worse, I can tell you! Should have stayed where I was and put up with the groping!' Another drag of her cigarette and she said, 'Go on, now you.'

'Now me?'

'Yeah, now you. You tell me why you don't want to go home.'

'Oh God.' Thea took a sip of her own tea. 'I don't really know where to start.' Cora stared at her and Thea felt suddenly pathetic. 'I've got a baby.'

'No? You're kidding?'

'No, I'm not. He's called Tom and he's three months old. That's not why I don't want to go home though.'

'No?'

'No, it's more complicated than that. It doesn't matter anyway.'

'No?'

Thea shrugged, but of course it mattered and she could see Cora knew that.

'Where's his dad then, this baby of yours?'

'I don't know. At home probably, with his parents. We met at university . . .'

'Told you you was posh.' Cora stubbed her cigarette out and started on her food again. 'Posh and stupid,' she said, shaking her head. 'Landing yourself with a kid.'

'It wasn't like that!'

'No?'

'No. I got pregnant but I was pleased, I was relieved, I—' Thea broke off. She was going to say that she'd had her mother's attention, for the first time ever, all of it, and for a while that somehow made it all worth while, but she didn't. That was too complicated, too much to explain. Instead, she said, 'Oh God, I don't know what I was, maybe I was stupid.'

'And the kid's dad, was he happy about it?'

Thea looked down. She didn't answer for a while and Cora finished her food, pushing the plate to one side, then picked up her tea. Her gaze never left Thea's face.

'No,' Thea said, 'he wasn't happy about it, it never really worked out between us.'

'Don't blame him.'

Thea glanced away to avoid Cora's eyes which had an odd knowingness in them, as if they'd seen too much.

'So where's the kid now?'

'He's at home.'

'Yeah?'

Thea looked back. 'Yes,' she said coolly. 'Where'd you think he'd be?'

Cora shrugged. 'How should I know? Might be in care for all I know, like me. It isn't any great shakes, you know, to be in care.'

Thea was embarrassed. 'No,' she said quietly, 'I'm sure.'

'So.' Cora picked her teeth with her thumbnail, retrieved a stray bit of bacon and popped it back into her mouth. 'You still happy about it?'

'About what?'

'Having a kid an' all.'

Thea smiled; Cora had no pretensions. 'I don't know,' she answered. 'It wasn't anything like I expected it to be.'

'Yeah? Tell me about it!' Cora pulled a face. 'Not for me, I can tell you, all those shitty nappies and puke and screaming.' She shook her head. 'Won't catch me going up that street, ta very much.' She stopped and looked at Thea. 'What did you expect then?'

'I don't know.' Thea hesitated, then said, 'I didn't expect to feel so lonely, so . . .' She hesitated again. 'So desperate.'

Cora shook her head.

'It probably sounds stupid but I had this image in my mind of . . . well, of like it is on the telly, on the baby ads, and—' Thea stopped. 'What's so funny?'

Cora was smiling. 'Yeah, it does sound stupid! What, cuddly little babies chasing rolls of bleeding toilet paper with that daft bloody dog? If it ran off with my bog paper while I was having a shit I wouldn't be laughing, I can tell you.'

And all of a sudden Thea, who had found nothing at all

amusing about her situation until that moment, burst into fits of giggles.

'All they bloody do is laugh about it on the telly and chase that friggin' dog round. Jesus!' Cora frowned. 'Wouldn't be like that in my house. I'd be shouting "Come here, you little bugger," and that's before I'd clock it one for wasting all that bloody bog roll!'

Thea was laughing so much now she could hardly breathe.

'It's not cheap, you know, that stuff!' Cora said earnestly and, pleased but slightly puzzled as to why her conversation was so amusing, announced: 'Far too nice to waste wiping your bum on, if you ask me.'

Cora walked home with Thea. She had nothing better to do, she said, except go home to her poxy bedsit and listen to the radio. When they arrived at the steps of 59, Park Road, Thea asked her in, but Cora, looking up at the house, a large detached red-brick Victorian building, declined. She didn't see it as Thea did, scruffy and ill kept, she just saw money and something out of her reach.

'I could put some ice on your eye, and I think I've got some antiseptic somewhere,' Thea said. 'And you could see my baby.'

'Nah.' Cora huddled into her coat. 'Thanks, but no thanks. I've got to go, it's a bit of a walk home from here.'

'Right.'

The two girls exchanged nervous smiles. They were both loners, neither had any friends to speak of and yet they'd found something they liked about each other, something that might be akin to friendship.

'Thanks for the grub,' Cora said. 'It was nice.'

'That's OK, thanks for saving me from coming home at eight o'clock.' They both smiled again.

'I'd better go.' Cora turned towards the road. 'I'll see you around.'

'Yes, sure, I . . .' Thea dug in her pockets for her key, then she looked over her shoulder and suddenly called, 'Where d'you live?'

Cora glanced back. 'Gilbert House, on Hubbert Road.' She shrugged. 'It's a dump but it's not council.'

'What number Gilbert House?'

'Why? You want to come over?'

'Yes. Tomorrow morning maybe? I could bring Tom.'

Cora pulled a face, then smiled. 'Number seven, lucky for some!' She hesitated for a moment, chewing on her lip and obviously considering something, then she said quickly: 'You couldn't bring us a packet of fags, could you?'

'No I bloody well couldn't!' Thea burst out indignantly. 'They're bad for your health and I wouldn't encourage you!' She stopped. Cora had shrugged her coat up and buried her face into the fluffy pink nylon collar. Embarrassed, she avoided Thea's eye. She hardly ever asked for anything, only took what was given her. Thea turned towards the front door, then looked back. 'Hedda smokes,' she said, changing her mind. 'I'll pinch a few of hers, OK?'

Suddenly Cora beamed and it set the seal on the friendship. 'Brill,' she said and, setting off down the road, she held her hand up to wave, calling: 'See you tomorrow morning then.' Her heels tapping smartly on the pavement were the last thing Thea heard as she went inside.

Chapter Seven

An unlikely friendship between Cora and Thea Marshall developed. They were very different. Cora was sharp and rough, cocksure and sometimes arrogant; she gave little, expected nothing in return and yet she longed to be loved. Thea in contrast was softer; she gave of herself easily but she floundered with lack of confidence and felt that she had nothing to offer. Cora gave Thea confidence and Thea gave Cora affection. They took from the other what they needed without really knowing it, and they formed a bond that tied them closer than they ever could have imagined.

They started out by having coffee together, first in Cora's bedsit, then at Thea's house, drinking coffee and talking, exchanging lives, to the fascination of them both. Tom lay in his car seat between them, or on a rug, and they played with him, simply, just making faces or tickling his fingers and toes. Then they went shopping together, wheeling Tom round in a second-hand pushchair Jake had borrowed from a neighbour, taking him on the underground and into women's changing rooms while they tried on a never-ending variety of clothing from Top Shop and Miss Selfridge. They experimented with lipsticks and eyeliners in department stores, painted every nail a different colour from the tester ranges and sat in Hyde Park as the weather got warmer for long afternoons, lolling around and gossiping about themselves.

As the spring gave way to early summer, they frequented the leisure centre in Islington most mornings, watching the aerobics class in the dance studio, noses pressed against the wall of glass, Tom in the pushchair mesmerised by the constant motion and beat of the bodies in brightly coloured leotards. They tried out the dance routines at home in Hedda and Jake's front room, practising the steps, taping bits of music that they liked, until one day Jake suggested that they go along to try it and gave them a fiver to pay for the class.

After that they were hooked. The money that Cora used to spend on ten cigarettes a day went instead to pay for her aerobics class and Thea offered to iron for the lady next door at five pounds a basketload to fund herself. Sometimes they left Tom at home with Jake and snatched an hour and a half of freedom, other times they took him along and put him in the crèche. But every time they went, they stood at the front of the class, both humming along to the tunes and making sure that they copied every step, every movement and every gesture that the instructor made. They were naturals.

Then one day, over a coffee in the snack bar after a particularly good class, Thea and Cora very nearly fell out.

'All right,' Cora said, stirring sugar into her coffee, 'come on, spit it out! You've got a face as long as a donkey's dick.'

'Choice use of language!' Thea replied. 'Thanks a lot.'

'Well you have! You've not said a bloody word and I've

had to do all the talking and I've had enough! Come on, out with it!'

Thea drank her coffee. 'Look, sorry, Cora, but it's too complicated, you wouldn't understand.'

'What, not as clever as you? That it?'

'No, nothing like that, I . . .'

'Yeah?' Cora had narrowed her eyes. 'I may not have got into some snotty university but I'm not bloody stupid, you know.'

'Yes I know, it's not that at all, it's just . . .' Thea suddenly threw her hands up. 'It's Hedda,' she said. 'She's started coming home mid morning from the Therapy centre, while I'm here, and doing things with Tom.'

'Yeah?' Cora, who had only once met Hedda and decided that once was enough, narrowed her eyes again. It was a habit she had, she thought it made her look sophisticated. 'What kinda things?'

Thea looked away for a few moments, sighed, then looked squarely at Cora. 'She's started on this whole educational play thing, subliminal learning I think it's called.'

'Jesus! What the friggin' hell does that mean?'

Thea sighed again. 'It's sort of feeding the brain messages but not being conscious of those messages. Like really faint whispers in the music played at supermarkets to entice you to buy things.'

'No! You've gotta be kidding! They do that at Tesco's?'

'I don't know for sure. Maybe.'

'Is that what your mum's doing?'

'Well, sort of, she's started using these flash cards, with words and pictures on them, and she shows them to Tom. She spends whole mornings doing it. She's convinced that it'll help him read early, help his development.' Thea was becoming increasingly tense as she spoke. 'It's just bizarre really, cramming a five-month-old baby, trying to force him to respond! It drives me mad, it's like she can't relax, she's got to have him doing things, things that'll in some way make him more clever, or more advanced, or brighter than anyone else! She can't just leave him alone, let him be happy, let him play and enjoy himself, she's got to keep on at him, on and on! I—' Thea broke off, suddenly aware that she'd been raising her voice and that people were staring. She was also suddenly aware that Cora had turned away from her and gone very quiet.

'Cora?' she said, reaching out and touching her friend's arm, 'Are you OK?'

Cora turned back. She looked at Thea, then at her hand and removed her arm from reach. 'I've gotta go,' she said quickly. She stood and snatched up her purse. 'Sorry. I'll see you around, all right?' She scraped her chair back and made off without looking at Thea again, without saying another word. She crossed the snack bar, almost running, and knocked a chair as she went, slamming through the double swing doors. Thea hesitated for a moment, then jumped up and ran after her.

'Cora!' she shouted, running down the stairs. 'Cora, wait!' But Cora ignored her and carried on, out of the building and into the street. Thea ran faster. She caught her friend at the bus stop and, out of breath, grabbed Cora's arm, spinning her round. 'Cora? What's up? What did I say?' She was upset and hurt. 'Cora? What is it?' Cora went to shrug her off; the bus was coming; but Thea held on to her arm. 'Cora! Tell me!'

'All right!' Cora suddenly cried. 'All right, I'll tell you, shall I? You and your bloody smug ideas, you haven't gotta clue, have you? You know nothing, carping on about your mum helping your kid to read and you haven't gotta clue! You haven't got the nous to be grateful, think it's some kind of problem, and all she wants to do is help him! God, you make me sick! She's trying to give him something that alotta kids never get, trying to give him a good start in life and you' – Cora jabbed her forefinger at Thea's chest – 'you just criticise her, you just whinge and whine like she's doing something wrong!' Cora's voice cracked and her eyes glistened with unshed tears. 'You haven't gotta clue . . .' she said again, her voice dying in her throat. Then she turned away and just at that moment the bus pulled up. Moving quickly towards the open doors, she fumbled for her purse and climbed up. 'One to Hubbert Road,' she said, recovering her composure. She waited for the ticket, took it and, without turning to look at Thea, moved along the bus to her seat.

Thea stood motionless and watched as the bus doors closed with a hiss and a belch of exhaust fumes accompanied its moving off. She had a sinking in the pit of her stomach, the familiar ache of hurt and disappointment, and as she walked back to the leisure centre to collect the sports bag she'd left in the snack bar, she honestly didn't know what she had said wrong.

That night, in the long, silent hours after midnight and before dawn, Thea was awake with Tom and thought about Cora. As she fed her baby in the shadowy darkness and touched the soft fold of his cheek pressed against her breast, she had time to reflect on what she had said and why Cora was so upset. She knew Cora couldn't read, she had helped her so often with signs and shop labels, menus and prices, but had never commented on it. How could she, when Cora ignored it herself and pretended that it didn't exist? She had immense cunning at skirting round anything that required the skill; she covered herself at every turn and she had never, not even once, asked for any help.

Thea glanced down at Tom, who had fallen asleep, and gently lifted him back into his cot. She sat down again on the chaise in the darkness and curled her legs up underneath her. Tom gently snored beside her and she thought about him, about his chances in life and about the things that came so naturally to her that she almost took them for granted, things that she was sure would come naturally to him as well; things like reading and writing.

Thea had never had to navigate her way around the underground by asking people if she was on the right platform, learning the stops off by heart and counting each one so that she knew which station was hers. She had never had to identify food in the supermarket by the colours on their labels or wait in a café until somebody ordered something she wanted so that she knew it was on the menu. And nor, she thought, would Tom. So why criticise Hedda for wanting to make sure of that? What had Cora said? That she hadn't got a clue, that she was just whinging and whining at Hedda trying to give Tom something that a lot of children never get.

Thea stood to look down at Tom asleep in the cot and was suddenly deeply ashamed. Ashamed of what she had always assumed was hers by right, ashamed – for the first time ever – of letting Hedda down. She bent, kissed him, and returned to her room. She took her dressing gown off the back of the door, pulled it on and crept downstairs. In the cupboard in Hedda's study, Thea found the flash cards; they were in a pack with a manual and several work books. She switched on the lamp, took everything across to Hedda's desk and sat down to read. What she had was a basic literacy package; it was the perfect tool and she knew exactly how she was going to use it.

The following morning, Thea was up before anyone else in the house. She had fed, bathed and dressed Tom ready for the day when Jake came down in his pyjamas and slippers, looking fuddled and drowsy.

'Tea, Jake?' she asked as he came into the kitchen.

'Hmm, please. And do a cup for Hedda too, will you? I'll take it up to her.'

'Sure.' Thea put the kettle on and started to lay out the tea things on a tray.

Jake looked up from rubbing his hands wearily over his face. 'What are you up to today, Thea? You're up very bright and early!' He stretched, yawning. 'It makes me feel rather unwell actually, the sight of all that efficiency in the morning.'

Thea smiled. 'I'm just off to Cora's.'

'What, again?' Jake was beginning to worry that this friendship with Cora was unproductive. Perhaps Hedda had a point, perhaps Thea should be thinking more about her future, rather than drinking coffee and doing aerobics.

'What on earth do you two girls do all day to keep your-selves occupied?'

There was an edge of irritation in his voice and Thea picked up on it. 'Up to now, not very much,' she said, 'but that's all going to change this morning.'

'Oh really?' Jake took the mug of tea Thea handed him. 'What cunning plans are afoot then? Trying a new lipstick? Buying another top?'

Thea looked at him. 'Sorry, Jake, did I do something wrong this morning?'

Jake sighed. 'No, not just this morning, Thea. I just wonder when you're going to *do* something with yourself, something positive, something productive, instead of all this laying about and wasting time!'

'I've got Tom to look after, remember, it does limit things a bit!'

'Don't I know it!' Hedda was getting increasingly edgy with a baby in the house and Jake had to confess he could see her point. 'Look, Thea, if you could at least show me that you were using your brain in some way, doing something positive—'

'What, like teaching Cora to read? Is that positive enough for you?' Thea plonked Hedda's mug on the tea tray and filled it with tea. When she turned back Jake was staring at her.

'Teaching Cora to read?' He walked across to the table and sat down. 'Is that what you're doing?'

'Yes! That's what I plan to do anyway. I want to start this morning, with the reading scheme that Hedda's been using for Tom.' She glared at him. 'I think that's using my brain, isn't it?'

Jake ignored her sarcasm and cupped his hands round his mug. He looked at her, genuinely impressed. 'What will you do with Tom?'

'He can come too, it'll please Hedda and he might learn something!'

Suddenly, they both smiled.

'Look, how about I have him?' Jake said. 'For a couple of hours each morning so that you can get off to a good start?'

Thea bit her lip. 'That's very nice of you, but I don't think so, you've got your own things to do, so Hedda keeps telling me, and I wouldn't want to impose Tom on you, I—'

'You wouldn't be imposing, honestly!' Jake's irritation had evaporated. This was more than positive and productive, it was ethical and selfless. He had to help, he wouldn't have been Jake if he didn't offer. 'I'd like to help, I'd like to be part of this great scheme. I mean, I look after Tom on and off already, what's making it a regular thing, eh?'

Thea crossed the room and pulled out a chair opposite him. 'Jake, are you really sure? What will Hedda say? Won't she be—'

He reached out and touched Thea's hand. 'Leave Hedda to me,' he said, with far more confidence than he felt. 'You go and get yourself ready to go and leave Tom and Hedda to me.'

Thea smiled, squeezed his fingers and stood up. 'If you're sure?'

'Of course I'm sure,' he said. 'Go on.' Certain that he'd done the right thing, he watched Thea disappear off upstairs and stood to take Hedda up her tea.

*   *   *

When Thea arrived at Cora's bedsit, the curtains on the small windows at the top of the house were drawn and there was no reply from the buzzer. She rang twice, waited, then decided to pop down to Woolies to buy a couple of notebooks and come back in an hour or so. This she did, returning to Cora's at nine-thirty. She rang the buzzer again, put her ear close to the little speaker on the intercom and moments later sprang back as Cora barked in her ear.

'If that's you, Thea, go away!' she snapped. 'I didn't finish work till late and I'm tired!'

'Cora, listen. I've got something I want to talk to you about. It won't take long, I promise. Please let me in.'

There was a silence; Thea held her breath. She carried a string bag with the reading scheme in and tapped it nervously against her thigh. Then, without Cora saying a word, the door lock released, Thea stepped into the musty-smelling, shabby hall and made her way up the narrow stairs towards the top floor.

'Door's open!' she heard as she climbed. There was no greeting and warmth in Cora's voice. Oh God, Thea thought, I hope I'm doing the right thing, and she reached Cora's small dark bedsit quicker than she usually did, only realising at the top that it was because she was without Tom.

'Cora?' Walking in through the open door, she saw that the curtains were still drawn and that only a dingy table lamp was lit, giving off a grubby light. Cora had climbed back into bed.

'Hello,' Thea said.

Cora pulled her knees up under the covers and sat with her chin resting on them, staring at Thea. She didn't reply.

'How was work?'

Cora had a job, six nights a week, stacking shelves for the Co-op. It was neither stimulating nor well paid but it kept her off the social. 'All right,' she said. 'Same as ever.'

'Good – well, I mean, not that good, I suppose, if it's the same as ever. I mean, boring really.' Thea came across and stood by the bed. She would have sat, but with the bed occupied there was nowhere else to sit in the room. She put the string bag down in front of Cora. 'Cora,' she said, 'I'm sorry for upsetting you yesterday. You were right, I didn't realise that Hedda means well and . . .' Thea was embarrassed; Cora was staring hard at her and she felt ridiculous. Perhaps she'd been wrong to come, perhaps she was assuming far too much. She hesitated for a moment, wondering briefly if she should abandon this idea and go home but she didn't, she was as stubborn as Cora. She had made a decision and she would stick to it. 'Look,' she said, braving the stare and summoning all her confidence. 'It was a misunderstanding, you feel strongly about the chance to read and write and I didn't realise that.'

'Yeah, well,' Cora said, not adding anything more. Thea looked at her. The defiance had gone and, without it, she just seemed sad and vulnerable.

'What it did do though, Cora, was get me thinking.'

'Yeah?' Cora leant forward and threw a couple of magazines off the end of the bed to make room for Thea to sit. 'What about?'

Thea tapped the string bag. 'Reading,' she said.

Cora was wary. 'Reading? What sort of reading?'

Thea opened the bag and took out the flash cards and the reading manual. 'This is what Hedda was using for Tom, it's a reading scheme, to teach basic reading skills.'

The wariness deepened. Cora said nothing.

'And I was thinking that if you want me to, I could teach you to read and write with this scheme!' Thea couldn't keep the note of triumph out of her voice. She was so thrilled with her idea, so filled with the overwhelming need to help her friend, that she completely missed Cora's reaction. It was one of acute embarrassment. Throwing the covers back, Cora jumped out of bed and strode across to the door.

'Cora? Where are you going?'

'I'm going for a pee,' she growled and disappeared, leaving Thea sitting alone with her flash cards. It was a good fifteen minutes before she returned, and when she did, she was washed and ready to get dressed. Picking her underwear up off the chair next to the bed, she put it on under her dressing gown, then went to the wardrobe to find some clothes.

'Cora?'

She pulled a sweater over her head and reached for her jeans.

'Cora? What did I say this time?' There was genuine distress in Thea's voice.

Cora turned. 'If you think that I'm going to do some poxy reading scheme that a baby does then you'd better think again!' She walked across to the bed and shook the covers to straighten them, scattering the flash cards and books on to the floor. 'I'm not thick, you know! Anyway, who told you I couldn't read? Eh?'

'No one told me. I just know, that's all. I know because I can see you struggle whenever you're faced with words and it doesn't have to be like that. And another thing, it's not a baby's scheme, it's for any age, all it is is the basics of reading, you can be five, twenty-five or seventy-five. Frankly, if you want my opinion, doing it with a five-month-old baby, as I told you yesterday, is a complete waste of time, but that's another matter. And it's not poxy! I read through all the stuff last night and it's really good, it's easy to follow and you could do it standing on your head drinking a pint of lager!'

'I don't like lager.'

'All right, gin and black or whatever other thing you drink!' This was the longest and most explosive outburst Thea had ever given. She stopped, drew breath and said, 'I think I'm more like my mother than I realised!' And Cora grudgingly smiled, then knelt to pick the flash cards up off the floor.

They had been sitting on the floor, next to each other, the reading scheme between them, for over an hour when Cora put down the book she was holding and said, 'So why'd you do this then?'

'Do what?' Thea was working out tomorrow's lesson, while Cora learnt the words in her book. She was miles away and it wasn't until Cora said it again that she looked up.

'Do this? D'you mean teach you to read?'

'Yeah. Nobody has ever done anything for me for free before, ever. No one cared that much. Teachers never cared when I dropped out of school, eleven I was and I couldn't even write my name. Mum never cared when I ran off. Gordon couldn't give a stuff. So, why you?'

'Why not me?'

Cora smiled and cuffed Thea on the arm. 'No, come on, tell me. Why? Why d'you do this for me? It's not like you've got anything to gain, have you?'

'No, I suppose not, except being able to be out with you and not hear "which way we going?" or "how much is that?" every five minutes.' Again Cora hit Thea on the arm, this time a bit harder. 'Ouch! That hurt!' Thea yelped. 'You really want to know why?' Cora nodded. There was a moment's silence, then Thea said, 'Because we're friends.'

Cora narrowed her eyes. She hadn't had many friends, none to be accurate, but it still sounded like a bit of a flimsy explanation.

'What, just because of that? There's nothing else?'

'No. Nothing else.'

Cora looked down. She fiddled with her hands, turning the book over and over, staring hard at it, then all of a sudden, she jumped up and dashed across to her wardrobe. 'Right!' she announced, rummaging through the pile of clobber at the bottom of it. 'We're friends then, are we?'

'Yes.' Thea began to feel uneasy, there was an almost fervent zeal about Cora's actions.

'Right!' Cora continued to sift, chucking out the odd bit of junk. Finally, she found what she was looking for.

'Ah ha!' she cried. Then: 'Here it is, the little beauty!' She threw a box of what looked like hair colour out behind her and dived back into the wardrobe for some clothes. She emerged a few minutes later with an armful of items.

'If we're friends,' she said, 'and if you're gonna do all this for me, then I'm gonna do something for you. OK?'

'Well . . .'

'You said we were friends.'

'I know, but . . .'

Cora had crossed to the sink and was filling a washing-up bowl with warm water. 'No buts about it,' she said, plucking the box of hair colour from the floor. 'If you're my mate then you can come here.'

'Where? There?'

'Yeah, here.' Cora pointed to the water.

'What are you going to do?'

'Nothing much.'

'Nothing much that involves a box of hair colour?'

'Yeah, and some hair gel, a bit of make-up and a few choice bits of clobber.'

Thea started to laugh. 'Choice bits of clobber. Oh God, why do I feel suddenly faint with nerves?'

'Just come here, Miss Posh Thea Marshall, because I'm gonna change how you look for ever.'

'You are?' Thea took a deep breath; for friendship, this could be make or break.

'Yes,' Cora said, 'I bloody well am!' And she opened the box of chestnut dye and reached across to the sink for her rubber gloves.

Jake had just got Tom off for a sleep when Hedda came downstairs in her dressing gown. He knew she didn't have patients that morning, she had refused her tea and slept in, but he was surprised that she wasn't up and about by midday, since he had assumed she was going to work for the afternoon session. He was washing up when she found him. The kitchen was a mess, Tom's things were all over the place and Jake had a small dribble of milk all down the sleeve of his shirt. Hedda stood in the kitchen doorway watching him for several minutes, trying to remember the man she had married, the man she once knew, but she wasn't sure she could. Had he changed so much? Or was it her? Hedda just didn't know.

Jake turned to collect the breakfast things from the table and said, 'Oh, hi.' He looked slightly uncomfortable, ill at ease, and Hedda wondered if it was her presence. 'Not dressed yet?' he asked.

'No, I thought I'd take a day off,' she answered, coming into the room. 'I thought, seeing as we have the house to ourselves, that it might be nice to spend a bit of time together, get some lunch from the deli, go to an exhibition maybe?' She smiled. 'Go to bed?'

Jake felt a knot of tension twist in his stomach. She walked across to him. 'It's been ages, Jake,' she said, reaching up to touch a strand of his hair, 'since we were alone.'

Jake nodded. 'Erm, Hedda . . .'

She kissed him on the mouth and he felt an instant flare of desire. 'Hedda,' he murmured, pulling back, 'I'm afraid . . .' He stopped. A piercing wail came through the floor from the bedroom above and Hedda's face froze. 'I'm afraid that we're not alone,' Jake said. 'Thea's gone out and I offered to have Tom for the day.'

Suddenly Hedda threw her hands up. 'Perfect,' she growled through gritted teeth. 'Absolutely bloody perfect!' She turned and walked away from him. 'Why, Jake?' she demanded, facing him across the room. 'Why do you do it? Why?'

'I didn't plan it, Hedda, I had no idea that you'd want to take the day off! I mean, if I'd known, then . . .' He shrugged helplessly.

'Then what? You'd have organised for us to go to soft play and Mcdonald's? Oh for God's sake! Why couldn't we have just one day together, just one day alone, the two of us, like we used to be? That's all I wanted, Jake, just one day.' She was close to tears and Jake made a move forward to comfort her.

'No!' she snapped. 'No, don't come near me, it'll just make it worse!' The wail upstairs had given way to a full-throttle cry and Jake was suddenly furious, with himself, with Thea and with Hedda. 'Fine!' he said. 'I won't come near you!' He brushed past her on his way to the stairs.

'You use Tom as an excuse!' Hedda called after him. 'You use Tom and Thea as an excuse for a life!'

Jake stood at the top of the stairs and turned round. 'Yes,' he said coldly, 'maybe I do, but I don't have much of one with you, do I?' With that, he walked away to see to Tom.

Chapter Eight

It was the height of the summer, late one evening, and Hedda had just arrived home. She had been working long hours for the past few weeks with a particularly rich but difficult patient and tonight was no exception. It was after nine by the time she walked in the door and all she needed was a long hot bath, a stiff drink and the supper which Jake was preparing downstairs. She didn't need any added stress. As she came up the stairs with a Scotch in her hand, she noticed that Thea's bedroom door was ajar and stopped off on the way to the bathroom to say hello. It was ages since she had had any real contact with Thea; they had passed on the stairs or spoken briefly over coffee in the morning, but that was all. It would be nice to catch up, Hedda thought, pausing outside Thea's room. Maybe I'll ask her if she's looked at the degree course brochures I've left lying around.

Standing in the doorway, Hedda peered in and saw Thea sitting cross-legged on the floor in just her underwear, sheer black bra and thong, drying a head of thick, glossy, now chestnut-coloured hair.

'Hello.'

Thea swivelled round and switched the hair-dryer off. 'Hi, Mum.'

Hedda gripped the doorframe. Mum? Mum? Where the hell did that come from? Hedda felt her hackles rise.

'Come in. I was just getting ready to go out.'

'Go out? It's half past nine.'

'Yes, there's this club that I'm going to with Cora. We don't want to get there too early.' Thea leant across and cleared a space on her bed. 'D'you want to sit down?'

'Oh, no, no thanks, I'm on my way to run a bath.' Hedda watched as Thea brushed her hair into its style, flicked the hairbrush to turn the ends under and then spritzed it with hairspray.

'Your hair's nice. When did you colour it?'

'Ages ago.'

'Really?' Hedda was surprised. Had she really been that insensitive not to notice that her daughter had coloured her hair?

'Yes, Cora did it for me. She showed me how to dry it too, so that it all sort of fits my face.' Thea lifted her arms to run her hands through her hair and, unable to stop herself, Hedda gasped. Thea followed her gaze to the red and black snake tattoo on her upper arm and said, 'It's OK, it's fake, a transfer. I'm too much of a coward for the real thing.' She lifted her arm a bit higher so as to be able to see the tattoo in the mirror. 'It's great though, isn't it?'

Hedda swallowed and forced a smile. 'Yes, great.' Stay cool, she told herself, keep calm. 'And you've lost weight,' she went on. 'It really suits you.'

'Thanks.' Thea stood up and Hedda thought: My God,

what a body! Thea had always been full figured, rounded, a bit lumpy, but the roundedness had gone. The full figure had now become voluptuous and sleekly curved. She had the flesh of youth, smooth, firm and unveined, that perfectly fitted her skeleton; there were no protruding bones, no sagging muscles.

Hedda found herself staring at Thea's breasts and Thea followed her gaze. Blushing, she said, 'It's having Tom, they just sort of, erm, grew.'

Hedda smiled tightly. 'Wonderful,' she managed.

'Did you want something?' Thea asked. 'It's just that I'm going out in about ten minutes and . . .'

Hedda felt old. She had always prided herself on not looking her age and certainly not feeling it, but tonight she did feel it, and more. Standing a little straighter, she sucked her tummy in. 'I didn't want anything really, just thought I'd say hello,' she replied weakly.

'Thanks.' Thea reached for her skirt, a tiny bit of faded denim that she pulled on and zipped up. She sat on the bed and picked up a pair of fish-net tights. 'Why don't you pop in and see your grandson?' she said. 'He looks angelic when he's asleep.'

Grandson. Hedda preferred to refer to him as just Tom, or Thea's baby; never grandson. 'Yes, I'll do that, after my bath.' The tights went on, then a pair of black base-ball boots and finally another of Jake's old sweaters, only this one looked sensational. It was a thin black cotton-jersey turtle-neck and it clung to the shape of Thea's body in an unselfconscious but highly provocative way. Hedda found herself swallowing hard again and forcing another smile. Thea applied a lipstick, mulberry pink, and fastened some big silver earrings on to her unpierced lobes.

'You found a colour that suits you then?'

'Oh, what? The lipstick? Yes, you like it?'

Hedda would have preferred something less obviously sexy, something a bit more subdued, but she nodded and watched Thea stuff the lipstick and a hairbrush into a small black shiny sixties-style bag, which looked vaguely familiar, then click it shut. 'Right, I'm ready,' she said.

'Great.' There was no enthusiasm in Hedda's voice. 'What sort of club is it you're going to?' she asked, standing aside to let Thea pass.

'I don't really know. Cora's meeting her boyfriend there and it's in Soho.'

'Soho? Perhaps it's a jazz club.'

Thea turned and gave Hedda the most peculiar look. Hedda felt as if she'd just landed from another planet. Then her face cleared, she shrugged and made for the stairs. 'I very much doubt it, Mum,' she called as she went down, slinging the bag over her shoulder. 'More likely to be strippers, I'd have thought, than trumpet players.'

'Strip—?'

And as the front door slammed shut and Hedda stood speechless on the landing, she realised exactly why the bag had looked vaguely familiar. It was hers.

'Strippers?' Hedda shrieked, stomping down the stairs. 'Strippers!' She stormed into the kitchen where Jake sat reading the paper. 'What the hell's going on, Jake? She's going to a bloody strip club!'

Jake looked up over the top of the *Guardian*. 'Is she?' He

rustled the paper to straighten the pages, then went back to his article.

'Jake!' Hedda suddenly shouted. 'I'm talking to you!'

'No you're not,' he said, calmly folding the paper away. 'You are shouting at me and you will wake the baby.'

'Sod the bloody baby!' she snapped. 'What the hell is going on with that girl? Dyed hair, tattoos, fish-net tights, black underwear, mini-skirts and strip joints! For God's sake, Jake! Why didn't you tell me it had got so out of control?'

'Because it hasn't, Hedda, it's all perfectly normal!'

'Normal? It's that bloody friend Cara—'

'Cora,' Jake corrected.

'Cora then! It's all her fault, it's—'

Jake had stood. He came across to Hedda, gently placed his hands on her shoulders and eased her down into a chair. 'Sit,' he said, 'and I'll get you another drink.' She began to protest but he held his hands up to silence her and poured a hefty measure of whisky into a glass. Handing it to Hedda, he said, 'Now. You want to discuss Thea?'

Hedda nodded. She drank down a large mouthful of Scotch and shuddered as it hit the pit of her stomach. She waited a few moments, swirling the amber liquid round and round her glass, then she said, 'Why, Jake? Why have you let things get like this?'

'Are we talking Thea or us?'

Hedda started. She glanced at him, knowing that they would have to talk at some point about themselves, but not feeling strong enough to do it now. 'Thea,' she answered. 'Why have you let this friendship with Cora get so out of hand?'

'Well, firstly, I don't think it is out of hand and secondly, I think it's good for Thea, I think it'll help her.'

'Good for her? Help her? In what way?'

'Because Cora is tough and bright and she can teach Thea a thing or two, that's why.'

Hedda threw up her hands in dismay. 'You know, Jake, I'm beginning to think that you really have lost it! Teach Thea a thing or two? You have got to be joking!'

'No, Hedda, sadly I'm not.'

'But—'

'If you wait a moment,' Jake cut in, 'then I'll tell you why.' He stood, went over to the sideboard and poured himself a shot of whisky, then he returned to the table and nursed the drink in his hands for a few moments.

'All right, I've waited,' Hedda said sharply. 'What do you mean?'

'Hedda, we both know Thea's very bright, she's had a good education and we've taught her everything we can. She knows her art, she can tell an alto from a soprano and argue philosophy, but she hasn't got a clue about life. We sent her off to Oxford and it was like letting her jump in the water without ever having taught her how to float, let alone swim.'

'So what are you saying? That she needs to know about strip joints and tattoos and looking like a siren when she goes out! For God's sake, Jake, she's made a big enough mistake already, we don't need her to make another one! End up with another baby or high on drugs!'

'But that's exactly it! Cora won't let her make any mistakes because Cora's got no intention of making any herself! Thea needs to learn, she needs to find out about herself, about what she likes, about what she's good at. She's spent her whole life trying to please us, trying to fit in, do what we wanted—'

'No! Wait a minute, Jake! That's not true. We always encouraged self-expression, we always tried to be liberal, let her find herself . . .'

'Did we? Or did we use that as an excuse just to let her get on with it? We were pretty wrapped up in ourselves, Hedda, always have been, in our own separate affairs, our work, our philanthropy!' Jake said the last word with heavy bitterness and Hedda winced. 'She wanted attention, Hedda, that's all. She wanted to be with her mum and dad, so she did the opposite to what most teenagers do and bent over backwards to please us. All that cleaning and cooking and domesticity, doing the things that neither of us could be bothered to do ourselves.' Jake shook his head. He drank his whisky and stood to get more. 'D'you want a top-up?'

Hedda looked at her glass. 'I think I might need one,' she said.

He brought the bottle over to the table and poured them both another drink. Jake sat, took a sip of his, then suddenly dropped his head in his hands. 'Poor Thea,' he said bitterly. 'You know what she asked me, several weeks back, completely out of the blue? She asked me if she could call me Dad. "Jake," she said, "Can I call you Dad?"'

Hedda said nothing.

'"Of course," I said, "if you want to."' He looked up at Hedda. 'D'you know what she said then? She said, "I've always wanted to." Just like that, no anger or remorse, just simply, "I've always wanted to."'

Hedda reached out and touched Jake's hand. 'Did we go very wrong?' she asked.

There was a silence, then Jake said, 'I don't know.' He removed his hand and cradled the glass of whisky. 'I think we kind of went askew, rather than wrong. And I think that what we ended up with was pretty much all down to Thea.'

Rebuffed, Hedda stood. She didn't seem to be able to get through to Jake. 'So that's back off, Hedda,' she said coolly, 'and let her be, right?'

Jake stared up at her, amazed at her lack of compassion. 'I don't know if it's back off, Hedda or, more, calm down.' He stopped and took a deep, weary breath. 'Look, I don't think Thea is ever going to be like you, Hedda, think the same way or want the same things. I don't think she's ever going to be a soul mate, but surely that's the whole point, isn't it? To have a strong-minded, intelligent child who thinks for herself?'

Hedda raised an eyebrow. Jake thought he had all the answers. 'Goodness me, Jake,' she said, 'I'm supposed to be the therapist!' Leaving her third glass of whisky untouched, she went upstairs for her bath.

Cora met Thea at the end of Park Road as arranged; equidistant for them both to the tube.

'You look great!' Cora said, slipping her arm through Thea's as they made off towards the station. 'That skirt is absolutely outrageous!'

Thea laughed. Cora was an expert mimic and did a brilliant take-off of her. 'You don't look bad yourself,' Thea retaliated.

'Oi!' Cora nudged her in the ribs. 'Don't be so ruddy cheeky, you!'

They walked on in companionable silence to the tube; both bought a ticket and made their way towards the platform. Thea watched Cora carefully. She stood in front of the tube map and found where they wanted to go, then she traced the route with her finger and said, 'We've got to go up to Finsbury Park and get the . . .' she hesitated, spelt it out in her head, then said, 'The Piccadilly line, is that right?'

Thea nodded and covered her swelling pride in Cora's hard work and ability. 'Then?' she asked.

'It's eight stops and we get off at Leicester Square. We can walk from there.'

Thea patted her on the back affectionately. Cora hadn't memorised it, she had read it off the map. 'Well done,' she said; then, not without wanting to make too much fuss: 'Come on, let's get going.' They headed off to the escalator and made their way down on to the platform as the train pulled in. Moments later, they sat side by side and looked at their reflections in the glass window opposite. Cora took out a roll of mints and offered one across. Thea took it, popped it in her mouth and said, 'So where exactly are we going?'

Cora dug in her handbag, a pink nylon retro affair, and pulled out a scrap of paper. 'It's a club, dunno what one, probably a dive, mind you, but Ewert's got a job as a bouncer and he told us to come along an' see him. Said he'd get us a few free drinks.'

She handed the scrap over to Thea and as Thea looked at it she realised that Cora hadn't been able to read it;

the handwriting was terrible. 'It says . . .' Thea looked up puzzled; she hadn't a clue what it meant. 'It says Manny's Muff Parlour.' She looked at Cora. 'It doesn't sound very promising . . .'

'Promising!' Cora snatched the paper away from her and stared hard at it, then crumpled it into a tight little ball. 'The bastard!' she cried. 'The bloody bastard! Promising! Thea, it's a bloody strip joint!'

'A strip joint? What, you mean—'

'Yes! Strippers! The bastard! How could he do this to me! Taking the piss, that's what he was doing, inviting me for a night up West and getting me all excited, and all the time knowing that it was one of those sex dives that you read about in the *News of the World*. Jesus! I'll kill him, that's what, I'll bloody kill him! He's trying to make a fool out of me!' Cora jumped up and stared at the tube map up above the seats opposite. 'We're not going,' she announced. 'I'm not taking you to some poxy, crummy dive where—'

'Cora, calm down!' Thea urged, taking her arm and gently pulling her back into her seat. 'Everyone's looking at us. Come on, it can't be that bad, I imagine it—'

'Have you ever been to Soho, Thea?' Cora interrupted.

'No, but—'

'Well, take my word for it, it'll be worse than you imagine, much worse!' Cora shook her head. 'Bloody hell! Here we are, all dressed up on a Friday night and nowhere to go. Typical! I feel a right blooming jerk!'

'Well, let's go then,' Thea suddenly said. 'Let's just brave it out. Besides, what's a few naked women? We see it every day in the mirror, they haven't got anything that we haven't got!'

Cora turned to Thea aghast. 'You know something? You're weird, that's what you are! *Weird!* You've got no idea, have you?'

Thea shook her head. 'No.'

Cora stared at her and narrowed her eyes. 'Are you really game for it, Thea? I mean, you wouldn't be shocked and disgusted and all that?'

'Probably. But I'm all dressed up for a night out and I want to go and have a few drinks.'

'You do realise that Ewert's trying to make a fool out of us, don't you?'

'So? Let's go and pretend we do it all the time. That'll put his nose out of joint!'

Cora looked sidelong at Thea as if she couldn't quite believe her. 'You think you could do that? I mean, it'll be pretty tacky: strippers, maybe even a sex act, loads of oiks jeering. You really reckon you're up to it?'

Thea didn't know, but one thing being with Cora had taught her was that if she didn't try she wasn't ever going to find out. 'I'll give it a go,' she said. 'Just to spite Ewert.'

At last Cora smiled. 'All right then,' she said, squeezing Thea's arm. 'Just to spite Ewert.'

The club, when they finally found it, was a bit of a surprise for both of them. Of course, Thea had absolutely no experience of strip clubs and had never been to Soho before, but Cora had been expecting somewhere dark, dingy and scruffy, so the sleek narrow staircase, its walls lined with red velvet and up-lit with Art Nouveau lamps, that led to a dimly lit, intimate and smoky interior was nothing like she had imagined.

They met Ewert on the door and he escorted them in. Thea had lingered over the posters outside while Cora gave Ewert what she described as a 'tongue sandwich'. They advertised Cheryl the sorceress, trying to look glamorous in bits of snakeskin, who did something peculiar with a drugged and blank-looking snake. They gave Thea some indication of what was to come.

The club itself was everything its owner Manni – second-generation Spanish, short, rotund and balding – had wanted it to be. It was kitsch in the extreme: velvet walls, gilt mirrors, a bar lined with buttoned pink satin and hearts everywhere – gold, purple, pink; velvet, feather, satin and lace. It was frequented by city types, businessmen, 'a select clientele', as Manni liked to call them, but to Cora it was still a strip joint and no amount of tarting it up would change that. She finally turned towards the stage just as Cheryl came on with a snake that looked as if it had died some time ago, and began to gyrate obscenely. As they ordered their drinks, she murmured, 'Jesus!' then, out of Ewert's earshot: 'That is disgusting!'

Thea said nothing; she just watched. The act was not really disgusting, more pathetic, but that didn't stop the audience. There was a stag night in, young men in suits, and as Cheryl did her bit, appalling as it was, they egged each other on to stuff fivers and tenners and the odd twenty-pound note into her long black boots, which, along with a snakeskin thong, were the only items of clothing that she kept on.

'You like it?' Ewert appeared, smiling, with their drinks.

'It's unusual,' Thea said. 'I'd fancy the snake more than I'd fancy her though.'

Ewert laughed. Thea smiled, then turned away. She didn't like him – how could she, knowing that he took life's stresses and strains out on Cora's face? But she could see why Cora did. He was attractive in a macho, muscular way, exuding huge amounts of testosterone that would overpower most women.

'I think your mate's getting turned on there, Cora,' he said loudly. 'I reckon she likes a bit of totty.'

'Shut your face, Ewert!' Cora snapped.

In a split second Ewert had swung round on Cora and grabbed her wrist. 'What'd you say?' he snarled.

Cora's eyes registered panic, but her face stayed exactly the same. Thea held her breath for a moment, completely helpless, then she said, 'I think you're right.' And she reached out to touch Ewert, running her finger gently along his tight, sinewy forearm. He released Cora and looked at her. 'It fascinates me,' she went on. 'The men love it, don't they?'

Ewert smiled. His violence seemed to erupt out of nowhere and evaporate just as instantly. 'Yeah, they love it. Mr Rodriguez, the boss, he gets a lot of them city types in, they come in to let off steam, Friday nights, stag do's, after a big day's trading. They got money to burn.'

'Is it always Cheryl?'

'Nah, it's changed on a weekly basis. Why, you like her?'

Thea smiled. 'Oh please. As I said, I'd rather have the snake.'

Ewert touched her thigh under the table. 'I bet you would.'

Thea moved her leg slightly, took a sip of her drink,

113

then stood up. 'I need to go to the loo,' she said. 'And I think you two could do with a bit of time alone.'

'Nah, I don't think—'

'Yeah,' Cora said sharply to Ewert. 'We could.'

'You want me to show you where the toilets are?' he asked hopefully.

'No thanks, I'll find my own way.' And darting off before Ewert had a chance to stop her, Thea manoeuvred her way through the tables, ignoring the catcalls from the men, and found her way backstage to the cramped, dark and completely inadequate ladies' toilet.

'Oi!'

Just about to go in, Thea stopped and spun round towards the voice. Cheryl with the snake was standing behind her, naked but for the thong and boots, with a film of sweat over her chest and upper arms. 'This bloody snake weighs a ton,' she said, dropping it down on to the floor. There was a hefty thud and Thea stepped back a pace. 'It's all right, it's dead. Bloody thing went and popped its clogs a few months ago so I had it stuffed.' She turned and unlocked a door behind her. 'Bloody sight cheaper, I can tell you, it ate me out of house and home! Here . . .' She swung the door open. 'You can't use them toilets, by the way, they're blocked and the management's only fixed the men's. Typical!' She shrugged. 'Sorry, thought I'd better let you know.'

'Oh, right, thanks. You wouldn't know where I could find one, would you? I'm desperate.'

Cheryl shrugged. She stared at Thea for a few moments, then, making her mind up suddenly, she said, 'I've got me own loo in here. Come on, you can use that. But don't let anyone else know. I don't want all and sundry traipsing through my dressing room for a pee.'

'No, of course not. Erm, thanks.'

Cheryl bent and heaved the stuffed snake on to her shoulder, then led the way into her dressing room.

'Don't get many women in here, that's why the management don't do nothing about the toilets. You a friend of Ewert's?'

'Sort of. Not me really, my friend Cora, she's his girl-friend.'

'Oh, poor cow!' Cheryl plonked the snake over a chair and sat down to unzip her boots. 'Go on,' she said, carefully removing every note that had been stuffed in there and laying them in a bundle on the side. She then rubbed her sore feet and nodded towards a grey door at the end of the dressing room. 'Help yourself.'

Thea did as she was told, peed as quickly as she could and washed her hands. She came out to find Cheryl rubbing cold cream over her face, neck and chest.

'How far does the make-up go down?' she asked.

'All over, pretty much. It's a bugger to get off an' all.' Cheryl stopped what she was doing and reached for a tissue. 'Have a pew if you like,' she said.

'No, I'm fine thanks.' Thea was fascinated. 'Would you mind if I asked you a few questions?'

'It's a free country. Ask away, lovey; don't know if I can answer them though.' Cheryl worked quickly with the cold cream and tissues and her natural skin colour began to emerge. It was fair and slightly blemished, with a grey tinge to it that the lighting did nothing to enhance. Her nipples, Thea saw, had been rouged.

'How long have you been stripping?'

'Dunno. Let me think – about five years.' Cheryl began work on her bottom with the cold cream, which Thea had to admit was in good shape.

'How do you get bookings?'

'I've got a booker, he does it all for me, for a hell of a whack an' all! Still, it means I get no crappy places and he negotiates the fee. The more I get, the more he gets.' Cheryl stopped what she was doing and looked Thea over briefly. 'Why? You wanna have a go?'

Thea flushed. 'Oh no, I . . .' She put her hands up to her face and Cheryl laughed.

'Nah, haven't got the bottle. You need quite a bit of that I can tell you, some of them blokes out there are shits and you gotta be able to handle them.'

'Did you make much tonight?'

'Oi! Mind your own business!'

Again Thea flushed. 'Sorry, I'm just curious, that's all. They get pretty carried away with the notes, don't they?'

'Yeah, pretty.' Cheryl finished wiping off the last of the cold cream and screwed the top on to the jar. She then rubbed herself all over with a towel and began to dress. Pulling on a pair of grey track-suit bottoms over large white knickers, she said, 'They're all pissed, that's why.' She tugged a blue sweatshirt over her head and ran her fingers through her hair to reshape it. 'It's about one-forty, one-fifty, if you must know.'

'What? In just one show?'

Cheryl tied a scarf round her neck, peered forward to the mirror to check her face and finally turned to Thea. She took a packet of cigarettes off the dressing table and lit one up. 'Yeah, just the one.' Raising an eyebrow, she said, 'I bloody well earn it, though. It's no more than I deserve and my booker don't get any of it.'

'No, no obviously not.'

Cheryl was ready to go. She placed the snake in a sports bag, curling it carefully so as not to damage it and zipped the bag up. The remainder of her stuff, the small snakeskin outfit and boots, she folded and put into another holdall along with her make-up and cold cream. 'I gotta go,' she said. 'My mum's got me kid and I don't want to be late tonight.'

Thea glanced at her watch; it was eleven-thirty. She followed Cheryl out into the passage backstage and waited for her to lock the dressing room. 'How d'you get started then?' she asked quickly.

'Dancing in a pub – you know, topless.' Cheryl smiled, smoked the last of the cigarette and dropped it on to the floor. She didn't bother to grind it out, but left it glowing as she turned to go. Thea felt obliged to tread on it.

'Money for old rope, that,' she said, 'strutting about showing me tits. At least this is art, there's a lot more to it than you'd think.'

'God, I'm sure,' Thea answered, although she seriously doubted the art bit. 'Listen, thanks, Cheryl,' she said, 'for the chat and use of the loo.'

'No probs, love.' Cheryl turned and looked at Thea, full length, from her breasts down to her ankles. 'You gotta nice little figure,' she said. 'If you ever want to have a go let me know.'

Thea blushed deeply. 'Yes,' she stammered, 'I will, erm, thanks.'

'Right you are then,' Cheryl said. 'Ta ta!' And heaving the bag with the snake in up over her shoulder, she smiled, waved and walked off. Thea watched her go. She stood there for a moment, breathing in the damp, musty smell, then she rotated her hips, did a pelvic thrust just like Cheryl's and laughed out loud. She wandered back out front, dodged the catcalls and groping hands a second time and made her way back to her seat.

Later, on the way home, as Thea told Cora about Cheryl, she had to admit that the whole thing fascinated her.

'Bleeding old trollop!' Cora exploded. 'Don't know why you gave her the time of day even! I think it's disgusting, I really do, and to think that Ewert's working in that dive seeing all those shows night in night out makes me bloody sick, it really does!' She dug her hands deep into her pockets and kicked a small stone on the pavement.

'The show was pretty tacky, I have to admit,' Thea said, 'but I don't think stripping necessarily has to be. I mean, if it was done properly, with a bit of style and class, I reckon it could be quite good fun. And there's a hell of a lot of money involved as well. Cheryl probably makes about two hundred and fifty pounds a night, with tips.'

'Two hundred and fifty quid? For that old tart! You've gotta be kidding!'

'No, that's what she said.'

'Yeah, well, what she told you and the truth are two different things, I bet!' Cora walked on a couple of paces then stopped. 'Anyway, what d'you mean: with a bit of style and class it could be quite good fun?! You're surely not thinking of taking up stripping?'

'No, of course not!' Thea stopped too. 'Well, not immediately anyway!'

Cora was aghast. She swung round, not knowing what to say and suddenly Thea laughed. 'Got you!' she teased.

'No,' Cora said, not laughing at all. 'You are joking, aren't you? I mean, you wouldn't do all that stuff that Cheryl did tonight, would you? Not seriously?'

Thea linked her arm through Cora's and they began walking again. 'I don't know to be honest, Cora,' she replied. 'It's very good money and Cheryl's only the middle market. Imagine what you could earn if you had a really class act.'

'There ain't nothing classy about taking your clothes off for a bunch of pricks and a boot full of fivers.'

Thea sighed. 'Yes, maybe you're right.' They walked on in silence for a while, then Thea said quietly, 'Or maybe you're not.'

Despite her outraged sensibility, Cora had to smile.

Chapter Nine

The following morning, Thea was up early with Tom and was sitting in the kitchen in an old faded silk kimono that she had bought for a pound in the Oxfam shop when Hedda came down, dressed, perfumed and ready for her Saturday morning clinic.

Hedda stood in the doorway for a few moments, staring at her daughter before she made her presence known. She was astonished all over again by the difference in Thea in such a short space of time. Had Jake been right? Had Thea been in such desperate need of attention that she had deliberately denied herself to fit in with what she thought her parents wanted? Or was it that only now she had developed beauty, as some women do, and a beauty that was intrinsically bound up with confidence and style?

Hedda sighed and as she did so, Thea glanced up and said, 'Hi, Mum. Would you like some tea?'

Hedda shuddered as she had done last night at the word 'Mum'. 'No thanks,' she replied hastily, 'I'll make myself some coffee.'

Thea continued to flick through her magazine – some

banal woman's affair Hedda noted – while Hedda made her coffee: strong, with a dash of milk but no sugar. She sipped, glanced at the time and felt instantly irritated by her constant clock watching. Thea was languidly sipping her tea, oblivious to any of the pressures and strains of ordinary life, and here was Hedda, slurping down a quick coffee, dashing off to the tube (which was sweaty and oppressive in the heat of mid summer), working long hours, stressed and, to cap it all, having to deal with the highly disruptive effects of a small baby. Hedda's jaw tightened, the back of her neck tensed and she felt the beginnings of a stress headache at the base of her skull.

'Thea?' she asked sharply, 'What are your plans today?'

Thea looked up. Tom gurgled in his seat by her side and she bent to offer him a rattle before she said, 'Nothing much. See Cora, I expect, maybe go swimming with Tom.' Then bending forward again, she murmured, 'Would you like that, darling Tom? A little swim with Mummy and Cora?' She smiled as Tom gurgled and Hedda found herself grinding her teeth with resentment.

'Well,' she said, before she could stop herself, 'I think it's about time that you started to think more clearly about what you do with your time, Thea. I think' – Hedda glared down at Tom – 'that it's about time we sorted a nursery for that young man and got you back into full-time education!'

Thea looked up. 'That young man?' She smiled at Hedda, not understanding at all the depth of Hedda's mood. 'He's a little baby, Mum, hardly ready for nursery, are you, my little darling?'

'Thea!' Hedda suddenly snapped, 'could we please have a two-way conversation for once, without you constantly having to include a six-month-old baby! I was not asking you, Thea, I was telling you, that you have to start thinking about your future. You either have to get yourself a job or go back to college! I will not have you idling round the house, doing aerobics, spending your cash in Soho and hanging out with an illiterate nobody! And,' Hedda added, 'whatever you choose, Thea, Tom is going into a nursery, there is no other option!'

Thea sat tight-lipped throughout this outburst and stared down at her hands. By her feet Tom's gurgling had stopped; he frowned as, perceptive as young babies are to moods, he sensed the anger and stress in the room.

Hedda gulped down more of her coffee, then chucked the remainder of it down the sink. 'I have to go to work,' she said. 'Some of us do, it would seem, but I have left some degree course brochures in the living room for you to look through and I suggest that you begin with them and then start going through the *Yellow Pages* for full-time nursery care.'

Still Thea didn't look up.

'Thea? I am talking to you!'

'No you're not,' Thea said, completely unaware that only twelve hours earlier Jake had said exactly the same thing. 'You are shouting at me.'

Hedda reined in a sudden, inexplicable anger and turned to leave. 'I will see you tonight,' she said, as calmly as she could. 'I'll look forward to hearing how you got on!' And, walking into the hall, she picked up her briefcase and slammed out of the house.

Thea was left alone. She let out a huge sigh, then bent to gather up Tom. Cradling him in her arms, she breathed in the wonderfully sweet skin smell that babies have and closed her eyes. Thea's transformation was complete. What had started with no sense of reality, with no clear idea of what it all meant, was ending in one sure and determined path. There would be no going back to college and no job that involved Tom in full-time nursery. She hadn't a clue what she was going to do, bar one immediate task. Taking Tom into the sitting room, Thea snatched up the small pile of university brochures that Hedda had left so obviously around and took them out to the back of the house. There she lifted the lid on the dustbin and dumped them in. That done, she smiled. Now she had the rest of her life to get on with.

Thea still wasn't dressed by the time Jake came down, but that sort of thing didn't bother him. In fact, he liked it, it was a relief after all the years he had spent going to work, leaving Thea dressed and ready for school, her apron on, tackling some grisly task like cleaning the oven before she had to catch her lift.

'Good morning!' Jake said. 'Tom asleep, is he?' He crossed to the sink to put the kettle on and stood waiting for it to boil. 'What're you up to today, sweetheart?' he asked, making himself a coffee and crossing to the kitchen table with the paper. He had taken to using terms of endearment to Thea, terms that he had never used in the past because Hedda thought them derogatory and chauvinist, terms which now gave him extraordinary pleasure.

'I'm meeting Cora for her reading lesson, and then I thought . . .' Thea stopped. She had been doing a great deal of thinking in the two hours since Hedda had left for work, but perhaps now wasn't the right time to talk about it. The pause was long enough to make Jake glance up from the paper.

'Thought what?' he asked.

'Nothing much. Look, Dad, what d'you think of strippers?' Thea enquired, as casually as she could. 'Do you approve or disapprove?'

Jake put the paper down. 'Strippers! Good Lord, what a question! Why on earth do you ask?'

'I don't know. Just curious, I suppose.'

'Oh, well, I don't think I approve or disapprove really. I suppose for some it's a way of earning money, but I don't think it's a particularly nice way, I should think it's pretty humiliating and tacky most of the time.' Alarm bells had started to ring in his head and Jake could hardly think what he was saying. *Strippers? God, if Hedda heard this conversation she'd blow a gasket! Strippers? What the hell was Thea thinking about? Had she been to a strip club last night?* Jake swallowed down a mouthful of coffee and said, 'So, what's brought this up? You weren't at a strip club last night, were you?'

'No, of course not! Nothing's brought it up, I just wondered.' Thea hadn't wanted to lie, but she didn't see the point in stirring things up, not just yet.

'If it's done tastefully,' Jake went on, feeling slightly better, 'I suppose one could argue that stripping is valid in its own right.' He felt that he had at least to be fair on the subject. 'Some might even call it an art form.' He smiled and picked up the newspaper.

Thea waited a few moments, then said, 'D'you mind if I look through your jazz collection this afternoon, Dad?'

Jake was taken aback; Thea had never expressed an

interest in any music other than classical. This had to be a step forward. 'Of course not!' he exclaimed. 'In fact, I'd love you to! We can look at it together with Tom, play him some quality music, get him started early!'

'Very early!' Thea said, smiling. 'Thanks, I'd like that.' That established, she left Jake to his paper and finally went upstairs to shower and dress.

Once dressed, with Tom settled happily with Jake, Thea left for Cora's a couple of hours early, intending to hit the Portobello Road before she did anything else. She had her savings – not a great deal, about twenty-five pounds, but probably enough for what she wanted. There was a stall there that sold antique clothes and she wanted to have a good old rummage round. She had an idea, a good solid idea, but before she tested it on anyone, she needed to see that she could assemble all the parts, see that it could, if given the time and the energy, work.

So, in the Portobello Market, chatting to the stall holder, Thea carefully worked through a basket of clothes, pulling out the odd item that interested her and bargaining hard for the sale price. She wanted something specific too, which the stall-holder didn't have, said he hardly ever came across. However, he thought Thea was an attractive girl, so he gave her the number of a woman he knew who specialised and told her to give his name as a reference. He also asked Thea for a drink and she was so surprised that she flushed deep red and stammered that she'd like that but would have to see about a baby-sitter. Somehow, after that comment, he found he was rather busy for the next few weeks and it was impossible to fix a date. Thea paid for her items, he put them in an old carrier and she went on her way. She may have been naïve but she wasn't stupid. Next time she would definitely not mention the baby-sitting.

Cora was still asleep when Thea arrived at her bedsit. Thea rang, waited a few minutes, then decided to come back later. She scribbled a note on a scrap of paper from her bag and went to the phone box up the road. She rang the number she'd been given earlier, spoke to the woman and made an appointment to see her in half an hour. She didn't have a shop, she kept her stuff in the back room of her flat and that was in Latimer Road.

'Bugger.' Thea muttered on hanging up. It was another journey across town, almost back to where she had just come from. She took out her *A – Z* and looked up the address, then she made her way back to the tube and took a train across to Notting Hill.

The flat Thea was looking for was on the ground floor of a tall white Regency building with a black glossed double front door and a shiny – obviously daily polished – brass doorknob and bell. Thea rang, waited, then, curious, peered through the glass panel in the door into a long wide hallway with cream walls, gilt mirrors and a black and white tiled floor. There was the crackle of a voice through the intercom; Thea jumped, regained her composure, gave her name and the door release went. Stepping inside, she waited nervously by the door and wished that she had worn something smarter.

'Hello? Thea Marshall?'

Thea turned. A mahogany door at the end of the hall had opened and a women – probably in her early seventies Thea guessed – stood just inside it. She was tall and well built, the rounded curve of her hips and stomach emphasised by a wide black suede belt that was pulled in tight around her full waist and gave rise to a fold of flesh over the top of it. It was fastened with a large gold buckle that matched equally large gold earrings and a scarf loop holding a fine peacock green chiffon cravat. She looked extraordinary, a face and body obviously aged but an attitude that had stayed determinedly young. She wore blue, a bright, intense periwinkle blue, wool trousers and a silk shirt, the fabric stretched over her ample bosom, gaping slightly at the buttons, and her hair was white, swept back off her face and stiffly lacquered into a neat chignon at the back.

'Come on, dear,' she called, 'Don't look so sheepish.'

Thea moved across the hall towards the woman and noticed the ropes of pearls, five of them, falling heavily into the dip between her breasts. 'Dolly Heally,' the woman said, extending a plump, blue-veined hand. 'Nice to meet you dear. Thea, is it? Not short for Dorothea by any chance? No, probably not, you don't look like a Dorothea, it's not a very popular name nowadays, I shouldn't think.'

Dolly opened the door a bit wider and smiled. Her lips were painted a deep magenta and she had yellowing but immaculate teeth. 'Well, well, come on in and we'll have a look at these clothes. Who did you say you worked for? Not one of those little independent studios I hope, they're so pushy and they never pay on time, oh dear me, not at all good, wouldn't have happened when I was in the business but then there were only the big ones you know. You only ever counted if you worked for one of the big ones.'

Thea was led through a dark hall into the most extra-ordinary set of rooms, three of them, that stretched into each other through square arches hung with jewelled beaded curtains pulled to one side. There was a chandelier in the room where she now stood and even unlit it glistened, catching any ray of light and bouncing it off onto the walls. The walls themselves were covered, from ceiling to skirting, entirely in pictures. There were paintings, prints, sketches, photographs, cartoons and row upon row of framed theatre posters. There was a fireplace, white marble, with its mantelpiece crowded with tiny pill boxes, several Art Nouveau bronze figures, faded sepia postcards, snapshots and the odd gilt-edged invitation. And finally there was the furniture, Louis XV chairs, card tables crammed with porcelain, a long faded yellow silk sofa with a deep braided silk fringe and the most incongruous chaise, covered in purple brocade and finished with deep red velvet cushions.

Thea stood amazed.

'Ah, you like the chaise,' Dolly said. 'Not many do but I can tell by the look on your face that it doesn't shock you. It's as ugly as hell, of course, but it belonged to Max, my husband. He was an artist, not well known, mind you, but he made a good living from the kind of work he did.' She came across and patted the back of the chaise. 'Came in very handy this chaise did, provided exactly the right sort of atmosphere for painting portraits of naked mistresses.' Suddenly she let out a loud, throaty chuckle. 'Came in very handy for other things too but that would be telling, now wouldn't it!'

Thea still stood amazed; she hadn't been able to utter a single word yet.

'So, what can I do for you, Thea? You said that you wanted to look at my things. Is there any particular period that you're interested in?'

'Well, erm, yes there is. Victorian, actually.'

'Ah, Victorian, how fortunate! I've lots of Victorian! What studio did you say you were from?'

'Studio? Oh, erm, the thing is, Mrs Heally, I'm not exactly from a studio, this is a private sale, I, erm . . .' Thea broke off, not at all sure how to continue.

Dolly narrowed her eyes. She stared at Thea for some time, taking in her whole appearance and making Thea anxious. Then she said, 'I don't usually do retail, I can't have any old body coming in off the streets to nose around, not at my age, not with the things I've got here, it's the security aspect, I mean . . .' She stopped, pursed her lips and shook her head. There was an uncomfortable silence as she looked Thea briefly up and down again, then suddenly, as if she'd just decided something, she said, 'Oh what the heck! You're here now, you might as well get on with it! Come on, come into the back room and have a good look.' She led the way through the archway towards the room at the very back. 'Oh, and it's Dolly by the way, no one's ever called me Mrs Heally . . .' She laughed her deep, hoarse chuckle. 'Never deserved the respect some might say!' The laugh continued. 'And they'd be quite right too!'

The room at the back was long and narrow with French doors at the end. It too was hung with pictures so close together that hardly any of the wall could be seen. But there was no furniture, just rails and rails of clothes and, underneath the clothes, racks of shoes and hats. Thea stared. She took in the evening dresses, the translucent, bead-covered gauze shifts, layers of organza, films of silk, but she couldn't see anything else that resembled normal clothing. There were no coats, day dresses or suits. She glanced behind her at Dolly, was about to ask, when Dolly said, 'Victorian that rail, Edwardian over there and we work our way up to modern day – well, sixties anyway, up the wall and along.'

Thea turned to the sixties rail: thigh-length vinyl boots, lace-up leather corsets, sparkling G-strings, feather-trimmed bikinis hardly the size of a postage stamp and realised, with a sharp intake of breath, exactly what sort of clothes Dolly Heally collected and sold. She flushed with embarrassment, her heart hammered in her chest and she began to stammer some sort of exit line. 'I, erm, I don't think . . .' Then suddenly Thea stopped. On the Edwardian rail she had just spotted a whalebone corset with tiny hooks and eyes at the back. Underneath it, Dolly had put a pair of creamy silk and lace camiknickers and hung fine silk stockings alongside. It was perfect, exactly what she had imagined and it purged her of all embarrassment. 'That is wonderful,' she said, pointing to the corset. 'It's just what I had been thinking of.'

Dolly, who had been watching Thea's face closely and who, despite seventy-two years, never missed a trick, said, 'I see.' She walked across to the rail and took down the underwear. 'Would you like to try it on?'

'Oh, erm, yes, yes please.'

'Good.' Dolly drew a velvet curtain across a brass curtain pole hanging in the corner. 'You can change here, it makes a nice little dressing room,' she said. 'And while you're doing that, I'll put the kettle on for coffee and get the full-length mirror out.' She handed Thea the underwear, then bent, slowly and arthritically, to pull a pair of cream silk Edwardian shoes from under the rail. 'Here.' She put them in Thea's hands. They were exquisite: narrow-toed, with a small heel and a strap across the ankle fastened with a pearl button. 'These'll make sense of it all, my dear,' she said. She turned to leave the room. 'I can't wait to see how it all looks,' she remarked, shifting a gilt mirror out of a corner. 'And then' – she glanced over her shoulder on her way out and Thea was certain that she had winked – 'then, Thea sweetie,' she continued, 'we can talk about your act!'

Behind the velvet curtain, Thea rolled the silk stockings up her thighs, pulled on the garters and adjusted them into place. She slipped on the shoes and took the corset off the hanger, held it round her and reached behind to fasten the hooks and eyes.

'You all right there, Thea?' Dolly called from behind the curtain. 'I've got coffee. It's Turkish, I do hope you like Turkish. Not many do but I love it, I won't make anything else.'

'Turkish is fine,' Thea called. 'Erm, I can't seem to reach these hooks on the back, is there any chance you could do them for me?'

'Course, sweetie, come on out.'

Thea drew back the curtain and stepped into the room. Dolly raised her eyebrows. 'Good Lord!' she exclaimed.

'Oh no! Do I look ridiculous?'

Dolly stood aside and let Thea get to the mirror. 'Hardly, lovey,' she said. 'Ridiculous isn't quite the word that springs to mind.'

Thea peered at herself. 'Oh, I see what you mean.' The effect was deeply erotic, in an old-fashioned, unselfconscious way. It simply looked as if Thea had been caught with her clothes off and it was this innocence that created the effect.

Thea turned and Dolly fastened the corset. It was tight around her waist and made the most of the curve of her hips. It also swelled her ample breasts and gave her the most spectacular cleavage. Thea began to giggle.

'Your problem's going to be getting it off,' Dolly said, scrutinising Thea from top to bottom. 'We could lace it and leave the laces loose so that once the top one is undone the whole thing slides down over your hips, but it wouldn't have the same effect, the same tightness over the waist and the spectacular bust.'

Thea had stopped giggling and was staring at Dolly. 'How did you—?'

'Instinct!' Dolly interrupted her. She came across, knelt down and, straightening one of the silk stockings, said, 'Put it this way, Thea my love, if you hadn't had stripping in mind then I think I might have tried to convince you.' She smiled and eased herself straight again. Her knees creaked and she pulled a face. 'Did it myself for years before I got into the theatre proper. Not the sort of stuff that goes on nowadays, of course, not all this rude rubbish, gyrating hips and all sorts. No, proper stripping, that's what I did, a strip-tease act, taking my clothes off carefully and artistically and leaving something to the imagination at the end.' She smiled. 'Used to get them going as well. Brought the house down once, Portsmouth it was, the Aldbry Theatre. I turned my back to give the sightly view of my bare behind, then turned, and covered the essentials with a large straw picture hat. As I walked sideways to the music, I went and missed my step, tripped and dropped the bloody hat! A roar went up out front, so I smiled, turned, bent over to give them the nicest perspective, retrieved my hat and walked off stage!'

Thea's mouth had dropped open.

'My dressing room was chock-a-block with flowers for weeks afterwards, even after I'd moved on with the tour.' Dolly gave one of her chuckles. 'The florists of Portsmouth loved me, every time I returned after that, they sold out of blooms!' Dolly walked across the room and took a large hat off a hat-stand. 'You've got a natural sexiness, Thea, I saw it at once. Born to strip, some might say!' Laughing again, Dolly handed her the hat. 'Here, put this on, hair up.'

Thea did as she was told and piled her hair up inside the hat.

'Now take it off,' Dolly commanded. 'Slowly, and let your hair fall down, turning your head slightly to release it.'

Again Thea did as she'd been asked. 'Brilliant!' Dolly said. 'You're a natural! If you move in time to the music as well as you move normally then you'll be spectacular! Now, do it again and have a look at yourself.'

Thea turned to the mirror, piled her hair up under the hat, then, watching her reflection, took the hat off, letting her shoulder-length hair tumble down her neck. Dolly clapped her hands.

'Bravo!' She took the hat and lay it on a chair beside the mirror. 'There's a silk robe over there, pop it on and we can have our coffee, there's a good girl.' Thea took the silk wrap off its padded hanger and disappeared behind the curtain. 'And then,' Dolly called, 'you can tell me all about your plans and I can tell you – because I may be old and a bit saggy round the ass, Thea sweetie, but I still know what's what – I can tell you whether or not your plans will work! How does that sound?'

Thea appeared, underwear over her arm, the silk wrap barely concealing her young curvaceous body. 'It sounds a bit bewildering,' she answered honestly. 'I only came here to see if I could pick up the odd bit of underwear.'

'And you'll leave with half an act under your arm,' Dolly said. 'Not a bad day's work, I'd say!' And she laughed once more, only this time Thea laughed with her.

Cora was up and waiting for her by the time Thea arrived at her bedsit. The windows on the top floor were open and she was sitting by one, her face in the sun as Thea crossed the street to her building.

'Hey! Thea!'

Thea glanced up. 'Hello. How are you?'

'Fine! All the better for seeing you!'

They both laughed; it was a corny in-joke between them.

'Don't come up,' Cora called, 'I'll come down! We can do my reading in the park, it's too nice a day to be stuck inside!'

'OK,' Thea called back. 'I'll wait here for you.'

Moments later, Cora was down in the street. She had her books and her small pencil case, her sunglasses and a tube of suntan cream.

'Thought we might get a bit of a tan in the park, kill two birds with one stone, so to speak!' She held up the sun lotion. 'Got my bikini on underneath,' she said.

'You haven't! You can't concentrate and sunbathe at the same time!'

'Course I can!' Cora disagreed. 'Come on.'

Thea smiled and they linked arms, walking off towards the park at the far end of the street. 'Anyway, what you been up to this morning, I thought you'd be here ages ago.'

'This and that,' Thea said.

'Oh yeah?' Cora nudged her hard in the ribs. 'What sort of this and that?'

'I'll tell you in the park and only once we've done some work.'

'Blimey!' Cora said, pulling a face. 'You were right, you know.'

'Really? About what?'

'You are more like your mother than you realised!'

Laughing, Thea nudged her back, also hard in the ribs, and made Cora yelp.

The reading and writing done, Cora lay on her back in the park, sunglasses on and her skirt hitched up round her hips to let the sun get at her legs. She was fair-skinned, her hair, before it had been so interfered with, was a light blonde and her legs had a down of almost invisible white hairs. She had taken her T-shirt off too, to reveal a small triangle of bikini top that just covered her breasts.

'So,' she said, making Thea jump. 'What you been up to that's so secretive then?' She didn't turn her head or move a muscle and Thea had thought she was asleep.

'Well . . .' Thea had been reading and now looked up from the paper. She tucked her knees up under her and hugged them. 'It's a bit of a long story actually.'

'Oh yeah?' Cora rolled on to her side and looked at Thea. 'Go on.'

'I'm not sure I'm ready to tell you yet.'

Cora gently pinched her leg. '"I'm not sure I want to tell you yet . . ."' she mimicked. 'Hey, what's the big secret? Blimey, Miss High and Mighty! Not ready to tell me—'

'All right, all right!' Thea interrupted. 'Promise you'll listen though and won't go flying off the handle or jumping to the wrong conclusions.'

'Oh blimey, this sounds serious. All right, I promise!'

'No really, Cora, I mean it! Promise that you'll just hear me out, let me finish! You will, won't you?'

Cora took off her sunglasses and narrowed her eyes. 'OK,' she said, 'I promise.'

'Right, well, the thing is that Hedda had a bit of a go at me this morning.'

'She never!' Cora sat up. 'Why?'

'It's all to do with going back to university and seeing me wasting my time – well, in her eyes I do anyway. I suppose that I don't really blame her, she wants me to do well, but . . .' Thea's voice trailed off as she thought about Hedda. She didn't really know what Hedda wanted. She never had.

'And?'

Thea started. 'Oh yes, sorry. Well, basically, she wants me to do another degree or get a job. I suppose that she thinks going back to college would be easier than getting a job as far as I'm concerned, but it's not, I just don't want to do it.'

Cora said nothing. Degrees and universities were out of her league.

'So I've got to get myself a job, a career I suppose, but the thing is that I don't want to put Tom into a nursery, I want to look after him myself . . .' Again Thea stopped. She said, more to herself than to Cora: 'I don't just want to, I've got to, he's mine and I want to be everything to him, I—' Suddenly she looked at Cora. 'Cora, I've had an idea. It started last night, at Ewert's club—'

'At Ewert's club? Oh God, this isn't what I think it is, is it? You're not seriously—'

'You promised not to interrupt!' Thea interjected. 'Come on, I can't tell you if you keep butting in and never let me finish a sentence, can I?'

Cora nodded. She chewed her lip, but shut up.

'Well, I've been doing a bit of research this morning. I thought about it all last night and I decided to look into it today, and, purely by chance, I came across this amazing person – Cora, you have to meet her – and, well, we sort of talked things through and I think I may have a bit of a proposition to put to you.'

Cora had begun pulling at blades of grass and didn't look at Thea.

'I went to look at some antique clothes that she sells – she's called Dolly – because, well, I had a germ of an idea that we—'

'We?' Cora was shocked. 'Don't you start getting me into this thing! I'm not interested, all right?'

'All right then, an idea that I might be able to put an act together.'

'An act!' Cora snorted. 'Taking your clothes off is hardly an act, it's just bloody stripping!'

'OK, stripping, but you're wrong, it is still an act and the one I'd do would be different. I went to see Dolly because she sells old clothes, antique clothes, and when I got there it turns out that she mainly sells antique underwear, sort of erotica, I suppose, and it also turns out that she used to have an act, years ago, and she made a small fortune with it!'

'Oh yeah? How old's this Dolly then?'

'I don't know, about seventy-odd, I suppose.'

'Well then, she made a small fortune – as you put it – in the days when showing an ankle was daring!' Cora shook her head. 'Look, Thea, I don't want to be a downer but you really haven't thought this through at all! Stripping isn't what you think it is, no way! You get loads of drunk blokes in a pub or a club and they want to see the whole thing! They don't want no antique underwear and titillation, they want hard-core stuff because they're ignorant pigs! They'll treat you like shit and all you'll get is a few hundred quid for it!' Cora snatched a handful of grass up and scattered it moments later.

'OK, maybe you're right, but that's at the bottom end of the market and I'm not talking about that, I'm talking about the top end, where there's real money and if we – Oh sorry, I mean, if *I* offer something completely different but bloody sexy and they buy it then it's a whole different thing!'

Cora continued to snatch up small handfuls of grass. She said nothing.

'Look, I know it seems bizarre but I think it makes perfect sense for both of us. For you it would mean working at night, like you do already and carrying on with reading and writing during the day, only we're talking much, much more money.'

'And you?'

'Well, for me it would mean that I could look after Tom. I would only need a baby-sitter at night, he would be asleep and wouldn't even know that I wasn't there, and during the day I could have him to myself.'

There was a sniff, which Thea took to mean approval. 'Listen, Cora, at Dolly's this morning I tried some things on and I did a couple of moves and frankly it was terrific! Maybe if you came along with me tomorrow and saw for yourself, maybe if you—'

'Look!' Cora snapped. 'Let's get one thing straight now, all right? I am not taking my clothes off for a bunch of pricks and that's final!'

'OK, OK!' Thea held her hands up defensively. 'But I don't see your problem, I really don't! I'd rise above it, that's what I'd do, I wouldn't let them treat me like shit! Besides, I've got one over on them, I'm the one in control up there on the stage, I'm the one with the power. I can turn them on or off whenever I want and for that privilege, they pay me!' Thea shrugged. 'Anyway, from what Cheryl said last night and from what Dolly said today, it's not a few hundred quid here, Cora, it's more like six hundred a week. Each.'

Cora jerked up. 'Six hundred quid each?' She took her sunglasses off. 'You've gotta be kidding!'

'No.'

'How's that then?'

'Well, a great deal of it is in tips, money stuffed into boots, thrown on the stage, handed over personally, but the booking fee is pretty good too. Providing you've got a regular slot and can bring in a crowd then you can more or less name your price. The money these places make over the bar when there's a good act on apparently goes into thousands.'

Cora was silent. She slipped her glasses back on again and turned away so that Thea had no idea what she was thinking. Thea uncurled her legs and lay down on the grass, rolling on to her side and propping herself up on one elbow. She didn't say anything, she just waited.

'So why d'you want me to do it with you?' Cora said at last. 'If the money's so good and you've got all the nerve, why d'you want me in on it too?'

Thea didn't look up. 'Because we're friends,' she said. 'You're my best friend in fact, and because you're very attractive. I think that together we could cause a storm.'

There was another silence.

'Besides, I'm not sure I've got the confidence to do it myself and' – she glanced sidelong at Cora – 'I actually think we might enjoy it if we were in it together.'

'Enjoy it?' Cora spluttered. 'You're barmy!'

'Yes,' Thea said, rolling on to her back. 'Maybe I am.' She ruched her skirt up so that her legs were also exposed to the sun. 'But maybe,' she said, 'if you don't turn up at Dolly's with me tomorrow then you're the one who's really mad. What have you got to lose, Cora? All you have to do is give it a go.' Closing her eyes, she heard Cora stand, pick up her things and leave. But knowing when enough was enough, Thea made no attempt to stop her.

Chapter Ten

The following day Thea was up early again, only this time Jake was waiting for her when she came downstairs. He had been worried all night, lying next to Hedda, desperate to talk and yet unable to say a word. Hedda had put up a barrier; talking about Thea made her uptight and she made no effort to hide it. So, lonely and troubled, at five a.m. Jake had risen, showered and come downstairs to look again at the records Thea had asked to borrow from his jazz collection. She was up to something, Jake realised, but exactly what he couldn't put his finger on. For one thing, the music she'd chosen yesterday had taken him by surprise; for another she hadn't wanted just to listen, to see what she liked, she had been making a choice of tracks, as if she wanted to use them for something. It didn't make sense but she hadn't told him anything, hadn't given him any idea why she was doing it.

The more Jake thought about it, now he was up and awake, the more he worried. So, unable to think of anything else to do, he sat down by the stereo, put the headphones on and placed the first record Thea had chosen on the turntable. He found the track she liked and played it, tapping his fingertip lightly on his thigh, in time to the music. It was 'Summertime' by Herbie Mann and he couldn't deny its sensuality. There was a mid tempo, a good strong sax and trumpet melody and a certain mood to it that he couldn't quite put his finger on. The track finished, Jake found the next record and track and repeated the procedure. Four records later, he switched off the stereo and stood to make himself a cup of coffee.

The same thing that had troubled him last night, that had kept him awake, still bugged him. What was it about all those pieces of music that baffled him? Why had Thea liked them so much? They were all strongly melodic, they all had good trumpet work, so it was easy to see the immediate attraction, but then so had some of the other pieces on the albums; pieces, as a jazz fan, he thought far better, more accessible.

Switching the kettle on, Jake stood pensively at the kitchen work surface and stared out of the window. Nothing came to him. He dropped a couple of spoonfuls of fresh coffee into the pot, placed it on the hob, then filled it with boiling water and turned the gas on. He hummed a few bars of the last track, went to the fridge for some milk and all of a sudden it hit him. The music he was humming was raunchy! It was out and out sexy, provocative, erotic, sometimes almost visual in its conveyance of mood. Jake smacked the milk down on to the work surface and swore. What the bloody hell was Thea up to? Talk about strippers yesterday, sexy pieces of music, long disappearances. He heard the coffee pot whistle but ignored it. She wasn't really thinking of stripping, was she? Going back to the stereo, he put the last track on again and picked up the headphones.

He swore a second time. As soon as the music started he saw it in his mind: it was perfect music for taking your clothes off to, it was perfect music for sex.

Tearing the headphones off again, Jake stormed over to the now squealing coffee pot and snatched it off the gas. He poured himself a cup, splashed some milk in and opened the back door. Walking out into the garden, he took a couple of lungfuls of cool early morning air to calm himself and slowly sipped his coffee. He would have to talk to Thea; he would have to confront her. If she really was into something seedy then Hedda would never forgive him. God, he would never forgive himself! Pulling out a garden chair, he wiped the dew off with the sleeve of his sweater and sat down. It was here that Thea found him when she came down into the kitchen just after seven.

'Hello, Dad,' she called, standing in the doorway.

Jake turned to look at her. She really had changed, his Thea, she had grown beyond all recognition and for a moment he wondered if she didn't know best about what she was doing. She had a poise and confidence he had never seen in her before; she had discovered herself as a woman. Even he, as a blind old father, couldn't deny her sexuality: she wore it like scent, it clung to her, enveloping people.

'Thea,' he said, 'I wonder if we might have a chat.'

Thea stepped outside. She was barefoot, and in her silk kimono she shivered in the fresh morning air. Laying a hand on his shoulder, she said, 'You look tired. Are you worrying about something?'

Jake patted her hand. 'Yes,' he answered. 'You.'

'Me?' Thea pulled out a chair opposite Jake and performed the same action as he had, wiping the dew off it with the sleeve of her dressing gown. Jake smiled. Ah, genetics, he thought and it made him feel slightly better.

'Thea, what did you want all that music for yesterday?'

'Oh, that? Nothing much, a few dance routines with Cora, just to listen to.' Unlike Hedda, Thea was a lousy liar. She flushed as she spoke and the blood flooded her face and neck.

'Is that all?' Jake fidgeted in his chair. 'I mean, you're not getting into anything you can't handle, are you?'

'What d'you mean?'

'I mean . . .' Jake hesitated, then said, 'I mean that things aren't always as easy as they look from the outset, Thea. You are one of life's innocents and I don't want you hurt. I don't know what you are planning but you must be cautious, whatever it is, think very carefully before you enter into anything, all right?'

Thea nodded, then she reached out and touched Jake's hand. 'Thanks,' she said. 'I think I know what I'm doing and I've got Cora with me, she's pretty streetwise.' She stood. 'Was that all?'

Jake sighed. No, it wasn't all, it was only the half of it, but as he'd sat there talking he had realised that he didn't really have the right to interfere in Thea's life. That right had to be earned, through long-term attention and interest, and he and Hedda had never done much to prove themselves on that score. 'Thea,' he said, 'you will talk to me about what's going on, won't you? I might be able to help.'

Thea smiled. 'OK.' Then she turned to go back inside.

'But, Dad,' she said, just before she went, 'I'm hardly an innocent any more. Having Tom changed all that.'

'Did it?'

'I think so. That and having Cora as a friend.'

'Yes,' said Jake. Then after she'd gone, under his breath he murmured, 'I only hope you're right.'

A bit later, Thea made her way to the bus stop where she always met Cora. She stood, glanced at her watch and decided to give it ten minutes. Cora was never late, she knew Thea had to be at Dolly's by nine-thirty and it was ten to nine now. If she was coming, she wouldn't leave it later than nine o'clock.

Digging her hands in the pockets of her denim jacket, she stared at the bus timetable to stop herself from gazing hopefully at the horizon and waited. She was anxious; the few words with Jake had unnerved her and she realised how much she wanted Cora to be in on this with her. In fact she wasn't sure she could do it on her own. Her friendship with Cora had changed Thea, it had given her a whole new confidence, but it was a confidence that was unestablished and thus fragile and Thea was only too aware of how easily it could be broken.

Glancing at her watch again, Thea counted five minutes down, five to go. She looked briefly up the road for an approaching figure then turned back to the timetable. She wished she'd brought a book or had a Walkman, indeed anything to take her mind off waiting for Cora. She began to add up the bus times and work out the entire time of the route from beginning to end. Her mental arithmetic was rusty and it took a while, so by the end of the first route, it was nearly nine o'clock and Thea heard the bus.

'Damn,' she muttered, looking up again and seeing no sign of Cora. 'Damn and blast.' She felt a moment of indecision and panicked, wondering if she should get on the bus or just forget the whole thing. Her hands began to sweat; her heart raced as the bus approached; she was momentarily weepy. Then the bus pulled up with a squealing of brakes and a polluted hiss, the doors slid open and she had no more time to think. She propelled herself forward and began to climb.

'One to . . .' Thea's mind went blank. 'Oh, I, erm, I . . .'

'Oi! Thea! What're you doing on the bus? I thought this old girl lived in Notting Hill.'

Thea spun round. 'Oh Cora! Thank goodness!' She beamed. 'Yes, yes she does!'

'What're you doing on the bus then?'

Thea glanced round at the bus driver. 'Oh dear, I shouldn't be here, I, erm, I . . . I'm sorry, but you pulled up,' she twittered at him, 'and I got on without thinking. I, erm, I don't need the bus, I need the tube.'

'It'd be helpful if you made your mind up, luv, before you got on,' he said.

'Yes, I . . . Oh dear!' Thea turned and jumped down the steps. 'Sorry!' she called as the doors juddered shut again and the driver indicated. He shook his head at Thea to emphasise his disapproval and pulled out. 'Oh dear,' she said again, 'I wasn't thinking. I . . .'

'Silly old fart,' Cora said. 'Don't get in a flap about it, everyone makes mistakes.' She pulled out a stick of chewing gum, a habit she'd developed since giving up the ten cigarettes a day. 'Here, you want one?'

Thea shook her head.

'Please yourself.' Cora popped the stick into her mouth and folded it before she started chewing. 'Come on,' she said, mouth full, 'I thought we were supposed to be there at nine-thirty.'

'We are,' Thea said.

'Right, let's get a move on then or we'll be late.' She started off in the direction of the tube and let Thea catch her up.

'I'm really glad you came,' Thea said, marvelling at how Cora could take such long strides in such high heels.

'Yeah, well,' Cora said, chewing hard.

'No, really, I really am glad—'

'Look,' Cora said, taking the gum out for a moment and stopping to face Thea. 'I came because we're mates, right? But I'm not making any promises. I'll have a dekko, see what it's like, then make my mind up. OK?'

Thea smiled. 'OK,' she said, but she knew Cora was interested; she wouldn't have turned up if she weren't.

Dolly had cleared a space in the middle room of the three and brought in her music centre, a 1967 Decca stereo in a teak veneer unit with a lid. It sat to one side, the lid up, plugged in and ready to go. It was the first thing that Cora fell upon when she came into the room.

'Wow!' she said, fingering the wood and peering inside it. 'This is really ancient! Does it still work?'

'Of course it does,' Dolly replied tersely, offended at the use of the word *ancient*. 'It may not be state of the art, I think the expression is, but yes, it still works. Very well actually.' She took the records Thea held out to her and placed them on the stacking shelf built into the unit, then turned to the girls. Cora and Thea made an unlikely pair, both tall but one model slim, pale and blonde, the other voluptuous, with creamy skin and heavy dark hair. They looked ill matched, but then that would be the attraction. Dolly could see, with her practised eye, that with a bit of work, being opposites would work to their advantage. She clapped her hands together loudly and made Thea jump.

'Now, girls,' she said briskly, 'we need the outfits. Thea, I think what we chose yesterday will work beautifully. Cora, we need to kit you out and see how it matches up.'

Cora narrowed her eyes. 'Kit me up?'

'Yes, yes, come along, dear, we need to find you something that'll complement Thea but give you your own identity.'

'Oh.' Even Cora was lost for words. They followed Dolly into the next room and stood while she started to sort through the Victorian clothes rail. Cora's jaw dropped. She had never seen black leather used in the way that Dolly had it displayed and the silver nipple covers with the long pink tassels drew her forward for a closer inspection.

'How do these stay on?' she asked, holding them up over her breasts.

'With a bit of glue, dear,' Dolly said over her shoulder.

'Ouch!'

'Yes, but well worth it for the effect. Some I've seen could make each tassel twirl in a different direction.'

'Never!'

'Oh yes, absolutely.' Dolly pulled a hanger from the rail and turned. 'You fancy a go?'

'Me?' Cora was astonished. 'No thanks, Dolly, think I'll miss that one!'

Dolly laughed. She lay the robe that she had pulled from the rail on to the back of a gilt chair and went across to a chest of drawers. She opened the first drawer, then the second and finally found what she was looking for in the third.

'Now,' she said, draping the camiknickers she'd taken out over her arm and holding up a pair of silk stockings. 'I don't think Cora wants a corset, she hasn't got the same curves as you, Thea, and owing to her look and colouring, I think we need something a little more sophisticated.'

Cora pulled a face at Thea that said: *Sophisticated, eh?* She walked across to the chair and held up the robe. It was a black-silk oriental kimono, with huge embroidered dragons and flowers on it. The camiknickers that Dolly held were also black – as were the stockings – but it was a sheer chiffon, finished with lace. Dolly handed them to Cora. 'You can change there, behind the curtain and, Thea, you need to go with her so that I can see you both together. Oh, and Cora, you'll need these.' Dolly went across and bent for a pair of Edwardian black kid ankle boots with a high Cuban heel. 'Here.' She stood up gingerly, rubbing her knees as she did so, and placed the boots on top of Cora's pile. 'Go on then! Let's get on, we haven't got all day, you know!'

Both girls scurried across to the velvet curtain and drew it. There was much rustling, a few giggles, the odd exclamation and swear word – from Cora – and finally the curtain was drawn back.

'Ah,' said Dolly. She motioned for the girls to walk

forward and turn, then she said, 'Nice,' and, 'Hmmm.' Finally, after several minutes of silence, she said, 'We'll have to change Cora's hair, it's got to be sleeker and—'.

'My hair?' Cora wailed. 'What's wrong with my hair?'

'Nothing, Cora sweetie, I just think we need to make it a little more chic, that's all.'

'Chic? What d'you mean chic?! I'm not having it all chopped off, I don't know if I'm even gonna get involved in all this stuff yet, I—'

Thea lay a calming hand on Cora's arm. 'It's OK, you don't have to do anything unless you really want to. Just let Dolly finish, OK?'

Cora nodded and Dolly said, 'I think we need shoes, not boots. But apart from that I think it all looks rather good! Come and have a look, girls.'

Cora and Thea exchanged glances, then walked across to the mirror. They stood side by side and stared.

'Bloody hell!' Cora murmured.

Thea said nothing.

'The hat!' Dolly cried. 'Put on the hat, Thea darling!'

Thea and Cora exchanged another look; Dolly handed Thea the hat and she scooped her hair up and piled it inside.

'Bloody hell!' Cora murmured again. She fingered the glossy silk of her kimono, opened it slightly and ran her hand down over her leg, touching first the pale downy skin of her thigh then the sleek, glossy silk-knit of the stocking. 'I look—' she broke off and turned to Thea. 'I look . . .' Again she hesitated, searching for the right words. 'I don't know what I look like,' she said truthfully. 'It's sort of tarty but then not really tarty, not common.' She shook her head, pinging the elastic suspender. 'Jesus! I don't know about this, Thea, I really don't!'

Thea smiled. 'You look sexy, Cora, not tarty, there's a difference.'

'Yeah?'

'Yes, yes there is.'

Cora pulled a face. 'Well, if I look sexy, then you'll make their blood boil!' She began to giggle. 'Your tits look unbelievable!' Thea had started to laugh as well, and as she did so, her spectacular cleavage wobbled.

'Oh my God!' Cora wailed, almost helpless with laughter. 'They're like two jellies on a—'

There was a sharp clap of hands and both girls were so startled that they instantly stopped laughing and looked up.

'Girls!' said Dolly, to a background of renewed but stifled giggles from Cora. 'We must get on. Now we've found you the clothes, we've got to get going on the act. Music? Thea, did you say that you had some music that you liked? Oh yes, that's it, I put it on the music centre.' Dolly crossed to the stereo unit and picked up the five LPs that Thea had brought with her. 'Now, let's see . . . What was it that you liked, Thea sweetie? Did you tell me? Or did you make a note of the tracks?'

'I put a note in with the LPs, Dolly,' Thea said. She walked across and found her slip of paper under the top album. 'The first piece is the second track side one. D'you want me to—'

'Good Lord no, lovey! I can manage, thank you!' Dolly fiddled with the LP, trying to find where the record sleeve opened, located it after a minute or so of torture for Thea and Cora and dropped the vinyl record on the floor. 'Oops!' She went to bend but Thea got there before her, retrieving it and handing it back to Dolly. After another couple of minutes of fiddling, the record made it to the turntable and Dolly began trying to operate the machine. It wasn't that she was inept in any way, more fumbly, in the way elderly people often get. Thea and Cora waited. Cora, Thea could see, was having her doubts.

'Ah ha!' Dolly suddenly announced. 'Got it!' She bent forward to turn the volume on the stereo up and suddenly soft melodic jazz filled the room. Dolly's face broke into a broad grin. 'Thea,' she said, tapping her foot in time to the music, 'this has class!' She began to move, very slowly, exaggerated actions, small steps here and there. 'And so, my dears,' she said, looking across at the two girls watching her, 'will you!'

Thea held her pose. She was breathing hard and her chest rose and fell as she struggled to bring the breathlessness under control. Sweat trickled down the side of her face.

'Hold for five more,' Dolly called. 'Five, four, three, two and one! Good, and relax!'

Thea slumped against the chair and took several big lungfuls of air.

'You were brill, Thea!' Cora patted her on the back. 'Here.' She handed Thea a towel and Thea wiped it over her damp sweating limbs. They were both in swimsuits – which should have been leotards – that Dolly had asked Thea to bring with her and as she finished drying her body, Cora passed her a sweatshirt which Thea pulled over her head.

'Right!' said Dolly. 'I think we can safely call that a wrap, don't you?'

Both girls nodded. They had been working with Dolly for three hours now, choreographing what Dolly called a traditional strip-tease act to a track from one of Jake's jazz albums. There was nothing lewd or easy about what they'd learnt, there was a huge amount to take on board about posture, counting time, small stage movements and perfecting a grace and style that neither of them had any idea they possessed. They were both exhausted; Dolly was of the old school of stage management, where you rehearsed until you got it right, even if you collapsed in the middle of it. Only they hadn't collapsed and they had got it right.

'Now,' she went on, giving them just a few moments to rest. 'What I'd like you to do is keep your leotards on, if one can call them leotards, of course, and put your costumes over the top. I'm going to pop out for a few moments and I'll be back by the time you're dressed and ready to start. We're going to run through this whole thing one last time, with the costumes on, to see how it all fits together. OK, darlings?'

Again both girls nodded; they didn't have the energy to reply and besides, Cora was on the verge of saying something rude and thought it better just to nod. Dolly clapped her hands, twice, and, exchanging a wry smile, the girls found their clothes and scurried behind the curtain to change.

The music went on, the girls counted the bars, waited until they hit their cue and on the third beat stepped out from behind the curtain.

One, two, three, four: Thea moved across to the chaise
that Dolly had set up for them; five, six, seven, eight:
Cora moved to stand behind it. One, two, three, four:
Thea placed her leg gracefully up on the chaise; five, six,
seven, eight: she rolled down a stocking and turned her
shoulder towards the audience. Over the next eight beats,
she dropped the strap of her camiknickers down off her
shoulder, ran her hand down her arm and tilted her head
to exactly the right angle. Cora leant forward and, frantically
counting the beats in her head, slipped her robe off her
shoulders, turned her back, wriggled her hips and stepped
out from behind the chaise. The act had begun.

Traditional strip-tease, as Thea and Cora had learnt,
takes perfect timing, confidence and an innate sensuality
that either makes the act or breaks it. With the lights on full
glare over their faces and the back room in semi-darkness
as a result, Thea and Cora worked to the music, doing
the routine they'd rehearsed, making the small provocative actions that Dolly had shown them and, as they
did so, something incredible happened. Dolly had been
right in her instinct; that instinct had paid off. Cora and
Thea exuded personality; they came alive with every twist
of the saxophone, every strain of the trumpet; and they
stripped with the sort of exuberant sexuality that Dolly
hadn't seen for many years. The act wasn't polished, they
dropped the odd beat, made wrong turns, let a hand
slip here and there that in the real thing would reveal
something they wanted to keep covered up, but the over-
all effect was stunning. If they worked hard to refine it
and kept that perfect balance of innocence and cheek
then, clapping her hands jubilantly in applause, Dolly

realised that Cora and Thea really might have something very special.

'Bravo, bravo!' Dolly cried. 'Hold for eight! Hold it . . . and relax!' She switched the lights off and both Thea and Cora fell towards each other and slumped down on to the chaise. They burst into fits of giggles.

'Well done, girls, that was super!' Dolly said, coming towards them. 'I'd like you to meet—'

The giggling stopped, abruptly. Thea stood up. 'Who on earth—?'

Cora stood up right behind her. 'You never said we were stripping for anyone, Dolly! That's not—'

'Girls, girls!' Dolly said, clapping her hands. 'Come on, who do you think you're going to be doing this to for real? Certainly not Mickey Mouse and his family!' She glanced behind her and let the man she was standing in front of step forward. 'Girls, Thea and Cora, this is Phil. Phil, this is, well, you know who they are, I've just told you.'

Thea and Cora stared. Into the light had just stepped the most handsome man either of them had ever seen. And handsome in the old-fashioned, Prince Charming sense of the word. He was tall, muscular and dark, with a face that looked almost sculpted, so strong was his jawline, so defined were his features. He smiled and his mouth stretched evenly across his teeth, dazzlingly white teeth that were probably worth a small fortune in dental work.

'Is he for real?' whispered Cora. Thea gave the faintest shrug. Phil ran a hand through his hair. It was wavy, swept back off his face and more than likely treated with an expensive wax.

'Hello,' he said, and Cora's heart fell.

'Oh,' she murmured in Thea's ear. 'Not available.' Thea glanced quizzically over her shoulder. 'Never mind,' hissed Cora.

'Your act,' Phil said, holding one elbow with the other hand. 'was simply fabulous!' He moved forward and lightly fingered the silk of Cora's kimono. 'And this, my dear, is quite divine!' Thea understood. Her mouth dropped open and, catching Dolly's eye, she made a conscious effort to clamp it shut.

'Phil lives upstairs,' Dolly said, 'and we, he and I, that is, have had a wonderful idea. Once you get this act up and running, both of you are going to need a booker and Phil would be only too happy to take on that task.'

'A booker? Phil?' Thea sat down on the edge of the chaise. 'Dolly, I don't know if—'

'A booker? What the hell's a booker when it's at home?' Cora interrupted.

Thea turned. 'He, or she, makes the bookings with the clubs, looks after us, and earns a commission on our fee. It's in his interest to get us the best deal because he takes a slice of it.'

'Whoa! Hang on a minute! If I'm out there taking all my clobber off, I'm not gonna give a whack of it to some tight-assed bastard in an office, ta very much!' Cora snatched her kimono together.

'It's not quite like that, Cora,' Thea said. 'We do need a booker, it makes things an awful lot easier, but I don't know, Dolly, it all seems a bit sudden. Yesterday I was just thinking about the whole thing, it was simply an idea, and today I've practised my act and got a booker. It's a little too quick to take everything in. Cora and I haven't exactly made up our minds for certain yet that we're going to do it.' Thea glanced at Cora. 'Have we, Cora?'

Cora, who was scowling for England, shrugged.

'Oh,' said Phil, turning to Dolly. 'I think we have a bit of a problemo. Shall I depart?'

Dolly patted his arm. 'No, Phil sweetie, you stay there, I don't think I've explained myself very well, that's the problem. Come on, girls, get some clothes on and we'll have coffee. Your blood sugar level has gone down, Cora lovey, I can tell. Is Turkish all right? I love Turkish, I won't drink anything else. Oh, did I tell you that already, dears?'

Cora and Thea nodded.

'Yes, thought so, problem of old age, repeating oneself. It's very tiresome, not least of all for me!' Dolly laughed her throaty cackle and shooed the girls towards the velvet curtain with the back of her hand. 'Go on, get decent and I'll make coffee. I think I've got some of those delicious little Viennese biscuits somewhere. Come on, Philip darling, you can help me find them.' And leaving Thea and Cora alone, Dolly disappeared to get the refreshments.

'This isn't for real!' Cora burst out as soon as they'd gone. 'What the hell's going on, Thea? I reckon this Dolly's gonna stitch us up good and proper. You heard about this bloke Phil before?'

Thea stared down at the floor and frowned. 'No I haven't,' she answered, after a few moments' contemplation, 'but I think that it could actually be quite a good idea, I mean if we decide to go through with this.' She glanced sidelong at Cora. 'I think Dolly's trying to do the best for us, trying to help, and we would need a booker eventually anyway. I hadn't really got that far in my great scheme of things, so I guess we should be thankful to Dolly for doing it for us.'

'Yeah, and what's in it for Dolly?'

'I would imagine that she'll charge us for training and costumes etc., once we're up and running.'

'Up and running? But we haven't made up our minds for sure yet, have we?'

Thea shrugged. As far as she was concerned the whole thing made perfect sense for her and Tom. She would have a job, just like Hedda had wanted, earn money, possibly a good deal of it, and she could have Tom as well: no nurseries, no full-time child care. OK, it wasn't an ideal career, hardly the most acceptable of professions, but if they did it right, got a really good act together and only worked the decent clubs, then it could be bloody successful! The only thing was, Thea thought, looking at her friend, that she didn't want to do it without Cora. Cora was a mate, she was there for her and she did something for Thea that no one else had been able to do. She gave her confidence. Just being with Cora made Thea feel good and being without her she knew that she didn't really have a chance at this game.

'Have we?' Cora repeated. She poked Thea in the ribs and Thea turned to protest. When she did, she saw that Cora was smiling. 'Well, I might not have made up my mind, but it looks like you have!' She poked Thea again and Thea grabbed her hand and held it.

'Thanks Cora,' she murmured, 'I couldn't do it without—'

'Yeah, yeah, yeah,' Cora said. She squeezed Thea's hand and dropped it. Turning towards the velvet curtain, she said, 'So, what's he gonna charge us then, this Phil bloke? And how do we know he's gonna be any good, look after us and stuff?' She took her clothes off the peg and drew back the curtain. 'Come on, Thea, let's get dressed before Dolly comes back. If you really have made up your mind, then we've got things to discuss!' And struggling to clip up her bra, she called, 'Tell you what, it's a hell of a lot easier to take stuff off than put it on.' She swore under her breath and turned to her friend. 'Oi! Give us a hand with this, will you? Or I'll still be in my pants by the time the coffee arrives! Turkish . . .' she muttered. 'What's wrong with instant, eh? Turkish, I ask you!'

Chapter Eleven

As soon as things were finalised at Dolly's that afternoon, appointing Phil as booker and general guardian of the duo, he got to work with alacrity and Thea and Cora's act – Silk and Lace – took shape at great speed. Neither Thea nor Cora liked the name, they thought it rather naff, but Dolly explained that there was no room for the avant-garde at the outset, they needed to let people know straight off what they were selling and both girls had to agree that, though not chic, the name was certainly apt.

It was a week after the initial meeting at Dolly's and Thea sat with Phil in the reception area of a very expensive Mayfair hairdressers, looking through his list of bookings and waiting for Cora. Hardly a list, to be precise, just three, but it was a start, a good start, seeing as Phil had been to each club personally to check out the atmosphere, clientele and facilities. He had also made his face known to the club owners, barmen and bouncers. It was now clear that he was with Silk and Lace and as long as everyone knew that, the act hopefully wouldn't get the usual run of the mill trouble.

'So,' Phil said, interrupting Thea's reading, 'what d'you think?'

Thea glanced up. 'I think it's great, Phil, thanks. This note here though, I can't read your writing. What does it say?'

'Oh, that's clients, Thea darling. Look here, on the next page I've done a little key and explained the note. That club has mainly city types, young men in their twenties and thirties, lots of money but not always the same amount of style. Traders, mainly dealers, spot forex boys, that sort of thing. I've called them BOSSOMs.'

'Bossoms?' Thea giggled. 'What, like in breasts?'

'Yes, with an extra S. Big On Spending Small On Manners.'

'Phil, that's brilliant! Oh I see, and this one is SAM, Smart And Mean, FOBS, Foreign Big Spenders, PULPs . . .' Thea burst out laughing. 'Posh Upper-class Loaded Prats! Phil, this is really mean!'

'No, darling, not mean, just accurate. You'll come across a lot of Johnnies in these clubs, and I don't want my girls to start off even the slightest bit naïve.' He looked at her, suddenly serious. 'I mean it, Thea, don't be fooled, those men are there for a good time. They want you to entertain them and they'll pay for that privilege, but don't start thinking that there's any more to it than that because that's the slippery slope down to a rotten time and you, my love . . .' He took her hand and kissed it. '. . . you are far too lovely for that to happen to.' Dropping her hand, he stood. 'Now, that little key is for you to keep for your records so that we all know what I'm talking about when I grade a club. One for you and one for Cora. Where is the wonderful Cora, by the way? I should think that she's done by now. I'm going to find out, Thea darling, you stay there and wait for Dolly.'

'Dolly?'

'Yes, she's meeting us here, didn't she say?'

Thea shook her head.

'Oh well, never mind. We've plans to decamp to the Arts Café for lunch. I've got a surprise for you and Dolly and I think that with everything more or less in place now, it's time we all had a little celebration. Ah, Cora!' Phil spun round. 'I was just coming to find you, wasn't I, Thea darling?!'

Cora stood, wrapped in a black nylon cape, a little uneasily behind her stylist. She took a deep breath and stepped forward, touching the nape of her neck and the base of her hair as she did so.

'My God, Cora! You look fantastic!' Thea was completely spontaneous in her reaction. She jumped up and embraced her friend, then stood back and stared long and hard at the newly coloured, shaped and styled hair. 'You look like a different person, it's just wonderful!'

'Oi! What was wrong with the one before?'

'Nothing, I . . .' Thea saw that Cora was smiling. 'You know I didn't mean that, I just meant that it really suits you, it's, it's so . . .'

'Elegant!' Dolly announced. She had just come into the salon and crossed to Cora, kissing her cheek. 'It is very chic and very expensive-looking, Cora sweetie, it transforms you.' Dolly turned to the stylist. 'Michael, it is just wonderful! You are a very clever man! Thank you!'

'All part of the service, Dolly,' the stylist said. He touched Cora's head and tilted it gently forward. 'I've coloured right the way through the hair as you can see,' he said, 'two tones, both warm blonde, a ten and an eight, and I've cut

162

it into the base of her neck at the back, here' – he turned Cora to show her neck – 'to show its lovely long curve, while keeping it reasonably long and sleek at the front, see, here.' Straightening Cora's head, he turned her back to face everyone and ran his hand along the curve of her hair. '*Voilà!* I think it works marvellously!'

'So do we all!' Dolly said. 'Well done!'

Michael beamed and flushed, shooting a look at Phil on his way to the reception desk to prepare the bill.

'I think I'll have to book myself in for a restyle, Michael,' Phil said, never missing the slightest nuance. He crossed to the desk to pay and the two men fell into quiet, intimate conversation. Thea and Cora exchanged glances, wondering if one of them should offer to pay, but Dolly said, *sotto voce*, 'Philip and I agreed that from now on he would incur your expenses. He is confident that he can recoup his investment in a very short space of time, girls.' She moved towards Cora and helped her off with the cape. 'Did you have a jacket, Cora darling?'

'No, just me cardigan, here.'

'Good. Well, if Phil has finished I think we can make our way along for lunch.'

'Lunch?' Cora said.

'Don't worry, Cora sweetie, it's just a quick bite and a glass of something to celebrate! We know Thea has to be back for the baby but Phil's got the photos—'

'Dolly!' Phil cried, spinning round. 'You fiend! That was my surprise!'

'Oh dear, sorry, Philip darling. Anyway, he has got the photos, haven't you, Phil, and he's dying to show them to you.'

'Right.' Cora pulled a face at Thea and whispered, 'Come on, darling sweetie darling.'

Thea nudged her and held down a giggle.

'Girls!' Dolly said loudly, with a small sharp clap. *'On y va!'*

'On a what?'

'Let's go,' Thea said. 'It's French.' And opening the door, she held it for the small party to exit and followed them out into the street.

Hedda was home early for once. She'd had a headache all day, probably connected to the weather. There was a sort of thick oppressive cloud that hung low overhead, trapping the warm polluted air close to the ground, making everything feel heavy and dirty. She was tense, liable to irritable eruptions and had shouted at her assistant twice in the course of the afternoon before she decided to call it a day. As she came up the steps of the house, she saw Jake in the living room, the carpet littered with toys and baby paraphernalia, while he sat in an armchair with the paper ignoring it all as if it didn't exist. She ground her back teeth – a habit that was becoming increasingly regular – and braced herself as she put the key in the lock.

'Hello, Hedda!' Jake called from his armchair. 'You're home early.'

'Not particularly,' she snapped, pausing in the doorway of the living room on her way through to the kitchen. 'Normal time for most people, it's just that I work such goddamn long hours so regularly that you all seem to assume it's natural!' She trudged on without waiting for a reply and dumped her handbag and briefcase on the kitchen table, going immediately to the fridge for a glass of wine. Filling a tumbler, she drank a large mouthful and leant against the wall. Hedda didn't believe in pills, she never recommended them and she never took them herself. A decent glass of wine to relax her and a lie down in a cool dark room would do the trick and Hedda had always been lucky enough to be able to do both. Not for her the swallowing down of endless paracetamol to keep problems at bay while struggling with everyday life. It was easy to have strong principles if they were never challenged.

'D'you want an early supper seeing as you're home at this hour?' Jake asked, coming through to the kitchen.

'Not particularly,' Hedda replied coolly. 'I'd like a bit of peace and quiet first.' She knew she was carping but she couldn't help it; it was just her mood. But as she left Jake in the kitchen and went upstairs towards the sounds of Thea in the bathroom with Tom, she wondered if it was *just* her mood. Jake had changed over the past few months; he was not, Hedda thought, her soul mate any more. What Hedda failed to see was that Jake had never been her soul mate, not in the true sense of the word. He had agreed with her a great deal, had gone her way for an easy life, but that wasn't spiritual togetherness. And now he didn't do that any more; he couldn't, he had other people to take into account. Jake had found, albeit better late than never, that someone else needed him and that there was more to life than just Hedda.

'Hello,' Thea said, meeting Hedda on the stairs. 'Tom's about to go in the bath, I came out to get a towel.'

'I see.' Hedda stepped past her daughter and went towards her bedroom. She said nothing else and so Thea, unable to think of anything that might start a conversation, took a towel from the airing cupboard and went back to Tom. He was sitting up now and placing him on his bottom in the bath, Thea sat close to the edge of it in case he toppled backwards. She was gently splashing water over his body to delighted squeals when Hedda appeared in the doorway, glass in hand. She'd had a change of heart, felt bad about ignoring Thea and so came at least to make an attempt to join in a bit.

'He likes the bath then,' she said.

'Loves it.'

'He's quite steady sitting up. I remember you were too.'

Thea turned. 'Really?' This was the first reference that Hedda had ever made to herself as a baby. She smiled and reached forward to move the towel and night clothes off the chair. 'Here, why don't you come in and watch for a while?'

Hedda hesitated, but extraordinarily her headache had eased and so she did as Thea asked, sitting down and placing her glass on her lap. 'He's what, seven months now?'

Thea counted on her fingers. 'Yes, that's right.' She rubbed the soap between her fingers and tenderly lathered his body, the small, plump limbs slippery in her hands. 'I can't believe it, it's gone so quickly.'

'Has it?' Hedda was surprised. For her it seemed that Tom had been part of their lives for ever. 'He certainly seems to have grown, he's more than ready for a nursery.'

Thea looked up. She bit her lip but said nothing.

Hedda took a gulp of her drink. 'I notice that the

brochures have gone from the sitting room,' she said, the rush of alcohol on an empty stomach and on top of a fatigue headache making her rash. 'I'm glad that you took heed of my words, Thea, I'm glad that you've finally seen sense.' Another gulp of wine and the tumbler was empty; Hedda couldn't remember drinking it that quickly. 'What did you think, by the way? Have you made any choices yet?'

Thea, who had been focusing hard on Tom, wondered if she could ignore that last question, but out of the corner of her eye she could see Hedda watching her, waiting for an answer.

'Thea?' Hedda prompted.

'Yes, I, erm, I think I've come to a decision,' she murmured. She glanced at the floor, then said, 'Oh God, I've left Tom's nappy cream in my bedroom.' It wasn't an answer but it might divert attention long enough to evade the subject. 'You couldn't take over here for me, could you, while I get it?'

Hedda stood. 'No,' she said, 'I'll get it. You carry on.' She made for the door. 'Whereabouts in your room?'

'On the chest of drawers I think, or if it's not there I might have put it back in Tom's room.'

'Right.' Hedda left and Thea breathed a sigh of relief.

In Thea's room, Hedda made straight for the chest of drawers and found the cream on the top of it. She should have simply walked out then, mission accomplished, nothing further to add, only she didn't. She turned, saw a brown A4 envelope addressed to Thea on her bedside table and without thinking, picked it up. It was obviously from one of the universities, very official looking, but it didn't have a stamp, and curiosity got the better of her. Hedda slipped her finger under the flap and pulled out the contents. She looked down at them and a black and white photograph of Thea and Cora, both in costume, both seductively posed, one breast of Cora's only just covered by her hand, stared back at her. She felt the breath constrict in her throat, the anger and revulsion of years of feminism rise up in her chest and, turning on her heel, she stormed out of the room and into the bathroom, the photos still in her hand.

'What the hell is going on?' she hissed, thrusting them under Thea's nose. 'What in God's name are these?'

Thea sprang up. 'Oh God . . .' she stammered. 'I, erm, I . . .' She couldn't think straight, the water was draining out of the bath, Tom's face puckered miserably as it did so and the photos swam before her eyes. 'Oh God, Hedda, I didn't want you to find out like this. I . . .' Tom began to cry. 'It's all right, Tom darling, I . . .'

'It is not all right, Tom darling!' Hedda snarled. 'It is far from bloody all right!' Hedda went out on to the landing and yelled down the stairs. 'Jake! Jake, get up here now!' Her voice had that hysterical note which set Thea's teeth on edge. Tom's cries got louder; Thea bent to scoop him up into a towel just as Jake hurried into the bathroom. The three of them stood there, with Tom between them, in five square yards of space, the air electric with fury.

'Have you seen these?' Hedda cried. 'Did you know about all this?' She jabbed the photos towards Jake, who took them and stared down at the image of his daughter. He rifled through the pictures, looking at the stamp on the back: 'Silk and Lace, Traditional Strip-tease. Agent

Phil Habben', with his address, phone number and fax underneath. Then he looked up at Thea.

'Is this what I think it is?'

'Well of course it's what you bloody well think it is!' Hedda cried. 'Don't be facile, Jake! Thea has deliberately betrayed us, she has gone behind our backs and got herself involved, yet again, in something ruinous and utterly, utterly stupid!' Hedda put her hand on the back of her neck; her headache had started up again with a vengeance. 'I just can't believe it,' she went on hysterically. 'After all that we've done for her, after everything we've given—'

'Hedda,' Jake said calmly, 'please. Let's just cool it for a few moments, shall we?' He turned to Thea. 'Thea, get Tom in his pyjamas and into bed and we will wait for you downstairs in the living room. We deserve an explanation, Thea.' He handed her the pictures. 'I hope it's a good one.'

Thea lay Tom in his cot, gave him his rabbit and bent to kiss the top of his head. He held Rabbit in a vice-like grip against his cheek and stuck the thumb on his other hand in his mouth. Thea whispered goodnight and crept out of the room, closing the door behind her. She stood leaning against it for several minutes, listening out for Tom and attempting to compose herself, ready for her explanation. But the truth was she didn't have one. Whatever she said, she felt, would hurt, would be misunderstood, would sound feeble and selfish to Hedda, if not Jake. She was doing this for Tom, because it made good sense, commericially and domestically, but was that the only reason? She wondered momentarily – and it was only the briefest moment – whether the reason might be that while she stripped, Hedda would never rest. Thea would always be in her mind, and for a child who had struggled to be noticed, wasn't that the ultimate coup?

Downstairs, Hedda and Jake sat in silence waiting for Thea. Hedda smoked and drank, her stress-related headache raging, fuelled by too much wine and emotion on an empty stomach. Jake did nothing; he just sat. They heard Thea come down, get herself a glass of water in the kitchen and come through to the living room. By the time she appeared Hedda was standing by the fireplace; she felt it gave her more authority.

Thea stood her glass on the coffee table and sat neatly and squarely on the edge of an armchair, folding her hands in her lap. 'Cora and I,' she began, 'have decided to go into business together.'

'Business!' Hedda snorted. 'Is that what you call it?'

Jake placed a hand on her arm. 'Why don't we let Thea finish?' he said quietly. 'Then we can try and talk it through.' Hedda said nothing, she coldly removed her arm from his reach.

'We have been training to perform traditional strip-tease,' Thea went on, 'and we've put together an act, with costumes; had a set of photographs done, the ones that you've seen; and we've hired a booker: Phil Habben. We've got our first booking at the end of the week at a club in the West End.' Thea reached for her water and swallowed down a mouthful. Her throat was bone dry. 'This isn't some tin-pot idea, we've gone into it all very professionally, with the backing and guidance of someone who was at the top end of the market for many years.' Dolly had told her to say that, if she had to explain to her parents. 'And it's all above board and legal. Once we're up and running we plan to hire an accountant.' She reached for the water again and felt an icy silence in the room. Staring straight ahead, she said, 'I know that it's not exactly the sort of career you'd had planned for me . . .' At this point Hedda let out a short sharp cry. '. . . but it is very lucrative, it means that I can work at night and still look after Tom during the day and that, well, it's my own thing . . .' Her voice petered out and she dropped her head down, unable to look at either Jake or Hedda. 'It's what I want to do,' she murmured, having completely lost her nerve. 'I'm sorry that it upsets you so much.'

'You're sorry?' Hedda said. 'That it upsets us so much?' Her voice was hoarse with the effort of holding down so much anger. She shook her head in disbelief. 'Not sorry that it's a seedy, demeaning, horrible thing to do, that it's the lowest of the low, that you've let us down, thrown your life's opportunity away . . . No, no, you're not sorry for any of those things, just that you've upset us.' Hedda reached for her wine and gulped down a mouthful. 'That's very considerate of you, Thea, to be so concerned about our feelings.'

'Hedda,' Jake warned. 'Come on, this is supposed to be a discussion.'

'A discussion, is it? What is there to discuss?' Her voice rose as the tight rein on her emotion slipped. 'Thea has made up her mind, she's set the whole thing up and from where I'm standing there's bugger all we can do about it!' Hedda turned to Thea. 'I'm right, aren't I? You have no intention of giving this up because we disapprove, do you?'

Thea was paralysed by the intensity of Hedda's fury.

'Do you?' Hedda suddenly shouted. 'Answer me!'

'N-no,' Thea stammered, 'I . . .' She couldn't finish, she had started to cry. All the new-found confidence, all the self-esteem and steely nerve deserted her.

'Good God!' Hedda cried. 'How the bloody hell you think you're going to get up on stage and take your clothes off to an offensive rabble of drunken, braying men when you can't even argue your case to your own parents I have no idea!' Hedda strode over to the coffee table and snatched up her cigarettes. She lit one, then stood by the window, silently smoking and looking out into the street.

Jake said, 'Why did you do this, Thea? If you wanted to earn money why couldn't you have come to us and asked our advice? We'd have helped you, we'd have done anything to make sure that you made the right decisions. Please, just explain to me why?'

Thea dug in her pockets for a tissue and blew her nose. She drank some more water. 'I'm sorry that I didn't ask you, but if I had, what would you have said? Hedda wants Tom in a nursery full time and I don't. Hedda wants me to go back to college and I don't. What sort of job could I get where I can look after Tom myself and, providing things go as we plan, where I can earn more than enough money to keep us both? Maybe even buy my own place one day?'

'Is that what you've been told? That there's a lot of money involved?'

'It's not what I've been told, it's what I know! Phil has agreed a fee of two hundred pounds a go for the first three bookings and that's only the beginning. If we're good enough and the word gets round, then that'll go up to three hundred then four hundred and finally maybe even a thousand a week.'

'Is that what you think?'

'It's not what I think, Dad, it's what I *know*! Why do you keep asking me if it's what I think, like I don't know the half of it?'

'Because, Thea, I'm seriously concerned that you don't! The people in that business, in the sex industry, they prey on young girls like you and Cora, on innocent young girls thinking that they can make a lot of money for nothing. They get them involved in drugs and God knows what else and before you know it it's just another word for prostitution.'

'Oh Jake, I know that side of it, we're both only too aware that that goes on, but if we do it right, if we're careful, then—'

'And what's doing it right?' Hedda asked, turning round. 'What makes you two so special?'

'We don't know,' Thea said quietly, 'until we try.'

Hedda shook her head. 'See,' she said to Jake, 'you can't get through to her! She thinks she knows best, she thinks—'

'I think that we've got a good product, that's what I think. We've worked hard, trained hard to get it right and I think that it could be a success. We've got Phil with us, he checks out the clubs first, makes sure that it's all above board, he drives us there, stays out front to keep an eye on us, he's got to know the bouncers at the clubs we're working in the next week so that we've got people on our side . . .' Thea stopped, short of breath. 'We've done everything we can to make a success of this and if it doesn't work then fine, but we've got to give it a go! Please, you must understand that!'

'Why?' Hedda demanded. 'Why must we understand that? Why do I have to understand you going against all my principles, against everything I believe in: rights for women, establishing them as real people with brains and opinions, not just objects for sex and slavery, burdened by motherhood, by male dominance. Why should I understand you doing something that undermines all that? Tell me, Thea, why?'

Thea swallowed hard. 'Because . . .' she glanced up at Hedda glaring down at her and her voice trailed off. There was a long silence, with Thea staring down at her hands and Hedda continuing to glare at her. Then, somehow finding the courage from deep inside her, Thea said, in barely a whisper, 'Because sometimes we have to swallow our principles in order to get on with life.'

'Swallow our principles!' Hedda cried. 'I can't believe I'm hearing this! What are you saying, Thea? That I should give up trying to live a politically correct life in order to keep you happy?' Hedda came back into the centre of the room and aggressively ground her cigarette out in a big green glass ashtray.

'No, I . . .'

'Then what are you saying? Come on, out with it! Do I detect a veiled criticism in that sentence? Do I?'

'She is saying,' Jake suddenly shouted, 'that it is about time you stepped off that fucking high horse of yours, Hedda, and got a grip on real life! That is what she is saying!'

There was a momentary stunned silence, then Jake stood up and rubbed his hands wearily over his face. 'Sometimes our principles can be so far removed from ordinary life that we lose touch, we lose sight of the real goals,' he said. 'I don't approve of what Thea is going to do, boy oh boy do I disapprove, mainly because it scares the shit out of me, but I can see where she's coming from and I can respect that she's got guts enough to get out there and go for it!'

Hedda looked at him. 'Are you saying that you condone this whole affair? Are you finally going to make a stand against me, Jake?'

Jake faced her. 'Yes,' he said, 'that is pretty much, more or less, what I'm saying.'

Thea held her breath. She could see Hedda's jaw lock tight and the sinews on her neck stand out as it did so. She watched her mother light up another cigarette, her hand shaking, and inhale a deep lungful of smoke, holding it down, then letting it out slowly and deliberately. There was a minute-long, awful silence. Hedda and Jake looked away from each other and the room was suffused with a sudden, intense, raw emotion.

'Then you give me no choice,' Hedda said at last. 'I would like both of you to leave the house, now, tonight.'

Jake jerked round. 'Leave? What on earth do you mean, leave?'

'Exactly that,' Hedda said coldly. 'Go, the pair of you, pack your things and get out of my house.'

'Your house?'

'Yes,' Hedda said. 'I think you will find that it's my name on the mortgage documents, my name on the deeds.' She wrapped her arms around her, suddenly feeling very cold.

'I am well within my rights,' she said, 'and I want you to leave. Get out!'

'Hedda, have you gone mad?' Jake was incredulous. 'You can't chuck a single mother and her baby out on the streets at night and expect her to fend for herself! Good God, Hedda! What the hell has happened to you?' He stepped forward towards her and she jumped back.

'I told you to go!' she cried. 'And if you come so much as one inch closer I shall call the police and say that you've threatened violence!'

Jake glanced fleetingly at Thea; there was pain and disbelief in his eyes. 'Hedda, don't do this,' he said quietly. 'I'll go, but don't do this to Thea, please.'

Hedda turned away. She walked across to the window and stood with her back to them both. 'I want you out by ten,' she said, without turning round. 'I am what I believe and if that means so little to either of you then I no longer want you in my house or in my life.'

Thea had stood and Jake took her hand.

'Hedda, please,' he tried, one last time. There was no reply. He swallowed down a terrible overwhelming grief and, without another word, led Thea from the room and upstairs to pack.

Jake and Thea sat in his car outside Gilbert House on Hubbert Road, Tom asleep in the back in his car seat. They had just collected the key from Cora at work.

'You OK?' Jake said.

Thea nodded.

'Are you sure you don't want me to come in with you, help you up the stairs with Tom?'

'No, thanks, I can manage.' Thea glanced behind at her sleeping baby. 'You will be all right, won't you, Dad?'

Jake shrugged. 'Of course.' He unclipped his seatbelt. 'Now look, you're not to worry about me, I'll be fine. I'm a grown-up, remember?'

Thea smiled.

'Anyway, she'll get over it, we've been through worse.' That was a lie and Thea knew it. 'You'll be home by the end of the week.'

Thea shook her head. 'No, I don't think so.' Jake winced. 'If you're there in the morning, I'll come back and get the rest of our things,' she said. She reached forward for her handbag by her feet. 'Jake?'

Jake turned to her and was, for an instant, so strongly reminded of Hedda as a girl that his heart felt as if it would burst.

'Thanks,' Thea said, 'for all that stuff about principles, for sticking up for me.'

He leant over and planted a kiss on her cheek. 'You don't have to thank me.'

'Yes I do,' she said. 'For a lot more than just tonight.' And opening the car door, she climbed out, then reached into the back for Tom. Within minutes she was gone, through the door and up the stairs to a whole new and different life, a life that Jake really didn't understand, but one that he had to respect, if he wanted a place in it.

Thea was just getting Tom off to sleep again when Cora came in. It was after eleven, but she should have had another three hours to run on her shift.

'Cora? What—'

'I told them I was ill, got off early. You all right?!'

Thea nodded, but put her finger to her lips. Cora came across to the bed, looked down at Tom and smiled.

'You look cold and shivery,' Cora whispered. 'Go on, get into bed and warm up a bit.'

Thea did as she was told. 'It's just being upset,' she said, pulling the covers up to her chin. 'I can't seem to get warm.'

'Nah, course not.' Cora unzipped her jacket and hung it on the chair. 'Blimey, you're shiverin'!'

'I . . . know . . .' Thea murmured, her teeth clenched together.

Cora said nothing more. Pulling off her top and skirt, she unhooked her bra and reached for her pyjama top. 'Go on,' she said quietly, 'budge up.'

Thea shuffled closer to Tom. It was only a single bed and they had agreed to sleep top to bottom, but Cora slipped in beside her friend and turned towards her, embracing her. 'You need a cuddle,' Cora whispered. Thea nodded, and as Cora's body began to warm her, the shivering eased. She closed her eyes, silent tears squeezing out from tightly shut lids as Cora murmured, 'Hush now, it's all right. We're mates, aren't we? I'll look after you.' Warm in each other's arms, the two girls eventually fell asleep.

Chapter Twelve

Jake had his head in the cupboard under Marian's sink, a toolbox by his feet, a screwdriver in his hand. He was fixing the door.

'Coffee?'

He ducked out and knelt back. 'Thanks.' Taking the mug offered, he said, 'Hmmm, this smells delicious! I thought you didn't drink coffee.'

'I don't, but I know you do, so I popped out to the deli to get you some.'

'Thanks, Marian, that was kind.'

Marian shrugged. 'It's kind of you to fix my cupboard.'

'It's the least I can do, I mean for putting me up at such short notice last night.' Jake had phoned her after he'd left Thea. The truth was that when it came down to it, he couldn't think of anyone else to ring.

Marian sipped her herbal tea and said nothing. She'd been surprised by the phone call – no, more than that: she'd been shocked, but Jake was as much her friend as Hedda, probably more so over the past few years. There was something so righteous about Hedda, something unbending, although Marian would never say so.

Jake put down his screwdriver and drank his coffee. Here he was, his life in chaos, in Marian's bathroom, fixing the cupboard door. It was bizarre. 'There's a lot that needs doing in this flat,' he said. 'I've had a look round, you don't mind, do you?'

'Of course not, why should I mind?'

Jake shrugged. It would have driven Hedda crazy, the thought of all this DIY. 'Hedda would say that my constant fixing of things is an excuse to try and cover the gaping holes in my life.'

'Hedda would say a lot of things that I wouldn't.' Marian smiled. 'I'm just glad to have things mended.'

'Well, I kind of thought that I could do it in return for putting me up. I mean on top of my share of expenses etc.'

'Don't be ridiculous, Jake! I'm not taking expenses off you, you can stay as long as it takes to—' Marian stopped. She'd been about to say: as long as it takes to patch things up with Hedda, but perhaps there wasn't any patching to do. 'As long as it takes to get yourself sorted,' she finished.

'No, Marian, I couldn't possibly not pay my way, not share things equally.'

Marian smiled again, only Jake couldn't see what was so amusing. 'Jake, you and I will never be equal!' she said. 'You're a man, I'm a woman; you are married, I am single; you have a child and a grandchild, I do not; I have a small private income and a good job in local government and, well, I suppose that it'll take time for you to sort finances out with Hedda and that you're probably a bit chaotic at the moment, cash-wise. So' – she took his empty coffee cup – 'let's forget all that crap, shall we? And just get on with it, you as my guest and me enjoying a bit of male company for as long as it lasts. OK?'

Jake looked at her. 'Marian,' he said, 'I had no idea that you could be so forceful.'

Marian arched an eyebrow. 'Jake,' she replied, 'I'm afraid that I think you simply had no idea.' Leaving him to it, she went off to start preparing breakfast.

Thea and Cora had been rearranging the bedsit for a couple of hours when the downstairs buzzer went. They were clearing a space in the corner for Tom's cot, having decided that the best arrangement was for Thea to move in for a while, until they made enough money to get properly sorted. But once they had cleared that space, they found that they didn't like the way the furniture was grouped, so they moved the whole lot around, only to find dirty torn patches on the wallpaper and stains on the carpet they never knew were there. The bedsit needed a thorough clean and there was an abundance of clutter strewn across the floor.

'Who the hell's that?' Cora snapped. Her head was down the back of the bed where she was trying to clean the skirting. 'That's all we need, visitors!'

Thea went to the intercom and pressed *speak*. She heard Jake's voice and released the door downstairs.

'My God! Your dad!' Cora wailed. 'What's he gonna think of this mess!'

Thea came back to pick Tom up before she opened the door. 'He won't mind at all,' she said. 'He's not like that. Besides' – she stepped out on to the stairs to wait for Jake – 'he's got enough to worry about, without thinking about this as well.'

Cora straightened up and whipped the scarf off her head. She heard the greetings outside and wiped her running nose on her sleeve just as Jake came in, followed by a woman Cora had never seen before, then Thea and Tom.

'Hello, Cora,' Jake said. 'This is my friend Marian, I'm staying with her for a while.'

'Hi, I mean, erm, pleased to meet you.' Cora stepped forward, offered her hand, felt acutely embarrassed and was relieved when Marian shook it firmly and smiled.

'We've brought Tom's things,' Jake said. 'His cot and stuff. Marian's got a hatchback, we just got it in.' Jake glanced around. 'Crikey, this place could do with a lick of paint.'

'Yeah, and the rest,' Cora said.

Jake smiled. 'I'll do it for you if you like, tomorrow. I'll slap some white emulsion on . . .' He looked down at the stained grubby carpet. 'And get you a rug for the floor.'

'No? You're kidding!' Cora was astounded.

'No, I'm not kidding.' He smiled again and turned to Thea. 'I take it you plan to stay here for a while?'

'Yes. We've been trying to find a space to fit in another bed.'

'Why don't you get one of those fold-up futon beds?' Marian said. 'Jake's sleeping on mine at the moment. They're not exactly slumber heaven but it would do I suppose and it folds into a chair.'

'Yes, good idea.' Thea looked at Marian. Out of Hedda's shadow, she seemed different somehow. 'When we get some money.' She turned to Jake. 'Shall we get Tom's things? He's been pretty grouchy, I think he's a bit disorientated.'

'Here,' said Marian. 'Give him to me and you can go down to the car with Jake.'

'He's a bit funny with strangers,' Thea answered. 'I don't know if he'll . . .' But Marian held her arms out and smiled and Tom reached for her. Surprised, Thea passed him across. 'Right, well, we'll be back in a few minutes,' she said.

Cora dumped her cloth on the bed. 'D'you want a cup of tea, Marian?'

Marian nodded. 'Love one. You wouldn't have any herb tea, would you?'

Cora looked blank. 'Herb tea?'

'Oh, never mind,' Marian said, 'I'll drink whatever you've got.'

Smiling at this sudden change of heart, Thea went down with Jake to the car.

'Are you all right, Dad?' she asked as they went out into the street.

Jake turned. 'Yes, I think so. Marian's going to put me up for a while, bed and board in exchange for fixing up her flat. Sounds a reasonable offer to me, so . . .' He shrugged. 'You'll need to come and get your things from the house, I got Tom's but didn't know where to start on yours.'

'I'll do it in the next few days. Is that OK?'

'Of course.' Jake dug in his pocket for the piece of paper he'd brought with him. 'Look, here's Marian's number, you can phone me there any time, Marian won't mind. We'll go over together.' He smiled wryly. 'Before Hedda changes the locks.'

'She won't do that.'

'Won't she?' Jake felt bitter, far more bitter than he had expected to feel. 'Have you heard from her? Hedda, I mean?'

'Yes, she rang last night.'

'And?'

'And I don't know really. She said she didn't retract any of the things she'd said, but at least she rang. She wanted to know that Tom and I were safe.'

'How considerate!' Jake's sarcasm made Thea wince. She'd never seen him like this before, ever. Then Jake said, 'Oh well, it's over now, what should I care?' He unlocked the car and went round the back to open up the boot. 'Here, come on, you take one end of this cot and I'll take the other.'

'What's that? In the cot?'

'It's a portable telly. Marian's. She's going to lend it to you.'

'To us? Why?'

'Well, not to you exactly, to me to be precise. I'll need something to watch when I babysit the nights that you're working.'

Thea stopped.

'Hey, don't stop, this is heavy!'

'Jake.' Thea put her end of the cot down on the ground. 'You don't have to, you . . .'

Jake put his end of the cot down too and came round it, taking Thea in his arms. 'Thea, I don't approve of what you're doing,' he said gently. 'I can't pretend I like it . . .' He broke off and looked down at her. 'It worries the hell out of me, to be honest, but the only thing I can think of to stop that worry is to make sure that I'm around, looking after Tom, and you, and keeping my eye on you both.' He smiled. 'That's very old-fashioned, isn't it? Hedda would never approve.' His smile broke into a broad grin. 'Bugger Hedda,' he said. For the first time since last night, they both laughed.

Chapter Thirteen

What with Jake painting the bedsit, Marian bringing over all sorts of odds and ends to make life more comfortable there, rehearsals, final arrangements, Phil constantly chasing them with things to do, and last-minute alterations to her costume because Thea had lost so much weight with nerves, the day of their first booking arrived, it seemed, before they had even had time to think about it. Thea woke on the morning they were due to perform, climbed out of bed, taking care not to wake Cora at the other end of it and went to the bathroom. There she was promptly sick.

She staggered back to bed, where Cora, who was now awake, said, 'Oh Christ! You're not ill, are you?'

'I don't think so.' Thea lay on her side, with her head hanging over the edge of the bed. 'Just nerves, I think.'

Cora climbed out, went to the sink and ran some warm water, soaking a flannel. She brought it back to Thea. 'Here, wipe your face. D'you want a cup of tea?'

Thea shook her head.

'I think you'd better have one, and a biscuit.' She pulled her cardigan over her pyjama top and crossed the room to fill the kettle. Tom was still asleep, so she did everything silently and stealthily. The tea made, she came back to the bed and sat on the edge of it. 'Here, drink this. I don't know why but they say that tea's good for the nerves.'

Thea sat up, glanced across at Tom in his cot and took the tea. She sipped. Her stomach turned but after the third swallow she did start to feel marginally better. 'Sorry,' she said. 'I don't know what's come over me.'

Cora tucked her legs up under her and hugged her knees. 'Stage fright,' she quipped. Thea didn't smile. 'No! Come on!' Cora said, 'You're not really scared about tonight, are ya? You're the one who started all this in the first place!'

Thea drank her tea, her head down, not looking at Cora, not answering her. She felt the same churning in the pit of her stomach that she'd had for days, her mouth tasted horrible, muggy and sour, and the thought of taking her clothes off brought a sweat up on the back of her neck.

'Thea?' Cora stared at her. 'Talk to me! You're having me on, aren't you?' There was a silence, a snuffle from the cot and Cora said, 'Shit!' She stood up and went across to make herself a cup of coffee. 'Shit,' she murmured. 'Shit, shit, shit.' She poured boiling water on coffee grains, added a heap of sugar and leant back against the sink, sipping. Then she came back to the bed and, standing over Thea, asked, 'You gonna back out?'

Thea gripped the cup. 'I don't know,' she said.

Cora took a towel off the radiator and her wash bag off the side. 'You got any change?'

'Yes, in my purse, help yourself.'

'Right.' Cora did so, gathered up a bundle of clothes and headed for the door.

'Cora?' Thea called. 'Where are you going?'

'To have a bath and then call Dolly,' Cora replied, pulling open the door. 'Maybe she can talk some sense into you.'

Dolly didn't do what Cora had expected. On the phone she told Cora to ignore everything and just focus in on herself and her part of the act. At the final dress rehearsal in the club that afternoon, she said absolutely nothing to Thea despite her poor performance and the obvious fact that it had scared the wits out of her. In the dressing room that night, half an hour before they were due to go on, as Thea sat alone in the corner, made up and in costume but insistent that she just couldn't do it, Dolly still didn't react. Cora paced up and down in the corridor with Phil, angry, disappointed, so wound up that she wanted to punch the wall, but Dolly sat with Thea and stayed silent.

Ten minutes before they were due to go on, Dolly said, 'There isn't any time left now, Thea. I'm afraid that you've got to go out and tell Cora that you're not going to do it.'

Thea looked up.

'It's not fair to leave it any longer, she's upset and anxious. You must be honest with her. If you're going to let her down, tell her now, so that Phil can go out front and warn the management and Cora can get dressed.'

Thea went to stand. 'I just can't do it, Dolly,' she said quietly. 'I'm sorry, I thought I could, I . . .'

'Cora thought she couldn't either.' Dolly smiled. 'In fact as far as I can remember you were the one who talked her into it! It's disgusting, she said. It's just doing what we do every night, getting undressed, you said, only it's in front of a few onlookers and for money.' Dolly shook her head. 'I can hear you now. It was rather logical, I thought.'

'I didn't know,' Thea said, 'how hard it would be.'

'No, of course not. It's been harder for Cora though, I think. She's done it for friendship, because she respects and admires you, and she thinks: Well, if Thea can do it, then so can I.'

Thea looked at Dolly.

'Cora's a good friend, Thea,' Dolly said. 'And I know because I've seen a few mates come and go in my life.' Dolly stood too. 'Still, there you are. Some things work out and some don't.'

There was a sharp knock on the door and a voice shouted, 'Five minutes to go, miss.' Both women turned and as they did so they were confronted by Thea's reflection in the mirror. Yet again it astounded Dolly in its sensuality. They stood for a few moments and stared; Dolly smiled, shrugged helplessly and looked away.

Suddenly Thea said, 'Where's my hat, Dolly? I can't go on without my hat!'

Looking back at her, Dolly touched her arm with affection and finally opened the door. 'Cora!' she called out into the corridor. 'Cora, come and get your lipstick on, darling, it's nearly time to go on stage!'

Cora and Thea stood behind the curtain, heard their name announced and, exchanging glances, counted the first three bars of the music together.

'Break a leg,' Thea whispered.

'I bloody well hope not!' Cora replied.

The base beat strummed its rhythm, the sax started up and to the count of four, Thea put a long, stockinged thigh out of the curtain. There was a thin obligatory round of clapping; her hand went out, then her arm, and on the count of eight, she stepped out into the glare of the lights. Four beats later, Cora was behind her and they stood back to back, the same height, one dark and voluptuous, one blonde and sleek. They turned their heads, looked at the audience and dropped the straps on their camisoles. Another clap broke out, this time spontaneously, and at that moment, the girls knew they had got it right.

'Blimey!' Cora gasped as the curtain went down and her chest rose and fell rapidly with the struggle to breathe evenly. 'That was . . .' Moments later, Thea fell towards her and they hugged, breaking out into breathless giggles. With their arms round each other, they headed for the corridor and their dressing room, the applause and wolf whistles ringing in their ears.

'Oh God . . .' Thea panted, 'that was unbelievable! I didn't think I could do it, I really didn't! They loved it! They really loved it!'

Cora elbowed her hard. 'Of course they bloody well loved it, stupid! We were brilliant!'

They were at the door of the dressing room and before they could get to the handle, Dolly flung it open and embraced them both. 'Spectacular!' she cried. 'Absolutely spectacular! Here, come on in, darlings, or you'll catch your death of cold! Here, put these on, Phil ordered them for you!' She handed them both a long white towelling robe. 'A surprise! Aren't they divine! Go on, get something warm on your bodies before you perish!'

Thea and Cora wrapped themselves up.

'Was it really OK?' Thea asked. She reached for a bottle

of mineral water and gulped some down, swigging straight from the bottle. She handed it to Cora.

'It was more than OK, it was fantastic!'

Phil knocked and came straight in, carrying Thea's hat. She had taken it off and left it at the front of the stage for anyone who might want to tip. It was stuffed with notes.

'Shit!' Cora murmured.

'No,' Phil said, 'cash, hard cash!'

They all laughed. 'Go on then,' he urged. 'Ask me how much!'

Thea leant forward and peered into the hat. 'I don't know, a hundred?'

'Two seventy-five.'

'Two hundred and seventy-five quid?' Cora was dumb-founded. 'You have got to be having me on!'

'No, not in the slightest, Cora my love. This is a mid-to top-range club, there are seventy rather drunk city gents out there and nearly half of them tipped.' He laughed, ran his fingers through the notes and dropped the hat on the side. 'You were perfect,' he said. 'Very, very classy.' He sat down. 'And the management want to book you for next week.'

'Next week? That's brilliant!'

'I told them no,' he said. 'I told them three weeks from now and if they advertise they'll get this place packed to capacity. They agreed, so the next date here is October.' He took a slim leather diary from the inside pocket of his jacket. 'We'll fill the remaining spaces easily. After tonight, I'd say there's no doubt—' He was interrupted by a knock on the door. Standing, he went across, opened it, paused, then said, 'Cora, there's a bottle of champagne here for you.'

'What, me?' Cora jumped up and hurried to the door. She took the card with the bottle and held it, staring hard at the writing. Slowly, she read out: '*To Silk . . . please . . . join . . . us . . . for . . . a . . . drink.*' Turning to Thea, she held the card out. 'That's right, isn't it?'

Thea read. 'Yes, that's right.'

Cora put the card back with the bottle. 'Tell the gentleman, thanks, but another time maybe.' She closed the door, turned and looked at everyone. 'What you all staring at?' she demanded. 'I'm not taking no drinks off punters, ta very much! Don't know where it'll end, do I?'

Thea smiled as Cora came back to her seat, but nodded as Cora said seriously, 'You gotta have rules, Thea!'

'Quite right,' Dolly added. 'Well said, Cora!' She was gathering up her things: handbag, jacket, the vanity case she'd brought with all her ageing stage make-up in. 'Philip,' she said, 'we must go out front and be seen while the girls get changed.'

Phil, who had started bundling the cash and was counting, held up his hand to indicate that he was almost finished. He put a rubber band around the last pile of tenners and slipped the money into an envelope. 'Right. As agreed,' he said, 'I'll hang on to this until the morning, then you split half of it, after my fifteen per cent, and we bank the rest along with the cheque. OK?' Both girls nodded. 'I'm ready when you are, Dolly.' Phil held out his arm and Dolly took it. 'We'll be back for you in twenty minutes. Lock the door after us and don't let anyone in, OK?'

Both girls nodded again and he blew them a kiss. 'TTFN, darlings!'

'Bye!' they called, and as soon as he and Dolly had gone,

Cora stood up to lock the door. 'Blimey, he's a queer one, isn't he?' she said.

Suddenly Thea burst out laughing.

'What's so . . .' The penny dropped and Cora dissolved. Thea was helpless with giggles and Cora fell against the door, almost hysterical. For a good five minutes they were paralysed with laughter. Every time they were almost over it, they looked at each other and fell about again. With tears streaming down her face, Cora slid down the door and collapsed on to the floor, weak with hysterics. Finally, having laughed themselves out, Cora got to her feet and came back to where Thea sat. She slumped into a chair. 'Bloody hell,' she said, blowing her nose, 'it wasn't even that funny!'

Thea wiped her face with a tissue, the giggles only just beneath the surface.

'Seriously, though,' Cora said, looking at Thea in the mirror. 'He and Dolly are pretty close. It's a bit of a—' She stopped and giggled, 'I nearly said queer again!' Thea snorted with laughter but brought herself under control pretty quickly. 'It's a bit odd, ain't it? I mean, have they known each other a long time?'

Thea's face ached from laughing. She rubbed her hands over her cheeks and massaged the muscles. 'I think,' she said, 'only Dolly hasn't told me all the details exactly, but I think that Phil's partner owned the flat above Dolly and left it to Phil when he died.'

'What, Phil's bloke died?'

'Yes, Dolly's never said what of. But apparently she helped Phil to get over it, supported him a lot, that's what he told me anyway. They've been good friends ever since.'

'So she got him involved with us?'

'Yes, she thought it was ideal, for him and us.' They had been talking to each other in the mirror and now Thea turned to Cora. 'He's been pretty good so far, hasn't he?'

'Yeah, I think so.'

They turned back to the mirror and Thea picked up the tub of make-up remover to start on her face. She looked at Cora. 'This has been pretty good so far, hasn't it?'

Cora nodded, then she smiled. 'With you it has.'

'Yes,' Thea said. 'Together.' She scooped a dollop of cream out of the tub and smeared it on to her face. 'Together,' she said, 'we can do anything.'

She handed the jar to Cora, who also took a handful, placing a large blob on her nose and both cheeks. She looked at Thea. 'Not like this we can't!' she said. And unable to stop themselves, they both dissolved into helpless laughter all over again.

Part Two

Chapter Fourteen

Thea stood outside in the warm early May morning, in nightshirt and wellies, watering her garden. The windows of the cottage were open, as were the French doors that led to the kitchen. 'Tom!' she called over her shoulder, in the direction of the house. 'Tom, I hope you're getting dressed!' There was a silence. 'Tom?' Thea called again.

'YES!' came the reply, in exaggerated tones of exasperation. 'I AM!'

Thea smiled to herself, dropped the hose on the ground and turned off the tap. Kicking her wellies off, she went inside, lay a place for breakfast and put the kettle on the Aga to boil.

She sat down at the table and looked around the kitchen of her cottage. She had been here nearly three years now, and still she wondered at her luck. It was bright primrose yellow, completely unfitted, just old pine shelves, two dresser bottoms, a butler's sink (original), Aga and a huge old scrubbed oak table. There was a clutter of mess: Tom's paintings, her post, catalogues, magazines, newspapers; there was a drying rack with herbs on; the pans, French cast-iron, hung from the walls on big brass hooks and a cast-iron rail held all her cooking tools. This kitchen was the heart of the cottage, the cottage she had always wanted: a small 1840s brick-and-flint farmhouse, with three bedrooms, three living rooms and a pitch-tile roof. A home, for her and Tom, bought at a rock-bottom price and fitted immediately with gas central heating.

'Can you do my collar, Mum?'

Tom stood in the doorway of the kitchen with his grey wool sweater askew. Thea stood, tucked his shirt into his shorts, pulled the collar of his shirt out over the top of his jumper and kissed the top of his head. 'Right, Rice Krispies or Shreddies?'

'Toast.'

'No, it's Krispies or Shreddies. We haven't got time for toast.'

'OK. Krispies. Can I have sugar on them?'

'No, it rots your teeth.' Thea poured the cereal from the packet, added milk and took the bowl across to the table. 'Here, sit down please.' Tom had found a Power Ranger on his chair and was dive bombing the cat. 'Tom! Sit, please! Breakfast's ready!' The cat snarled, Tom made whooping noises and Thea snapped: 'Tom! Sit down!'

He did as he was asked, muttering, 'Soorrry!' Thea smiled because he really was very comical and because, quite simply, she was happy, then went upstairs to dress.

Thea's life had turned out all right. And so, albeit differently, had Cora's. The girls were still close friends, they still worked together three nights a week and two days. The nature of the work had altered: they had expanded their business into a franchise of kinds, training girls in traditional strip-tease routines that they choreographed themselves and taking a percentage of the profits these acts earned, above and below the line. Phil still worked with them, only he now headed up a team of bookers who booked the new acts across the country and took a fifteen per cent booking fee. His team of bookers, five in all, Manchester, Birmingham, Glasgow, Leeds and Newcastle, ensured the same degree of protection that he offered in London, checking out clubs, driving the acts to and from their bookings, making sure they were safe and well looked after. The business was called Silk and Lace Limited, it was small, friendly and completely legitimate.

Cora and Thea still performed. They were much in demand but had cut back to three nights a week. In the beginning, after the initial huge success, they had found themselves working six nights a week, packing the clubs out and living the peculiar existence that shift workers live. Tom had suffered: Thea had a great deal of money put away, but she was anxious during the day, short-tempered and exhausted. They did that for a year, got the business well under way and then started to think around the act.

Thea had moved out of London a year after that. One sunny Saturday morning, just after Cora had passed her driving test, they had driven Tom down to the Sussex coast and got thoroughly lost. Thea had seen the house for sale in a small village east of Petworth, a village they should never have been in and took its discovery as a sign of fate. She had enquired about it, and found that the cottage was in perfect order, albeit old-fashioned and in need of redecoration, but structurally sound. So taking a large cash deposit out of the business, she had secured a mortgage, guaranteed by Jake, and bought it.

'Mum!' Tom shouted up the stairs. 'Aunty Cora's on the phone!'

'Blast,' Thea muttered, closing her bedroom window on the scent of lavender blossom and early honeysuckle. She smiled: Aunty Cora sounded so funny! 'Tell her I'll call her back, will you, Tom? We'll be late otherwise!' She glanced in the mirror, grabbed a brush, ran it through her hair and hurried for the stairs.

'She said she'll call you later,' Tom told her, sitting on the stairs with his reading book. 'Here, you forgot to write that I did my homework.'

Thea took the book, scribbled a note for Tom's teacher in it, dropped the pencil into her pocket and opened the front door. 'OK,' she said. 'Bag, homework?'

'Yup.'

'Anything else?'

'Nope.'

'Right, let's go then.'

They walked out to the car. 'Back door!' Thea said. 'I forgot to lock it.' She threw the car keys at Tom. 'Here, catch.' He dropped them on the ground as she darted round the back of the cottage to lock the French doors. That done, she re-emerged through the front door and climbed into the car. Tom was already in the passenger seat with his seatbelt done up.

'Did Cora say anything else?' she asked, starting the engine.

'Nope.' Tom was reading a Rupert Annual, one Jake had given to him. 'Is Gramps coming down tonight?'

'He sure is,' Thea said. 'But that doesn't mean football until all hours and late to bed.'

'Yes it does.'

Thea glanced behind her and slammed the car into reverse. 'All right,' she said, 'it does.' She jabbed out a finger to tickle Tom who burst into shrieks of giggles. 'But don't you dare be grumpy in the morning.' And swinging the car round, they pulled out into the main road and headed off to school.

Thea dropped Tom off a few minutes late, chatted for a time to one of the other mums, then made her way back down the lane towards her car. As she turned the corner, a black Land-Rover came racing up and took the bend so close that she had to jump back and into the nettles. 'Ouch!' She had bare legs and the stings were sharp and intense. 'Bloody idiot!' she cried. The Land-Rover swung into the spaces in front of the pre-prep; someone, she couldn't see who, jumped out, shouted at two boys who climbed out after him and the three of them ran off towards the building.

'Who on earth was that?' Thea exclaimed.

'Daniel Ellis,' Pascal Norden said. Thea turned. She didn't know Pascal Norden but she'd heard of her. 'He's new,' Pascal went on, 'and he's absolutely gorgeous!'

Absolutely gorgeous! Thea thought; shades of Dolly. God, I can't wait to tell Cora. She said, 'Shame he can't drive!'

Pascal laughed. 'Are you around on Saturday by any chance?' she said. 'I know it's short notice but we're having drinks and supper, in the garden, spur of the moment, as it's such nice weather.'

Thea smiled. Spur of the moment meant someone had

dropped out. She went through her mental list of refusals and wondered which one to utilise.

'Daniel Ellis is coming,' Pascal said. 'You could meet him and berate him for nearly running you over. I'd say it was worth accepting just for that!'

Suddenly Thea laughed. 'OK,' she said, 'Thanks, I'd love to come.' What was she doing? She never accepted invitations!

'Good.' Pascal pressed the alarm pad in her hand and the lights flashed on her car. The doors unlocked. 'I'm glad you're coming,' she said, 'I've wanted to get to know you for ages.'

'Oh, erm, have you?'

'Yes! You're an artist, is that right? Tom told Oliver.'

'Yes, sort of.'

'How wonderful! I'd love to see your work some time!'

Thea held down the urge to laugh.

'Seven-thirty then, on Saturday. We're at Mallow House, Widcomb. It's casual, wear anything you like.' Pascal climbed into her car. 'Bye!'

'Yes, bye, and thanks!' Thea held up her hand to wave and carried on to her own car. As she climbed inside, her mobile went; it was her work phone.

'Dorothy Marsh.' Years ago, just after they started, Dolly had suggested that Thea and Cora use pseudonyms for work. She'd said it would leave a clear dividing line between work and their private lives which they would eventually need and, as Thea had found out, she was exactly right.

'Hi, Thea, it's me!'

'Hi, Aunty Cora. How are you?'

'Oi! Less of the aunty, you! I'm only just a quarter of a

century!' Cora's accent had all but disappeared but every now and then it slipped. Thea smiled. 'Anyways, I'm fine thanks, Dorothy! You?'

'Yes, I'm well. I'm at school actually, on my way home. What's up?'

'Saturday,' Cora said. 'We've had a last-minute booking, a party at the Mayfair Club. I know you don't usually work Saturdays but it's big money and they really want us. Phil said no, but Lenny, the owner of the club, rang me direct so I thought I'd give you a ring and see what you said.'

'If he really wants us, then why didn't he book us months ago? That's what most clubs do, Cora.'

'It's last minute apparently. This bloke, the one who's booked the club, only rang up on Monday night.'

'What, and Lenny's given him the club at such short notice?'

'Yeah, he's loaded. Some city type, just got a big pay-off or something. He said he wants a really class act, so Lenny asked us. It's a fifteen-hundred fee.'

That wasn't unheard of but it was about five hundred over the odds. 'Cora, I've just accepted an invitation to a party, I literally just said yes!'

'Can't you cancel it?'

'Yes I can, I suppose . . .'

'But?'

'It's just that I said yes and it looks bad and, well, there's this chap from school, he just nearly ran me over and I'd like to—'

'Say no more!' Cora said, laughing. 'If it's a bloke involved then I'll tell Lenny we can't—'

'No, Cora, wait! It's nothing like that!' Thea stopped. She thought for a few moments, then said, 'What time do they want the act?'

'About eleven-thirty. They've got a dinner first, then they've booked the club from ten-thirty.'

Thea's heart sank. 'Oh, I don't know, Cora, I hate staying out that late at the weekend. I mean, Sundays are for Tom and . . .' Thea also hated letting Cora down. Cora was friends with Lenny, sometimes drank with him after the act. 'If it was earlier, I mean I . . .' She really didn't know what to do.

'Look, don't worry.' Cora hesitated for a moment, then said, 'There's always Debbie.'

'Debbie?'

'Yes, she's offered to cover for you any time you can't make it. She's not as good as you, but if we rehearsed, I don't think it would make that much difference. If you didn't mind, that is?'

'No, I, erm . . .' Debbie was one of the girls they had been training up, she was young and attractive, and she was good. But she was also silly and irresponsible, and if it hadn't been for Cora striking up a friendship with her Thea wasn't sure she'd have had her in the team. 'No, I don't mind,' Thea said.

'OK, I'll ask her then.'

'Make sure that Phil squares it with Lenny though, won't you?'

'Sure.'

'Are you picking her up or is Phil?' It was one of the ground rules, that the girls were always escorted to and from their bookings.

There was a brief tense silence, then Cora said, 'Look, Thea, Phil's not actually going to be there.'

'What? Why on earth not?'

'He can't do it, he's got some long-standing engagement and he can't work.'

'I see.' Thea and Cora never worked without Phil. 'Can't he break it?' Thea wasn't happy, she really didn't like the idea of Cora working without Phil.

'Apparently not.'

'Look, I don't know about this, Cora, we don't work without Phil, that's the rule. No one works without their booker.'

'I know, but it is Lenny and the club is very up market. Thea! How long have I been doing this? Come on, don't be so paranoid! Besides, we've never, ever had any trouble there before.'

'I know that but . . .'

'No buts, I know what I'm doing, all right?'

Thea was silent as she mulled it over. 'All right. I don't reckon that much can go wrong, can it?'

Cora laughed. 'No, of course not! Nothing can go wrong! We've done this hundreds and hundreds of times now, what could possibly go wrong?'

Thea still didn't like it, but despite this, she said, 'Nothing.' Then, as an afterthought: 'I suppose.'

It was Saturday night and Thea had organised Betty to baby-sit because Jake had been down once that week already and she didn't like to ask him at weekends. He had supported her throughout but he needed his own life, now that things with Marian had taken on a new dimension.

Betty was a lady from the village, forty-nine, two grown-up children and in need of a small job to help keep things ticking over, now that her husband had gone self-employed. She had been working for Thea for two years now, three days and two nights a week. She didn't know what Thea did for a living, she had not been told very much and didn't like to ask. She assumed it was something to do with the huge bold canvases that Thea painted for relaxation in the garage and hence Thea's small reputation as an artist had sprung up. Of course a trained eye would have spotted a thoroughly bad attempt at art first off but only Betty ever saw the work so that was never a problem.

Tonight, she knew that Thea was off out to the Nordens' party, and as she let herself in and called up the stairs, Thea came out of the bedroom in a short sleeveless black silk dress, make-up on and her hair in heated curlers. 'Hello! Tom's in his pyjamas watching telly; *Superman* I think it is.'

Betty nodded, then stood for a moment and stared. She had never seen Thea dressed up ready to go out before. When she was working, she went in jeans, made up before the show and came home in jeans. When she wasn't she was very low key, wore nothing showy, barely any make-up and nearly always flat shoes. It was a direct contradiction to her working life. As she removed the curlers, Betty saw that her hair had a fashionable kink to it, not the fuzz that always resulted from heated rollers in Betty's own hair. Thea's skin too, her bare legs and arms, had a light golden tan to it that Betty had never noticed before. 'You look very nice,' she said. 'Very chic.'

Thea smiled. 'Thanks. Don't look so surprised!' She took

the last roller out and ran her fingers through her hair. 'I'm off in a few minutes. Tom can stay up till eight but no later, OK?'

Betty nodded.

'There's supper in the fridge,' Thea called as Betty went towards the sitting room to join Tom, 'and a glass of wine.' She went back into her bedroom, brushed her hair and wondered about a bit of perfume. She decided against it. Leaning towards the window, she also decided against closing it. Instead, she drew the curtains to keep the bugs out and switched on the lamp. Now she would be greeted by the smell of lilac through the window when she came home, it was better than any perfume.

'Right,' she said, peering into the sitting room at both Tom and Betty curled up on the sofa glued to the television. 'I'm off.'

'OK, Mum.' Tom didn't take his eyes off the screen so Thea walked in and stood in front of it, blocking his view.

'Kiss please.'

'Oh Mum!' He scampered off the sofa, darted across to her and Thea leant down. He kissed her, throwing his arms around her neck and hugging her tight. She closed her eyes for a moment and wondered why on earth she was going out and not sitting next to him watching telly. 'Bed on time,' she said as he released her and leapt back on the sofa. 'When Betty says so, OK?'

'Yup.'

Thea moved aside and he was once more goggle-eyed. Betty stood and walked out into the hall with Thea. 'I may be late,' Thea said, 'then again I may not.' She smiled. 'Is that OK?'

'Fine with me,' Betty said. 'You just go and enjoy yourself.' She'd always felt sorry for Thea, going up to London in the week to work, weekends at home with Tom, no boyfriends, no social life to speak of except her friend Cora and her father. It was good to see her dressed up and ready to go out; she could do with a bit of fun.

'Give us a poke if I'm asleep on the sofa when you come in. I said I'd ring Norman and he'll come and walk me back home.'

'I hope I won't be that late,' Thea said, smiling. 'Anyway, I wouldn't dare poke you, you might bite me!'

Betty laughed. 'Go on, off you go and have a nice time.' She stood by the door, hand on the catch, and watched Thea climb into her car. Thea waved, started the engine and drove off.

Mallow House was originally sixteenth century. It had been added to over the centuries and was now a hotch potch of architectural styles that lacked composition but had a great deal of charm. It sprawled, the main part of the house long and narrow, beamed, with cross brickwork, its two additional wings wider with high sash windows, and the back part added on somewhere around the Victorian period, brick with a wonderful detailed chimney. Thea loved it. She had parked, as instructed by a sign, in a field to the right of the house and now walked up the cherry-tree-lined drive and looked over the gardens: uneven rolling lawns and densely planted herbaceous beds. There was a hum of conversation coming from behind the house and the sound of music: jazz, which made her smile. Perhaps they'd ask her to do the entertaining. As she reached the front door it was opened by a young man in black jeans and a white shirt who said, 'If you'd like to go round the side, madam, there's drinks and Mr and Mrs Norden to receive you.'

'Oh right, thanks.' Thea's stomach lurched. Drinks and some supper in the garden, Pascal had said, casual, wear anything you like. She took a deep breath and walked on. Around the side was through a high iron gate and along a rose walk on to a terrace at the back. 'Wear anything you like' had obviously meant Versace to most of the guests and Thea's confidence was boosted by her little black dress. When had the country got so townish? she wondered, and then a waiter offered her a drink which she declined, seeing as there were only two glasses of champagne on his tray and she had to drive.

'Would you like a soft drink?' he asked.

Thea nodded, glancing over his shoulder to try and locate her hosts. 'I'd love an orange juice, if you've got one,' she said.

The waiter looked at her, smiled – a peculiar, rather startled smile, she thought – and walked away. 'How rude,' she muttered. Some caterers considered themselves more important than the guests. Moving off the terrace, away from the crowd, Thea found herself drifting down towards the end of the garden. She couldn't see anyone she recognised and was beginning to feel uneasy.

'Your drink, madam,' the waiter suddenly said at her elbow.

Thea spun round. 'Oh, crikey! You made me jump!'

The waiter burst out laughing. 'Crikey!' he said. 'Good God, I haven't heard that expression since my sister was at school!'

Thea's face set. She didn't mind a joke but this was patronising and rude. Who did he think he was? 'I'm sorry? What would you rather I said? Christ, you scared the hell out of me, asshole?'

The waiter stopped laughing. He caught the steely glint in Thea's eye and took a pace back. Thea thought: Oh God, I've gone too far, I work too many clubs, I'm out of place. She flushed deep red, then put her hand out to his arm and said, 'I'm sorry, that was rude. I'm just not used to parties, that's all, I don't like them and I'm a bit uptight. Sorry.'

The waiter glanced down at her hand. Her nails were perfect long ovals, cut short as usual and buffed to a natural polish. She wore no rings at all, no bracelets and only a small black Swatch watch.

'Apology accepted,' he said. 'Now, would you like that drink?'

'Please.' Thea took her orange juice and wondered why he remained. Still, she wasn't going to drive him away, she was just relieved not to be standing alone.

'I don't know anyone,' she said, not wanting to stand in silence either. 'It's embarrassing when that happens.'

'Yes, yes it is.' He took a glass of champagne off the tray, dropped the empty tray down by his feet and sipped. Thea's eyes widened in surprise, she stared at him for a few moments but when he seemed completely unfazed by this she looked away. 'Look, I'm terribly sorry,' she said, turning back to him.

'What, again?'

Thea suppressed her sudden irritation. 'I'm not sure you should be doing this,' she went on, 'I mean, standing here with me, drinking champagne. You might get into trouble.'

'Really?' He smiled and it infuriated Thea. 'Why would standing here with you get me into trouble?'

Thea couldn't hold her temper any longer. 'Well, really!' she exploded. 'I—'

'Ah, Thea! There you are!' Pascal appeared, almost out of nowhere, and bore down on them in a cloud of Calvin Klein scent. 'I see you've met Daniel Ellis! Well done, you're the only woman at the party who has so far!' She embraced Thea, kissing the air either side of her face.

'Daniel Ellis?' Thea stammered.

'Yes! The man who nearly ran you over! Remember?' Pascal shook a forefinger at the waiter and Thea flushed crimson. 'This is Thea Marshall,' she said. 'And you, Daniel my darling, very nearly knocked her down with your appalling driving the other day.'

'Ah.' Daniel Ellis looked at Thea. 'The legs in the nettles,' he said. 'I'm terribly sorry.'

'I think it deserves more than that,' Pascal went on. 'I think it probably deserves a dinner at somewhere very posh and expensive! She's here to tell you off, you know. It was the only way I could convince her to come!'

Daniel continued to look at Thea, who continued to blush. Her face pulsated. 'I think she's already done that!' he said, and suddenly he laughed.

'Did I miss something?' Pascal asked.

'No, of course not, Pascal!' He downed his glass of

champagne in one. 'You couldn't find me an unsuspecting waiter, could you? I'm gasping for another drink!'

She looked momentarily affronted but, too polite to react, said, 'Oh, yes, of course. If I can't lure you away to circulate.'

'I'd rather stay here for a while.' He smiled at Pascal and Thea saw why she'd called him 'absolutely gorgeous' a few days ago. He had that look: it was clean and masculine but slightly awry, like his shirt, expensive yet lightly creased, and his brown hair, well cut but uncombed. He had shaved and missed a patch under his chin, and when he smiled, an easy, warm smile, his eyes held a glint of dark blue humour. He ran his tongue over his front tooth, just at the bottom where it was chipped, and Thea thought he was the most attractive man she had ever seen. Not handsome, just powerfully attractive. She stared at him for the few moments more that he smiled at Pascal and then, as he looked back at her, she glanced away.

'So why,' he said, 'would standing here with you get me into trouble? You didn't answer my question.'

'That was unfair,' Thea said, turning back to him. She almost instantly wished she hadn't. His gaze was so intense that it took her breath away. 'You posed as a waiter and made a fool of me,' she went on, staring down at her drink. 'It was unkind.'

'No, I didn't, in defence of your first two accusations, and no, it wasn't, to your third. I didn't pose as a waiter, you mistook me for one; I didn't make a fool of you either, how could I have done? There was only us two involved and I certainly don't think you a fool. Attractive yes, possibly the most attractive woman I've ever seen and unbelievably sexy when you blush, but definitely not a fool. And no, it wasn't unkind, it was rather funny actually.'

Thea looked up. She had heard more chat-up lines than she cared to remember – most, if not all, were immediately forgotten, should never even have been uttered in the first place – but this, this was ridiculous, insulting almost! She started to reply, sharply, when Daniel said, 'I don't like parties either, and the only reason I accepted was because Pascal told me that you'd be here. I'm not very good at this sort of thing, I don't do dates, I was married too long for that, so what I've just told you is the absolute plain truth.' Thea was about to interrupt, but he stopped her. 'No, let me finish,' he said. 'I'm a barrister and we must have our say. I've seen you at school, for months I've wanted to speak to you but you're so damned aloof I never got the chance. So here we are. There's a back way out of this place, along the side of the duck pond at the bottom of the garden and through the gate into the meadow. My boys told me, they've been here for tea. Dad, they said, if it gets too much and Mrs Norden keeps talking at you, then there's a secret way out. They drew me a little map.' Daniel dug in his pocket and brought out a piece of paper. 'Here, the first piece of evidence.' He handed it across to Thea. 'Shall we do a runner? Before Pascal gets back?'

Thea looked at the map, read the small, neat handwriting and the signatures underneath. She folded it, handed it back and thought for a few moments. It was probably a mistake, there was no good reason for doing it, it was rude and childish and she would have to face Pascal on Monday and make an excuse. But there was no denying the sharp, exquisitely painful longing she felt when he spoke and now, when he smiled at her, she saw that his tooth was not only chipped but slightly crooked as well.

'All right,' she said. 'Only don't expect me to navigate. I gave up Geography for Latin.'

Daniel took her hand, glanced over his shoulder and, seeing the all clear, led her off in the direction of the pond. 'Oh dear,' he said, 'so did I.' He pulled her close. 'Never mind, as long as we get through that gate we can be lost for days as far as I'm concerned. In fact' – he took the map out of his pocket and suddenly scrunched it into a ball, throwing it high up over the trees to the pond – 'I think it's preferable,' he said.

Once through the gate, halfway across the meadow and out of sight of the house and garden, Thea and Daniel stopped to look back. They could just see the top of Mallow House, hear the buzz of distant conversation and, suddenly, they both began to laugh. They stood in the middle of a field in the warm summer evening and laughed until they were helpless, hot and weak with hysterics. Then Thea wiped her face on her bare arm and Daniel took the arm, running his tongue along the smooth supple flesh. Thea shivered. 'Salty tears,' he murmured. Locking his fingers in hers, he pulled her towards him and kissed first her hand, then her mouth. 'I have two boys at home,' he said, gently pulling away. 'We can't go there.'

'And I have one boy and one Betty.' Thea moved away from him. Her heart was pounding so hard in her chest that it was making her breathless. She took a lungful of air.

'I've never done this before,' Daniel said. 'I mean, so

soon, I don't know the—' Thea silenced him with the tip of her finger. He sucked it.

'Where's your car?' she asked. She had never done it before either but she didn't want to say so, she sensed that she needed to be in control.

'My car?' He was surprised. 'It's in the field.'

'Well,' Thea said, moving back towards him, 'let's go for a drive, somewhere quiet, remote.' She put her hands on his face and eased it down towards her own, briefly kissing his lips. This was insanity. She had no idea why she was doing it, but she didn't care. The attraction was too strong, too sudden and extraordinary to resist.

Daniel smiled. 'Are you serious?'

She nodded and smiled back. 'Deadly serious,' she murmured. 'What else would you use that bloody great car for?'

Daniel pulled the Land-Rover into a small parking space carved out of the trees at the end of a narrow unmade-up lane, right under the dark green shadow of the Downs. He stopped the car, switched the engine off and they sat in silence. The light was fading, there was the fresh heavy scent of woodland, leaf mould and damp air, and there was silence. Not a sound, except their breathing.

'I know nothing about you,' Daniel said. 'I can't believe I'm doing this.' He turned to Thea. Her skin had a sheen to it and as he reached out to touch her arm he thought it looked and felt like satin.

Thea stared at the velvet cushion of the land, great pillows of emerald darkening with the movement of the clouds across the sky in the fading light. 'No,' she said, 'nor can I.'

His fingers stroked her shoulder and she wondered how long it was since she had been loved. Years. Not since Hal, not once since Hal. She wasn't sure she had the nerve to go through with it, if they hadn't lost something in coming here, planning it. Then Daniel said, 'What should we do? Shall I put my seat back or something?' and it was so plain and unromantic, so honest and nervous and unpretentious that she turned to him and without hesitation, leant forward to kiss him. He caught his hands in her hair and the kiss deepened.

'I think,' she whispered, pulling back, 'that things will just happen.'

'Will they?'

She nodded, reached behind her and unzipped her dress. Then, kneeling up on the seat, she lifted the dress over her head.

'Jesus!' Daniel whispered. She wore just a lace thong underneath. In that and her heels, she moved across and straddled him.

'You see?' she murmured as he took her nipple in his mouth. But that was the last thing she uttered. In the time that followed, there was no energy or space for words.

'So, Thea Marshall,' Daniel said, tracing the outline of her collar bone with his fingertip. 'Now I know you intimately in the physical sense, I should like to know you intimately in the mental sense.' They were naked, lying in the back of the car, their limbs tangled together, Thea's head on Daniel's chest. 'Tell me all about yourself.'

'What, *all* about myself? Like my O level grades and when I went to France with the school, that sort of thing?'

'Well, not exactly that sort of thing, but I'll let you be the judge.'

Thea shuffled and turned on to her side. She propped herself up on her elbow and nearly knocked Daniel off the seat. 'I think – oops, sorry,' she said as he righted himself. 'I think that I've done enough of the verbals tonight, don't you?'

Daniel smiled. 'I rather liked that moaning, it was—' He broke off for thought. 'Enthusiastic!'

Thea poked him. 'You rotter!'

He laughed.

'I think that you should tell me all about *yourself*,' Thea said. 'Start with your boys and work backwards if you like.'

Daniel was silent for a while. 'Are you sure?'

'Yes, go on.'

'Right, well, I've got two boys at the Marlow Prep, Charlie and Wills, seven and eight and a half.' There was another brief silence but Thea couldn't see Daniel's face. 'My wife died three years ago, she was killed in a road accident . . .'

'Oh God, I'm so sorry,' Thea said. 'I didn't know.'

Daniel stroked her hair. 'It's OK, I find it easier to deal with now. That old adage: time and healing etc.' There was another silence. It seemed to go on for ever, then Daniel cleared his throat and said, 'We – the boys, a rather dopey but endearing nanny called Petula, who has been with us for four years and whom I could not bear to part with, despite repeatedly making me late for school and hence work through her lack of organisation – we, live in Hornsby Ash, in the Willow House, and I am a barrister, working in a Chambers in Chancery Lane.' He stopped stroking and tweaked Thea's earlobe. 'Now your turn.'

'Oh God, really?'

'Yes, really.'

'I don't know if there's much to tell,' Thea said. 'I've got one boy, Tom, five, at Marlow Pre-prep, and I'm single, always have been.'

'Why?'

'It never worked out with Tom's father.'

'Hmmm. Do you still see him?'

'No, not really. He keeps in touch with Tom – Christmas, birthdays – but it's no more than that. He's got his own life, we're not really part of it.'

'Does that matter?'

'No, not at all!'

'Hmmm,' Daniel said again.

Thea was getting edgy. She hated talking about herself. She had no intention of telling the truth – where the hell would that get her in a place as small as this? 'What does "Hmmm" mean?' she asked.

'Nothing. And you live?'

'In West Burton.'

'Ah.'

'What does "Ah" mean?'

Daniel looked down at her. 'Stop it!'

'Stop what?'

'All this paranoia! You've got nothing to hide, have you?'

'Of course not!'

'You're not the great axe murderer of Bignor swamp, are you? About to chop my head off and drop it in a bog?'

Thea started to laugh. 'Good, that's better!' Daniel turned towards her and kissed the tip of her nose. 'Thea, can I see you again?' he asked. 'Like tomorrow? Or the next day, or the day after that?'

Thea held her breath. 'I don't know,' she said. 'Can I call you?'

Daniel turned her face up to look at him. 'Of course you can call me, but the answer had better be yes, Thea. I really, really have to see you again. OK?'

Thea closed her eyes and imagined, just for the briefest nano-second, that things really could work out for them together. Then she opened them on reality and shrugged. 'We'll see,' she said. 'We'll see.'

Thea wasn't late in. Betty was watching the Saturday night movie on the television when she put her head round the door. 'Hello. Everything OK?'

Betty looked up. 'Oh, hello. Yes, fine. You're back early, I didn't hear your car.'

'No, I had a couple of drinks at the party and someone brought me home.'

'Oh really? Who?'

Thea sighed and came into the room. 'Daniel Ellis, his boys are at school with—'

'Yes, I know Daniel Ellis, the barrister chappie from Hornsby Ash. Everyone knows everyone round here. Norman does the odd job for him. Nice man, dreadful shame, and still young.' Betty shook her head. 'Oh well, nice of him to bring you back.' She got to her feet and rubbed her back. 'I'll ring Norman if I may?'

'Of course.'

Betty came out into the hall and picked up the phone. 'You friendly with him then?' she asked as Thea went through into the kitchen.

'Not particularly,' Thea replied, 'I—' But she was interrupted by the line connecting and Betty talking to Norman. Saved, she thought, putting the kettle on for tea, but for how long, she had no idea.

Chapter Fifteen

Cora was ready to go. Like Thea, she rarely wore anything to travel up to London for work except jeans and a T-shirt but tonight it was too hot for jeans and so she wore the coolest thing she could find in her wardrobe: a short, light, floral silk dress, with shoe-string straps and a skirt that flared out over her narrow hips and ended just above the knee. She put on a pair of flat ballet pumps, changed them for high-heeled strappy sandals, then took those off and decided to drive in plimsolls.

Leaving her bag by the front door, she went across to draw the blinds on the balcony windows, then on the skylights in her bedroom. She glanced round the flat, rearranged the big glass vase of red amaryllis and finally switched on the lamps. She hated coming home to a dark apartment; she liked it lit up like a fairground.

Cora's flat in Chichester was as near to Thea as she could get without being rural. Cora didn't *do* rural. It was the entire first floor of a row of three church cottages, which a visionary and slightly misguided architect from London had designed and redeveloped into one large wood-floored living space divided by glass brick walls. It was light, owing to all the windows and skylights; airy, owing to the lack of doors and the lack of clutter, but it was totally inappropriate for Chichester's large retired population. The architect had built it and then been lumbered with it, unable to sell. The property market had slumped and Cora had bought it only days before he was about to go bankrupt. She'd got herself a real bargain.

And Cora loved it. She wasn't a cottage type, she wasn't even particularly homely. It was Phil bullying her to invest her money that had convinced her she should buy and now she had, she wouldn't have swapped it for the world. It was the first and only real home Cora had ever had. All she had to do to move in was buy a bed and a sofa and that was pretty much all she had now, two years later.

Making her way to the front door, Cora checked her face in her bronzing powder compact. She removed a smudge of lipstick from the side of her mouth with her perfectly manicured fingertip and shut the compact with a sharp click. Cora had changed so much that sometimes these days she hardly recognised herself. She was chic and smart, revelling in the designer labels that Thea had no time for. She had manicures and pedicures, facials and aromatherapy massage. She had reflexology and worked out regularly at the Goodwood Country Club. She was blonde and sleek, she had an air of confidence that years ago she would never have dreamt possible, but somehow, underneath all this, beneath the polished accent, the glossy veneer, she was still as fragile as the days of the pink fur coat. She still didn't know who she was or what she was worth.

It was different for Thea; Thea had Tom. She had a structure to her life and a purpose. They both worked hard, Cora and Thea, had worked bloody hard over the first three years and Thea spent her money wisely: on Tom's school, on investments, on her future. Cora wasn't even sure she had a future. What man was going to take on a stripper for a wife? The sort of man who came to gawp and crow, who cruised the clubs and slipped tenners into her shoe or threw fifty-pound notes into the hat for show. That's what sort of man. It was all very well, the business she was in, Cora thought, she'd been successful, more successful than she ever imagined, but it was hardly choice, all the groping punters and the stale whiff of sex. Thea rose above it, she had a reason for it all, but what reason did Cora have, except the money? And what good was money for money's own sake?

Cora glanced at her watch. She spent too much time thinking nowadays, it was probably all that reading she did. There was a job to be done tonight, no time for dawdling, for thinking herself into a hole. She bent to pick up her bag and rummaged in it for her car keys. Locating them, she clutched them in her hand and slung the bag over her shoulder.

'Bye-bye, flat,' she said, but it seemed to echo and made her feel lonely, so she shut the door quickly and went down the outside staircase to her car.

Cora collected Debbie at the house she shared in Tooting and together they headed up the A3 towards central London. They chatted a little on the way but the traffic was heavy so Cora had to concentrate and it was tough going. They made it to Mayfair at ten where Lenny had reserved a parking space for Cora right outside the club.

'Good old Lenny,' she said, spotting the grey authorities bag he had slipped over the meter to stop others from using it. 'Can you pop out and get one of the boys to take the bag off for me, Debbie? Just go in the front and one of them will come out with you. OK?'

Debbie jumped out of the car and walked into the club. Cora wasn't happy with the way she was dressed: tight black mini-skirt (if you could call it a skirt), bare legs, high-heeled shoes and a crop top. She looked young and tarty and if she hadn't been so nervous, Cora would have said something. But as it was, Debbie was obviously petrified and Cora didn't want to upset her further. They had an act to perform and for the amount of money on offer tonight, she couldn't afford for it to be marred by upset or nerves. She waved as one of the bouncers came out to do the meter and drove into the space as soon as he'd finished.

Slipping her plimsolls off, Cora bent to fasten her sandals before she climbed out of the car. As she did so, she showed a long expanse of thigh and high heel and was embarrassed to see the bouncer gawping.

'I'll keep my eye on it,' he said, jangling change in his pocket.

'Oh, erm, right.' Cora didn't know him, he was new and she wasn't at all sure about the way he looked at her. 'Thanks,' she said. Then, straightening her dress, she nodded at him and went on inside the club.

'Evening, Cora!' Lenny came forward and kissed her cheek as she entered the darkness. 'How are you?'

'Fine, fine, thanks, Lenny. You?'

'Can't complain, Cora love, not with business like this coming my way.'

'No, I expect not.'

'I've met your lovely young lady there, Cora, I was just getting her a drink. What'll you have?'

Cora glanced across at Debbie who was up on a bar stool chatting to the barman and showing the odd flash of red knickers.

'Nothing, thank you, Lenny,' Cora replied. 'And nothing for Debbie either, thanks, I've got a bottle of water in my bag and we need to start making up. Thanks all the same. Debbie?'

Debbie glanced across.

'Come on, no time to waste, I'm afraid,' Cora said. She handed Debbie her bag and with a gentle hand in the middle of her back, propelled her towards the back of the stage.

Backstage, Cora said, 'Debbie love, we don't usually sit up at the bar when Phil's here, it doesn't look good, it sort of invites the wrong impression.'

'But Phil's not here tonight, is he?' Debbie glanced over her shoulder at Cora. 'So it doesn't matter what sort of impression we give, does it?'

'Well, it's not as simple as that, it's not Phil we should be concerned with, it's—' Cora broke off. She could see that Debbie wasn't listening to a word she was saying. She was staring at her nails and buffing the bright red polish up to an implacable gloss. 'Never mind,' Cora said. There was plenty of time to talk about this after the performance. 'Come on, into the dressing room, you'd be amazed at how long it takes to get that make-up even over your backside!'

The act went surprisingly well. That's what Cora told herself as she followed Debbie back stage, sweating and pulsing with the adrenalin. Debbie wasn't Thea, she didn't have Thea's grace or sensuality, but what she lacked there, she made up for in cheek and sexiness and she had managed to carry it off, despite a couple of wrong moves and missed bars. Cora was pleased; she wouldn't like to repeat the experience, but the standing ovation and the hat full of cash were a clear indication that it had been a success.

Inside the dressing room, she kicked off her shoes and pulled on her towelling robe, then sat to peel off the stockings. She glanced up at Debbie, standing naked, drinking from the bottle of water, and said, 'Did you bring something to put on Debbie?'

'No, I don't normally.'

'I see.' Cora said, tight-lipped. 'Thea and I usually sit and relax for a while before we take our make-up off. I find if you've been sweating you can get cold very quickly.' Cora wasn't into nudity, she liked to draw a distinct line between work and leisure, but Debbie missed the subtle hint.

'Oh, right,' she said, but she did nothing to cover herself up and Cora held down a flash of irritation. It wasn't worth it, she'd be home before too long, tucked up on the sofa with a nice glass of wine and a good book.

There was a knock on the door and she walked across to open it.

'Debbie, I don't think . . .' But Cora was too late, she had opened the door and was smiling at the new bouncer. He took a pace back, then smirked at Debbie.

'I've got a message,' he said, 'from a party of gentlemen out front. They'd like to know if you ladies would join them for a drink.'

Cora stood up. She pulled her dressing gown a little tighter round her body and walked across to the door. 'Debbie,' she said coldly, 'put something on please.' She faced the bouncer. 'Could you please say thank you but no, perhaps another time.' And closing the door, she locked it and turned to Debbie.

'Rule one,' she said, 'we never answer the door in costume, and that means naked, OK? Rule two, we never have a drink out front.'

'But that barman said earlier that you drink with Lenny whenever you work here. He told me you were a regular at his bar.'

'Well, that just goes to show you how the wrong impressions can be formed, doesn't it?' Cora was cross; Debbie was overstepping the mark. 'I sometimes have a drink with Lenny after the show and only ever as his guest at a special table he reserves for entertaining. I never sit at the bar.' Cora told herself mentally to calm down. This was stupid, she was getting riled about nothing; she was tired, it was late and she was uneasy without Phil.

'Come on now, Debbie, let's just get showered and dressed and go home. All right?' Debbie was leaning against the dressing table and Cora could see the reflection of her bottom, brightly lit by the twenty bulbs around the mirror. 'Come on,' she said again, a bit more kindly, 'I'm exhausted.'

Debbie looked down at her nipple. 'I'd like to have a drink with the gentlemen out front,' she said. 'If it's all right with you.'

Cora tensed. She took a deep breath and said as calmly as she could manage, 'No, it's not all right, I'm afraid. I have no wish to do that and you are not going to drink out front on your own.'

'Why not?' Debbie had a truculent, defiant look in her eye that reminded Cora of Tom.

'Because it doesn't reflect well on Silk and Lace Limited, that's why not. You are our employee at the moment, that is until you buy your own franchise for the act, and we don't allow employees to fraternise with the punters.'

'It's hardly fraternising! It's only a bloody drink!'

'It may start as a drink but you never know where it'll end up, so it's best not to take the chance. OK?'

Debbie shrugged. 'Presumably I'm not an employee twenty-four hours a day, so if I want to drink in here on my own free time then it's my business, isn't it?'

This was beginning to annoy Cora; she really didn't have the patience for it. 'Look, Debbie,' she began, 'do I have to spell it out for you? You are eighteen and I have no intention of letting you go out and drink with a bunch of rowdy drunken men on your own.'

'Then you'll have to come with me,' Debbie fired back, 'to look after me. That's what my booker would do, isn't it?'

Cora gritted her teeth. 'I am not your booker!'

'No, but you are responsible for me, aren't you?'

'Only up to a point!' Cora snapped. But Debbie was right; of course she was responsible for her, she wouldn't dream of letting a young girl loose in a club like this, particularly not after a performance. 'Look, Debbie.' Cora decided to try again. 'You have just stood on a stage and performed a very erotic act; those men are aroused by you, they think you're *it*. Believe me, they'll be salivating all over you.'

'That's half the fun, isn't it? The power!'

Cora dropped her head in her hands. There was no getting out of this. Debbie had dug her heels in and she was going to have a drink, whether Cora liked it or not. 'All right,' Cora said, 'I'm not going to stand here and argue all night with you about it, we'll go for a drink, if that's what you want, but I think you'll find that it's not quite as glamorous as you'd imagined.' She pulled her robe off and dropped it on the back of the chair. Reaching into the sports bag for her pot of make-up remover, she rubbed it all over her face, then started on her body. 'But it's one drink, that's all, just one!' she warned. 'After one, you're on your own!'

But of course it didn't turn out like that, one drink led to another, then another, and although she had said it, Cora was too responsible to leave Debbie on her own after the first drink. So she stuck to Perrier water, because she was driving, and sat quietly, keeping an eye on Debbie but ignoring the party as best she could. Debbie was going for it in a major way. She downed two double vodkas in a matter of minutes and then a bottle of tequila was produced for tequila slammers. She took the first go, did it to much applause and as Cora stood up to intervene, a voice at her side said, 'I'm not sure if I should stop it, what do you think?'

She turned.

'Oh, sorry, Jason Wakes.' A young man held his hand out to her, a young good-looking man, tall and slim and blond, like her. 'It's my party but I don't want things to get out of control.'

Cora took his hand and noticed how smooth it was. He

had a large signet ring on the little finger of his left hand, it was stamped with his family crest and it dug into her palm as they shook.

'Corinne White,' she said. She never gave her real name. 'I think you should intervene, then perhaps I can get off home.'

He smiled. 'Not enjoying yourself?'

She looked across at the rabble of men, mostly drunk, dishevelled and jostling for Debbie's attention in a way that looked pathetic. 'No.' She looked back. 'Are you?'

'Not really.' They dropped their hands down and he dug his in his pockets. 'It wasn't my idea, someone booked it for me. Not my scene really – Oh, erm, I didn't mean . . .' He pulled a face, embarrassed. 'Your act was very good, it wasn't that, I liked that bit, it's just . . .'

Cora smiled. 'It's OK, I get your drift!'

Debbie was on her third tequila slammer. She had taken her top off in the few moments that Cora had looked away and the party were laying bets.

'A fiver to take it off,' Cora heard. Someone was acting as bookie. 'What the hell's she doing?' she exclaimed.

'I think they're betting that if she doesn't drink the slammer, she's got to take her bra off,' Jason said.

'Oh no!' Cora moved forward, but the men around Debbie were several bodies thick. She elbowed her way through, digging her heel into several pairs of highly polished brogues as she went and got to the front just as Debbie picked up the third tequila slammer. She raised it to her lips, the crowd went suddenly silent and as she opened her mouth her eyes went blank and she toppled backwards.

'Christ!' Cora leapt forward and knelt down by her side. 'Debbie? Debbie? Are you all right?' She gently slapped her cheek. 'Debbie?' She let out a sigh. 'OK, party's over, boys,' she called out. 'Debbie keeps her top on and you keep your money.' Debbie was out cold.

With the help of Jason Wakes, Cora got Debbie into the front seat of her car and strapped her in. She wound down the window so that some cool air would blow on her face and put a carrier bag on her lap in case she threw up.

'I'll wait here with her, if you want to go in and get your stuff,' Jason said.

Cora nodded. 'Thanks, I won't be long.' She ran into the club and made her way through to the back to collect their bags. She was so quick that no one saw her come and go.

'Great, thanks again,' she said to Jason, opening the boot and chucking the bags in. 'God knows how I'm going to manage her the other end, I've phoned her house but there's no one there.' She slammed the boot shut and came round to the driver's side.

'Look,' Jason said, 'why don't I hop in the back and give you a hand dropping her off. You can either run me back here or I can get a cab back. You could do with some help by the looks of things, especially if she starts puking up.'

Cora hesitated. God, where was Phil when she needed him? It was sod's law that the only time he wasn't with her, this had to happen. 'It's really kind of you to offer, but I . . .'

'It's no trouble, really. I'd like to help, I feel sort of responsible for those pricks in there.' Jason was standing in his shirt sleeves with his jacket over his arm. 'I'm ready to go now. I've settled up, I've got my jacket . . .'

'Oh, all right then.' Cora made a flip decision. 'Thanks, I could really do with the help.'

She got into the driver's seat and Jason let himself into the back of the car. 'Where does she live?'

'Tooting, would you believe?'

Jason smiled. 'Yes I would believe.'

Cora looked at him in the rear-view mirror and smiled back.

'What about you?' he asked.

'West Sussex.' She didn't like to give much away.

'Me too! What a coincidence! Horsham actually, I bought a house on this new development, Berkeley Homes, very upmarket. It's an investment really, I'll live in it for a couple of years and then sell.'

'Right.'

'I've kept my flat in London, I use it mid-week if the work's tough.'

'Really?'

Jason smiled. 'It's OK, I won't talk to you if you don't want me to. Another duff punter, I suspect.'

Cora pulled up at the lights and glanced behind her. 'Oh no, it's not that, it's . . .' She saw him grin and shake his head. 'All right,' she said. 'Sorry, but we do get quite a lot of them. It's nice of you to help.' Still he grinned. 'No, I mean it, it is nice, thanks.'

'The lights,' he said.

'Oh yes!' Cora shoved the car into first and pulled off.

'You're not a Sussex girl though, are you? That accent, or rather trace of it, it's London I'd say.'

Cora suddenly smiled again. 'I've not had elocution lessons, I've just got a very posh friend. I picked it up from her.'

'The one who usually does the act with you?'

'Yes. How did . . . . ?'

'My mate who booked the club told me about you. I just guessed that Debbie here wasn't your usual . . .' he stopped. 'I'm lost for words. Wasn't your usual what? Team-mate? Fellow artiste?'

'My usual partner.'

'Oh right, that's it. Sorry.'

'That's OK.'

They fell silent for a while. Cora drove, Debbie lay inert, breathing heavily through her mouth, and Jason looked out of the window.

'How long have you been stripping, Cora?' he asked, sitting forward.

'A few years.'

'D'you enjoy it?'

She looked round.

'Sorry, only asking.' He laughed. 'Forget it.'

'No, no, it's OK, I'm paranoid, that's all, don't like talking about myself. Sometimes I enjoy it. We don't perform very much any more, once or twice a week only. We train mostly, it's a business and I like that side of it more.' She stopped at another set of lights and turned. 'What about you? What do you do?'

'I work in the City, I head up a Eurobond fund.'

'Sounds very clever. D'you like it?'

'Sometimes.'

They both smiled, the lights changed and Cora drove

on. She liked him, she decided, he was nice, nice and ordinary, not pushy at all. She took a packet of mints from the dashboard, had one herself and offered them back.

'Thanks.' Jason took one and left the packet in the tray between the seats. Cora liked that too: no physical contact. Most men she met through the club just had to touch her, all the time, as if they couldn't believe that she was real. 'We're nearly there,' she said, 'I think it's the next on the right. Gulliver Avenue.'

'Oh, back there! You just missed it!'

'Damn.' Cora pulled in to the side of the road and stopped. 'Can I do a U-turn, d'you think?'

Jason looked behind him. 'Yes, I don't see why not. It's all clear behind me.' She indicated, checked both ways, then swung her little car right round to face the opposite way. 'Here,' Jason called out. 'Right here!' She turned, recognised the road and found the house, just minutes later. Drawing up outside Debbie's front door, Cora thought how nice it was to have company. She stopped, switched the engine off and pulled on the handbrake. Jason had got his mobile phone out of his jacket pocket.

'I'll just ring a cab, then I'll help you in with her. Has she got keys?'

'I bloody well hope so or we'll have to break in!'

He laughed, dialled and waited for the line to connect. 'Yes, hello, I'd like a cab please.' Cora watched him and thought again how good-looking he was. Not that she fancied him, not at all; she'd only just got over Ewert, finally dumped him after all these years. 'From . . . hang on a second . . . Corinne, what number house is this?'

'Twenty.'

'From number twenty, Gulliver Avenue, Tooting, to Horsham please. Yes, West Sussex.'

'Horsham?' Cora stared at him. 'You can't do that, it'll cost you a fortune!'

'Sorry, could you hang on a moment? Thanks . . .' He looked at Cora. 'It doesn't matter. Anyway, I realised on the way over here that I gave my flat keys to my mate, so I've got no choice.' He went back on the line.

'Look, Jason, hang on a minute!'

'Sorry about this, can I call you right back? Thanks.' He switched the phone off. 'What's the matter?'

'I'll take you home,' Cora said suddenly. She'd just made another flip decision. She wasn't thinking, she was tired and she felt terrible, bringing him all the way over to Tooting and then dumping him to get a cab back to Sussex. It wasn't on, it was rude and ungrateful. 'I drive right past Horsham on the A24,' she said, 'I can take you, it's not a problem.'

'No. Thanks, Cora, but honestly I couldn't put you out.'

She smiled. It may have been flip but it was the right decision; he was considerate enough to refuse. 'Of course you can. As I said, it's not a problem. Really it's not.'

Jason looked concerned. He hesitated, chewed his lip, then finally said, 'Are you absolutely sure?'

'Yes, I'm absolutely sure.' She unclipped her seatbelt. 'Come on, let's get Debbie inside.' Leaning across, she unclipped Debbie's and Debbie fell to the right. Cora turned to look at the house. 'Oh great! There's a light on, it looks like someone's in. We can leave her safely and finally get off home.' She propped Debbie up and went to open the door. 'I don't know about you,' she said to Jason, 'but I'm certainly ready for it.'

*   *   *

The journey from Tooting down to Horsham was better than Cora had thought it would be. Jason was good company, clever and amusing and, despite being tired, she found that she was actually enjoying the chat, enjoying not being alone for once.

It was an occupational hazard, being lonely. With a working life so full of men, and not exactly the best specimens, neither Thea nor Cora had much time for them in their private lives. That was why Cora had kept up with Ewert for so long: not because she loved him but because she couldn't be bothered with anyone else. He still bullied her, gave her the odd slap now and again, but that was nothing really, not compared to the emptiness of being on her own.

Cora pulled off the A24 at the first sign to Horsham as Jason asked her to and took a left at the roundabout. The estate that he lived on had an almost surreal feel to it. It was a network of huge houses, all in different styles, all with their own drives and triple garages. Cora drove on, took a right, as directed, then a left and pulled into the drive of a large mock Georgian mansion.

'Blimey!' she said.

'Yes, it is a bit, isn't it, but it's appreciated over the past twelve months by about twenty per cent. I can put up with it at those rates.'

'Oh no, I didn't mean that it was awful or anything, I just meant, blimey, it's big. Huge, actually.'

Jason smiled. 'D'you want to see inside? I bought the show house, it's got all sorts of gadgets and gizmos.'

'Oh, erm . . .' Cora was tempted. She liked Jason, liked

him a lot actually, but it was late and it was just one of those things that she never did. 'No. No thanks, I mean; I ought to get back, it's late and—'

'Go on, just for five minutes. I'll make you a coffee, I've got an espresso machine and a good strong black coffee will keep you awake on your drive back to Chichester.'

Cora sighed. Oh God, what should she do? She really wanted to go in, she'd love to see round and have a coffee, but the sensible thing was to say no.

'All right,' Jason said. 'Forget the coffee, but come in and let me write down your number, I haven't got a pen on me.' He looked at her. 'Please.'

Write down her number! He wanted to see her again, she could hardly believe it. She smiled. 'OK.' Switching the engine off, she clicked the lights out and unclipped her seatbelt. Jason held out his jacket. 'Here, it's getting chilly, put this on over your dress.'

'Thanks.'

They climbed out of the car and she followed him up to the front door. Unlocking it, an alarm buzzer sounded and Jason darted inside to decode it. 'Come on in,' he called, 'I'll just get the . . .' It was dark so Cora stayed where she was. '. . . lights!' he said, and in an instant the whole hall was lit up, a big, wide, open hall, with a black and white tiled floor and an enormous dazzling chandelier that hung from the ceiling.

'Blimey!' Cora said again as Jason came across to stand next to her.

'You like it?'

'Yes, I . . .' She stopped and looked at him. 'It's amazing, I've never seen anything like it.'

'Come on through to the kitchen, you'll love that too.'
He took her hand; Cora glanced down but said nothing.
The truth was, it felt good.

Turning lights on as he went, Jason led her from the
hall into the kitchen, a high-tech fitted affair in light ash
and granite with chrome trim. There were framed black
and white architectural prints on the walls, a long heavy
ash dining table and six tall-backed chairs, covered in a
dark grey velvet.

'Blimey!' Cora said a third time.

'You like that word, don't you?'

She smiled.

'Coffee?'

'Yes, please.'

Jason busied himself while Cora watched. He seemed
different all of a sudden, more in control, sharper. She
liked that, that felt good too.

'Come on, while the coffee's brewing let me show you
the rest of the house.'

'OK.'

Again he took her hand but this time she thought nothing
of it. He took her round the house, the sitting room, dining
room, TV room, study. Upstairs, the bedrooms for guests,
bathrooms and finally the master suite. He opened the door,
let her go in first, then followed her, closing the door quietly
behind him.

'Gosh, this is incredible.'

'What, not blimey again?' Cora glanced at him and saw
that he was teasing. She smiled. 'Come on, feel this bed.'
It was a water bed, a great moving pillow of H_2O covered
in royal-blue sheets, with a midnight-blue sky above it,

painted with silver stars. Jason sat on it and patted the space beside him. Cora walked across, sat gingerly on the edge and felt the whole thing move under her weight. 'My God!' she wailed. 'It's horrible.' She made to stand up but Jason caught her wrist.

'No, don't get up.'

She looked at her wrist, then at him, the smallest flutter of panic in the pit of her stomach. He smiled and the flutter vanished.

'Come on,' he said. 'It's really weird, have another go.'

Cora sat. Jason bounced and sent a ripple of water under her so that her body moved without her control. 'God, I see what you mean, it is weird, isn't it?' Cora then bounced herself, sending her own ripple of water. As she did so, something jangled in Jason's jacket pocket.

'What was that?' Cora put her hand into the pocket and felt around. She brought out a set of keys, looked at them, then at Jason. He grinned and shrugged.

'My flat keys,' he said. 'Oh dear.'

Cora was momentarily flummoxed. 'But I . . .'

Jason, who still had her wrist, pulled her towards him. 'How else was I going to get you back here? I had to do something.' He kissed her mouth. She felt the soft pressure of his lips, the motion of the water under her, then she pulled away.

'I don't think . . .'

Jason turned her wrist up and kissed the pale smooth skin on the inside. He slipped the jacket off her shoulders. 'Come on, Corinne,' he whispered. 'You didn't just come in for coffee, did you?'

Cora tensed. She gently pulled her wrist free and stood

up. 'Look, sorry, I think you misunderstood me, I did just come for coffee and I'd better go now.' Her voice was calm, it gave away nothing of the sudden panic she felt inside. She went to move off and Jason caught her round the waist with his arm.

'Not so fast, Corinne baby!' He was smiling, as if this was all some kind of big joke. 'There's no need to be such a cock-tease. I'm ready for you, Corinne, you don't need to do all this to get me going.' He pulled her in hard against him so that she was trapped between his legs, her breasts level with his face. He licked the skin on her chest and she flinched.

'Look!' she cried, 'I don't want you to do this! I—'

In a split second Jason had cupped his hand over her mouth. 'Of course you do,' he said, his voice breathless. The sudden violence of it all inflamed him. 'You've been gagging for it all night, haven't you?'

Cora stayed perfectly still, her whole body rigid with fear. She shook her head.

'Yes you have, taking your clothes off for me; this slip of a thing only just covering your tits!' He let go of her mouth and tugged at the strap of her dress, pulling it down. Cora gasped.

'God, you're beautiful, you . . .' He pressed his face into her breasts, kissing and biting the flesh while he fumbled across her back for the catch on her bra. 'You want me, I know you do . . .' His legs relaxed open as he eased her in to his body to press against his groin. 'God, I know you want it, I . . .'

It took only seconds. Cora shoved him back with all her might and lunged away towards the door. Her ankle twisted on her heels, but she was there in four paces.

She grabbed the handle, yanked it down and pulled at the door. 'Oh God,' she cried. 'Oh God, please . . .' It wouldn't open, it wouldn't budge. Shaking and crying, she pulled and tugged, kicked it, then looked down for a key, a catch, anything that would open it. She saw a brass knob, fumbled hopelessly for a few seconds, then finally managed to turn it. She heard a click. But as she tore open the door, Jason grabbed her hair from behind and yanked her back. She fell against the doorframe, cracked the side of her face and started to cry.

'You stupid bitch!' he shouted. 'You could have broken my fucking door!' He was standing above her, bigger, much bigger than she'd thought, and he smacked her across the mouth, the side of his ring catching her nose.

'You like to play rough do you, you little tart! Like a bit of rough and tumble! Eh?' He knelt over her, pinning her arms down with one hand, the strength of him overpowering her. With his other hand he undid his flies, shoved her legs apart and ripped at her pants. They tore and the violence of it bruised her thighs and groin. Cora struggled. She wrestled to try and free herself, tossing from side to side, trying to kick out with her legs but it aroused him even more. Kneeing her in the stomach to quieten her he moved down her body and jarred her legs apart. He didn't say a word but his breathing was laboured, heavy and he was sweating, it ran down the side of his face. Cora closed her eyes. She clenched her jaw and teeth tight together and braced herself.

Nothing prepared her for the pain.

She screamed, a piercing, animal scream and then she began to sob.

* * *

When it was over, Jason rolled off her. He lay on his stomach with his face turned away and Cora curled up into the foetal position. She had stopped sobbing but she was shaking so violently that she couldn't move. After several minutes, she managed to get on to all fours and, leaving a trail of blood on the carpet, she crawled out of the room.

She didn't know how long she was on the stairs, she lost all sense of time and reality. It might have been minutes, it might have been hours. When finally she was able to move, she pulled the strap of her dress up over her shoulder and stumbled down and out to her car. She wasn't sure if she was crying or not, her face was wet but she wasn't conscious of anything. She started the engine, put the car into gear and drove away. As she did so the lights in the house went out.

Chapter Sixteen

Thea woke with a start. There was the sound of banging and Tom was by the side of the bed saying, 'Mummy! Mummy, wake up! There's someone downstairs, at the front door.'

She rolled on to her side and looked at her watch. It was five a.m. Dropping her legs down on to the floor, she sat up, shook her head to clear it and pulled on a T-shirt. She stood. Muzzy with sleep, she said, 'It's all right darling, go back to bed, I . . .' Whoever it was was banging hard on the door, rattling the letter-box. 'I'll get it.' Thea walked across to the window and lifted the blinds. Cora's car was outside, slewed up on the grass in front of the cottage. The gate to the drive had been left open. Thea grabbed her dressing gown and hurried downstairs. 'All right, Cora,' she called, 'I'm coming! Hang on!' She decoded the alarm and went straight to the front door. Her unease mounted when Cora didn't call out. Releasing the Chubb locks, she unlatched the chain and opened it.

'Oh my God!' Cora stood, her arms wrapped tight around her body, shaking violently, her dress ripped, her nose and face bloody and swollen. 'Christ, Cora! Not Ewert?' Thea held her arm and pulled her into the house. 'Cora, what's happened, Cora . . .'

'It was all my fault,' Cora whispered. 'I asked for it, he said I asked for it, it was all my fault. Oh God, Thea, it was—' She broke off and started to cry.

Thea put her arms around her. 'It's all right, Cora,' she murmured. 'It's all right.'

'Mum?' Tom was at the top of the stairs.

Thea looked up. 'Tom darling, go back to bed, it's all right. Aunty Cora isn't feeling very well so Mummy's going to look after her.'

'Aunty Cora? Are you all right?'

'Tom,' Thea said, her voice rising, 'go back to bed, OK? Be a good boy for me, would you? Just get back into bed and I'll come up and see you in a few minutes.' She glanced up at him, Cora's body shivering in her arms. 'All right, Tom?' The tone of her voice changed from request to order. Tom nodded, sulked for a few moments, then did as she asked.

Thea held Cora for as long as it took to stop her shaking. She kept one eye on the stairs and prayed that Tom would do as she said. Whatever had happened, she didn't want him to witness this. When Cora was still, she pulled away gently and looked at her. 'You need to see a doctor,' she said. 'That nose is very swollen. Come on, come and sit by the Aga, you're cold, your hands are like ice.'

Cora let Thea lead her into the kitchen. She sat, wincing at the pain. Thea knelt in front of her. 'Cora,' she said softly. 'Tell me what happened – can you?'

Cora's face was blank. Her hands started to shake again and with uncontrollable fingers she lifted her dress. Thea saw the blood and the bruising and closed her eyes. 'Oh God,' she murmured. 'Who was it, Cora?' she asked gently. 'Was it Ewert?'

Cora shook her head but she couldn't speak. She had started to cry again and Thea thought: She's been raped, she's been raped. A knot of fear and panic and grief exploded in the pit of her stomach and for a moment she thought she was going to be sick. She stood up. 'Cora, I'm going to phone Jake, I need him here to look after Tom and then I'm going to phone the police. OK? Do you want to come with me or stay here?'

Cora shook her head. 'Here,' she said, 'I'll stay here.'

Thea nodded. 'I won't be long.'

'Not the police,' Cora said, as Thea began to walk away. 'Not the police, it was my fault, I shouldn't have gone there, I shouldn't have gone in for coffee.' She looked at Thea. 'He held my hand, I went up to his bedroom, I shouldn't have done that, I . . .'

Thea came back and knelt down again. 'Cora,' she said, 'you've got to tell me what happened. I'll write it down. You've got to tell me the whole thing. OK?' Thea took her hands. 'You must tell me, Cora, I have to know.'

Cora nodded.

'Who did this?'

'Jason. He was at the club tonight.'

Oh Christ, Thea thought, a punter. 'How did it happen? Did you go home with him?' Thea was speaking slowly, as if Cora were an idiot. She felt suddenly embarrassed. 'Please, Cora,' she said. 'Please tell me what happened.'

'I drove him home,' Cora said. She looked at Thea, but didn't really see her, there was no expression on her face.

'He lives in Horsham, he was kind, he helped me with Debbie and I couldn't just leave him there. So I gave him a lift. He liked me, he said he did, he wanted my number and I went in, for coffee and to see the house.' She blinked rapidly, then shook her head. 'It was in his bedroom, he wanted to show me the water bed and his keys were in his jacket, all the time they were there.'

Thea squeezed her hands. Cora was confused, this wasn't making any sense and she felt helpless, out of her depth. 'Cora, I've got to ring someone,' she said. 'I'll be back in a moment.'

Thea stood and left the kitchen. In the hall she stopped, leant against the wall and pressed her hands to her head. She felt sick. She stayed like that for several minutes, unable to move, until she heard Tom say, 'Are you all right, Mum?' Then she stood straight, looking up.

'Yes, Tom, I'm fine, just a bit tired,' she said. 'Now come on, into bed and try and get some sleep.' She climbed the stairs and followed him into his room. As he got into bed, she tucked the duvet round him and bent to kiss his head. God, there was such evil in the world, however would he survive? she thought. Tom put his arms around her neck and hugged her. Thea closed her eyes. However would Cora survive?

''Night, Mummy,' Tom said, releasing her. 'Love you.'

Thea stood. ''Night, Tom darling. I love you too.'

Downstairs in the hall, she called Jake. She spoke quietly into the phone and he agreed to come at once. He said he'd bring Marian and Thea was glad; Marian had experienced this before with the women's refuge. He told her to ring the police right away and to ask them to come to the house. 'They are trained,' he told her. 'They'll know what to do.'

Thea rang 999.

She spoke to an operator and gave a few details, along with her number. The operator said someone would ring her back. Then she returned to Cora.

'Are you OK?'

Cora had pulled a coat around her. She nodded. The phone rang. Thea went to answer it and again she spoke quietly. It was as if, she thought, someone had died. Minutes later, she went back to Cora. 'I phoned the police,' she said. 'I had to, Cora, we have to get this straight.'

Cora didn't react.

'They're sending someone over. They said not to wash or drink anything, OK?'

Cora looked up.

'I'm sorry, it's awful but they need forensic evidence.' Thea came and sat down on the floor in front of Cora. 'I gave our work names,' she said.

'Because it's a punter, isn't it?'

Thea didn't answer.

'Because it's connected to the job, isn't it?'

Thea nodded. She saw a look of such revulsion pass across Cora's face that she immediately reached forward to take her hands, to comfort her, but Cora stood up and backed away.

'It's because of that filthy, lousy, disgusting job!' she cried. 'Because if I hadn't taken my clothes off, if I hadn't teased him then it would never have happened. I'm low life, that's what I am, we both are, low life, so low that we can't even use our real names!' Thea stayed silent and Cora's anger drained away. 'We are, aren't we?' Cora whispered. 'It's my fault! It's all my fault!' She started to sob.

Thea jumped up and held her. 'It's not your fault,' she said. 'Please, Cora, believe me, it is not your fault.'

Jake arrived first. It was six-thirty and almost time to get Tom up and organised for school. Marian sat with Cora in the bedroom while Thea got things ready for him downstairs. She packed his school bag, wrote in his homework book and left his clothes out for Jake. Upstairs, Cora was silent and withdrawn. Marian chatted, trying to buoy her up enough to give a statement to the police but she was in shock, confused and numb.

The police arrived at seven in a plain dark blue car. There were two of them, one a WPC, who asked if Cora would prefer to deal only with female officers. She said no, but she didn't seem to take the question in so Thea said, 'I think she might prefer to be examined by a woman. Is that possible?'

'Yes, of course.' The WPC got on the radio and made the request. Afterwards she explained about the house. 'It's more comfortable for interviews,' she said. 'It's in Crawley but it's not connected to the station. We'd rather take you there if that's OK?'

Cora nodded. 'Can Thea come with me?'

'Of course.' The WPC took Thea aside. 'Can we take a statement from you first? Before we leave?'

'Yes, but—' Thea broke off. 'Look,' she said, 'I'm sorry but I don't remember that much and she didn't really make sense. I think she was too shocked to be able to tell me.'

'That's normal. If you could just tell me what you remember, that'll be fine.'

Thea gave her statement. At seven-thirty, just before Tom woke up, she took a small bag and packed a few clean clothes for Cora, some wash things and a towel. She wrapped a blanket round Cora's shoulders and together they were helped into the unmarked police car. In a tense, private silence, they were driven up to Crawley to be interviewed.

The safe house was a small nondescript detached house on the end of a cul-de-sac in suburban Crawley. It was already occupied by the detective and medical officer by the time Thea and Cora arrived. They were shown in, there was a brief exchange and they were told that the medical examination had to take place first, before anything else.

'Is that all right?' the WPC asked.

Cora nodded but she had started to shake again. She was taken upstairs into the medical room at the back, a bland and sterile room, painted pale grey. Cora thought the sterility comforting, it felt anonymous. The WPC came into the room as well as a Scenes-of-Crime Officer and Cora was gently asked to go to the couch behind the screen and take off her clothes while the medical officer got things ready. She did so, put on the white gown that was there for her and lay down, then she looked down at the bruises on her thighs, curled herself into the foetal position and started to cry like a child.

When the examination was over, Thea came to sit with her. Cora was so cold and numb that she couldn't dress, could hardly even move, so Thea had to help her, pulling the clean clothes over her head and slipping her feet into the shoes. The examination had been humiliating, invasive and painful and Cora's face was swollen from crying.

'Can I clean my teeth?' she whispered. 'My mouth tastes of blood and sick.' Thea wrapped the blanket round her again as the medical officer came across.

'She wants to clean her teeth, is that OK?'

The woman nodded. 'We've got some toothbrushes and toothpaste there, in the box. Help yourself.' She glanced at Thea. 'She could do with a sedative. Do you know if she's allergic to anything?'

'No, no I don't think so.'

'OK. Corinne? I'm going to give you a couple of pills here, I'd like you to take them after you've given your statement to the officers downstairs. Is that OK?'

Cora nodded.

'There's nothing you're allergic to, is there?'

'No.'

'Good.' The doctor gave Thea a small brown bottle. 'There's six Temazepam in there, she can have one every six hours. Can you get her to her GP tomorrow?'

'Yes, of course.'

'Good.'

Thea left Cora to brush her teeth. When she had finished, she was given a coffee and taken downstairs. Thea was waiting for her.

'You all right now?' Thea hugged her briefly. Cora nodded. 'We have to go and sit down in there. They want you to give a statement, nothing too serious, just a brief one and then we can go home and rest. Is that OK? D'you think that you can manage that?'

'Yes.'

Thea led the way into the front room of the house where the two waiting officers stood up. There were three armchairs and a sofa in there, floral curtains at the window and a coffee table with a large ashtray in the middle of it.

'Hello, Corinne,' the taller of the two men said. 'Come and sit down.'

Cora frowned. 'That's my work name,' she said. 'My real name is Cora.'

'Right. Cora, then, come and sit down please, anywhere you like.'

She chose the armchair, on her own, and sat down.

'Dorothy?'

Thea hesitated but if Cora wanted to be honest, she had to be too. 'It's Thea actually,' she said, 'Thea Marshall. Dorothy Marsh is my stage name. I use it for business as well.'

'Right. OK, no problem. Thea, come on in and sit down as well, if you wouldn't mind.'

Thea did so, on one of the other armchairs. 'I'm Detective Sergeant David Lawrence,' the officer said, 'and this is my colleague, Detective Constable Louis Judd.' The DC nodded. 'We'll be heading up this investigation and you'll deal directly with us, OK? If you have any worries, anything at all, you come to either one of us and we'll handle it.' The DS took a packet of cigarettes out of his pocket, offered them around and Cora took one; she hadn't smoked for over five years.

'Now, Cora, what I'd suggest is that you make a brief statement now regarding the assault and then you go home with your friend here and get some rest. The sort of details we need from you in a proper statement can take hours to do and as it's nine-thirty now and I gather that you've been up all night, I think we'd be better to do it either later today or tomorrow. Does that sound reasonable to you?'

Cora nodded.

'Good. It's very easy, all you need to do is give your name and say that you are reporting the attack, who it was by – if you know the name of the attacker – and where it took place. Is that all right?'

Again Cora nodded. She smoked her cigarette but said nothing and Thea wondered if she was going to be able to do it. Neither of the police officers seemed in any hurry, they just sat and waited. When Cora had finished smoking, she took a slug of coffee and held the cup in her hands. 'Can I use my work name?'

'Why is that, Cora?' Lawrence asked.

'I'd just feel safer, that's all.'

Lawrence hesitated, then said, 'OK, I think that'll be all right.'

Cora knotted her hands together in her lap and began. 'I am Corinne White,' she said, her voice only just audible. 'I am reporting that I have been attacked and—' She broke off and there was a long painful silence. 'Attacked and sexually assaulted . . .' Her voice went down to a whisper and Thea's heart ached. '. . . by Jason Wakes, at his home in Horsham, at three o'clock this morning.' She looked up. 'What's the date, I don't even know the date?'

'May the fourteenth,' the DS said.

'On May the fourteenth.' Cora stopped. She put her head in her hands and stayed like that for some time.

'Is that all?' Thea asked. 'She's exhausted, she needs to go home.'

'Yup, that's all we need. Cora? If you could just add that you're tired and you need to rest and that you'll give a full statement later. Could you do that for me, Cora?'

Cora dropped her hands away. She held her head up and stared straight ahead. 'I am very tired now,' she murmured, 'and I would like to rest. I will make a full statement later.'

'Thank you, Cora, that's fine.' The DS stood up. 'If you stay here, then I'll organise the car to take you back to your friend's house. OK?'

'Yes.'

'D'you want more coffee?'

'No, thanks.'

'Right. Well done, Cora.' The DS left the room and Cora turned her gaze from the window to Thea. She looked so lost and helpless that Thea moved across to her and knelt down to hug her.

Outside in the hall, the DS waited for his DC to come out and said, 'Jason Wakes, Horsham. Get on to the duty sergeant, get the address and then put in for a warrant for preservation of evidence. I want it ASAP.'

The DC nodded.

'And when you've done that, let's go and nobble the little bastard!'

Chapter Seventeen

DS Dave Lawrence stood with Dr Lucy Cairns in the hall of the house after Cora had left. 'Three a.m., she put in her statement,' he said. 'Does that sound about right to you?'

'Yes, judging from the bruising, I'd say round about that time.'

'But the friend says she didn't arrive at her place until five a.m. and it's only thirty minutes from Horsham. She's pretty sure about it too. I wonder where the hell she was in the two hours between three and five?'

'Well' – Dr Cairns picked her bag up – 'if she went anywhere else, we'll know from her clothes. Perhaps she didn't have much conception of time, she was pretty shocked, certainly very distressed. It was a fairly violent attack.'

Dave Lawrence lit a cigarette – his fifth that hour – and inhaled deeply. The stress of a violent sexual assault case was intense. 'When can we have the report?'

Cairns glanced at her watch. 'About five tomorrow afternoon.'

'No quicker?'

'No, Dave, no quicker, not even with all your charm!' She

smiled at him and opened the door. 'See you tomorrow. Call me later if you like and I'll tell you what I've got so far.'

'Right, thanks, Dr Cairns.' He turned as DC Judd came back into the house.

'Got the address, boss,' Judd said. 'Warrant request's in place and the car that brought the victim in has been registered.'

'Good.' Lawrence picked up his jacket. 'Where does this Mr Wakes live, then?'

Judd held out the bit of paper and Lawrence looked at it. 'Oh, I see,' he said. 'Very nice. Nob Hill.' He opened the front door, dropped his cigarette down on the grass outside and left it smoking. 'Right, Louis, let's get over there then, shall we?' And opening his car door he threw his jacket carelessly in the back and climbed in.

Jason Wakes answered the door in his dressing gown. It was ten a.m. on Sunday morning, he was unshaven and groggy with sleep.

'Yes?'

Judd and Lawrence were both in plain clothes but as Judd moved forward with his badge, a patrol car pulled up and three uniformed officers jumped out.

'What the hell—?'

'Jason Wakes?'

'Yes, that's right. What the hell is going on?'

'Jason Wakes, I am arresting you on suspicion of rape. You do not have to say anything . . .'

While Wakes was cautioned, DS Lawrence walked on into the house. He could smell burnt coffee, a deeply acrid smell, and crossed the hall trying two doors before he found the kitchen. It was immaculate, only the smell lingered. In the sink he found an Italian espresso coffee pot charred and burnt. Nothing else, no cups, no sign that anyone had been there.

He returned to the hall. Wakes was sitting in a chair in the hall, his head in his hands. 'I don't believe this is happening,' he said. 'I just don't believe it.'

'What clothes were you wearing last night?' Judd asked as Lawrence came over to him. 'Suit? Casual? Come on, Mr Wakes, we'd like to know what you were wearing.'

'I can't remember!'

'No? But it wasn't all that long ago that you got undressed, was it?'

'Boss?' One of the uniformed officers had been through the kitchen to the laundry room. 'Boss, the washing machine's been on, there's a load in there, it's still on spin.'

'I thought you'd just woken up, Mr Wakes. It isn't last night's shirt and underwear in the machine by any chance?'

'Very probably! I only get home once or twice a week, I'm doing my weekly wash, like most normal people do on a Sunday!'

'Bag all dirty clothing you can find, OK? And the sheets on the bed.'

'You can't do that!'

'Yes, I can,' Lawrence said. 'I'm well within my rights, Mr Wakes.' He looked at Judd. 'Take him upstairs to get some clothes on him and then let's go.'

'I'm not going anywhere!' Wakes cried. 'I want to ring my solicitor! This is about that silly bitch Corinne, isn't it? This is about her!'

Lawrence turned away.

'I didn't do anything! She wanted to have sex, she begged me for it. Likes it rough too, likes a bit of—'

'I'd suggest that you keep quiet until your brief arrives, Mr Wakes!' Lawrence snapped. 'You have been cautioned, all right?!' Wakes shut up and Lawrence walked out of the house to wait for him to dress.

Wakes asked to make his phone call before he left his home but he didn't phone his solicitor, he called his father. Michael Wakes, at his country house, with his new wife still in bed, went immediately down to his study and called the head of the law firm he had been using for years.

'I want the best criminal man you've got down in Crawley this morning and I want you to start sorting through defence barristers,' he said. 'I don't care how much I have to pay, I want the top guy. Jason's been stitched up and he's got a hell of a lot more to lose than some two-bit stripper!'

There was a reply of sorts but Michael Wakes didn't listen to it. He was an overbearing, arrogant man and he rarely listened to anyone. 'I want a full report from your man as soon as he's spoken to Jason, all right? He can get me at this number all morning.' Michael Wakes read out his number, switched on his pager and, without even saying goodbye, hung up.

His new wife stood in the doorway in a long black silk nightdress. She was just thirty, thirty-three years younger than Wakes almost to a day, and, as wife number three, she had little to offer in the way of companionship. It was straightforward ego massage and sex.

'Go away,' he said, 'I'm busy.'

Knowing when not to offer herself was one of her skills as much as coaxing an erection was another. She yawned, shrugged and left Michael Wakes alone.

Daniel Ellis left Petula in charge of the boys for half an hour on Sunday morning, something he rarely did, and went out to get his paper and some freshly baked bread from the farm shop. He also bought home-made marmalade, fresh coffee and strawberries. Putting his booty in the car, he drove the four miles to Tanbry Cottage where Thea lived, pulled up outside the house and, with carrier bag in hand, knocked on her glossy dark green front door. There was no answer.

He called out and, going round the back, saw Thea, in shorts, T-shirt and welly boots, watering her vegetables. She looked wonderful, natural and sexy, despite the wellies, and even better than she had last night. He stood there for a moment unseen and smiled. Christ, sometimes things just worked out and he had a feeling that this was going to be one of them. He glanced at Tom, who was sitting at the table on the terrace under an umbrella eating an ice-cream and he thought: It's about time too, it's about time something worked out for me. He walked forward into view. 'Hello?'

Thea spun round. 'Oh my goodness! Daniel! You gave me a fright!'

She looked tired, pale and drawn, and although he wasn't an expert, he'd have sworn she'd been crying.

'Yes, Daniel, remember me from last night?' Thea flushed and his reaction was so physical that he found himself standing there in shorts and a T-shirt having to cover his erection with the carrier bag. 'I brought breakfast,' he said.

'Oh, oh thanks, but—' Thea broke off and brushed her hair off her face with her wrist. 'Look, hang on, I . . .' Again her words tailed off. She walked across to the garden tap, turned off the hose and dropped it down on the floor. 'Tom, this is Daniel Ellis, he's got—'

'Yes, I know, Wills and Charlie. I know Charlie.'

'Oh right.' Thea and Daniel exchanged smiles and Thea felt an exquisite pain, immediately tempered by sadness. This wasn't going to work; it just couldn't work, not now.

'Look, Daniel, come for a walk round the garden with me,' she said.

'So you're going to lead me up the garden path, right?' Thea smiled again, but it was a weary smile, there wasn't much humour in it.

'All right, so my jokes are appalling, I know, but—'

Thea turned and looked at him. She decided to be frank, or at least as frank as she could be. She took a breath. 'Listen, thanks for breakfast, Daniel,' she said, 'but the thing is that you can't stay. I'm sorry, but I've got a friend here and it's awkward, you being here too, it might . . .' Oh God, this was awful, this wasn't at all how it was meant to sound.

'I see.' Daniel looked away from Thea and stared into the distance. He had misunderstood.

'It isn't how it sounds,' she said in a desperate attempt to make things clear. 'I mean, it's my partner . . .' That was the only word she could come up with, it made sense, Cora *was* her business partner. 'Look, it's—' She stopped. What more could she say, without telling him the whole truth?

He was an intelligent, honest man, how could she tell him the truth about Cora, about herself and still expect him to stick around? She couldn't, and he was too nice, far too nice to lie to. 'It's a bit embarrassing,' she finished lamely. 'I'm sorry.'

'Yes, quite,' Daniel said. Partner. The word held a whole stack of meanings for Daniel that Thea hadn't anticipated. He held out the carrier bag. 'Well, you ought to have these. Pet will have got the boys' breakfast and I'm not very hungry any more.'

Thea took it and swallowed down the most powerful urge to cry. 'Thanks, it's really kind of you, I—'

Daniel held up his hand to silence her. 'Don't, it's nothing, really.' And turning heel, he just caught sight of Jake inside the house, dug his hands into his pockets and walked away.

Minutes later, he was gone.

'I don't believe this is happening to me,' Jason Wakes said. He looked at his solicitor. 'I have just been subjected to an hour of the most painful and disgusting fucking tests known to mankind and you can't do a fucking thing about it, is that what you're telling me?' He paced the interview room, too irate to sit down. 'This is appalling! I tell you, when I get out of this fucking place I'm going to sue the West Sussex fucking Constabulary for every penny they've got!' He stopped. 'How much longer are they going to keep me waiting?'

His solicitor said, 'As long as they want to, I'm afraid. They've charged you and until we're up in front of the magistrates for bail you're detained here.' The solicitor,

Peter Killen, stood up. 'I'll go out again and ask about the delay but the best thing you can do is sit tight and keep your cool.'

'Keep my fucking cool?' Jason exploded. 'You've got to be joking, haven't you? Some lousy stripper, a right tart stitches me up, gets me locked away for having sex at her request and I'm supposed to keep my cool?' He smacked his fist against the wall and there was a sharp crack. Killen winced. 'Fuck!' he shouted.

Killen said nothing but he did stand up and leave the room. A bit of time out would do them both good.

Approaching the desk, he said, 'I'd like to know when my client is going to be interviewed. Have you any idea?'

The duty sergeant shrugged. 'No, not yet, I'm afraid. I'll let you know as soon as I have.'

Killen nodded. 'Where's DS Lawrence? Can I have a word with him?'

'Not at present, he's in interview, but I'll pass on the message.'

'Thanks.' And taking a seat in the corridor, Peter Killen sat outside for half an hour to give his client time to calm down.

At ten-thirty that night, Jason Wakes was brought up from the cell to be interviewed. Outside the interview room, DS Lawrence and DC Judd briefed his solicitor. They had wanted to get Cora's statement on record, she had come back to the house that afternoon and it had taken four hours, but it was done. They now felt happy to interview the suspect.

'We've charged him with statutory rape,' Lawrence said,

'and that's what we're going for. The victim alleges a violent sexual assault at three a.m., she has bruising on her face and thighs, as well as bruising and tearing internally. We've got her statement, we've got forensic to prove that it was your client and we'd now like to interview him.'

'Fine. I'll have a word with him first then.' Killen went into the interview room to talk to Wakes and emerged ten minutes later. 'My client is ready to co-operate fully with the police on this matter,' he said. DS Lawrence sighed. It was going to be a long night.

'OK, Jason, let's go over that again, shall we? You asked Corinne to come into the house for sex. You made that quite clear to her, did you?' They had been interviewing for two hours. Wakes admitted sex but with full consent.

'Absolutely. She said something like, I'm ready for it. Yes, I think it was that, I'm ready for it.'

'So you took her inside and straight upstairs?'

Wakes looked at his solicitor. 'Yes.'

'You didn't go into the kitchen for coffee? Or a drink at all?' Again Wakes looked at his solicitor.

Killen said, 'Could we suspend this interview for a few moments? I think my client would like a word with me in private.'

Lawrence nodded. 'Interview with Jason Wakes suspended at . . .' He glanced at his watch. '. . . one a.m., on Monday May the fifteenth.' Lawrence switched the tape off and stood up. 'Five minutes,' he said. 'All right?'

Killen nodded and Lawrence and Judd left the room.

'What the fuck is going on?' Wakes said. 'That's the third time they've asked me about coffee!'

'I would think that they have something about coffee in the victim's statement.'

Wakes was silent. He stood up and paced the room for a couple of minutes, then he said, 'I did make coffee, now I come to think about it, but we never drank it, we got too carried away and forgot about it. I offered her a cup at the end but she didn't want any. She just wanted to get home.'

Killen made a note on his pad. He said nothing, but privately he was bloody irritated. This was the third time Wakes had changed his story. 'Is there anything else you might have forgotten?' he asked.

Wakes shrugged. 'No, not that I can think of.'

'Right, I'll ask DS Lawrence to come back in then, shall I?'

'Yes.'

Wakes sat down again and a minute or so later the interview recommenced.

'My client would like to add something about the coffee,' Killen said. 'Jason?'

'I did make coffee,' Wakes said. 'Or rather I started to make coffee but we got carried away kissing in the kitchen and went straight upstairs, and I forgot about the coffee. I think I asked her if she wanted a cup when we'd finished but she didn't want one, she wanted to get home.'

'What? You asked her if she'd like a coffee after hitting her about the face? You asked her if she wanted coffee, even though she was bleeding like a pig all over your carpet?' Lawrence shook his head. 'How very polite!' He leant forward. 'Come on, Jason, wasn't it that you put coffee on to brew and then took her on a tour of the house? Wasn't it that while in your bedroom, you initiated sex and she didn't want it, so you gave her a thump, you hit her about the face, threw her against the door and then violently raped her? Isn't that it?' Lawrence raised his voice.

'Isn't it?'

Wakes shook his head. He sat silent, his head down and shook it.

'For the benefit of the tape, the suspect is shaking his head.' There was a silence.

'It's exactly as I've told you,' Wakes said.

'Exactly as you've told us?' Lawrence snapped. 'Is that why you keep changing your story? No, you didn't make coffee; yes, you did! Come on, make your mind up!' He stopped and reached for his cigarettes. Lighting up, he pulled the ashtray towards him and said, 'You hit Corinne with your left hand, didn't you?'

'No, she fell.' Wakes repositioned himself in his chair. 'I told you, she liked it rough. We tussled and she fell. She hit her face on the door, she was bleeding and I wanted to stop but she didn't. She said the taste of blood turned her on.'

'Jason, she was crying. You hit her across the face and caught her nose with your ring, your signet ring.'

'I don't have a signet ring.'

'You hit her on the face when she tried to get away and you caught her with your ring.'

'I do not have a ring,' Wakes snapped. 'Look! See? No ring!'

'For the benefit of the tape the suspect is holding up his left hand. There is no ring on it.' Lawrence sighed. 'OK, let's imagine that it is exactly as you said. You offer coffee, get carried away in the kitchen and go straight upstairs to the bedroom. You both want sex, so why the violence? The bruises, the ripped dress?'

Wakes shrugged. 'Some people like it like that. It's not my preference, but she was hot for it so I went along with it.'

'She was hot for it, was she?' Lawrence shook his head. 'Really?'

'She's a bloody stripper, for fuck's sake!' Wakes suddenly cried. 'What sort of woman takes her clothes off in front of a rabble of drunken men, eh? She's a fucking tart, she'd do anything for it, she—' He stopped as Killen lay a hand on his arm. He was quiet for a few moments, then he said, 'Corinne White wanted to have sex with me and she wanted it rough. I did not rape her, I did not do anything she did not want me to do. I am completely innocent of this charge.'

Lawrence looked at DC Judd and reached for the tape machine. 'This interview is terminated at one fifteen a.m., Monday the fifteenth of May. Those present were myself, Detective Sergeant Lawrence, Detective Constable Judd, Police Constable Bryan, the suspect, Jason Wakes, and his solicitor.' He switched off the machine and stood up. Without another word, he walked out of the room.

Daniel was up early; the truth was he hadn't been able to sleep. For the first time in months he had dreamed his dream, his nightmare really, about Charlotte and the car crash. He never witnessed her death, never saw the car afterwards, but in his dream he saw her again and again, trapped in the car, calling out to him and he was powerless to help her. He kept trying to run but couldn't move, he was rooted to the ground, screaming and panic-stricken as the car burned. Then he woke up and, as he always did, he found that he had been crying.

'You're up early,' Petula said, coming down in her dressing gown and finding Daniel already dressed and eating breakfast. 'Have you had tea?'

'Thanks, yes I have, Pet.' He looked up from the paper. 'I'm going into work early this morning and I think I'll drive up, OK? You can use the runabout for school. I won't be in for supper either, I'm afraid, I need to catch up on a few things.'

Petula nodded. She stared at him for a moment and knew that he hadn't slept. When he didn't sleep, he overworked, trying to blot things out, she supposed, and he ended up exhausted. 'I'll do a chilli and you can heat it up when you come in,' she said. 'You must eat.'

He smiled. 'Thanks, although they won't thank you in Chambers tomorrow!'

Petula laughed and turned away to put the kettle on for tea.

Daniel was just checking his briefcase when the phone rang. He answered it from his study and sat down at his desk when he heard who it was.

'John,' he said. 'Nice to hear from you. To what do I owe this pleasure?' John Edwards was an old friend, head of a legal firm and a very good contact.

'I've got something for you, Daniel, it's important, likely to be quite high profile, I should think, and I want you to do it. You're right for it, or rather it's right for you.'

'Really? Is that why you've come direct to me and not gone through Chambers?'

'I don't want to be fobbed off with someone else, thank you, as brilliant as they are, of course . . .'

Daniel laughed. 'OK, what is it, John?'

'Defence. It's a rape case but it's a question of consent. My client is innocent, he says the girl initiated sex, she accuses him of rape.'

'That sounds pretty straightforward. Why me?'

'Because my client has asked me to find the best criminal barrister available, that's why.'

'Who's the client?'

'The defendant is Jason Wakes, but the client is his father, Michael Wakes.'

'The Chairman of Hind Industrial?'

'That's the one.'

'Ah.' Daniel smiled.

'Yes, one of our biggest commercial clients. I can hear you smiling, Daniel.'

Daniel laughed. 'Send the brief over and I'll look at it. When did all this happen?'

'This weekend. Jason is up in front of the magistrates this morning, but his father wants things hurried along. He doesn't want a trial hanging over his son's career and what Michael Wakes wants he usually gets.'

'I'm sure.' Daniel glanced at his watch and for some peculiar reason he thought: Thirty-five hours ago I was with Thea. 'John,' he said, 'Send it across this morning and I'll go over it as soon as I get in, OK? I must warn you, though, rape isn't usually my thing.'

'I realise that, but it's big money, Daniel.'

'Pays the school fees I suppose.'

John laughed. 'And the rest: universities, PHDs, law school, Prue Leith's cookery school, would you believe? Which is where my darling daughter is insistent she wants to go!'

Daniel laughed. 'I'll look at it, John, OK?'

'That's fine. Thank you, Daniel. I'll courier it and we'll speak later on today.'

'Right. Make it tonight though. I'm in court tomorrow and I've a lot on.'

'Tonight it is then.' Pleased with the result so far, John Edwards hung up. He immediately dialled his client and was on the phone to Michael Wakes before Daniel Ellis left for work.

Chapter Eighteen

Jason Wakes climbed into Killen's car outside the magistrates court and sat for a few moments, his head in his hands. Killen stared out of the window.

'Thank God that's over,' Wakes said. 'It had to be the worst ordeal of my life.'

Killen turned and looked at him. 'I'm afraid that it's far from over, Jason,' he said. 'We got bail by the skin of our teeth, literally. I had to do some serious talking to get you out and there are conditions, you heard them, they're not to be taken lightly. In my opinion—'

'You're my solicitor,' Wakes snapped, 'not my father! I don't want your opinion, I'm not paying for your opinion!'

Killen started the engine. 'I'll drive you home,' he said.

'No you won't, you'll drive me to see my barrister! I want to speak to him now, get some things sorted!'

'Your barrister hasn't been appointed yet,' Killen said.

'What d'you mean, hasn't been appointed yet? My father told me we'd got the best that money can buy!'

'We've asked someone and he's considering the case now.'

'Considering? Christ! I don't believe you lot! Considering? That's my fucking life he's considering!'

Killen shifted into first gear and indicated. He was tired, it had been a hell of a long twenty-four hours and if he hadn't been a senior partner in the firm, he'd have told this little bastard where to get off. 'That's the way it works, Jason,' he said, pulling out into a space in the traffic. 'Now why don't you sit back and—'

'Sit back?' Wakes laughed sardonically. 'Sit back and what? Think about how one night of crude sex could ruin my entire life? Sit back and remember the little tart that started all this? Christ!' He put his hands up to his face and for a moment Killen thought he was going to cry. There was a long silence and Killen was glad of it. He drove on. Then, dropping his hands away, Wakes stared straight ahead and said, 'I'm going to get that bitch.' Killen glanced sidelong at him. 'I'm going to make sure,' he said, 'that she regrets the day she ever decided to crap on me.'

It was mid afternoon that same Monday and DS Lawrence had called a meeting in the station canteen. It was a relaxed debriefing for the past twenty-four hours and all the team were present.

DC Judd carried a tray of teas and coffees across to the table and put it down, slopping some of it over the top of the cups.

'Sorry. Tea's on the right, coffee's on the left, milk and sugar there.' He took his own cup, handed one across to Lawrence and sat down.

'Right,' Lawrence said. 'So where were we? Wakes is out on bail, having put up forty grand for the privilege. His solicitor, Peter Killen, is a senior partner in one of London's top law firms, Winter and May, and a specialist in criminal law. They are presently trying to hire a top barrister and we're down to sex with consent.' He took a sip of his coffee, black no sugar, and lit a cigarette. 'At the moment, there's only one thing we can be sure of, and that's that this is going to be one hell of a tough baby.' He inhaled deeply. 'Cath, what do we know for certain so far?'

Cath was a bright DC but this was her first rape case and she had taken it badly. She was anxious and tense about it. 'The assault took place at three a.m. Sunday morning,' she said. 'That's been confirmed by forensic. We know the assault was violent and sexual. We know that Corinne drove Wakes home, alone, in her car and that he had been at the Mayfair Gentleman's Club, watching her strip-tease act earlier that evening.'

'Right. What don't we know for certain?' Lawrence finished his coffee and stubbed out his cigarette. 'And what do we need to find out? OK, first, why did Corinne drive Wakes home? We've got her statement but were there any witnesses to any of their conversation? Who saw them leave? What did they say to each other? We need to get Debbie Pritchard in, what does she remember?' Cath was making notes as Lawrence spoke. 'We don't know for certain that it was Wakes's ring that hit Corinne, he says he doesn't have one, so we need to find it. Do any of his friends remember seeing him wear a ring? Photos of him with it on, anything you can find. We know that Corinne left the house at twenty past three, a neighbour saw her car leave but where did she go between three and five, when she turned up at her friend's house? Any sightings of the car?

Check twenty-four-hour garages on the way, Little Chefs, anything that was open in the area.' Even though he had just put a cigarette out, Lawrence lit another one. 'Obviously we have no witnesses to what actually went on in the house, it's his word against hers and we can't know for sure. So, we need to dig up what we can find on Wakes, his history, character, friends, hobbies, see if there's anything, anything at all that points to this sort of attack. And the same goes for Corinne. The defence will do everything they can to defame her character, so we need to build on what we know. She is a businesswoman, a quiet, private, single woman, with few friends. We need to collect as many character witnesses as we can: club owners, business associates, her partner, Thea Marshall, known to us by request as Dorothy Marsh, Phil Habben, anyone who knows her. OK? Cath, I'd like you to do that one, and Louis, if you could take on Wakes.'

Louis Judd nodded and made a note of it.

'I'm going to drive down to see Corinne at her friend's this afternoon and let her know what's happening. Is there anything else that anyone wants to add?'

Cath looked up. 'This time between three and five, what about her ex-boyfriend? She couldn't have visited him, could she?'

'Good point, Cath. I don't know, look into it, would you?'

'Yes.'

DS Lawrence put his cigarette in his mouth and stretched. 'Right, nothing else I take it?' There was a silence. 'OK, we'll have another briefing in my office, tomorrow morning, nine-thirty.' And picking up his cigarettes, he walked out of the canteen.

* * *

Cora sat in a deckchair in Thea's garden and watched Tom kick a football around. It was still warm, too warm for May, she thought, unnaturally warm, and she found the heat oppressive.

'Did you see that one, Aunty Cora?' Tom called.

She dipped her sunglasses to the end of her nose and said, 'Good shot!' even though she hadn't seen it.

Tom came over with his ball under his arm and sat on the grass at her feet. 'Phew! I'm steaming!'

Cora put her hand on his hair and smiled. 'What a funny expression,' she said. 'Who taught you that?'

'Henry Pearson.'

'Oh, Henry Pearson, eh? What a posh school you do go to, my darling Tom.' She ruffled his hair and the front door bell sounded.

'I'll go!' he chirped, jumping up with his ball under his arm. He disappeared inside the house and Cora was briefly uneasy on her own. Moments later, he re-emerged with a figure behind him. 'It's someone for you, Aunty Cora,' he said, but as Cora looked up she couldn't see who it was because their back was to the sun and a sudden knot of panic exploded in her stomach. She jumped up and DS Lawrence stepped forward. He saw her face.

'I'm sorry,' he said, keeping his distance. 'It's DS Lawrence, I didn't mean to scare you.' He took his ID badge out and held it up for her. Cora stood rigid, her heart hammering in her chest. 'Is your mother around?' Lawrence said to Tom.

'Yes, I'll go and get her. MUM!' He headed towards the house, shouting at the top of his voice. 'MUM! There's someone to see Aunty Cora! Can you come out? MUM!'

Cora remained standing. Her face had drained of colour and DS Lawrence wondered if she was going to faint. It was with relief that he saw Thea come out of the cottage and take Cora's arm.

'You all right?' she murmured. 'It's one of the police officers, he's . . .'

'I'm fine,' Cora said. She moved back to her deckchair.

Thea said, 'I'll put the kettle on for some tea. Would you like a cup, erm . . .'

'DS Lawrence, and yes, yes please, I'd love a cup.' He watched Thea go into the cottage through the French doors and recognised the grace and rhythm of a dancer in her movement. He found himself wondering about her act and had to mentally stop himself. It was unprofessional.

Walking across to the table, he pulled out a director's chair and sat down. Cora was staring at the end of the garden and he said, 'It's a lovely garden. What's at the bottom there?'

'A stream,' Cora said. 'Thea used to worry terribly about Tom when she first moved here, in case he fell in.'

'Yes, I can imagine.'

Thea appeared with a tray of tea things: brightly coloured mugs, a jug in the shape of a cow and a home-made cake.

'Wow,' Lawrence said. 'That looks good!'

Cora turned to him. 'Not quite what you expected from a couple of—' Thea glared at her and she stopped, seeing Tom over her shoulder. 'Thea's very talented. She went to university,' Cora said. 'Oxford.'

'Really?'

Thea flushed. 'I dropped out actually, I got pregnant

with this wonderful monster here!' She pulled Tom into a hug and he wriggled to be free. 'Poor old me!'

'Yes, poor old you!' Tom said. 'Can I have some cake?'

'Yes, after DS Lawrence.' Thea unloaded the plates. 'The kettle's boiling, I'll just make the tea,' and she disappeared inside.

'I need to talk to you,' Lawrence said to Cora. 'Privately.'

'I'd like Thea to be there,' Cora said. 'Is that OK?'

Lawrence glanced at Tom. 'Tom, how about if I ask Mummy to put a video on for you for an hour or so?' Cora suggested.

'What, before supper?'

'Yes, special treat.'

Tom threw his fist in the air. 'YES!'

When Thea came out with a large white teapot, Cora asked, 'Thea, can Tom watch a video while we talk to DS Lawrence?'

Thea nodded. 'Come on, monster, what's it going to be?'

'YES!' Tom crowed again in victory and they went inside. Again DS Lawrence found himself watching Thea. She was incredibly attractive. It wasn't really looks, there was just something physical about her, something inherently sexy.

Lawrence picked up the teapot and poured three mugs of tea. 'Cora, d'you have milk and sugar?'

'Just milk,' she said. He added some to her cup and passed it to her. 'What about Thea?'

'Both.'

He added both to Thea's cup and when she came out again he handed her the mug. 'Thanks,' she said. 'Cake?'

She cut it, passed it round and they all sat there for a few moments, drinking and eating, politely having tea. Cora thought it bizarre.

'Is it all right to talk?' Lawrence asked when he'd finished his cake.

Thea glanced over her shoulder. 'Yes.'

'Good. I've really only come to let you know what's been going on so far. And also to ask couple of questions. Is that all right?'

Cora nodded. She had folded her arms across her body, a defensive gesture, and Lawrence added, 'It won't take long, I promise.' She nodded again.

'Wakes is out on bail,' Lawrence said. 'That's the first thing I need to tell you.'

Cora sat forward. 'You're joking!' she exclaimed. 'After raping someone?'

'Yes, I'm afraid so. But, Cora, I'm afraid that it's also a bit more complicated than that. Wakes has admitted having sex with you and he's said that you consented.'

'What?' Her face was stricken. 'I consented? What the hell does that mean?'

Thea placed her hand on Cora's shoulder.

'It means that although we treat this as a violent sexual assault, the case that goes to court will be whether or not you consented to sex.'

'So it's his word against mine, is that it?' Her voice had taken on an hysterical edge. 'Is that what you're trying to tell me? That it's some big shot in the city against me, a stripper, someone who got what she deserved?' She let out a sob and bit the back of her hand.

'Has Cora got it right?' Thea asked. 'Can they do that?'

Lawrence nodded. 'But we've got a good case, as good as his, believe me! And we'll do everything we can to prove that this was a sexual assault, we're sure—'

'You can't be sure of anything,' Cora said.

Lawrence and Thea looked at her.

'You cannot be sure if it's going to rain tomorrow or not,' she said quietly. 'Or if the nice man you take home will turn out to be a violent rapist.' She stood up. 'There's nothing left that makes any sense any more.' And leaving her tea and cake unfinished, she walked inside.

Thea sat down. 'I don't know what to do with her,' she said. 'I don't know how to help.'

Lawrence took his cigarettes out of his pocket and, not thinking to ask, lit one up. 'We can offer counselling. D'you think she'd agree to that?'

'She might do. I honestly don't know at the moment.' Thea sipped her tea. She thought for a few seconds, then said, 'What were the questions? Can I help?'

'We're missing a couple of hours, between three-fifteen and around five, when Cora turned up here. Have you any idea where she might have gone? Has she mentioned it to you?'

'No.'

'What about the ex-boyfriend?'

'Ewert?' Thea put her cup down. 'She might have gone there, but I think she'd have remembered if she had. You'd probably want to ask him, I think. My guess is that she just drove around. She was very confused when she arrived, I don't think she knew what she was doing.'

'Well, we're checking that.' Lawrence drained his cup

and stubbed his cigarette out on the sole of his shoe. He put it in his pocket.

'You don't have to do that,' Thea said.

'What?'

'I could throw it away for you.'

He smiled and Thea thought how different he looked. Quite nice-looking, in fact. 'No, it's all right, it's a very old habit, hard to break.'

She smiled back. 'I'm sorry I can't help any more.'

'No. Think about the counselling, won't you? You can call me, you've got my number.' Thea nodded and Lawrence stood. 'Thanks for the tea.'

'That's OK.'

Smiling briefly at her, he left.

Daniel Ellis pulled into the drive of Willow House, switched his headlights off and sat for a few moments in the comforting silence of the country. It was late, the boys were in bed and Petula had switched most of the lights off in the house. He climbed out of the car, walked to the front door and put his key in the lock. The wistaria was in flower, a mass of pale lavender blooms that hung heavy and swollen with pollen, pulled towards the ground. Daniel stood looking at it, at the knotted branches, the feathery leaves and the ripe sensual flowers, then, completely on impulse, he took his key out of the lock, got back into the car and drove to Tanbry Cottage.

He knew Thea's bedroom was at the front and, risking making a fool of himself, he threw a handful of gravel up at the window, hearing it ping as it hit the glass. A minute or so later the blind went up, a lamp was switched on in the room and Thea came to the window. She looked down, saw Daniel and disappeared. He waited. The wait seemed to last for ever.

'Daniel?'

He turned. Thea had a silk thing on, a sort of dressing gown, he supposed, but it was thin and clingy and he had to swallow down a lump that rose in his throat. Was he here just for sex? Was he going insane, driven mad by lust for a younger woman? Oh God, he thought as she came nearer, I hope this isn't some kind of mid-life crisis, but then she smiled at him and said, 'This is ridiculously, insanely romantic!' and he knew that it was far more than that. She stepped a pace closer and he bent his head to kiss her.

'It is, isn't it?' He pulled back. 'Can we . . . ?'

'The car?'

'Yes, the car.'

Daniel opened the door for her and she climbed in the back. Her robe fell apart as she did so and her thighs were the colour of orange blossom honey.

'Are they real?' he asked, climbing in beside her and touching her leg.

She pinched her thigh. 'Ouch! Yes, I think so.'

He smiled. 'I'm sorry, I shouldn't be here, I know, but I can't get you out of my head and I, well, I just thought—'

Thea put her finger across his lips. 'I'm glad you're here.'

Daniel put his arm out and Thea moved into his embrace. 'We must look ridiculous,' he said, 'sitting here like this.'

'Who can see us?'

'No one.' He kissed the top of her head. 'God, I had a shitty day! I can't tell you how nice this is.' He kissed her again.

'Why so shitty?' She turned to look at him.

'I took a case that I don't really want to do, just for the money, and it bothers me. I don't like doing that, I think it's unethical.'

'Welcome to the real world,' Thea said. 'We all have to pay the bills.'

'You're very cynical for a young one.'

'Not that young,' she replied, turning her body further towards him. Her breasts pressed against his chest.

'Oh God, that's not fair.' He bent and kissed her mouth. 'That is definitely not fair,' he murmured as she snaked her fingers inside his shirt.

Thea sat up suddenly. 'OK, sorry. Let's just talk then.'

Daniel grinned. 'It wasn't that unfair!'

'No, really, come on, tell me about the case. Why don't you want to do it?'

'I'm not allowed to say that much, but it's not my thing. It's defence for a rape case and—'

Thea suddenly moved away. She moved from his embrace, folded her arms across her chest and stared out of the window.

'Hey? What did I say?' Daniel put his hand on her shoulder. 'Thea? What's up? Did I do something, say something?' She shrugged and he gently turned her to face him. 'Thea? What is it? You can't just turn away like that without any reason.'

She looked at him for a moment, then she said, 'Why would you defend a rapist?'

'Because that young man is innocent until proven guilty and he has a right to a defence.'

'Do you really believe he's innocent?'

'Yes! Of course I do! I wouldn't defend him if I didn't.'

'Not just for the money?'

Daniel sat up. 'No,' he said coolly, 'not just for the money. I have ethics and I'm an honest man, Thea. If you don't think that then you should get out of the car and walk away from me now.'

Thea continued to look at him. 'I'm sorry,' she said after a while. 'I didn't mean to offend you.'

'No, well . . .' She reached forward and kissed him. 'All right, apology accepted.' Taking her hand in his, he said, 'I'm sorry that it upsets you. It's a highly emotive subject, Thea, that's one of the reasons I don't want to do it. My junior is a young woman, Sophie Reece, and it's a sensitive issue all round. Especially when it's a question of consent.'

'Is it?'

'I'm not at liberty to say,' he replied, then he smiled. Kissing her hand, he pulled her towards him and said, 'Can we meet up? Tomorrow maybe?'

Phil had cancelled all their bookings, she was free but there was Cora to consider. 'I'd like to but my friend . . .'

'Ah, the friend.' Daniel looked away for a moment. Turning back, he said, 'Thea, I have to be honest, this isn't some silly fling as far as I'm concerned, I'd like it to be more, but I need to know if your friend, the man I saw here yesterday, is important to you.'

Thea looked down at her hands. She tried really hard to stop the bubble of glee that rose up in her chest but she couldn't. 'Yes,' she said, a snort of laughter escaping. 'He's very important to me.' Daniel stared at her. 'He's my father,' she said and burst into giggles. Daniel grinned.

'Jake was down from London,' Thea explained, calming down, 'he often comes down to see Tom.'

'I see.' There was a short pause. 'So who's the friend?'

Thea sobered up. She didn't know how much or how little to say, so she just said, 'It's my best friend, she's not well and she's staying with me. I don't want to leave her on her own, that's the problem, and she's not up to company.'

'OK.' A sudden relief flooded through Daniel and he grinned again. 'What about meeting here, tomorrow, same time, when everyone else is in bed?'

Thea glanced behind her at the house, then up the drive. 'Come at ten,' she said, 'and if you park the car round the corner there by the garage, it can't be seen from the house.' She turned back to him. 'OK?'

He pulled her to him and held her close, breathing in the warm scent of her. Then he released her and she jumped down out of the car. 'Tomorrow,' she said quietly.

'Yes, tomorrow.' He watched her disappear round the side of the cottage and smiled to himself. Then he too jumped down from the car, climbed back into the driver's seat, started the engine and drove off. He was home by eleven-thirty and in bed by midnight. He slept like a brick and woke the next day with the sort of excited, joyous feeling he hadn't experienced for years.

Chapter Nineteen

Cora sat with Phil in the drab, stuffy reception at Crawley police station, waiting for DS Lawrence. It was still hot, well into June now, and she wondered if this bloody weather would ever break. She wanted some rain, cool, cleansing rain, but all she got were deep blue skies, scorched earth and searing heat. She hated it. She hated it because it made no sense, it was another thing that made no sense, an English summer of sweltering, torrid weather.

'Miss White? Corinne White?'

Phil squeezed her hand. 'That's us.' He stood and waited for Cora to get to her feet. She pulled the cardigan she was wearing tight around her and a small trickle of sweat ran down the side of her face.

'D'you want to take that off?' Phil asked.

Cora shook her head and he sighed, taking hold of her hand again. In an ankle-length dress and long-sleeved cardigan, she was covered from the neck to the feet, as she had been since the attack. Her face was pink with the heat, but her hands, in contrast, were icy cold. Phil led her towards the interview room and the faceless WPC who, despite the smile, was unwelcoming.

DS Dave Lawrence was waiting for her. 'Corinne, come in and sit down, please.'

Cora and Phil did as asked, Cora clasping her hands tightly together on her lap. 'I'm Phil Habben,' Phil said, offering his hand, 'Cora's business partner and friend.'

'Nice to meet you, Phil,' Lawrence said. He sat down with a pale brown folder in front of him and opened it. This was difficult, probably the worst scenario in a case like this and Lawrence was dreading it.

'Corinne, I've asked you here to let you know what's happening with your case at the moment. We've got a case hearing in court tomorrow and the CPS have asked me to let you know, forewarn you to some extent, that things might not run as smoothly as we'd hoped.'

'What d'you mean, not as smoothly as you'd hoped?' Cora was immediately tense and Phil glanced sidelong at her.

'Well.' Lawrence glanced down at his file. 'The defence are going to question whether we really have a case and I'm afraid that it's going to be difficult to prove that we do.'

'Difficult? What's difficult about it? He raped me, surely you believe me, surely—'

'Of course we believe you, Corinne, of course we do. There's no question in my mind or in the minds of anyone here that we have a case, that a sexual assault against you was made by Jason Wakes, but I'm afraid that it's not as simple as that. His defence are arguing that you consented to sex and they have built up a very good case.'

'How? How can they do that?' Her voice had risen and Phil felt a knot in the pit of his stomach.

'The defence team have a witness who said that he saw

you leave with Mr Wakes on very good terms, intimate terms.'

'Who?' Cora was panic struck. 'Who said that? Who was it? They're lying! No one saw me leave, no one . . .' Suddenly she broke off. 'The new doorman,' she said. She shook her head. 'The new bouncer, I'd never seen him before and he gave me a really weird look when I arrived, like I was trash. He came to the dressing room and Debbie opened the door in costume, she—'

'He alleges that you and Debbie Pritchard were both naked when he called at the door with his message,' Lawrence said.

Cora gasped. She put her hand up to cover her mouth.

'Look, I'm sorry, I know this is very difficult for you. It's difficult for us too, we—'

'Difficult for you—?' Cora broke off, her voice failing her.

There was a brief silence which Lawrence felt it better to fill. 'I'm afraid that they also have witnesses in the club,' he said. 'Friends of Mr Wakes who state that you and Debbie Pritchard were both drinking heavily in the club after the act and that—'

'It's not true!' Cora cried. 'I was only there to make sure Debbie was all right. She's my responsibility Tell him, Phil, tell him that I never drink after the act, never! I never drink anywhere except at home or at Thea's house, do I, Phil? I never do! Tell him, Phil!'

Phil stood up. He moved across to Cora and knelt down in front of her, taking both her hands in his. 'It's all right,' he said. 'We've got my statement, Thea's statement, Debbie is a witness, and Lenny spoke up for you as well.

That's right, isn't it?' He glanced at the policeman, who nodded.

'Our case is strong too, Corinne,' Lawrence said. 'You must believe that, but I have to inform you of what the other side are going to put forward. It doesn't mean that they'll win, OK?'

Cora tried to swallow down a lump that was stuck in the back of her throat. She nodded.

'Are you all right for me to continue?'

Phil squeezed her hands and stood up. 'Cora? Are you OK?'

'Yes,' she said. 'Go on.'

'The defence are arguing that when you left the club with Mr Wakes you were on intimate terms with him. They are saying that you consented to sex, that things got a little aggressive, at your insistence, and that you accidentally hit your head on the doorframe. Mr Wakes tried to help you, but you told him you were fine. Now this next bit is speculation, the defence team's version of events, it bears no relation to what really happened, but I'm afraid as we are missing the time in question we can't prove irrefutably that it *didn't* actually happen. D'you see what I mean?'

'Yes. Go on.' Cora found she was bracing herself.

'OK. They are also going to argue that after you left Mr Wakes, you visited your ex-boyfriend, Ewert Lockhart, and that in a fit of jealousy he hit you. That accounts for the bruising on your face and thighs. He has used violence against you in the past, is that right?'

Cora nodded. She hung her head down and closed her eyes.

'To make matters worse, unfortunately Mr Lockhart isn't available to refute this. He has disappeared—'

'Disappeared?' Cora interjected. 'How the hell has he disappeared? What, like a bloody magician?! I don't understand!'

'Cora.' Phil reached out and touched her arm again. 'Let DS Lawrence finish, please. Hear him out.'

'But how can he have—' She broke off as Phil squeezed her arm and glanced up at Lawrence. 'OK, sorry,' she murmured. 'Go on.'

'Mr Lockhart seems to have left his known address and we have no idea of his present whereabouts. You wouldn't have any idea of where he might have gone, would you?'

Cora shook her head.

'No, well, the long and short of it is that we have no way of contacting him in order for him to make his own statement as to what happened.'

'Nothing happened!' Cora exclaimed. 'I didn't even see Ewert that night. I—'

'Corinne,' Lawrence interrupted. He wasn't good at handling this sort of thing, other people's pain made him uneasy. 'I'm sorry,' he said, 'I know this is distressing for you but I can't go on if you keep interrupting me! It's important that you listen to what I'm saying and that you understand the procedure! Is that clear?'

Cora ground her teeth and on her right Phil was close to snarling.

'As I was saying, we need Mr Lockhart to refute what the defence are saying, otherwise it could damage your case. They are arguing that he has recently disappeared because of what he did to you.'

'That's ridiculous!' Phil burst out. 'For starters Ewert wouldn't disappear because he gave Cora a slap. You're right, he has done it before and it's never bothered him in the past! Second, she finished with him months ago, so why would she want to go and see him? The whole affair was washed up and done with, what good would visiting Ewert have done her? Also, how did she get from Horsham to Balham and back to West Sussex in an hour and a half?'

'That's exactly the point the CPS are putting to the judge.'

'Good! I'm glad to hear it!' Phil said. 'At least they seem to be doing something!' He was irritated now; this business about Ewert was really taking the piss. 'If you'll forgive me for being blunt, it strikes me that your CPS people haven't got much of a clue and that the defendant gets to hire a brilliant barrister simply because he's loaded and he's the defendant. It's a bit weighted to one side, isn't it?'

'I don't think so,' Lawrence said. 'We do our best in the circumstances.'

'What circumstances are they, then?' Phil demanded.

'The circumstances of a very difficult case!' Lawrence fired back. 'With all due respect, we have a case that hinges on consent. On the one side we have the defendant with no previous convictions, a good solid reputation, an intelligent, hard-working, honest man by all accounts, and on the other we have a strip-tease artist, with an ex-boyfriend who used to knock her about and nowhere near the number of character witnesses that the defendant has! The jury will have to believe one of them and the defence are arguing that there's no contest!' Lawrence glared at Phil.

'We haven't exactly got a clear run at things, have we?' he snapped.

'Stop it!' Cora suddenly cried. 'Stop carping on about me as if I'm not here!' She stood up and Phil saw that her hands were shaking. 'What are the chances of the defence winning, of them saying I have no case?'

'I don't know . . . I couldn't be sure at this point, I . . .'

'Just tell me!' Cora cried. 'On a scale of one to ten, what are their chances of throwing the case out?' She was squeezing the fingers of one hand with the other so hard to stop them shaking that her hands had completely drained of blood.

'I don't think it's appropriate at this point to—'

'Just tell me!'

Lawrence was highly uncomfortable. He hesitated, glanced at Cora's stricken face, then said, 'It's seventy – thirty, in their favour, I'd say.'

'No . . .' Cora shook her head in disbelief. 'No, it can't be.' She put her hands up to her face, let out a strangled sob and that moment seemed to go on indefinitely, the sob echoing round the room. Phil went to stand, but Cora backed towards the door. 'That means he'll get away with it,' she hissed through clenched teeth. 'That he'll do it again and I—' She broke off and stared at DS Lawrence. 'That means that I . . . I'm all the things they say I am, that . . .' She shook her head again. 'He can't get away with it!' she suddenly cried. 'He can't, I don't believe it, I . . .' The next moment she turned and ran to the door. Phil jumped up, knocking his chair over, but she was too quick. Yanking the door open, she flew out into the corridor, shoving someone against the wall in her panic to flee.

Phil dashed after her. 'Cora!' he shouted down the corridor. 'Cora, wait!' But she ignored him and ran on. 'Cora!' He hurried down the steps and out into the street, looking both ways to see if he could spot her, but she had gone. The street was packed, it was hot and dusty and the traffic fumes left a haze in the air. She was nowhere to be seen.

'Oh fuck!' he snarled. He kicked the wall hard and briefly wondered about going back to give that police officer a piece of his mind. He slumped against the same wall and decided not to. What good would it do? It wouldn't change anything. 'Fuck!' he said again. He was as powerless as the next man. And digging his hands in his pockets he made his way back to the car.

Cora walked for miles. She walked around shops, along melting tarmac pavements, through alleyways and across a park. She didn't hear the traffic or the noise of the crowds shopping. She didn't see anything. At some point she found herself in a multi-storey car park and climbed the stairs to the top floor, eleven flights up, to see if the world made any sense from there. But it didn't.

At the edge, she sat on the wall and let her legs drop over the side, looking down on the small cars and the dots of people. It didn't make any more sense, but it was better, having everything in miniature, it was manageable. That was the problem, she thought, the size of everything. For months now nothing fitted, nothing was in its place, everything was too big, everything overpowered her. This was good, this was finally in proportion.

She saw a police car stop on the road below and a small crowd form. She wanted to call out, to tell them that it all looked far better up here. But she didn't. If she jumped, if she just slid off this wall, then she'd be down among them in seconds, she'd be able to tell them then. She smiled. I wonder what it's like to fly, she thought, and inched forward towards the falling air.

'Hello?'

She turned.

'Are you OK?' It was a woman.

'Fine.'

'Would you like a hand down?'

Cora looked behind her again. Would she like a hand down? What a stupid question. 'No thanks,' she said, 'I can jump.'

'I wouldn't, if I were you.'

'Wouldn't you? And why's that?'

There was no answer. Typical, Cora thought, no one has the answer.

'Because people care,' the woman said.

'Yes.' Cora glanced over her shoulder. The woman was ordinary looking, in a long M & S summer frock, flowery and badly cut. 'You see, the point is that I don't.'

'No?'

'No.'

'Why not?'

'For God's sake!' Cora said irritably. 'If I wanted to talk I'd have phoned a bloody chat line!' She glanced over her shoulder again. 'Please, just go away and leave me alone!'

'It might make it easier if you shared it with someone.'

Cora snorted. 'Oh please!' she said. 'Spare me!' A sort of senseless irritation was taking hold. Who the hell *was* this bloody woman? Christ, if this was the government's new caring society they could keep it! She couldn't even top herself in peace!

'If that's what you really want, but I don't think it is, is it?'

Cora swung round, a sudden bloodburst of anger hitting her brain. 'What the fucking hell would you know about what I want?' she cried. 'What does anyone know about it?' She slid off the wall and stood facing the woman. 'That bastard said he knew, he said I asked for it, that I wanted it, he told them he knew what I wanted and no one, no one ever asked me, not Thea, not my mum, not Ewert! No one! No one ever fucking asked me what I want! Not ever! Not . . .' Suddenly Cora began to cry. From deep inside her the pain welled up and haemorrhaged. She put her hands up to her face and the tears seeped out through her fingers and ran down her wrists. She slumped back against the wall, sinking to the floor. 'Oh God,' she wept, 'I just wanted to be loved.' And for the first time ever, it began to make sense.

Daniel Ellis sat with his oldest friend in a restaurant in the city. They were on coffees, having had just one main course because Daniel had to see clients that afternoon and because he wasn't a fan of big boozy lunches.

'And?' his friend asked.

'Yes, Matt, yes is the answer to that one and it was incredible!' Daniel glanced nervously over his shoulder. 'It is incredible,' he said. 'I can't believe it's happening to me!'

His friend smiled. 'Why not, Dan, you deserve a good time.'

'No, this is more than a good time, this is knee-trembling,

take-her-home-to-meet-your-mother stuff! Christ, Matt, she's the most extraordinary woman I've ever met.' He stopped and took a breath. The need to talk about Thea, to explain to someone was totally overpowering. 'I'm sorry,' he said, 'I've got to talk, you don't mind, do you?'

'Not at all.' Matt ordered more coffee and their cups were refilled. 'Fire away.'

'She's not like Charlotte, she's totally different, which I suppose is a good thing. There's nothing steady about her, she's the most capricious woman! She is so hot sometimes it takes my breath away, and other times, she's as cool as hell, aloof, which of course makes me wild for her!' He smiled. 'I'm like a schoolboy, I walk around with a permanent erection! It's bloody ridiculous!'

Matt laughed. 'Don't knock it, my friend!'

Now Daniel laughed. 'No, seriously, it's like being a youth again, we do it in the car and on rugs in fields in the moonlight.' Matt laughed again, this time raucously. 'I've got bloody gnat bites on my ass, for God's sake!' Daniel stopped and took a sip of his coffee. 'But it's not just the sex, it's the way she talks to me, listens to what I have to say, really listens, and the way she smiles and laughs. She gardens in a bikini and wellies, you know?'

'Really? Has she met the boys?'

'Oh no, it's all very secret. She's got this friend who comes and goes, so we tiptoe around this woman and she doesn't want anyone to know.'

'Why's that?'

'I guess in case it doesn't work out.' Daniel thought for a moment. He didn't really have a smart answer to that one.

'So where's all this going?'

Daniel signalled for the bill. 'Well, immediately, to Amberly Castle Hotel, for one night of unbridled passion in a huge comfy bed. Tonight actually, it's quite a step forward that she agreed to it.'

'And then?'

Daniel sighed. 'To be honest, Matt, I don't know. As far as I'm concerned, all the way, but she's holding back, I don't know why. It's as if a part of her just can't let go.'

Matt was smiling.

'I mean personality wise! You dirty old man!'

'Less of the old, Ellis,' Matt said, standing as the waiter came across with the bill. 'I'm thirty-four, which is a year younger than you!'

Daniel put his card on the tray and stood as well. 'Ah, but I look twenty-five, where as you, my friend, you look—' But before he could finish, Matt blew him a raspberry and walked away.

Daniel called his junior into the office on his arrival back from lunch. 'Is this the Wakes brief?'

'Yes. We're in court tomorrow morning and he's due in Chambers in . . .' She looked at her watch. '. . . ten minutes.' She smiled. 'Doesn't leave you much time.'

'I've had less,' he said and she left him to it.

In ten minutes he had looked over the file, got up to speed and called Sophie back in for a quick chat.

'Did we agree to this use of business names?'

'Yes, there was a special plea, owing to the nature of the case. The victim said she felt safer using her pseudonym.'

'OK, fine. Is there anything else that I need to know?'

Sophie raised an eyebrow. 'I'm putting something together on the business – Silk and Lace, it's called – but we don't really need that for tomorrow.'

'Silk and Lace, eh?' Daniel smiled.

There was a knock on the door and Charlie put his head round. 'Mr Wakes is here, Mr Ellis.'

'Thanks, Charlie, show him in, will you?' He glanced at Sophie. 'Let's hope he's a little better behaved than the last time we met him.'

She smiled and Wakes came in with Peter Killen.

'Mr Wakes.' Daniel stood and shook hands with Wakes, then Killen. 'You know my junior, Sophie Reece.' Sophie held out her hand but only Peter Killen shook it. Jason Wakes ignored her and sat down.

'Right, well, let's get on then, shall we?' Daniel usually offered tea but he didn't take kindly to anyone offending his junior. 'As you know, we're in court tomorrow morning and we're going for a dismissal. We are planning to argue that the CPS don't have a strong enough case.' Daniel opened the file. 'Now, you know the details, Mr Wakes, Mr Killen will have kept you up to speed on what we're doing but we wanted to know this afternoon if there was anything else you might want to add, anything at all.'

Wakes shuffled in his chair. He was a glossy character, Daniel thought, with his tailor-made suit, striped shirt, gold cufflinks and silk-weave tie. No wonder the CPS didn't have a case. His hair was immaculately cut and his nails had an unnatural sheen to them. Manicured, Daniel noted, and for some reason he found that slightly distasteful.

'I don't think there's anything I want to add verbally,' Wakes said, 'or to my statement, but I did find this in my desk some weeks back and I thought it might be useful.' He bent, lifted his briefcase on to his lap and, opening it, he took out a photograph. 'It's a card to advertise Corinne White's act and it's pretty provocative.'

'Well, I don't know that it's terribly relevant,' Daniel said. Wakes held the photo out and Daniel felt obliged to take it, even though he wasn't interested. He held the picture for a moment before looking at it, then he put it on the desk in front of him and glanced briefly at the image. He looked up at Wakes, but somewhere in his brain the image registered and he looked back down at it.

For a moment the room was completely still. He stared, stunned, his heart pounding.

'I, erm . . .' He glanced up at Wakes. 'Who is this?'

'That's Corinne White and her usual strip-tease partner Dorothy Marsh.'

Dorothy Marsh – Thea Marshall. Daniel stared at the photograph. It was her! It was Thea! It had to be, he'd recognise her anywhere! He blinked rapidly several times and a small sweat broke out on the back of his neck. 'I, erm . . . excuse me for a moment!' he said. And picking the picture up, he suddenly stood and strode out of the room.

'Daniel?' Sophie Reece stood on the steps of Chambers and looked at him pacing the ground. 'Daniel? What's up? What's happened?'

He stopped. 'It's far too complicated to go into now, Sophie.' He still held the photo. 'Look, can you do something for me?'

'Yes, of course. What?'

'Go back in there and tell Wakes that I've had to be called out on an emergency and I can't see him. OK?'

Sophie narrowed her eyes. 'He won't buy it, Daniel. You're not a GP, for God's sake!'

'Oh, that I were!'

He crossed to her and held her arms. 'Sophie, I can't take this case, I simply cannot do it, all right? I can't explain now, not until I've spoken to Geoffrey.' Geoffrey was head of Chambers. 'But I need you to sort it for me, OK? Tell Wakes I've had to go out, I'd forgotten that I was supposed to be in court and I'll call you later this afternoon. All right?' He felt in his jacket pocket for his wallet and car keys. 'I'll be back in Chambers tonight, I don't know what time but I will be back and I'll get someone else to do this brief, OK?'

Sophie nodded. 'OK.'

Daniel released her and glanced at his watch. 'Good girl, thank you.' He headed off in the direction of the car park. 'And good luck,' he called over his shoulder. 'I owe you one, Sophie!'

Phil parked his car, switched the engine off and picked up his mobile. He tried Thea again, his fingers drumming nervously on the dashboard as he waited. 'Come on, Thea,' he murmured; she had been engaged all afternoon. 'Bugger!' he said aloud. There was no connection. He started the engine and indicated to pull out. He didn't know where he was going next but he had to keep looking for Cora.

Thea was upstairs in the cottage, she had the door to her bedroom closed and her portable CD player blasting out

Puccini. There was no Tom to complain, he had been packed off to Jake's for the night and Cora was going back to her flat in Chichester with Phil after she'd seen the CPS. Thea was packing. She had one glorious, hedonistic night with Daniel ahead of her and she was as high as a kite with excitement. She had been trying on clothes all afternoon, deciding what to wear for dinner, for breakfast tomorrow, for arriving in, for leaving in and now she was about to pack the new silk slip she had bought for sleeping in. It was a slither of pale grey silk satin, with a deep inset of lace over her breasts so that her nipples were just visible through it. It was knee-length and had a long slit up the side, all the way to her hip. It was the most ridiculous and fanciful thing she had ever bought, but she loved it. She was about to lay it in the bag when she heard her name, but only just, over the noise of the music. She went to the window with the slip still in her hands.

'Daniel?'

He was standing by his car and calling up to her.

'Hang on!' she shouted. 'I'm just coming!' Leaving the music playing, she dashed down the stairs and out of the front door.

'Hi!' she said, reaching up to kiss him. 'Look, isn't this divine?' She held the slip, which was still in her hands, up for him to see. 'Oh, you shouldn't really see it before tonight.' She took a pace back and looked at him. He was pale and his eyes were blazing. 'Daniel? Are you—'

'Is that part of your act?' he asked coldly. 'One of your costumes perhaps?'

Thea took a sharp breath in. She stood where she was

and held herself a little straighter, lifting her head up. 'So you know,' she said.

'Know?' Daniel suddenly exploded, 'Know? Jesus Christ, Thea! Why the hell couldn't you have told me? Why? Yes I know! I only found out that I've been sleeping with the chief bloody witness in the case I'm supposed to be defending, haven't I? Jesus Christ! Why in God's name didn't you tell me?'

'Tell you? What do you mean sleeping with the witness?'

'I'm defending Jason Wakes!' Daniel cried. 'Or rather I was until this afternoon when I found out that you are a main witness in the case! Is that your friend? Corinne White?'

'Yes. Cora, her name is Cora.'

'And you're both—' He broke off.

'Go on, say it, Daniel!'

'All right! You're both strippers, are you?'

'Yes!'

'Christ, this is a mess! I've been sleeping with a stripper who's a witness in my case.' He put his hands up to his head. 'Have you any idea how difficult this is, how embarrassing?'

'What, Daniel? The fact that I'm a stripper or the fact that I'm a witness in this case?'

Daniel looked at her. 'I don't know,' he said. 'I really don't know.'

'I see.' Thea turned away from him.

'No,' Daniel said. 'I don't think you do, Thea. You should have told me, you should have—'

'What? Confessed all, begged for forgiveness? Oh please,

I'm not that sort, Daniel, and you know it! I do what I have to do to earn a living, it's not dirty, it's not dishonest and on top of that I run a bloody good business as well. It keeps me and it keeps Tom and frankly that's all—'

'What's that noise?' Thea stopped. She turned towards the house and heard a high-pitched screeching noise. 'I don't know.' She headed towards the front door.

'Is it an alarm?'

'No. It's the phone, it's been off the hook.'

'I see.'

She replaced the phone and they stood there for several minutes in silence; Daniel half inside the house, half outside it. Then the phone rang and made them both jump.

Thea picked it up. 'Phil? Where are you, I was going to phone you later, I—' She broke off. 'No, no she hasn't! Have you tried the flat?' She looked at Daniel and he saw the panic in her eyes.

'She can't have done! She can't just have disappeared, Phil! Where have you looked? Have you tried Jake? She's definitely not at home?' Thea stopped. 'Oh God, perhaps she's had an accident, Phil, perhaps—' Again she broke off. 'All right, yes, if you think so, yes, we'll leave it a couple of hours.' She slumped back against the wall. 'Yes, yes, come over, I'm not going anywhere. Yes, OK, see you then.' She hung up and covered her face with her hands.

'Thea?' Daniel moved forward, then stopped himself. 'Thea, what's happened?'

Thea dropped her hands down and looked at him. 'Cora found out this morning that the CPS might have to drop the case and she took it really badly.'

Daniel glanced away for a moment. 'And?'

'She was in a terrible state!' Her voice broke and was thick with tears. 'Phil said she ran out of the office almost hysterical, he tried to go after her but . . .'

'Oh God, Thea, I'm so sorry.'

'You're sorry?' she cried. 'You do it just for the money, you destroy her and you're sorry?'

'Where is she?' Daniel asked. 'What's happened to her?'

'That's just it! We don't know!' She looked at him and he longed to touch her. 'Cora has disappeared,' Thea said, 'and the state she was in, God knows what might have happened to her.'

Chapter Twenty

Hedda woke early, around four-thirty in the summer, just when the light began to filter into the day and the birdsong started its noisy chant. She turned on to her back and slowly let herself come to full consciousness. That was the most exquisite pleasure, the slow awakening to each day, the mellow anticipation of what was to come, and the birds. Sitting up on that Tuesday morning, Hedda cursed – good-naturedly, as she always did – the birds. God, if only someone had told her that rural life was made up of far more intrusive noise than city life ever was. If only someone had told her that there was no complaining to the noise-abatement people about her feathered neighbours, that there was no such thing as political correctness in rural France and that a life without any of that crap would be blissful. She reached for her cardigan and climbed out of bed to make herself some fresh coffee. Opening the shutters, Hedda looked out at a purple sky streaked with orange and at a landscape drenched in iridescent light. She took a deep breath, smiled at the birds and turned to go downstairs to the kitchen.

Hedda's house was small and well designed. It had been

constructed out of local stone and timber some time in the last century, a farm building, sturdy and solid, with cool stone floors. Once the house in London had been sold and Jake had taken his share – Hedda was egalitarian to the last – she had gone to Paris for a while, to escape, and had seen the house in an agent's window. She hadn't ever intended to buy something in France, but she had the money, had planned to take a year or so off from the practice and thought, on seeing it: What the hell? The following day she had driven down to Provence, fallen in love with a pile of stone and negotiated a price for it there and then. She hired a French architect and a local builder, very Peter Mayle, very slow and chaotic. But she'd become involved with the builder and somehow the time and the disorder didn't seem to matter as much as it should have done.

Henri was a man older than herself, a robust, Cognac-drinking French countryman who took no nonsense and who argued with her fiercely, never letting her gain ground that she shouldn't have won. He was rather old-fashioned, expected more of Hedda than she was prepared to give, but it added a certain frisson to the relationship and she never tired of telling him so.

Hedda pottered downstairs into the kitchen, moved Henri's boots from the hall to outside the front door and stood for a moment taking in the cool stillness of the dawn. She didn't live with Henri, he had his own place down in the village, but she expected him for breakfast. He was working on a project beyond her house, up towards the next village and he liked to call in for coffee, bread and a quick lie down before he started his day.

Turning back inside, Hedda put the coffee on, a small

task she had always left to Jake but something she now realised that she enjoyed. She pulled her cardigan a bit tighter round her body and cut herself a chunk of bread, standing where she was at the work surface to eat it greedily without butter or jam. Henri would bring a fresh loaf with him when he arrived and the breaking of warm new bread with good Colombian coffee was a pleasure so complete yet so simple that Hedda – whose life had always been complicated to the ninth degree – found it truly surprising.

She heard the coffee hiss as it came to the boil and turned, moving first to the fridge to take out some milk and then to the hob to turn the gas down. She put a pan of milk on to heat, a car came up the drive and Hedda smiled at such perfect timing. She took the coffee pot off the hob, resting it on a mat while she found her *café au lait* cups and placed them on the table. A car door slammed, Hedda slipped her cardigan off her shoulders and laid it over the back of the chair. As footsteps came up the stone path, she went to the door in just her slip of cotton, hair tussled and the smell of sleep still on her skin.

'*Bonjour, mon chéri!*' she called, unbolting the door. As she swung it open, the smile on her face froze, she blinked rapidly, three times, then frowned for an instant trying to remember the face. 'Cara!' she said suddenly. 'Good God, it's Cara, isn't it? That friend of Thea's!'

'Yes, Cora, not Cara.' Cora stood in yesterday's clothes, crumpled and white-faced. 'I'm sorry to call so early, I . . .' She hugged her arms tight across her chest and stared blankly at Hedda. 'I thought . . .' She shook her head, disorientated. 'I mean, I . . .' She broke off and Hedda, who had seen enough cases of mental disorder in her time to instantly know the signs, leant forward, took one of Cora's arms and gently pulled her inside.

'I've made coffee,' she said calmly. 'You've come just in time.' She eased Cora into one of the kitchen chairs and took a cup off the table. Cora was shivering and Hedda fetched a rug off the sofa before she did anything else. She draped it over Cora's shoulders.

'Cora, here. Drink this, you're cold and tired, it'll revive you.' Hedda handed Cora a large cup of milky coffee with a dash of brandy in it. 'I've put a bit of Cognac in there, Cora, it'll do you good.' After all the years of alternatives, Hedda had now come to the conclusion that doing what had been done for generations often worked best. 'You sit there and drink it, take your time, there's no rush.'

Hedda turned away and busied herself at the sink while Cora drank. She told herself not to be shocked, but her hands shook and although she could never have blamed Cora for the way Thea's life had turned out, the very sight of her filled Hedda with a fierce and quite unexpected resentment. She washed and dried a couple of things from last night, not that she was house proud in any way, but simply so that she didn't have to look at Cora. Years, she thought, years of trying to mellow, early retirement, a new life, a completely different life and one glimpse of that girl and my stomach churns as if it were yesterday. I should be able to let it go, to face her without recrimination, but I can't. She turned, finally, to look at Cora, to question her and find out what the hell she was doing here. She opened her mouth to speak, acutely aware of the effort it cost her to keep calm, but Cora glanced up just as she did so and she saw a look of such pain and humiliation on the young woman's face that it rendered her speechless.

'You look different,' Cora said.

'Do I?' Hedda's jaw clenched. 'A lot older, I expect.'

'No, not really.' Cora stared at Hedda for a few moments and Hedda felt the bags and sags of age clearly visible through the thin slip of cotton. 'I shouldn't have come.' She looked down at her hands and picked at a torn and bloody bit of skin by her fingernail. 'I didn't know where else to go. I . . .' She bit it and it started to bleed. 'I don't have anywhere else to go.'

Later, Cora slept. Hedda didn't want her there but she couldn't turn her away; it wasn't in Hedda's nature to turn her back on a problem. She helped Cora undress, shocked at her loss of weight, ran a bath for her in the plain white, uncomplicated bathroom and lent her an old linen shirt to sleep in. The sheets were cool and flat and Cora felt her limbs slip over their cotton sheen. She rolled on to her side and looked at the white-shuttered balcony window. She could smell honeysuckle outside and said, 'I never thought that you would be like this.'

Hedda went to touch Cora's hair, to comfort her, but withdrew her hand. Somehow she just couldn't manage it. 'There's an order in keeping a home that I've found I like. I'm not really domestic, but I muddle through.' She watched as Cora closed her eyes. She had no idea what the girl was doing in her house or how she had found her way across France to it, but she wasn't going to ask. In the last hour she had realised something. She had understood that if she could get over her resentment, then Cora was a bridge back to Thea and Hedda needed that link.

Henri called in again at lunchtime, having understood that he had been intruding earlier on in the day. He knocked lightly on the door and Hedda answered it, moving into his embrace the moment she saw him, in need of his strength, of physical reassurance. Cora's appearance had thoroughly upset her.

'You must ask her,' Henri said. 'You have to find out what has happened, or you must call your daughter. Come on, *chérie*, you must not worry like this, you must make a decision.' They had been sitting on the sofa, Hedda on the edge facing Henri. He looked at his watch and shrugged. 'I have to go,' he said. 'You must talk to her, Hedda, you must ask her what you want to know.'

Hedda nodded. Everything with Henri was black and white, there were no grey areas, no muddle or chance to get lost. Decisions were made, things were done and whether they were right or wrong you simply just got on with them. Hedda hadn't worked out yet if this way of life was preferable but it was easier on the mind, for there was no room for anguish.

Henri stood and Hedda walked him to the door. 'Will I see you tonight?'

Hedda shook her head. 'Leave it for a day or so. Thursday would be good.'

Henri smiled. 'Good.' He shook his head. 'It is so restrained, so English,' he said. He kissed her on the mouth and walked away, climbing into his car with only a wave. Hedda stood there for as long as it took his car to disappear down the drive and out on to the lane. He tooted the horn twice and as she turned to go back inside she saw Cora standing on the stairs watching her. She started and put her hand up to her chest. How long Cora had been there she had no idea.

'You speak good French,' Cora said.

Hedda smiled. 'Thank you.' She and Henri always spoke in French; his English was almost non-existent. 'D'you want lunch?' Cora looked as if she hadn't eaten for days. She shrugged and Hedda said, 'I'm not much of a cook, but I've got some local tomatoes and some fresh bread. I could make a salad – nothing special, but the tomatoes round here are very good.' She offered a tense smile. 'You look as if you could do with something to eat. It might make you feel . . .' She was about to say better but stopped, conscious of the fact that Cora had said nothing about the way she felt.

'Feel what? Less bleak?' Cora came down the stairs. The linen shirt hung on her, her collar bone prominent under the deep V of the neckline. 'They must be good tomatoes.'

Suddenly Hedda smiled, with ease, and Cora smiled back.

'Come on.' They walked into the small kitchen and Hedda pulled out a chair for Cora. 'Sit,' she said, going across to the sink and taking a couple of plump and glossy crimson tomatoes off the draining board. She found a knife and chopping board and began to slice.

'This is kind of you,' Cora said as Hedda cut. 'I didn't expect it.'

'No?' Hedda kept her head down, focused on the chopping. 'What did you expect then?'

'I don't know,' Cora answered. 'I just thought I had to come and see.'

'See what?'

'What you'd say.'

Hedda looked up, puzzled, but Cora offered no further explanation and she was momentarily torn between her own emotions and what she knew as a counsellor to be the right response. Her professional side won; she left it at that and changed the subject.

'How did you find me?'

'Thea told me the name of your village, ages ago. We were looking at a map of France with Tom and she said, "Granny lives there," and pointed it out.' Cora spoke quickly, her words tumbling out unconsidered, much as a child would speak. 'I never forgot it, I rarely forget anything, actually. I got the ferry yesterday afternoon, to Calais, and drove here through the night. I hadn't a clue where you lived, but I asked the baker in the village, he was the only one up.'

'Good thinking.'

Hedda had looked up and Cora froze for a moment. But when she went back to the chopping, this time herbs, Cora said, 'I had to get away, you see. I needed some space. I had to see things from a distance, they were getting too big, bigger than me and I—' She stopped and bit her lip. There was a silence which Hedda made no attempt to fill. She lay the slices of tomatoes on a plate and dribbled some dark green olive oil over them, sprinkling them with herbs and a pinch of good salt.

'I felt frightened,' Cora said.

Hedda turned. This time the need to ask more overwhelmed her and she said, 'Why?'

Cora looked at her. It was the first time she had faced Hedda squarely since she arrived. 'I was raped,' she said.

'By a punter, a man I gave a lift home to and I—' She broke off but continued to stare at Hedda. Hedda kept her face as impassive as she could but her mind was reeling, her body stiff with shock. 'I can't feel safe,' Cora said quietly. 'Not any more, not even when I'm asleep.'

Hedda came across to the table and sat down next to Cora, taking her hands. All sense of resentment had gone and she was overwhelmed with such pity and sadness that her chest ached with the burden of it.

'I wanted to know what you'd think,' Cora said. 'It's perverse, I know it is, but I wanted to hear what you'd say.' She moved her hands out of Hedda's reach. 'That it's my own fault probably, that I'm a common tart and that I deserved everything I got. You were always against me, against stripping, said it was degrading, humiliating. I got what I deserved, didn't I? Isn't that right? Isn't that what you're going to say?'

Hedda sat very still. Principles: this is where they'd got her. Cut adrift from her daughter and her grandson and thought of as harsh and judgemental. She stared at the red tomatoes on the yellow plate with the bright green herbs and saw none of it.

'My dear Cora,' she murmured, 'how could I ever say any of that?' She stayed with her head down for some time and when she finally looked up at Cora, the skin on her face was wet with tears. 'You have suffered a terrible crime,' she said quietly. 'It wasn't and never could have been your fault, *never*.' She wiped her face with the back of her wrist. 'You don't deserve the pain that you're in, no one deserves pain like that.'

Hedda stood up and went to the drawer for some cutlery.

In all her years as a therapist she had never found a cure that surpassed kindness and time. 'You must eat my tomatoes,' she said, taking out a knife and fork and bringing them over to the table. 'And then you must rest again. It's warm, you can sit out in the garden and read.' She placed the cutlery in front of Cora. 'You know, I was always so proud that you learnt to read, Cora,' she said, quite truthfully. 'I have lots of books; Thea told me in one of her letters that you are an avid reader now, you can borrow what you like.'

Cora looked down at the tomatoes. She could smell them, sharp and sweet, and the basil, with its peculiar, slightly aniseed scent, and for the first time in months her mouth produced saliva. She glanced up at Hedda. 'Thank you,' she said.

For the first time in her life Hedda was flooded with something as near to maternal kindness as she would ever get. She wanted to hold Cora, surround her and protect her, but she didn't. She shrugged and said, 'You can stay as long as you like, Cora. You are safe here with me, I promise you.' Cora nodded, then began to eat. In all her life, nothing had ever tasted as good and as sweet as that tomato salad.

Thea stood at the window in Cora's Chichester flat and stared out at the rain. At last the weather had broken; the heat had given way to sheets of cold, biting rain that washed over the hard, dry ground and ran away in rivulets taking the topsoil with it. She shivered, wrapping her arms around her, and wondered how the hell to turn the heating on in this high-tech, barely lived-in apartment. Turning, she walked across to the far wall and flicked on a light switch. All the up-lighting suddenly came on and the place felt better, less cold and sterile. God, she wished she knew where Cora was! She stared around her, at the clean, smooth lines, the lack of clutter, and wondered if she had missed anything. Once again she crossed to the bureau where Cora kept her papers and once again she rifled through everything to see if there was a clue as to where she might have gone. The only obvious thing was a missing passport, but then Thea wasn't absolutely sure that Cora kept it in this drawer. She sighed, closed the drawer and wandered through to the bedroom. She peered into the wardrobe, saw the few expensive and understated clothes that Cora kept for each season and realised again that nothing had gone. Nothing that is, except Cora. Thea dropped down on to the bed and put her head in her hands. 'Where are you, Cora?' she murmured. 'Please, let me know where you are.'

Hedda poured wine into two glasses and took a sip of her own before carrying the tray out on to the terrace. It was a warm evening, the breeze had dropped and the scent of mimosa from the clay pots filled the air. Cora sat with a book. She wore an old pair of Hedda's shorts tied in round the waist with cord and a vest top. Her feet were bare and her long limbs had tanned to a pale gold in the few days she had been there. As Hedda came out with the wine, Cora immediately stood to help her, taking the tray and laying it on the faded beechwood table.

'Is this mine?'

Hedda nodded and Cora took her wine. She sipped, then sat back down with her book. Hedda placed a cushion on her own chair for her back and she too sat down, but she didn't read, she simply stared out at the landscape. She had spent far too many years keeping track of current affairs with heavy weekend papers, medical journals and reports; she had pondered too long over each Booker Prize list and every well-reviewed biography to want to be bothered with it all now. Now she was happy to sit and stare, to talk to Henri about plumbing and heating, stonework versus brick or even to sketch, badly, her view.

Cora put down her book and looked at Hedda. It was impossible not to see the change that had taken place, she was hardly recognisable from the woman that Cora had begrudgingly respected five years ago. And yet she was still the same and in many respects it was Cora who had changed, it was Cora who could now see things in Hedda she had never been able to understand before. She sipped her wine and watched Hedda over the rim of her glass.

'I make an interesting study, do I?' Hedda said, without turning her head.

'Yes.'

'And what can you see that's so fascinating, Cora?'

Cora put down her glass and stared down at her hands. She hadn't spoken much over the past two days, she had slept and read, eaten Hedda's food and drunk her delicious wine and fresh coffee without any explanation apart from the few sentences that first morning. If she was honest with herself, she had to admit she hadn't spoken much at all over the past months, too weary to be bothered with talk, too confused to make sense of what people said to her. She hadn't seen the point in talking. What was there to say anyway?

Now, she looked up at Hedda and said, 'I'm trying to work out if it's you or me who's changed the most.'

Hedda turned to her. 'And what conclusions have you drawn?'

'I don't know.' Cora reached for the bottle of wine and refilled Hedda's glass, then her own. 'I don't really know anything any more.'

'Shall I help?'

Cora said nothing.

'I think that we've both changed, Cora, we've both changed a great deal, but that at heart we're still the people we were five years ago. Me, I've learnt that I made mistakes and I've had to realise the consequences of those mistakes. I exchange letters with my daughter but nothing more and I know that I failed as a mother. That's been hard, the hardest thing to own up to actually: that I was wrong, that Thea wasn't me and I should have accepted that right from the beginning. I've also learnt that through all those years of therapy, I lost the skill of listening. I thought I had all the answers and I never stopped to think, to really consider the problem and the fact that there might not have been any answers. But the core of me still believes in what I've always believed. I still have the same principles, I've just rounded them off a bit, made them fit a bit better.' Hedda paused and reached for her wine. She took a mouthful and let the liquid roll around her mouth for a few moments before swallowing it down. 'And you, Cora, do you think you've changed at all?'

'Yes . . . and no.'

Hedda smiled. 'Is that yes I've got a new hairstyle and lost twenty pounds and no I'm still the same person or is it that you think you've changed but you're not sure how or even why?'

'The last bit, I think.' Cora drank, then said, 'I thought I was doing all right, I thought that I'd got somewhere, and then, then I found that I hadn't got anywhere, that I was still the same stupid girl who asked for it and who got it.' Cora cracked her fist against the palm of her hand. 'Smack! Take that, you silly bitch!'

Hedda kept quiet. She focused her eyes on the distance and willed Cora to go on. Cora drank down more wine. 'All the things I'd done,' she said angrily, 'all the money I'd got, my own flat, interior designed no less, the clothes, my own car, nothing flash but still my own and yet I hadn't got anywhere, I ended up just as used and abused as I'd always been.' Again she cracked her fist against her palm. 'Smack! Take that you silly stupid bitch!'

Hedda looked at her. 'But you learnt to read, Cora. You have something that no one can destroy, a pleasure that no one can take away. Surely that has changed you?'

Cora shrugged, but she didn't deny Hedda's question.

'You think you're still the same because you suffered something – through no fault of your own in my and everyone else's opinion – something that you've suffered before and that this thing, this inviting of violence, is a part of you, a part of your inmost being. Am I right?'

'Are you charging me for this?' Cora asked.

Hedda had the grace to smile. 'No, this is not therapy, this is basic common sense. I think you are still the core person that you were because you will get over this, because you have the strength to move on, as you had the strength – and the guts – to achieve all that you have, the flat, interior designed as you so proudly point out, the car, the fact that you have learnt to read and have the nerve to drive hundreds and hundreds of miles to the south of bloody France and turn up at my house!' Hedda drained her glass. 'Five years ago you were a feisty, determined girl, you haven't lost that, that's still there.' She leant forward and placed her hand on Cora's chest, just above her heart. 'It's still in there, Cora, that's the essence of you. Think about it, but believe me, that's the bit that won't change.'

Cora put her hand where Hedda's had been and stared off into the distance. Time, Hedda reminded herself, it will take time. So she stood, leaving Cora alone with her thoughts, and went inside to prepare supper.

Chapter Twenty-One

Thea had just made tea when the front door sounded. She brought the pot to the table and, abandoning it, dashed out into the hall. 'It might be Cora,' she called over her shoulder. 'Or at least news of her . . .'

Phil stood up and moved to the doorway. Tom was already at the door, opening it, with Thea right behind him. Phil saw her face tense for a moment, then relax, falling with disappointment. Moving out into the hall, he saw DS Lawrence, who was standing with Thea, then he returned to the kitchen to sit down.

'Oh, hello,' Thea said. Lawrence looked different, less scruffy, and she found herself staring at him to see why. 'You've had your hair cut,' she said suddenly.

'Yes, I was hoping to keep it quiet but she took so much off it seems to have become a national event.'

Thea smiled. 'I've just made tea. Would you like a cup?'

Embarrassed, DS Lawrence said, 'I seem to make a habit of this, turning up at tea-time. Sorry.'

'Not at all.' Thea liked him, she decided. 'Come on in, there's cake. Again!' She glanced behind her. 'I seem to be forever making cakes, it's a radical reaction to my mother who never even opened a packet of Mr Kipling's, let alone baked.'

Lawrence laughed. 'Don't make excuses, it's very nice. Nice and homely!'

'Homely?' Thea shook her head smiling. 'Thanks!'

'OK, not homely then, sort of . . .' He searched for the right word.

Thea said, 'Homely?'

They both smiled and walked on into the kitchen. Phil stood up. 'Detective Sergeant Lawrence, this is Phil Habben,' Thea said.

'We've met,' Phil commented and sat down again. He felt uncomfortable with the policeman, in many ways blamed him for what happened with Cora.

'Oh yes, of course. On Monday, when Cora—' Thea broke off and stared down at the floor. It was now Friday and there had been no word and no sight of Cora. 'You haven't heard anything, have you?' she asked.

Lawrence shook his head. 'Nothing concrete.'

He hovered by the door and Thea said, 'Please, sit down, I'll get another cup.' She reached up into the cupboard and brought a third mug over to the table. 'God this is so awful!' she said. 'This whole thing just seems to get worse and worse.' Phil reached out and patted her hand. 'I've got no idea where Cora might have gone, except that it's very probably abroad, and I'm worried sick about it. She was hardly sane when she disappeared, I can't help thinking—' She broke off as Tom came into the kitchen.

'Any cake?' he said.

Thea took a deep breath and smiled at him. She picked

up the knife and positioned it over the cake. 'Guests first. DS Lawrence, cake?'

'Please.'

'You too, Phil?'

'No thanks, Thea.'

Thea cut Lawrence a slice and, as she passed him the plate, he noticed how slim her wrists were, how they were covered in very fine, pale hair and thought it unusual for a brunette. 'Thanks.'

'Tom?'

Thea went to cut a generous slice but Tom said, 'No, a bit more please.' She glanced sidelong at him and cut where she'd originally intended.

'Don't push your luck, monster!' she said quietly. Tom grinned, picked up his plate and took it away back to his bedroom. 'Don't make a mess,' Thea called after him. 'He's got some kind of massacre going on up there,' she said. 'Action Man is battling it out with Batman and the Teletubbies seem to be the first casualties. I found one hanging from the banister strangled with my leather belt.'

Phil smiled. 'He's got one hell of an imagination, Thea.'

'No, I think it's all kids. But males, in my opinion, seem to have a stronger leaning towards death and destruction from an early age.' She shrugged. 'My mother was a firm believer in crossing the gender barrier but I'm afraid that the doll I bought him just gets garotted every time she comes out of the toy box. He had it impaled on a bamboo cane in the garden last week.' She turned to Lawrence who was grinning. 'Do you have children, Mr Lawrence?'

'It's Dave, please, and no, no I don't. I'm not attached in any way. I've heard it helps.' Thea grinned back at him and Phil felt the smallest undercurrent of attraction between them. He was susceptible to these things and picked them up way before anyone else did.

'You're not gay by any chance are you, Dave?' Phil asked. He still didn't like him, nothing personal, more that he was just someone to blame.

'No, but I'd have thought you'd have known that instantly, Phil.' Lawrence smiled good-naturedly and Phil was forced to acknowledge a truce. Thea passed round the tea and for a few moments conversation was suspended.

Putting his mug down Lawrence said, 'So Cora hasn't made contact then?'

Thea shook her head. 'I'm pretty sure that she's gone abroad. Her passport is missing, I think, but I'm not absolutely certain. It wasn't where she usually keeps it but I didn't want to go around searching her flat. It made me uncomfortable being there without her.'

'Any idea where she might have gone? Europe, the US?'

'No. Europe, almost certainly. Her car is missing. She probably got a ferry across to France, or there again she might have driven to an airport . . .' Thea dropped her head in her hands. 'God, I really don't know! I've been round and round in circles like this since she disappeared. I just don't know.'

'Well,' Lawrence said, 'I'm afraid that one thing is for certain and that's that we need her back if we're going to have a case.'

Thea looked up.

'The longer she's gone, the less likely it is we can hold this whole thing together. We got through the committal proceeding on Tuesday purely because we are insistent that it goes to Crown Court, but the CPS still aren't convinced. We need Cora here and standing her ground. We're up against a very tough defence.'

'I know.' Thea instantly thought of Daniel and her stomach lurched. She took a sip of tea, gripping the cup tightly in both hands and thought: Why the hell do I feel like this? Why did her stomach lurch every time she thought about him? Good Lord, it was hardly serious, just a brief passionate fling.

'You all right?' Phil asked.

'Yes, yes, fine thanks.' He knew nothing about Daniel, nor did anyone else. 'So if we can't find Cora, where does that leave us?'

Lawrence shrugged. 'To be honest with you, Thea, at the moment, I wouldn't like to say.'

Later, when Lawrence had gone and Tom was in bed, Phil and Thea sat in the kitchen with a bottle of wine and made yet another attempt to try and guess where Cora might be. Only the more they did it, throwing ideas at each other, the more confused and distressed Thea became. 'I can't do this any longer!' she suddenly said, getting up and walking away from the table. 'I can't pretend that she's safe and happy somewhere in Europe when in all honesty I'm worried sick that she's lying in a gutter somewhere dead or only half alive! God, Phil, I just can't bear this not knowing!'

Phil rubbed his hands wearily over his face. 'I don't think anything has happened to her, Thea, I really don't, and nor should you! You've got to believe that she's all right, at least until we know! You've got to!'

'But how can I? You saw the state she was in, I lived with it for weeks, she was nearly insane, that rape all but destroyed her and—' Suddenly Thea broke off. She swallowed hard and bit the side of her fingernail.

'And what, Thea?'

She looked down at the ground. 'And I can't help thinking that if only I'd gone with her that night, if only I'd been there instead of Debbie Pritchard, then none of this would have happened, none of it! Cora would be here now, laughing, joking, being—' She broke off again and swallowed down her tears. 'Being the person we both loved so much.'

'Oh, Thea,' Phil said, standing and crossing to her, 'it isn't your fault, you have nothing to do with this, I promise you. It was just an arbitrary act of violence that happened, that nothing could have stopped and—'

'But it could have been stopped! If I'd been there then Cora would never have stayed, she'd have come straight home with me! You know that as well as I do! We often travel together in the same car, especially on a Saturday. If I hadn't been so bloody selfish and gone to a stupid party instead of working with her then none of this would have happened.' She looked at him. 'It wouldn't, would it? None of it would have happened!'

'No,' he said. 'It wouldn't.' He put his hands on her arms and turned her to face him. 'But, Thea, if I hadn't had something to go to then I'd have been there too! If Debbie hadn't got drunk then Cora wouldn't have stayed or had to take her home; if Lenny had kept more of a careful eye on proceedings then he might have got Debbie a taxi . . . Jesus! It goes on for ever, this hindsight thing! If, if,

if. There are no ifs, Thea, it happened and we have to deal
with that as best we can. As does Cora.' He looked at her
but she didn't face him. 'Thea? You do understand that,
don't you? You are not to blame, nor am I, nor is Debbie.
No one can take the guilt for this except that bastard who
did it to Cora.' Phil gently shook her. 'Thea?'

All this time Thea stared down at the floor, not looking
at him, not, he thought, even hearing him, but when he
released her, she lifted her head. 'Yes, I understand,' she
said. 'But it doesn't make me feel any better.'

'No, nor me.' Phil sighed and turned away. 'The only
thing that will, I suspect, is to see Wakes get the justice
he deserves.'

'Yes,' Thea said. And because he had turned away and
because he was thinking about Cora, Phil didn't pick up
the edge of hatred in her voice or see the way her eyes
burned with an anger she had never known before.

It was Friday night and Daniel Ellis had stayed late in
Chambers, working on a new case and catching the nine
o'clock train back to Sussex. He was tired, could have done
with a good lie-in and a day with the cricket on TV, but he
and Pet planned to take the boys to the beach tomorrow,
if the weather was dry, and let them paddle about with
the inflatable dinghy. He had hired a beach hut for the
summer at West Wittering and had stocked it with a new
barbecue, games, a wind break, deckchairs, umbrellas,
everything he could think of to make life on the beach
ultimately comfortable. He'd been looking forward to it
for months too; he had planned to take Thea there, had
imagined family days by the sea, Tom with his two boys,

all playing some sort of war game or trying to drown each other in the dinghy.

'Bugger!' he said aloud and the lady next to him rustled her *Evening Standard* and tutted loudly. Why the hell had Thea lied to him? And why the hell did it seem to matter so bloody much? Good Lord, it was only a brief affair, no one except Matt even knew about it! It wasn't as if – Daniel stopped his thoughts right there and bent to take some work out of his briefcase. He elbowed the lady with the *Evening Standard* by mistake as he did so and she lowered her paper to glare at him. 'Sorry,' he mumbled. He put the work on his lap and took a pen out of his jacket pocket, but the moment he glanced down at it his mind wandered off in the wrong direction and he found himself wishing that he didn't have to spend the weekend on his own and wondering why the hell that bothered him so much now.

'Bugger!' he said aloud again, but this time he didn't bother to look apologetic to the lady on his left; after all, it was exactly how he felt.

Cora was washing the things through Hedda had lent her at the sink when Hedda came into the kitchen. Cora had been into the nearest small town that morning and bought herself a few items of clothing: some underwear, several T-shirts, a pair of shorts, a swimsuit and a summer dress. The dress was a remarkable find for a provincial French town: short, fine cotton with a small white dot on a navy background. It suited Cora and it was the first time in months she had been able to look at herself in the mirror and say: 'Yes, that looks good.'

'You don't have to do that,' Hedda said. 'You could have put it all in the machine with my stuff.'

Cora turned. 'I wanted to wash them by hand, this linen shirt says hand wash and, well, it's nicer, isn't it, to have things hand washed?'

Hedda smiled. 'I suppose so. Thanks.' She stood and watched Cora for a few minutes, then she said, 'So you've decided to stay for a while then?'

Cora glanced up. 'You don't mind, do you?'

Hedda touched her gently on the shoulder. 'Of course not, I'm glad to have you.' She took the wet shirt off the draining board and walked towards the back door to hang it out to dry in the garden. 'Shouldn't you ring to let Thea know where you are, though? I have a feeling that she'll be worried about you.' And without waiting for a reply, Hedda walked out.

Cora wrung out the last piece of washing, enjoying the physical effort of it, and followed Hedda into the garden. There was a rope washing line strung between two trees and Hedda had already pegged the shirt up. Cora bent and took a handful of pegs, stuffing them into her pocket, and hung out the remaining clothes. 'I've decided to drop proceedings,' she said when she had finished. 'That's if it's not been dropped by the CPS already.'

Hedda said nothing.

'I just don't think I can cope with it, I can't bear to keep trying to forget it, trying to put it out of my mind, only to have it all dragged back up in court. Besides, there's no guarantee that he'll be convicted, not with a hot shot barrister on his side and, well, it all seems a bit pointless really.' She stared down at the ground. 'You do understand that, don't you?'

Hedda shrugged.

Cora looked up when Hedda didn't answer. 'D'you think I'm wrong?'

Hedda did in fact think Cora was very wrong, but that was personal, that was tied up with Hedda's own views of justice and retribution. 'I think that only you can decide what to do,' she said. Time, she reminded herself yet again, but she had always been an impatient woman.

'But you think I'm wrong to let it go, is that right?'

'It doesn't matter what I think,' Hedda said.

'Yes it does!' Cora looked at Hedda. 'It matters a great deal what you think. Please, tell me what to do!'

Hedda moved forward and gave Cora a hug. Why did Cora evoke all those maternal feelings that she had never felt with Thea? Was it lack of expectation that made Cora easier to love? Had she always wanted too much of Thea? Pulling back, she said, 'Cora love, I can't tell you what to do, you must decide on your own, but I can tell you that no one should get away with what they did to you, expert defence or not. Why don't you ring Thea and tell her where you are and how you're feeling? She might be able to help. She'll certainly know what happened at the committal hearing.'

Cora shrugged.

'Talk to Thea, discuss it with her for one last time and then put it from your mind.'

'Is that what you think I should do?'

Hedda sighed; she couldn't tell Cora what to do. 'If you really want to know what I think,' she said, 'then, in my opinion, it wouldn't be wise for you to make any decisions right now, one way or the other. You're too close to it to think straight. Settle things for the moment: talk to Thea, find out what has happened and then you can rest, put it aside until you feel ready to cope with it. If you still feel the same way in a few weeks' time then fine, but don't rush yourself, Cora love, don't decide now.'

Cora dug her hands in the pockets of her shorts. 'Where's the nearest phone?' she asked and Hedda smiled.

'Usually in the post office but at this time of day we can ask Michel in the café, he usually lets me ring if I need to.'

'I'll walk, I think,' Cora said.

'Yes, do that.' Hedda linked her arm through Cora's and they wandered back to the house. 'I tell you what,' she said, opening the back door. 'I'll come with you if you like and we can have a drink there. It is Saturday night, after all!'

'Yes, I'd like that,' Cora said. 'If you don't mind.'

Cora was always so unsure and Hedda said, 'Of course I don't mind, I wouldn't have said it if I didn't mean it.'

'No,' Cora murmured but she turned and looked at Hedda before easing her arm free. 'Perhaps not.' And Hedda saw then that for Cora, trust was something that just didn't exist.

Thea sat on the sofa with Tom eating tortilla chips and watching *Superman*. It was their Saturday night in front of the telly with supper on their laps: sausages, baked beans and mash, followed by Arctic Roll, a suspicious concoction of sickly sponge filled with vanilla ice-cream that Tom loved and Thea could probably have lived without. Often Cora used to come over and stay, bringing a sloppy girls' video to watch after Tom had gone to bed and a bottle of wine. Tonight Thea drank Coke and had already made up her mind to go to bed at nine as soon as she had tucked Tom up. Tonight Thea felt lonely.

It was a new experience for her, something she'd not ever really considered before: the prospect of being alone. She'd always had Tom, who left her no time to worry about men or relationships, no time really to dwell on the lack of sex. Then there had been Cora, for all the friendship bits and companionship and talking things through; and Jake, down often, sometimes with Marian, always managing to fix things and do all the male stuff that Tom needed. Thea sighed, shuffled about on the sofa and tucked her legs up into the lotus position. She knocked Tom who was holding the bowl of tortillas and he said, '*Mum!* Mind out!'

'Whoopsy,' she murmured. 'Sorry.' She stared at the television. Maybe it was the sex that she really missed, maybe it was that that made her feel so lonely. It *was* pretty good, she had to admit; it was definitely worth waiting five bloody years for!

'What're you smiling at, Mum?'

Thea flushed and said, 'Oh, erm, nothing, Tom sweetheart, just happy, that's all.'

Tom smiled back and immediately refocused on the TV.

Thea stood to go and put the sausages under the grill. 'Supper will be about ten minutes,' she said.

Tom made no answer; he didn't even move his eyes.

'Tom,' Thea said, more insistently, but again he ignored her. 'Supper,' she said, moving across the room to stand directly in front of the television screen, 'will be in about ten minutes and when I call I'd like you to come and get the trays ready. All right?'

Tom nodded.

'Yes, Mum,' Thea said.

'Yes, Mum,' Tom answered and grinned.

Thea moved aside and made her way through to the kitchen. Maybe it was simply missing Cora, she thought, the aching loneliness striking her again as she went to the fridge, maybe it was just the reaction to her disappearance. But as she lay out four sausages on the grill, they looked so pitiful, two for Tom and two for her, that she put the whole string on, eight sausages in all, and felt decidedly better. Life with Tom was wonderful, always had been, she'd never regretted for one moment doing what she'd done and having him so young, but what about now? Was life with Tom enough now?

'Oh bugger you, Daniel!' she said aloud. If it hadn't been for him she would never have questioned any of this, never have felt as she did. If it hadn't been for him . . . Thea took a deep breath and stopped. If, she thought, if, if, if. It had happened. What had Phil said? 'It happened and we have to deal with that as best we can.' She was just wondering how the hell she was going to do that when the telephone rang.

Cora stood in the back of Michel's café and heard the line to Thea connect and then ring. She held her breath. She desperately wanted to speak to Thea but she didn't want to be challenged in any way, she didn't want even to have to talk about what had happened. I want it all to go away, she thought, I want to escape it, but the line was answered and Cora heard Thea's voice.

'Hello?'

Cora's voice failed her. Why had it been her and not Thea? Why had Thea still got everything?

'Hello? Who's there? Hello?'

'Thea, it's me.'

In her small cottage in Sussex, all those miles away, Thea slumped back against the wall as relief swamped her. 'Cora? Cora, where on earth are you? Are you OK?'

Cora heard the relief, the pain and the fright in Thea's voice and for a moment she recognised that she was glad. Was that why she'd run away, to make Thea suffer as well? Did she blame Thea in some way? She bit her lip and was silent, then, plucking up courage, she said, 'I'm fine, Thea. I'm in France, with your mother.'

'With my mother?' Thea was stunned. 'How did you get there? How did you know where she lived?' She shook her head, trying to take it in. 'With my mother?' Thea hadn't seen Hedda since the night she had left 59, Park Road, Islington. They had spoken once or twice, exchanged the odd letter, but that was the extent of their relationship. Why Cora would choose to go to her mother Thea had no idea. 'Is she, I mean, are you all right there?'

'Yes, I'm fine. Hedda's been very kind, I've been here since Tuesday morning.'

'All week?' Thea felt the sap of anger rise. 'Why didn't you call me before? Why haven't you rung?'

'I couldn't face it, I—' Cora broke off and bit her finger-nail. Looking into the bar she could see Hedda sitting with a glass of wine, smoking and chatting to Michel.

'I'm sorry, Thea,' she said quietly, 'I'm not thinking right at the moment, I seem to have had some sort of breakdown I think.'

'Oh God . . .' Thea's anger fell, then rose again, like the swell of the sea. 'It's a good job you're with Hedda then,' she said coolly.

Cora winced and immediately the tears started. She stayed silent and Thea, who read through the silence, was immediately full of remorse. 'I'm sorry, that was a stupid thing to say, it's just that I've been so worried about you and, well, I just wish that you'd rung me and that I'd known you were with Hedda.' Why Hedda, she kept thinking, why did she go to Hedda? Why not me? But she forced these questions down and said, 'Is Hedda well?'

'Yes. And she's been marvellous, she's really looked after me, helped . . .'

'Yes, I'm sure she has.' It was there, in her voice, she couldn't help it, just the smallest edge of spite, the faintest trace of – was it envy? 'When are you coming home? We need you here for the case to proceed. DS Lawrence has been worried as well, he called round the other day and—'

'Thea?'

'Yes?'

'Thea, I can't come home yet. I don't know how I feel about things, about, well, everything that happened and well, I, I just don't know if . . .' Cora hesitated and Thea held her breath. She knew what was coming and she could see Hedda's hand in it. Hedda who didn't believe in the – what did she call it? Archaic and élitist, yes that was it – archaic and élitist British justice system; Hedda who

331

believed in personal healing and private triumph winning over the system.

'I don't know if I want to go ahead with the case, Thea,' Cora said. 'I'm thinking of dropping proceedings.'

'Dropping proceedings? Cora, you can't do that, you really can't!' Thea was close to tears. 'If you drop the case then it means he's got away with it, it means he—'

'It means that I don't have to be publicly humiliated in court!' Cora cried. 'That I don't have to have my personal life paraded in front of twelve men and women, that I don't have to see him again or go through all that pain and then have it thrown back in my face when he walks free . . .' Cora made a huge effort to calm herself, taking several deep breaths and clenching her hands tightly by her side. 'God, Thea,' she said moments later, 'I just don't think I can do it, I just don't think I can!'

Thea lay her head back against the wall and closed her eyes. Cora; strong, determined and fearless Cora. This is what she had become, this is what that bastard had done to her! The tears slid out from beneath Thea's closed eyes and ran down her face. There was a silence, the line clicked every twenty seconds as the units stacked up and finally Thea said, 'You must do what you want, Cora.'

And Cora, who had literally had the fight beaten out of her, murmured, 'Yes.' Moments later she hung up.

Thea sank down the wall to the floor and put her head in her hands. One act, one awful, mindless act of violence, five minutes, ten at the most and a life was shattered. It was nothing new, Cora wasn't unusual, these things happened every day somewhere to someone and very probably had the same effect. What was Cora's breakdown in the mire of misery that swamped the world? Not much. What was one person's pain amidst the universal suffering of whole nations? Nothing. Thea wanted to cry, to weep and sob and wail at the injustice of it all but no more tears would come. So she stayed with her hands over her face for some time until she heard Tom, who said, 'Mum? What's that funny smell?' and, looking up, she suddenly realised that there was smoke coming from the kitchen. Just as she did so, the smoke alarm went off.

'Bugger!' she cried, jumping up and running into the kitchen 'Tom! Go out and stay out!' The grill pan was on fire and the kitchen was filled with thick smoke. Grabbing an oven cloth, she pulled the pan from the grill and smothered it, hitting the flames down with one hand and covering her mouth with the other. Then she ran to the French doors and flung them open, gasping in lungfuls of clean air. Out in the garden she stood for several minutes, coughing and trying to calm down. Then she turned as Tom came out and gave him a hard, long hug.

'You all right, Mum?'

She nodded. 'Bloomin' sausages,' she said. 'Is the rest of the house OK?'

'Yes, it's only the kitchen that got the smoke.'

'Good.' Thea released him and headed inside. She uncovered the grill pan, stared down at eight blackened, charred sausages and at that moment she decided. She decided that Cora's pain wasn't something that had to be lumped in with everybody else's and it wasn't something she could forget or ignore. She decided that Jason Wakes was not going to get away with it and finally she decided that somewhere, somehow there had to be something that would catch him out. There had to be a case to answer and she was going to make it. She'd skewer that bastard, no matter how long it took.

'Tom,' Thea called, taking the grill pan to the bin and tipping the sausages in. 'Let's go out and have a pizza, shall we?' Tom's face lit up. What Phil had said yesterday, Thea realised, was right. The past was done, there was no going back but there was a way forward, a different way for everyone and Thea had just found hers. For the first time in weeks, Daniel Ellis had gone from her mind.

'Pizza Express?' Tom asked, kneeling to pull on his trainers.

'Yup,' Thea said, 'Pizza Express.'

'What about the sausages?'

Thea shrugged. 'There's nothing we can do about them,' she said, 'so we may as well forget them.' There was the difference: acceptance of what she couldn't change – Daniel; and the changing of what she couldn't accept – Cora. She smiled. 'Come on, Tom,' she said, holding out her hand, 'let's go.' Locking up quickly, they got into the car and drove off in search of supper.

Chapter Twenty-Two

It was school sports day and Thea pulled on a pair of pale cream linen shorts and a sleeveless white linen shirt. She fastened a brown suede belt around her waist and slipped on loafers to match. Glancing in the mirror, she pulled a comb through her hair, slid a pale lipstick over her lips and checked she had got both earrings in. She had.

'Right,' she said, turning and heading down the stairs. 'Sports day here I come.' She picked up her bag and her car keys, glanced one last time in the hall mirror and, finally confident that she looked OK, said, 'Daniel Ellis, eat your heart out,' to her reflection and opened the front door. Just as she did so, the phone rang. 'Blast!' she muttered, waiting for the answerphone to click on. It didn't; she'd forgotten to switch it on.

Turning back, she grabbed the phone off the hall table and answered it. 'Yes? Hello?' she said, rather more aggressively than she'd meant. She stopped. 'Oh, yes, yes I did! Look, can you hang on a minute, I just want to take this on another phone. Thanks.' Flinging the receiver back, Thea glanced quickly at her watch and saw that she had ten minutes to spare. She dashed back up the stairs, into her bedroom and across to the dressing table drawer, from which she pulled out a blue folder and a pen. Picking the bedside phone up, she said, 'Sorry about that. Yes, I did call in at the Duck and Ferret, I'm glad someone passed the message on.' She flicked through the file, holding the phone in the crook of her shoulder, until she came to a sheet headed Ewert. She pulled it out, reached for a magazine to lean on and continued to listen. 'Oh yes, right, yes, I see. No, nothing connected to the police at all, it's for his ex-girlfriend actually, Cora Whitby? Oh you did, did you? What, last year? Yes, she is attractive, yes.' Thea frantically scribbled while the voice on the other end of the phone talked. 'No, that's the problem, he didn't say a thing and we wanted to get hold of him but couldn't. Yes, yes, of course, no, I wouldn't reveal where I found out, of course not—' She broke off. 'Ah, I see.' There was a pause while she thought it through. 'OK then, if you give me the address in full then I'm sure I can arrange a small transfer of cash, say thirty quid?' She stopped again. 'No, sorry, thirty is my only offer and it's not bad for five minutes on the phone!' Bloody cheek, he wasn't getting anything until she'd checked this out. 'Yes I can, tomorrow morning. Good, glad to hear it!' She wrote down: *Cash, £35* and the name of the pub. 'OK, fire away.' Then the address and phone number that the so-called friend of Ewert's gave her. 'Yup, got it, thanks. Yes, yes I will, it'll be there in the morning at opening time.' She underlined the amount and wrote: *Ring Phil* next to it. 'And you're absolutely sure that he's there, are you?' The voice on the other end insisted that he was. 'OK, thanks, thanks a lot. I'll check this out and get the money right to you.' And without waiting for any reply, Thea hung up.

Standing, she put the paper back into the file and returned the file to the drawer. She didn't have time to look at it now but she'd ring the number later on, once she'd spoken to Phil. Closing the drawer, Thea congratulated herself. One morning in London, going round the old haunts that Ewert used to frequent and she'd got this, two days later: her first lead.

She glanced at her watch and hurried down the stairs, clicked the answerphone on, grabbed her bag and ran straight out of the door. So far so good, she thought, climbing into the car, perhaps I've got another career as a detective.

Tom's prep school was set in acres of prime Sussex land that ran down to the River Arun and had the South Downs as its backdrop. As Thea turned into the drive and parked behind the long line of cars stretching most of the way up it, she thought, as she so often did, that it beat the local primary in Finsbury Park hands down. She pulled on the handbrake, climbed out and reached for her bag. School sports day for the little guys was a low-key affair, rugs on the cricket field, lots of cheering and tea afterwards in the walled garden. When the sun was out and the breeze blew across the pitch it was idyllic, typically English, sharp voices carried across the wind, the sound of boys shouting and a prize for everyone, in that fairer-than-fair public-school tradition.

Thea took her rug out of the boot. Of course it wasn't plaid, it was fuschia pink and had an orange check on it.

She rolled it up under her arm, waved at one of the other mothers from Tom's class who called, 'I see you've got that groovy rug again, Thea!' and joined her to wander up to the field for the afternoon's events.

The sports over, tea was served in the walled garden and Thea stood with her cup and saucer in one hand, a small home-made cake in the other, making polite and very English conversation with the headmaster and one of the other mothers.

'So lucky this year, considering that we've had rain for most of last week and this!' the headmaster said.

'Absolutely,' Thea agreed. 'My poor garden's flattened.'

'Are you a keen gardener, Mrs Marshall?'

'Very.' Thea had never confirmed her title one way or the other and just let the school assume what they liked. It wasn't that she particularly wanted to lie, or that she was ashamed of her single status, it was more a question of ease, for Tom's sake, as well as her own. 'I have a reasonable-sized vegetable patch, some fruit and of course the obligatory herbaceous border!'

The headmaster smiled. 'Jolly glad to hear it! And does Tom help in the garden?'

It was one of the things that Thea loved about the school, the fact that the headmaster knew all the boys' names. Her own left-wing militant headmaster at school had been able to name every member of the Labour shadow cabinet but he hardly knew the names of his own staff, let alone the pupils. 'He's very good at digging,' Thea said, 'Particularly digging up the plants!'

The headmaster laughed. 'Like me, I'm afraid, can't tell

a Nerium from a nettle!' he said. He looked over Thea's shoulder. 'Ah, Daniel!' he said. 'Do you know Mrs Marshall? She's a keen gardener.' Thea blushed, she couldn't help it.

Daniel Ellis stepped into the circle and said, 'Yes I do, hello, Thea. How is the garden?'

'Fine thanks,' she murmured. He turned to the other mother and kissed her. 'Hello, Audrey. Thanks for tea the other day, Charlie had a great time.'

'My pleasure, Daniel, he must come again.'

'No, it's our turn next. I'll get Petula to give you a ring, I'm no good at organising the social diary.'

'OK.'

'Can I get anyone more tea?' the headmaster asked.

Thea shook her head but Daniel said, 'Yes please, I'd love a cup.'

'Good, I'll send one of the boys over with it. Audrey?'

'No, not for me, thanks, but I might wander over and find myself another slice of that delicious cake. Thea, more cake?'

'No, no thanks, I ought to be going soon.'

'Daniel?'

'No thanks, Audrey.'

'Right, well, if you'll excuse us?' The headmaster and Audrey made their exit together and Thea watched them go. Turning back to Daniel, she saw that he was staring at her and she blushed again. Daniel felt the knot he'd had in his stomach all afternoon twist a little tighter.

'Are you all right, Thea?' he asked quietly.

'Yes, fine,' she answered coolly.

'Good. And Tom?'

'Fine.' Thea glanced away, then, moments later, back at him. 'You didn't tell anyone, did you? I mean about me, what I do.'

'No.' Daniel was cross that she could even consider that he might. 'Why should I?' he asked irritably. 'I shouldn't think that anyone gives a toss about what you do for a living.'

'Except you.'

He stared down at the ground. God, this was hopeless. Here he was, having spent all afternoon with one eye on the boys and one eye on Thea, who she was talking to, what she was doing, how she looked, whether she looked in his direction at all, and now all he could do was incite her anger. She wasn't going to give an inch, that much was certain. He finished his tea and made one last attempt.

'Have you heard from Cora?'

Thea nodded. He watched her face: for a moment it changed and he couldn't read her expression at all. 'She's in France,' Thea said, 'with my mother.'

'Your mother?' Daniel knew only the bare essentials about Thea's background, but he did know that relations with her mother were Arctic. 'Oh, right. Is she OK?'

'She's as well as you'd expect I should think, in the circumstances.' Thea's voice was icy. 'I mean, she's had some sort of breakdown and she's convinced that she wants to drop all proceedings against Jason Wakes so . . .' Thea shrugged.

'I'm sorry,' Daniel said. 'It must be awful for her.'

Thea softened slightly. 'Yes it is.' She stared straight at Daniel and said, 'He is guilty, you know. Cora *was* raped.'

Daniel held her gaze. He knew what he was about to say was unethical but for that moment he didn't care. 'I know,' he answered, 'I don't doubt that she was.'

'Then you can help me!' Thea suddenly said, her eyes blazing. 'Surely, if you think he was guilty then there must be a case! I've got find out more about it, Daniel, I've got to find out what's behind Wakes, I don't believe all this character witness stuff, not knowing Cora as I do! There's no way she would have encouraged him, she was totally paranoid about that sort of thing, had been ever since we started, she had strict rules and to my certain knowledge she never broke them, not once. There has to be more to him than meets the eye, than the police have found out, he has to have some sort of previous, I just can't believe it otherwise! I—' Thea broke off as one of the older boys in the school brought Daniel's tea. Her face was flushed and her eyes had a wild glint in them.

Daniel thanked the boy and took a sip, looking away from Thea, painfully aware that the way that she looked now was the same as when he made love to her. He swallowed the liquid down, despite the fact that it burned his throat, and used the silence to rein in his feelings.

'Daniel, you could help me,' Thea said, 'if you wanted to. If you believe that he's guilty then you could put things right. You really could!'

Daniel bent and put his cup down on the lawn by his feet. He didn't care who saw him, he'd gone beyond that now. He took Thea's hands in his own and said, 'Thea, I cannot help you. I have been professionally embarrassed by this whole thing and if I became involved now I would seriously compromise myself and my career! I have principles, you know, and I have to abide by them.'

'Principles!' Thea pulled her hands away. 'I'm sorry but I don't think much of principles, not when they get in the way of doing what's right!'

'But I am doing what's right!' Daniel was upset now. Why did Thea always have this effect on him? 'I can't risk my career for this! You must understand that! Whatever I may know about this case I am simply not at liberty to say!'

Thea bit her lip. She too was upset and they stood there, locked in a painful silence, oblivious to the gentle chit chat that went on around them.

'Thea, please,' Daniel said at last. 'Can't we meet up and at least talk things through?'

Thea said; 'My best friend has been destroyed by this and you cannot bring yourself to help me or her. What more is there to talk about, Daniel, that you are at liberty to say?' She glanced at him one last time, then turned and, without waiting for his answer, walked away.

Tom sat at the kitchen table with his card rosette and counted his stickers. He'd got a sticker for every race, some of them winning stickers, some of them second or third place and some simply saying: *I did my best* or *Well tried*. 'Eight,' he called out to Thea. 'Eight stickers!'

'Brilliant,' she murmured, her head bent over the pudding she was making. She glanced up at him and smiled, forcing herself to put the incident with Daniel behind her. I will not let it ruin today, she told herself repeatedly, but she couldn't help the sinking feeling that swamped her every time she thought about it. 'You're a star, Tom Marshall, well done!'

'Can I see now?' Tom asked.

Thea shook her head. 'It's a surprise and you can see it after supper.'

'Oh please!' Tom whined. 'Please let me see it!' But the phone ringing diverted him and, as he leapt up to answer it, Thea put the pudding in the fridge out of sight.

'It's Dave Lawrence,' Tom said, standing in the doorway.

'Oh, right, can you tell him I'm just coming?'

'Yup.'

Thea rinsed her hands and dried them on a tea-towel. She went to the phone. 'Hello, Dave, sorry to keep you. How are you?'

DS Dave Lawrence sat in his car half a mile away from Thea's house and said, 'I'm fine thanks, Thea. Actually, I'm in the area, I had a call to make locally and I wondered if I might drop in?'

'Yes, of course! Was it anything in particular?'

Lawrence took a breath. 'Erm, no, actually, I just wanted to pop in and see you.'

'Oh, oh I see.' Thea was surprised, then quite unexpectedly pleased. 'Well, that'd be great!' She glanced behind her into the kitchen at the large dish of lasagne she had sitting on the side – half of which she'd planned to freeze – and her mind did a double somersault. Lawrence could be useful; this was an opportunity not to be wasted. 'Why don't you come for supper?' she asked. 'We're having a bit of a celebration meal, it was sports day today and Tom did pretty well.'

'Oh no, no, I wouldn't want to intrude.'

'You won't. Come on, Tom would like the company, I'm sure he gets sick of just me all the time.'

Lawrence smiled. 'I very much doubt that . . .' He paused. 'But, if you're sure you don't mind?'

'Yes, I'm sure. D'you want to come right over? I'd planned to eat in about an hour.'

'Yes, I'll do that. I'll stop and get a bottle of wine on the way and be with you in about fifteen, twenty minutes. Is that OK?'

Thea smiled. Who knew where a casual supper could lead her, as long as she kept it relaxed and informal? 'That's absolutely fine,' she replied. 'I'll look forward to it.' And with that, she put down the phone.

Dave Lawrence was exactly on time. He arrived fifteen minutes later with a bottle of Australian red and a box of Bendicks.

'Yummy,' Thea said as he handed them across and he laughed, wondering why it didn't sound completely ridiculous coming from her.

'You look nice.'

Thea turned. 'Do I?' Her linen was well crumpled and she hadn't brushed her hair all day or reapplied her lipstick.

Lawrence smiled. 'Yes, you do.' He found her expensive, lived-in look a real turn on but that was something he didn't want to add. Yet.

'Come on in. Shall I open this, or would you like a glass of white?'

'Red would be nice,' Lawrence said. 'Something smells wonderful.'

'It's lasagne, nothing too spectacular but Tom loves it and I'm afraid I rather pander to him, especially on days like this.'

'That's good.'

'Is it?' Thea smiled. 'I'm not sure if I spoil him. I was never spoiled, you see, so I think I've gone a bit the other way.'

'A bit of what you want never does any harm – in my opinion, anyway.'

Thea looked at him. He had a way of talking that seemed completely straight on the surface but he had a way of looking at her that gave his words a whole different meaning. She felt herself blush and moved across the kitchen to find a bottle opener – a diversion.

'Hello,' Tom said, coming into the kitchen. He was still in his sports kit, pale blue T-shirt and navy shorts. He looked angelic, Thea thought momentarily, all lanky legs and mop of dark hair. 'Are you the policeman?'

'Yes.'

'Do you have one of those cars, with the siren on top?'

'Yes.'

'What, here? Wow! Can I see it?!'

'No, not here, back at the station.'

'Oh.' Tom looked crestfallen.

'I tell you what I have got though, and that's a blue flashing light for the roof of my normal car. Would you like to see that?'

'Cor! Yes please!'

Lawrence smiled. 'Come on then.' He dug in his pockets for his car keys and led the way to the front door. He opened it and handed Tom the keys. 'Press the alarm pad to open the doors,' he said as Tom bounded out in front of him. He turned to Thea. 'Isn't he great?' he said, smiling, and Thea smiled back.

'Well, I think so,' she said, wondering if he knew that the way to a mother's heart was to love her children.

After supper, Thea produced her pudding, a gooseberry cheesecake, heavily coloured with green food colouring and decorated to look like the sports field at school. She had put several miniature plastic running figures on top and told Tom that the one at the front was him.

'It's amazing!' Lawrence said. 'How on earth did you—?'

Thea held up her hands to stop him. 'It's not amazing at all, it's terribly indulgent and a bit silly, but who cares? Tom, d'you want some?'

'Yes.'

'Yes what?'

'Yes please!'

'Dave?'

'How could I refuse?'

'Quite easily I should think, judging from the grass-green colour!' She cut two slices and handed them across, then cut herself a thin slither. 'I'm saving myself,' she said when she saw Lawrence looking at her plate, 'so that I can stuff myself with Bendicks! They're my favourites!'

'Good, I'm glad I got it right.'

She smiled. There was a silence as they all ate, then Tom said, finishing at an indecent speed, 'Thank you for supper, Mum, may I get down please?'

'Of course. You can finish your video, then I'd like you to go upstairs and start getting ready for bed.'

'What? No bath?'

'No, you can have a shower. Go on, off you go and give me a shout when it's finished.'

Tom jumped down from the table and disappeared. Thea watched him go, was silent for a moment, then decided to try her luck. She would have preferred it if Dave had drunk more and been more off guard but that wasn't going to happen so she took a breath and said, 'Dave, I hope you don't mind me asking this, but, erm, how come things went so wrong with Cora's case? I mean, things just don't seem to add up, do they?'

Dave finished his cheesecake, put down his spoon and fork and looked at her. 'No,' he said. 'They don't.' He took a sip of his wine, then his water. 'You've been building up to this all evening, haven't you?'

Thea stared down at her hands.

'I could feel your tension.' He reached out and took one of her hands. 'Thea, what is it you want to know?'

She felt herself relax. For one awful moment she thought he was going to ask her what she was up to and she wasn't sure she had an answer that he would believe. 'I just want to know what went awry,' she said quietly. 'I want to know what's missing and why things don't make sense.'

'For what purpose?'

Thea held her breath. 'I don't know,' she said quietly, not daring to look up. She was only too aware of the fact that she couldn't lie. 'I suppose I want to put the record straight, in my own mind.' She kept her gaze averted, 'And I want to be able to tell Cora exactly what's going on when she asks.'

There was a silence and Thea thought she'd messed it up, but after a few moments more Lawrence said, 'There are two major things that don't add up, Thea, and we just can't seem to find a way round them.' He sat back in his chair and looked at her. 'The first,' he began, 'is the missing time and Ewert Lockhart's disappearance . . .'

Thea silently let out a long, tense breath. She'd been right then, she'd picked up the scent. 'Go on,' she said and DS Lawrence, unaware that he was opening Pandora's box, went on to explain the whole thing.

Chapter Twenty-Three

Thea sat in bed with the lamp on, a cardigan over her nightie and a cup of tea on the bedside table, reading through her file. She was despondent, tired and beginning to feel that this whole thing was hopeless. In the two weeks since she had made her decision to find out what was going on for Cora, she had got nowhere fast. There were no leads, no clues and no answers. Nothing. Even the thirty-five-pound tip-off for Ewert had been a duff. Thea sighed and reached for her tea, flicking briefly through the file once more, then letting it slip from her lap on to the floor. She glanced up at a knock on her door and, bending to shove the file under her bed, called out, 'Come in, Dad, I was reading.'

Jake, in tartan dressing gown and old leather slippers, came into the room and across to the bed. Thea moved her legs and he sat down on the edge of it.

'Are you all right, Thea love? You seem very down at the moment, very preoccupied.'

She smiled. 'Do I? Sorry. No, I'm fine, thanks.'

'You sure?' Jake looked uncertain. 'It's just that Betty said you've been dashing here, there and everywhere. She seemed a bit, well concerned really and—' Jake stopped.

'And you'd like to know what's going on, right?'

He looked at her. 'Yes, to be honest with you, I would. I was rather hoping that it might be a relationship. It's about time that you—'

'Don't, Dad,' Thea said, reaching out and touching his arm. 'Been there, done that. It didn't work.'

'Oh?' He patted her hand. 'I'm sorry. You deserve a bit of fun, Thea, you work very hard and since what happened to Cora, well, you need some companionship. Anyway, enough moralising. You're sure you're OK?'

'Yes, fine.'

Jake stood but as he did so he caught the heel of his slipper under the divan bed and it came off. 'Blast!' He bent to retrieve it and pulled out the blue folder. 'Good Lord, what's this?' He picked it up. 'I bet you haven't seen this for yonks.' He went to hand it over but one of the pieces of paper came loose as he did so and dropped to the floor, so he knelt to put it back. 'I never liked these files, they always come apart on me . . .' He held the paper for a moment and glanced down at it. Something caught his eye and, unable to stop himself, he read the first few lines. He looked up at Thea. 'What's this?' He held the piece of paper out to her. 'Is there more?'

She nodded.

'The same? About Cora's case?'

Again she nodded, then dropped her head down and stared at her hands in her lap.

'What the devil are you playing at, Thea? It says here; *Made contact with Ewert lead*, then you've got an arrow down to an address and a line through it. What does it all mean? Are you interfering with the police investigation in some way?'

'No! I'm not interfering!'

'Well, what then?' Jake's voice was stern and ungiving. 'Tell me, Thea! Is this what all this dashing around has been about? Is this why you're so moody and preoccupied?' He sat down on the bed and opened the file, flicking through. 'It is, isn't it?' He was cross and it was one of the few occasions that Thea had ever seen him like it. 'Thea? Are you going to explain or am I going to telephone the police with this? I'd have thought they'd be very interested to know that someone else is on the case! I'd have thought that—'

'All right!' Thea snapped.

Jake stopped and looked at her.

'All right,' she said, more calmly, 'I'll tell you what it's about.' She reached forward and took the file, opening it and laying the papers out on the bed. 'All I'm doing is trying to find out what really happened . . .'

'You know what really happened! You know that Cora was raped! What more do you want to know?!'

'I want to know why Wakes is so squeaky clean, that's what I want to know! I want to know how he's managing to get away with this, why his defence have built such a watertight case for a complete bastard! I want to know why, when I spoke to one of the friends that was there on the night it happened, one of Wakes's *"best"* friends – who has apparently made a witness statement to the police about Wakes's good character – why, when I asked him when he last saw Wakes, he couldn't remember? Good mate, eh? Best friend? And then when I asked him when he last spoke to Wakes on the phone, he stammered, had to think hard, flushed dark red and finally said, "I can't remember, probably last week!"' Thea dropped her legs over the bed and stood up, too agitated to stay where she was. She paced the floor for a moment. 'The other so-called friend wouldn't say a word, for or against Wakes, he just wouldn't speak to me!'

'Thea, how on earth did you get in contact with these people?!'

'Lenny gave me a list of the people who signed up for his mailshot on the night Cora—' Thea broke off. She couldn't bear to keep saying: *the night Cora was raped.* She regained her composure and said, 'I rang them all and asked who had spoken to the police.'

'Don't you think that was rather presumptuous of you?' Jake just couldn't believe what he was hearing. 'Don't you think that the police might be a bit upset when they find out?'

'How will they find out? I'm not going to tell them!' Thea was unrepentant. 'There is something going on, Jake! I know it and I bloody well want to find out what it is! I know Cora, I know her like she's my own sister and I know full well that she wouldn't have encouraged Wakes. She wouldn't have given an inch, she's just not like that!' Thea came across to him. 'She isn't, is she?'

'No, you're right, she isn't. I have to admit that I was pretty shocked when they went for sex with consent. I just didn't think it would wash, not with Cora's character, but they don't seem to have taken that into account.'

'Sex with consent! It's a joke!' Thea picked up her paper. 'Then there's this Ewert thing. Where the hell is he? How come he's suddenly disappeared? By the time the police got there he'd cleared out and gone. Where? And what was the hurry? Someone must have got to him, Jake, someone must have paid him, threatened him, I don't know what, but it's one hell of a coincidence that he just vanishes and is then used in the defence's case.'

Jake shook his head. 'Hang on a minute, you can't make those sorts of accusations! You could get yourself into terrible trouble – that's slander! And what evidence do you have to back it up, apart from an over-stimulated imagination?' He held up his hands. 'No, no I won't accept that line, I simply won't!'

'All right then, let's go back to Wakes. He's been at his bank for just over a year and everyone loves him. The secretaries, his colleagues, his boss, they all think he's the business!'

'How do you know that? You haven't been to his workplace and—'

'No,' Thea interrupted. 'No, don't worry, I'm not that obvious!' She shook her head, momentarily concerned that Jake would think her so stupid. 'DS Lawrence told me that, it's one of the things that he doesn't like about the case, he said, and I quote: "It smells funny, a bit too nice, like air freshener covering something nasty." It's just one more thing that doesn't add up.'

'I don't really get where you're coming from, Thea. Are you saying that Wakes and all his friends and all his colleagues are lying? And if you are, not only is that frankly ludicrous, it's also totally unprovable! It's not going to help Cora, not one iota!'

Thea stopped and looked at Jake for a moment, then she dropped her head into her hands. 'I know,' she murmured.

'I think it but I can't prove it so it's absolutely no—' She stopped and glanced up. 'My God! What's that noise?!'

Jake jumped up. 'It sounds like a cat, like it's injured . . .'

They both darted to the window and Thea flung it open. The screeching wail rose up into the night. 'It's Mrs Betts's cat,' Thea said, scrabbling for a pair of shoes. 'Christ, it sounds as if someone's half killed it! I'd better go and see if I can find it, she's away for the weekend, it might have been run over.' Shoes on, she ran to the door.

'Shall I come with you?' Jake asked.

'No, not at the moment. If I can't find it, I'll come back and get you.' Her face had drained of colour, she hated animals in pain, the whole idea made her feel sick.

'Thea?' Jake hurried out on to the landing after her but she was already down the stairs and out of the front door. 'Thea, wait!' he called. She didn't hear him; she had gone.

'Artie?' Thea ran down the drive towards the lane. 'Artie? It's all right, darling, I'm coming!' she shouted. The screaming continued and her stomach churned. It was dark, there were few stars and only a crescent moon. 'Bugger!' She missed her step and wondered for a moment about going back for a torch. 'Artie?' she called again. The screaming had gone down to a whine, a pathetic whine, the terrible rasping of last breath. 'Artie,' she said quietly, 'where are you?'

Suddenly something hit her in the face. Smack! It was heavy and wet and warm, and as she put her hands out to touch it she felt a paw. 'Oh my God . . .' she gasped, then she went down. The blow was from behind, a hard crack over her shoulders and it knocked her to her knees, the pain wrenching her stomach. She hit the gravel, wincing as the sharp stones cut into her bare flesh, and opened her mouth, screaming just as a kick landed in the side of her body. She doubled up on to her side. 'Jake?' she yelled. 'My God . . . JAKE!' Another kick, this time to her upper body and she curled up, senseless with pain.

'THEA?' Jake was out of the house and running down the drive. She heard footsteps and the sound of crunching gravel but they seemed to be running away from her, not to her. She started to cry. 'Jake . . .' she whimpered. 'Jake, please . . .' She closed her eyes.

'Thea!' Jake was there. He dropped to his knees. 'Jesus! Are you . . .?' He gently lifted her head.

She opened her eyes and felt his hands on the side of her face. 'Yes,' she whispered. 'Yes, I'm OK, I . . .'

'Don't speak, it's fine, I'm here, it's just fine.' Jake stared down at her, at her face covered in blood, and he had the terrible urge to cry, with relief, with fear and anger, he didn't know what. 'Can you move at all?'

'Yes, I . . . I think so.' She uncurled her legs and eased herself up to a half-sitting position. Jake had a torch, he'd left it on the ground by her side and its beam went off up into the trees. 'Something hit me in the face, I don't know what it was, then someone hit me over the back.' She rubbed her shoulders. 'I couldn't see . . . it's too dark, I couldn't see a thing.' Thea glanced behind her up at the trees where the torch shone. 'I think it came from—' Suddenly she stopped and put her hand up to her mouth. 'Oh Christ.' Bile rose in her throat and from out of nowhere her stomach heaved. 'Christ, Jake, it's Artie . . .' she breathed, then she leant over and was violently sick.

Jake looked behind her. Hanging from the tree by a rope and split open from its neck to its tail was a cat. It was caught gruesomely in the glare of the torchlight, its tortured eyes wide open in terror. He stood up and swallowed down his own nausea. Around the animal's neck there was a card. It said: *Curiosity killed the cat*.

It was just luck that DS Lawrence was in the station that night, but he preferred to think of it as fate. He had been going over some paperwork when a call came in for CID and, being the nosy bugger that he was, he listened in to his colleague's conversation and heard the name of Thea's village.

'Hey, Mike? What's going down?' he called out.

'An assault, some village out near the Downs. A young woman's been assaulted in her own garden. We're just going over there now.'

'You got the victim's name?'

'Yes. It's Mrs Marshall . . .'

Lawrence was up and across the office in seconds. He snatched the bit of paper DS Mike Mitchell was holding and glanced at it. 'Jesus Christ!' He looked up. 'This all you got on it?'

'Yeah, we're just heading over there now.'

'Right!' Lawrence grabbed his jacket and car keys off his desk. 'I'll see you there,' he said, already on his way out of the office. 'She's a key witness in my case!'

At Tanbry Cottage, Thea sat wrapped in a blanket, a mug of hot sweet tea laced with brandy in her shaking hands and Jake, fully dressed, pacing the floor in front of her.

'I'm sorry, Thea,' he said, 'but I had to do it, I had to.' He stopped and looked at her. 'This has gone far enough, the police simply have to be told.' Thea said nothing. 'And as far as I'm concerned,' he went on, 'they should know the full story!'

'Don't, Jake, please . . .' She was still very weepy from the shock. 'Please don't go on.' She looked at her hands and lifted the mug to her lips, but she was unable to drink anything. 'What have you done with Artie?' she asked quietly.

'I've put him in a sack at the bottom of the garden.' Jake shook his head. 'Thea! Stop avoiding the issue! Are you going to tell them or am I?'

'Tell them what?' she cried. 'This has nothing to do with Cora's case!'

Jake crossed to her and knelt in front of her. 'It has everything to do with Cora's case. It's a warning, you've got to tell the police.'

'So you believe me now, do you? That there's something really weird about this case?'

Jake took a breath. 'I don't know, Thea,' he said. 'I can't think about that now, it's not the case I'm concerned about, it's you. Hand it over to the police and let them do their job.'

Again Thea said nothing, Jake stood up in frustration and continued to pace the floor.

DS Lawrence shoved the flashing blue light on the top of his car and drove full pelt along the A24. At the right junction he came off, hared down the country roads, through several villages and off on to the lanes. He came to Thea's village, slowed – only marginally – to get through it, then turned into her lane, an unmade-up road with only four houses off it. At her drive, he screeched to a halt, right behind the patrol car, left the light flashing and jumped over the five-barred gate, running up the drive towards the cottage. There was no police reason for his haste, this wasn't an emergency, but Lawrence didn't give a stuff. Thea Marshall wasn't only a key witness in his case, in the past two weeks he had started to think that she might be a great deal more than that.

Daniel Ellis drove back from a sedate supper with friends in Haycott, the next-door village to Thea's, listening to a new CD. He was a cautious driver, he liked to stick to the speed limit, and as he came to Thea's village itself, he took it slowly, peering at the cars in the village hall car park to see if any of them might be hers. And, despite telling himself repeatedly that there was nothing to see down Thea's lane, as he drove past it he couldn't stop himself from slowing right down to a snail's pace to peer up it in the darkness, although what he expected to see he had no idea. Suddenly he stopped dead in the middle of the road, with no warning to any cars behind; he just stopped. He gripped the steering wheel. At the top of the lane, just in front of Thea's gate, were two police cars, one with a light flashing its frightening blue signal. 'Oh fuck!' he snapped. And without thinking further, he slammed the car into first and sped off up towards the light.

DS Lawrence ran into the house. The door was open as one

of the uniformed officers was outside with Jake, looking at the cat.

'Police!' he said, holding up his ID at the WPC. 'Where's Thea? Mrs Marshall?'

'In the kitchen.'

'I'm in here, Dave,' Thea called out. He hurried through and found her standing in front of the Aga to keep warm.

'Christ, Thea! Are you all right?' He crossed to her and held her arms.

'Ouch!' she said and tried to smile.

'D'you need a doctor?'

'No I don't think so. I took a bang on the shoulders and a couple of kicks, but I think I'm OK. I'll get checked out tomorrow by my GP.'

'What happened?'

'Thea?'

Thea looked up as she heard Daniel's voice. 'Daniel?'

He hurried into the room followed by the WPC. 'I'm sorry, is he—?'

'Yes, yes, he's a friend, it's OK.'

Daniel stood just inside and took in every detail of the situation. DS Lawrence had moved aside but there was an intimacy between him and Thea that Daniel picked up.

'Thea? Are you OK?'

She nodded, suddenly swamped with embarrassment. 'What are you doing here?'

'Would you believe I was passing and I saw the police car and well . . .' He shrugged. There was a brief silence and he murmured, 'Thank God you're all right!'

Lawrence said, 'What happened, Thea? Did you disturb them? Was it burglary?'

'No, it was—' She broke off as Jake came back into the cottage.

He was followed by the uniformed officer who recognised DS Lawrence and said, 'Sir, I think you'd better come outside and have a look at something.'

Thea stared down at the floor.

'Thea?'

'Yes, go on.'

Lawrence went out and Daniel moved further into the room. 'Did you tell him?' Thea said to Jake. He shook his head.

'Tell him what?' Daniel asked.

Thea closed her eyes for a moment, then she said, 'I was assaulted tonight. It was a warning because I've been interfering. I've been asking questions about Jason Wakes and Cora.'

'You've *what*?'

'I contacted a couple of Wakes's friends, asked them some questions, that's all, and I tried to follow up what happened to Ewert.' Thea threw her hands up. 'Good God!' she snapped, 'Everyone's going on as if I committed a crime or something! All I was trying to do is find out some answers, all I want is to get to the—' She broke off and stuffed her fist in her mouth. The sight of Artie flashed into her mind, then out again a split second later, but it was enough for tears to spring to her eyes.

'Tell him about the cat.'

Thea shook her head.

'OK, then I will. Someone, whoever it was who assaulted Thea, also murdered the cat that lives next door. They slit it from its neck to its tail and left it hanging—'

'Stop it!' Thea cried. 'Stop it, Jake, please!'

'No I won't. They left a note on it that said: *Curiosity killed the cat*. It was a warning, all right, it was a bloody threat and she could have got herself killed.' He looked at Thea. 'Next time it could be you, Thea, or Tom!'

Thea started to cry and Daniel's stomach hurt. 'Thea,' he said gently. He stopped as DS Lawrence came back into the room.

'What the fuck is all this about?' Lawrence snapped. 'Thea? What the hell is going on?'

Thea gulped down her tears and bit her lip hard. 'I've been—' She stopped and took a breath. 'I've been asking questions, about Ewert and Jason Wakes, I—'

'Jesus Christ! You stupid fool!'

'Now hang on a minute!' Daniel snapped. 'There's no need for that!'

Lawrence glared over his shoulder at Daniel, but he did take a moment to calm down. 'Do you realise that you could put this whole case in jeopardy? That there're procedures to be gone through, rules, protocol, that if not followed, can bring a case down?' He was still seething but he kept it under control. 'What did you think you were doing? What, Thea?'

'I had a lead on Ewert, I got it from the pub he used to go to and, well, it just sort of went on . . .' Her voice trailed off.

'The lead that told you he was in Newcastle, right?'

She jerked up. 'How did you—?'

'We're the bloody professionals, Thea! We're not some tinpot operation who haven't got a fucking clue!' Lawrence shook his head. 'Did you think that we wouldn't go down every avenue open to us? Christ Almighty! Spare me the Miss Marple act!'

Thea dropped her head in her hands.

'This is a serious threat, Thea! You were lucky, you might not be so lucky next time!' Lawrence looked over his shoulder as the two officers from CID arrived.

'All right, Mike?'

'Yeah, what's going on?'

Lawrence had the grace to notice that Thea was crying and said, 'Come on, we'll go outside and I'll brief you. I could do with a cigarette.' He glanced at the WPC. 'You couldn't make Mrs Marshall a cup of tea, could you?' She nodded and, without looking again at Thea, DS Lawrence led his colleagues outside.

Much later, when the police had finally gone, Daniel stayed on. He found a bottle of Cognac in Thea's cupboard and poured three glasses, placing them on the table. Thea looked drained, physically and emotionally, and as she sat down he had to stop himself from reaching out to comfort her.

'OK,' he said, taking a sip of his brandy. 'What's all this about? You're not stupid, Thea, there must be something that's really bugging you for you to have got this involved.'

Jake glanced sidelong at Daniel. He liked him, but the way Thea was reacting to him, she very obviously didn't. 'Thea?' he said. 'Are you going to tell Daniel?'

Thea shrugged. She took a large gulp of the brandy and coughed as it hit the back of her throat. 'I'll give you my file,' she said directly to Daniel. 'You can see what I'm thinking from that.'

Daniel nodded and finished his drink in one. There was no point in wasting any more time here, he'd got the message. 'OK, I'll have a look at it.'

He stood and Jake said, 'I'll get it, it's upstairs.'

'Thanks.' As Jake left, Daniel stared down at the top of Thea's head and said, 'None of this is my fault, you know.'

'I never said it was.'

'But you seem to blame me in some way. If it wasn't me putting the case together it would have been someone else, some other barrister.'

She looked up at him and the effect was to make him physically pull back. 'You could have helped,' she said.

'No I couldn't. If you have principles, then you should stick by them, otherwise there's no point in having them.'

'And if you have principles you should know when they apply and when they don't,' Thea said. 'That was always my mother's problem.'

Jake came down the stairs and Daniel turned. He took the file and said goodnight. As he left the house, Thea didn't even raise her head or say goodbye. She just couldn't be bothered; nothing seemed to make any sense any more.

Chapter Twenty-Four

DS Lawrence had been up all night. He sat in his office with the Corinne White case file on his desk and went over and over every piece of paper, every statement, every scrap of forensic and every loose end that they couldn't seem to tie up. He wasn't tired, he was fuelled by caffeine and nicotine, an array of empty plastic cups was strewn on the floor around him and his ashtray was overloaded with butts. He had that strange rush of adrenalin that comes from lack of sleep and it made everything around him appear sharper.

He knew why he'd lost it with Thea last night now; he could see it, own up to it. It wasn't just the case, she couldn't seriously damage things, it was the feeling that he'd been conned, that the dinners, three in total, had been set up, an excuse to use him to find out the score. That had angered him; it made him feel stupid. Of course he fancied her, who in their right minds wouldn't? Maybe it was more? He lit another cigarette and sat back in his chair. Then again, maybe it wasn't. Christ, this case was littered with uncertainties! There was one thing for sure, though, and that was that nobody got away with the sort of shit he'd seen last night; nobody made threats like that on his turf.

Lawrence rubbed his hands over his face and, cigarette between his lips, stood to go to the bathroom. If it hadn't been Thea, would he have cared so much, been up all night? He took a last drag and dropped it in the ashtray. Another uncertainty, he thought, and the way he had behaved towards her last night, he wasn't sure if he was ever going to get the chance to put it straight.

On the way to the bathroom Lawrence passed DC Louis Judd. 'Morning, boss,' Judd said. 'What's the call?'

Lawrence stopped. 'The Corinne White case. File's on my desk. Get some coffees in, will you, Louis, for everyone? I'm just going to have a wash and a crap and I'll be back in about ten minutes.'

'Right-oh, boss. Have one for me!' Judd walked on into the office, took the file off Lawrence's desk and sat down to have a good look through it.

'Right, morning everyone,' Lawrence said, washed and shaved but in yesterday's clothes. 'Informal briefing this, I want to get to work again on the White case. I think we've left a couple of things undone and I want them put right.'

There was an uncomfortable shuffling on chairs. As far as the team were concerned they'd gone through it with a fine-toothed comb, left nothing out that couldn't be put in.

'Like what?' Cath asked.

'Film footage. Cath, I'd like you to contact every twenty-four-hour garage you contacted before, only this time I'd like you to look through their surveillance film.'

'You're joking? That'll take days!'

'Correct!'

'But why, when no one has come forward with a positive sighting of her or her car?'

'You asked verbally, but people are fallible. Somewhere out there Corinne White stopped for a couple of hours. She was confused and frightened and my guess is she stopped at a petrol station, maybe got a drink, maybe just sat parked for a while. If she did, then we may strike lucky and find her on camera. I'm sorry, Cath, I know it's a bore but . . .' He shrugged.

'Louis, work on the Ewert Lockhart angle again. That Newcastle lead was a red herring, he's hiding somewhere, somewhere in London is my guess so get on to it.'

DC Judd nodded and made several notes in his book.

'Pete, do more on this signet ring problem, all right? Check every friend again for photos on the night, find out if there's any evidence that Wakes might have had one. How do you get a signet ring? Not every Tom, Dick and Harry has one so they must be reasonably élite. Check city jewellers, check every avenue you can think of, OK?'

Detective Constable Pete Dowe was newly promoted, serious and tenacious; the very reason Lawrence had given him the flimsiest lead.

'The rest of you get back to the invitation list to the Wakes party that night and re-call the names on it. I want more. Let's put the pressure on and see if anyone will crack. There must be someone out there who doesn't like Wakes!' Lawrence smiled. 'Apart from us, of course.' There was a brief burst of laughter.

'Good. Any questions?'

'Yes, where's this leading, boss? I thought we had a case,' Judd asked.

'We do, but it's not good enough. This has to be as tight as a drum to stop the CPS pissing around trying to make up their minds whether or not to go ahead. Understood?'

The team nodded. 'Good, let's do it!'

Daniel Ellis was in Chambers before anyone else. He asked Charlie for the Wakes brief, got himself a coffee and sat down to read. It was early, he had been up most of the night worrying about Thea and the coffee tasted good. He sipped, cradled the cup in his hands for a few moments, staring out of the window, then got to work. There was something that had been bothering him, something that had come to him in the middle of the night, one small comment, prompted by Thea's words, and he knew it was in here somewhere. Searching through the character witness statements, he dismissed each one as he read through it, making the odd note here and there, then finally, three statements from the end, he found it. Wakes's boss, the man who headed the fund management team had originally said: '*Jason Wakes is a much-valued member of the team. He has only been with us for a year and although there were problems at first, with his lack of experience, dealing with staff, and of course taking on such a big fund, he has settled in exceptionally well.*' That's what Daniel remembered. The second statement, corrected on his recommendation, only referred to teething problems, there was no mention of lack of experience or the new fund. Daniel had what he wanted. He stood up and taking the piece of paper, went outside to the corridor to photocopy it. Minutes later, he replaced the original back in the file and returned the file to Charlie.

'You off then, Mr Ellis?'

'Yes, Charlie,' Daniel had planned a few days' break.

'Going anywhere nice?'

'If the weather's nice, to West Wittering, if it's not then cricket on the telly.'

'Very nice too. Couple of tinnies and the test match. Just where I'd be if I had half the chance!'

'I'll think of you as I'm raising my can! Thanks for your help, Charlie, I'll see you soon.'

'Right you are, Mr Ellis. Cheerio.'

With his photocopy safely in his briefcase Daniel headed back to Victoria and the first train home to Sussex.

Thea was at the sink washing up when Jake came down. Tom had started his summer vacation and was still asleep, catching up on all the early starts he'd had to endure during termtime, so the cottage was quiet. Quiet and a little depressed, Jake thought, as he put the kettle on the Aga for tea.

'I'll do that, Dad,' Thea said, taking the kettle from him. 'What would you like, tea or coffee?'

'Tea, please.' Jake wasn't dressed. To be honest, last night's scare had knocked him for six. It was a sign of old age, he thought, the inability to take things in your stride.

'Would you like some toast?' Thea went to the fridge. 'I made some gooseberry jam, I had rather a glut of them and—'

'Thea?'

She stopped, took a deep breath and turned.

'Thea, I'm sorry to have to bring this all up but I really do think that you owe me an explanation.' He looked at her. She was so pale that he could see the veins in her neck and the faint blue shadows under her eyes. 'I don't understand it, you see, I don't understand how you could have put yourself and Tom in such danger.'

'I . . .'

'No, let me finish. You see, I don't understand, Thea, what drives this terrible vengeance. Why you seemed to have taken the mantle of justice and retribution for Cora on to your own shoulders. Why it has affected you so very much. I mean, we're all upset, all of us, but this, this call to arms seems a bit far-fetched to me.'

The kettle whistled and Thea turned to make the tea. She let it brew for a few moments, stirred it and poured, bringing a cup over to the table where Jake sat.

'Sit down, Thea, and talk to me,' he said.

She did as he asked.

'I'm sorry to have to ask this, but I need to know. Is there something between you and Cora, something that runs deeper than friendship? Is this the reason for your anger and pain?'

'Are you asking me if Cora and I are lovers?'

Jake swallowed. He was surprised at how unliberal he felt about all these things now, after half a lifetime with Hedda. All he wanted for Thea was happiness and security, he didn't want her to have heartbreak and prejudice, to struggle to be accepted. He wanted her to have all the children he had never had and all the love. He said, 'Yes, I suppose I am.'

Thea was silent.

'Do you love Cora?'

She looked at him. 'Yes. Yes I do, I love her very much, but . . . but not in the way you mean. I love her in the same way that I love you, I suppose. You are a huge part of my life, Jake, mine and Tom's, and so is Cora. I couldn't live without you and I'm finding it very hard to live without Cora.'

Jake reached out and took her hand in his. 'Is that all?'

'Yes. Yes and no.' Thea squeezed his fingers. 'To be honest with you I don't really know why I feel the way I do about all of this. I've never felt so angry, never felt so much pain!' She let out a sigh. 'All I can think about is how Cora has struggled all her life, struggled to get away from care, struggled to be something, to learn to read, to talk nicely, to be all the things she wanted to be and in one night, in what, barely an hour, that bastard ruined it all!' She pulled her hand back and clasped both of them together in front of her, making one fist. 'You know she trusted me, Jake, she didn't want to get involved in stripping all those years ago and she did it because I said it would be OK. I failed her – I let her down big time! I got her into a career that she was ashamed of and in the end I wasn't there for her.'

'It wasn't your fault, Thea, you aren't to blame.'

'Oh I know that, I've been through that part of it. I feel she let me down too. She copped out. She's the one person I always respected but she didn't have what it takes. She ran away to France, to Hedda. It was insulting.' Thea stared down at her hands.

'Is that part of it too? Are you trying to win her back from Hedda by proving to her that there's a reason to come back?'

Thea jerked up. 'You should have been the therapist!'

Jake smiled and said, 'That's what Hedda used to say to me.'

Thea looked at him for a few moments, then finally she smiled back.

'Is there more?'

'A bit.' She took a deep breath, then said, 'I was having an affair with the man who turned up last night, Daniel Ellis. It was going well, brilliantly actually, I was really happy, then . . .' She bit her lip. 'He turned out to be the barrister for Jason Wakes.'

'Good God! Are you sure?'

'Of course I'm sure! He told me himself.'

Jake could hear the tears in her voice. 'And?'

'And nothing. He dumped me.'

'Dumped you?'

'Yes, walked out on me, didn't ring! Get the picture?'

Jake looked at her. 'I'm sorry, Thea.'

'Yes.' She swallowed hard. 'To be honest, Jake, so am I.'

'Does he know that?'

She shrugged. 'What, that I'm sorry? No, he couldn't care less.'

Jake said nothing. From the way Daniel had looked at Thea last night, from the way he'd spoken to her and handled himself, Jake knew that wasn't true.

'So now you know,' Thea said.

'Yes, now I know.'

'Do you understand any of it? Does it make sense to you?'

Jake shrugged. 'I don't know.' He stood up and went to

pour himself another cup of tea. The doorbell sounded and Jake said, 'I'll get it.' He walked into the hall and opened the front door.

'Hello, Daniel,' Thea heard. 'Come on in.' She stood, momentarily panicked, but Daniel was in the doorway before she had a chance to move anywhere.

'Thea, I've been thinking about what you said last night, and, well, I . . . erm, I want to help.'

'You do?'

'Yes, I do.' He was in a city suit, dark navy, tailor-made, with a royal-blue shirt and a red tie. He didn't look like a barrister at all, but then he was infamous for that character-istic. 'But you must promise me two things, if you want me to get involved.'

She looked at him. 'Go on.'

'No, not until you promise.'

'How can I promise when I don't know what you're going to ask of me?'

'You have to trust me if you want my help. You have to trust me completely.'

Thea hesitated, but only for a moment. What choice did she have? She couldn't do this on her own. 'OK, what do I have to promise?'

'First that you'll have nothing more to do with this case.' He couldn't bear it, he couldn't bear for something to happen to her. It was too dangerous, she had to let it go.

'Daniel! I can't promise that! You know I—'

'Next time it might not be a cat, it might be you, or Tom. You have to let me handle it, Thea. If you don't, then I shall have nothing more to do with it.' He was calling her bluff, he hoped to God that she'd fall for it.

372

She did. 'OK,' she said. 'You've got my word.'

'Thank you.'

'And the second promise?'

'That what I am doing will never go further than these four walls. I am putting my whole career in jeopardy, I must be sure that you won't tell anyone that I'm involved. As far as you're concerned, we've never had this conversation. OK?'

'Yes,' she said, suddenly aware of the seriousness of what he was doing. 'I promise. Of course I promise that.'

'Good.' He dug his hands in his pockets. 'Then there's no more to say.'

'No.'

He turned to go but Thea stopped him. 'Can I ask you something, Daniel?'

'Yes.'

'Why? Why have you decided to help?'

He dug his hands deeper into his pockets and stared at her for a moment. Now was his opportunity, now he could tell her why he was here. He'd been building up to this since the moment he saw her last night, he'd gone over and over the words in his head, rehearsed it out loud, but it wouldn't come out. He wasn't just trying to help, he was here because she meant more to him than his principles, than his career even. He was here because she wanted him to be and yet he just couldn't say it. 'Because . . .' He stopped. 'Because I think it's right to do so.'

'I see.'

'Do you, Thea?' He continued to stare at her for a moment longer, then he dragged his eyes away and headed for the door. Before Thea could call him back and ask him what he meant, he had opened it and disappeared outside. Moments later she heard his engine and he was gone.

'So?' Jake asked, coming back into the kitchen after his discreet removal to the sitting room.

'So nothing,' Thea said miserably. And she stood to pour them both more tea.

Out of sight, Hedda watched Cora from across the terrace. Her skin was dappled by shadow and she was reading, or at least she looked as if she was, but her leg jerked up and down off the ball of her foot, continuously, and there was no way she could have concentrated on the words. Hedda lit a cigarette and stayed where she was.

It was nearly three weeks now since Cora had arrived and in that time Cora had changed. The alterations were subtle, of course, perhaps apparent only to a professional, but Hedda saw them. Cora had gone from weepy and confused to simply withdrawn. There were no more tears, no more remonstrations of guilt and anger, no more indecision, only a cool, impenetrable silence. They had talked once or twice but Cora had been reticent, had spoken only of final retribution and true justice, in a way that Hedda couldn't expand on or delve into, and it worried her. It was beginning to worry her a great deal. Hedda walked over to where Cora was sitting.

'Cora?'

Cora turned. She had begun to take more notice of her appearance, in the most bizarre and inappropriate way. She wore the navy and white dress all the time now, rinsing it out overnight, and she styled her hair elaborately into a chignon or a French plait, changing the style two or three times a day. She wore one of several pairs of large flashy earrings that she had bought in town and painted the nails on her hands and feet a deep magenta pink. Now, as she turned, Hedda saw that she wore gold and diamond clips, shaped like a flower with a fake diamond in the middle, and lipstick, a red slash of it, in the centre of a still pale face.

'Cora, I might go up to the village tonight and have a drink with Henri. Would you like to come?'

Cora put down her book. 'No, I don't think so, Hedda.'

Hedda pulled out a chair from the table and sat down. 'But you look so nice, it would be a shame for no one to see you.'

'I'm saving myself,' Cora said.

'Oh? For what?'

Cora smiled. All the time she sat there, her leg jigged up and down, up and down. 'Nothing much,' she said.

Hedda sighed. She smoked her cigarette in silence, then she said, 'Cora, have you thought any more about going back home? About facing up to things?'

Cora put her book down on the table. 'Yes,' she replied, 'I have.'

'You have? And?'

'I am going to get the justice I deserve.'

Hedda looked at her. 'Good! I'm glad to hear it!'

But Cora didn't seem to hear her. She had dropped her head down and was rolling the hem of her dress between her fingers, a look of intense concentration on her face.

'Have you rung Thea?'

Cora jerked her head up. She looked momentarily disorientated. 'Thea?'

'Yes, does she know that you'll—'

Cora shook her head and smiled. 'I told you, Hedda,' she said, reaching out and placing a stiff, icy-cold hand on Hedda's warm brown skin, 'I am going to get the justice I deserve.' With that, she went back to her book.

'I don't like it, Henri,' Hedda said that evening over a drink at the café. 'I feel nervous. She isn't right and I don't know what to do to get through to her. My training, my instinct says leave her alone, let her get through it, but there's something volatile about her, she's an unknown quantity.'

Henri didn't know how best to advise. He found the girl very peculiar. She interrupted his routine with Hedda, was a depressing influence; she made him uneasy, even – the one time she'd been to his home – uneasy in his own house! But she had been through a terrible experience and although opinionated and rather set in his ways, Henri was not an unfair man. 'Leave her, Hedda,' he answered. 'Leave her for a bit longer and see if she comes round. Another week perhaps. Maybe we should get her more involved with people her own age, get her to go out a little bit, see a couple of the girls from the village. Marie with her family might be a good choice.' Henri drained his glass and stood. 'Now, one more drink here and then home to my house for a nightcap. OK?'

'OK,' Hedda replied, and gave him her empty glass.

Cora was back in Hedda's house well within the thirty-minute time limit she had allowed herself; The trip to Henri's had been easy; 'Easy peasy, lemon squeezy,' she chanted, over and over again. She smiled and fondled her prize. God that man was such a fool! He'd really thought she was eyeing him up after the shoot last week, giving him the come on! What an idiot! She'd been watching how he loaded the gun, unloaded it, where he kept it and after he locked the cupboard, where he hid the key. She held the gun close to her chest and let out a sigh. All those poor flapping birds. Bang! Out of the sky and down they fell. Bang, bang, you're dead! Cora smiled again. Then she stood and took a towel from the bathroom, wrapping the gun lovingly inside it and laying it at the bottom of the holdall she had packed earlier that day, covering it with her few clothes. She pulled the covers of the bed up over the pillows, smoothed it and walked out of the room.

Hedda would stay tonight with Henri. A few drinks followed by a nightcap and she'd fall asleep in his bed, too relaxed, too sated to get up. By the time she came back tomorrow Cora would be gone. A note of thanks, some flowers and goodbye.

Cora came down the stairs, tidied the few things out of place in the small stone house and took one last look round it. She didn't see it though, she hadn't seen anything for days, except a red glaze, a burning red glaze. She took the key from the front door, walked outside on to the drive and locked it behind her, placing the key under the mat. Then she climbed into her car, started the engine and without even a backward glance, drove off. She had a ferry to catch – she had booked it a week ago – and at the moment, she was running precisely on time.

Chapter Twenty-Five

DS Lawrence was feeling depressed. Twenty-four hours he'd been holed up in the office waiting for results after their renewed assault on the White case, a self-inflicted torture and they'd had nothing: zero, sweet FA, bugger all.

'Why don't you go home, Dave?' DS Mitchell had said, passing his desk and seeing him with his head on his arms, his eyes closed and the perpetual cigarette burning on his desk.

'You wouldn't understand,' he mumbled, keeping his head down. To be honest, he wasn't sure if he understood it himself. It wasn't Thea, that much he'd ascertained in the past day and night, it was more, it was to do with not letting Corinne White down, not letting that sleek, expensive little bastard get away with it. It was professionalism taken to its limits, and pride. Yeah, he thought, raising his head as the phone rang, that old killer dog: pride. He snatched the phone up and barked into it, then moments later sat bolt upright and reached for his cigarette.

'You're sure, Cath? Yeah, hang on, I'll double check it. It's M465FRC, a blue Vauxhall Corsa. It is? Jesus Christ! You're a fucking genius! Well done you, Cath! Yup, please do, bring that tape right in and we'll have a look at it!' He slammed the phone down and stood up.

'You all right, boss?'

'I'm more than all right, I'm fucking marvellous! She's got it, Cath's got a tape with Corinne White parked in the corner of a twenty-four-hour garage just off the A24. We've not done it before because it's not *en route*, but Cath thought she'd give it a go! Bloody genius, that's what it was! And Corinne White was there for the whole missing time, all one hour fifty-five minutes of it and it's definitely her!' He stubbed his cigarette out and immediately lit another. 'Now all we need is you, Louis, to strike gold and we've stitched that little bugger right up!' He took a long drag of nicotine and felt a rush to his head. 'We've stitched him up good and proper,' he murmured, 'from the bottom all the fucking way to the top.'

Daniel Ellis looked up from the notes he was making as his fax machine bleeped and began transmission. 'Ah ha!' he murmured, standing and stretching. He walked across to the machine and the phone on his desk rang. He answered it. 'Hello, yes, yes I did thanks, it's just coming through. Oh did you? Great, thanks. Yes, it is, for the *Daily Telegraph* finance page. Of course, let me take a note of your name again and I'll send you a copy through when it goes to press.' A few small lies could be very useful, he had discovered in the last twenty-four hours. He'd been researching into employment figures for the Department of Trade and Industry and now he was writing an article for the *Telegraph*. From barrister to researcher to journalist in just one day. Not bad. He wrote down the name of the girl in the bank's PR department and thanked her again for her help. Then he went to the fax, collected the papers that had come through and took them back to his desk. It was a list of major funds under management, their current value and the teams managing the funds. Daniel glanced through it and sank down into his chair.

'Oh my goodness . . .' He underlined the name of the firm with the biggest amount of money under management and shook his head. It was Hind Industrial. Jason Wakes managed a portion of their billion-pound pension fund, the bank spread the rest over several different teams. Daniel picked up the phone and dialled the number he had on the top of his fax.

'Hello, may I speak to Kylie, please? Oh it is, hi there, Kylie, it's Tom Rogers here, the journalist? We spoke a few moments ago? Yes, hi! Listen, Kylie, I wonder if you could find something out for me. I was wondering how long the bank has been managing the Hind Industrial pension fund? I'm thinking of adding a piece about client loyalty and how service counts for more than . . . Oh you can? Great. Yes, of course I'll hold.' He tapped his pen against his front teeth, suddenly anxious. 'Hello? Yes, hi. Last year? August last year, oh really, from First Mid-Western? Right. OK, thanks again, Kylie. Bye for now.' Replacing the receiver, Daniel sat back in his chair. Hind Industrial move their pension fund across to Premier Bank from First Mid-Western, Jason Wakes is taken on at the same time, maybe as part of the package, maybe not, but whatever the case, it was almost certain that nobody was going to talk about the son of a major bank client. It was a cover-up, that's what it was, a cover-up of sorts. No one would risk upsetting the balance, losing face with Hind Industrial, no matter how awful Jason Wakes turned out to be. What if, and Daniel was speculating now, what if there had been a directive, from the very top, that everyone should keep their mouths shut, say nice things and it would all be OK. What was it John Edwards had said, when he asked Daniel to take on the Wakes case? 'What Michael Wakes wants he usually gets.' So Wakes wants his son defended by a top barrister and he wants whatever faults little Jason might have to be hushed up, glossed over – lied about.

Daniel rifled through his papers and found the employment list that he'd had faxed through to him that morning by Premier Bank's Human Resources department under the impression he was researching for the DTI. He glanced through it, underlined a couple of things, made a note of two names, then picked up the phone again and dialled the employment agency who serviced Premier Bank.

'Yes, hi, I wonder if, erm, Maureen Parks is in yet? Oh she is? Yes, I would please. Yes, I'll hold.' Mrs Parks was the company director and no one, a secretary had said earlier, could give out any information except her. 'Hello? Maureen Parks? Yes I hope so. My name is Tom Rogers and I'm a journalist working on a feature for one of the national newspapers about sexual harassment in the city. It's mainly financial institutions I'm interested in and I know that you provide secretarial staff for a number of—' He stopped as Maureen Parks asked him what paper and wondered which one to choose this time. 'Yes, of course, it's the *Times*. The features editor Susan Hiller who commissioned the piece said she wanted me to concentrate mainly on secretarial staff because we feel that they seem to be in the main firing line.' Daniel paused for breath, but only very briefly. 'I was wondering if you might have any first-hand experience of this sort of thing with any of your staff?' He glanced at the employment list, a list of staff and how long they stayed and the two names he'd made a note of. They were both secretaries from Wakes's department, they had both left in quick succession, barely there a couple of months each and they were both supplied by Parks Secretarial. It might be nothing, just normal staff turnover, but then again . . .

'You have? Yes! Yes, of course I can come in. When would be convenient? The sooner the better for me to be honest, I'm on a bit of a tight deadline. Tomorrow morning?' Daniel reached for his diary. 'Yes, seven-forty-five will be perfect. No, it's not too early, not at all. Thanks, yes I know where you are. I look forward to meeting you.' And with that, he hung up.

Cora's ferry docked at five a.m. It was one of those luxury cruise liners that sails overnight and lists on board such things as swimming pools, nightclubs and hairdressers. It was here, in the hair salon, that Cora spent a good part of the passage and emerged on British soil, no longer a blonde with an elegant shoulder-length bob, but a brunette, her hair cut razor short to an inch all over. It completely changed her face, made it smaller and more angular and with the new narrow sunglasses on, she was barely recognisable.

She drove first to a car hire office and hired a car, leaving her own in their complimentary car park for a small fee. Then she filled the hire car with petrol and headed for the M25. Half an hour later, by six-thirty a.m., she was on her way to London and to the offices of Premier Bank.

It was Friday morning, five-thirty a.m., the third day of Daniel's short break, and he was up, showered and dressed, wearing a suit and collar and tie. He made tea, breakfasted and collected his notes, stuffing them into his briefcase. When Petula came down at six, he was just on his way out of the door to drive to Gatwick and catch the Gatwick Express to Victoria.

'I'll be back at lunchtime, Pet! Take the boys to Drusilla's today, will you?'

Drusilla's was a zoo in East Sussex. Petula frowned and Daniel said, 'I know! I know it's bad form but there's nothing I can do about it. I've got something important to do, something very important. OK?'

Still Petula frowned, so Daniel put down his case, came back into the house and kissed her cheek. 'I'll be around tomorrow,' he said, 'I promise.'

She nodded and he picked up his case, heading back to the door. 'Have I ever broken a promise, Pet?' he called just as he went out and Petula finally smiled. No, no he hadn't. Daniel Ellis was the most loyal man she'd ever met.

Maureen Parks's office was off Oxford Street, a smart affair that took up the ground floor of what was formerly a shop and the second floor of what was formerly the shop's flat. It had been interior designed to office spec, had deep, striped comfy sofas and swag and tail drapes, reproduction mahogany desks and well-framed fake Victorian botanical prints. Parks Secretarial employed a full-time staff of six women, who were all required to wear suits and who dispatched smart young things from the Lucie Clayton and St James's secretarial schools to posh jobs in the City, where they hopefully found themselves gainfully employed for a couple of years and then a rich young husband.

Maureen Parks was alone when Daniel arrived. Her team didn't start until eight-thirty, which gave them, she said, looking at her gold ladies' Rolex, forty minutes. 'I hope you don't mind,' she said, pouring him coffee from a percolator, 'but I'd like to finish before any of my staff arrive, I'd rather that only the two of us knew about this meeting.'

'Absolutely,' Daniel replied.

'Milk? Sugar?'

'No, as it is.' Daniel took his coffee and they sat down.

'So, Mr Rogers—'

'Tom, please.'

'Tom. You wanted to know about sexual harassment?'

'Yes, you said that you have first-hand experience of it? Is that right?'

'I do.' Maureen Parks was in her late forties, Daniel guessed, an upright, manicured lady, with a very expensive suit and a few items of classic jewellery. Her manner was clipped and he thought he could detect the faint trace of a northern accent. She seemed on edge. 'But I have to say that I'm not at all sure about sharing it with you. It's really only my growing sense of injustice and the fact that one of my girls, my best girls, has been—' She broke off and looked down at her hands for a moment. 'This article,' she said. 'Does it have to use real names?'

Daniel shook his head. 'Not at all. If you wish to remain

anonymous, then that's your prerogative. I would just say, for example, "a top London employment agency". There must be several of those to choose from.'

'Not that many.'

'No, of course, but it does ensure a certain amount of anonymity.'

'And I'd have your assurance on that? Your word?'

'Of course.' Believing a journalist, he thought, that's her first mistake.

'You see, the thing is, Tom, that for some time now I've had a rotten feeling about something. I'm an honest woman, a rare thing in business, I know, but I've built my reputation on it. What you see is what you get from Maureen Parks and, well, I, erm . . .' She stopped again and fiddled with her watch. 'I've had a problem with one particular City institution; I've had two of my girls leave because of sexual harassment. One case in particular, the second, was very nasty, well . . . terrible really . . .' There was another pause; it lasted for some time. Finally Maureen said, 'And I think it's time to speak out, get things straight. When you called me yesterday and left that message I had a good old think about it and I decided that fate had stepped in. I've had a warning, you see, to keep *stumm* about it, about what happened, that is, I was told that no more business would come my way if I made a fuss and to a reasonably small business a big bank is a major client. So I kept quiet but my girls aren't happy, word has got round and they don't trust me any more, I can sense it. What happened wasn't my fault but I think that some of my regular temps blame me, think that I was—'

'Mrs Parks?' Daniel interrupted. 'What exactly happened?

I'm sorry, but this doesn't make much sense unless you tell me what this is all about.'

Maureen took a moment. The whole subject obviously upset her.

'Why don't you tell me the whole thing, in your own words, from start to finish.'

'OK.' She was clearly a woman who usually had a tight grip on her feelings, but it was costing her some effort to do so now.

Daniel took a Dictaphone out of his case. 'Would you mind if I taped you?' he asked. 'It's really just for my own notes, it makes things clearer.'

Maureen hesitated, then said, 'No, no, that's all right.' She looked at the Dictaphone, waited for Daniel to switch it on and took a deep breath. 'It started almost a year ago to the day,' she began. 'I had a lovely girl, Laura, she started with one of my best clients, a good job, PA to a team of fund managers. There was an incident, she hadn't been there more than a month when a new chap made a pass at her.'

'A pass?'

'Yes, well, she wouldn't say more than that, not to me she wouldn't, but I heard later from one of my staff that the chap was a really nasty piece of work, abusive and aggressive. She declined his pass – she was engaged, supposed to be getting married this August, and for three weeks after that suffered what I would call abuse – that's the only word for it: abuse, mental and physical! This chap apparently touched her up repeatedly, made lewd innuendoes, jokes at her expense, thoroughly humiliated her and in the end she resigned, from the job and from my agency!' Maureen Parks shook her head. 'Of course all this came out after she'd left and I never got the chance to talk to her personally. But I was livid! I went to see the bank immediately, had an interview with the head of department who denied everything. He said it had been a "simple misunderstanding" and that my girl was "hysterical"! And d'you know, I believed him! God, I must have been gullible. This girl hadn't been on my books before, she was young and I'd never had any trouble with this bank, never! The whole incident was played down, made to seem inconsequential, so I did nothing about it. More fool me! I found them another secretary, one of my best temps, to tide them over and took a big bonus to do so. It was to shut me up, the money, only I didn't realise it at the time.'

Daniel, who was making furious notes, glanced up as Maureen Parks stopped speaking. Not such a tight grip, he thought, as she blew her nose on a white linen handkerchief.

'I'm sorry,' she said, 'but it's like opening the flood gates, this. I've kept the whole thing to myself for so long, worried about it so much, that telling you has thoroughly upset me . . .' She blew her nose again. 'I'm sorry.'

'Not at all. I can quite understand your distress.' Daniel stopped writing. 'Would you like to stop for a while?'

Maureen glanced at her watch. 'No, we'll run out of time if I do.' She folded the handkerchief. 'When this girl, Laura, left the bank, as I said, I sent them one my best temporary secretaries, a girl called Kate. She started with them the following week. Now, Kate is very capable. She's an attractive girl in her late twenties, single, independent, a really good girl. She was with me for seven years before

the situation at the bank and when I found out what had happened to her, there was absolutely no doubting her word.'

'What did happen?'

'Well, in the first instance, exactly the same as before.
This young man made a pass at her, but Kate handled it
better, she was older, more in control. Only then, I gather,
things took on a new perspective. He started courting
her against her wishes, sending her flowers, ringing her,
sending her intimate E-mails, asking her out all the time
and even though she tried to keep him at a distance, things
just got worse. She came to me and I went in again to see
the head of department. This time what he said didn't wash
and I demanded an inquiry and that Kate leave. He said he'd
discuss it with her and that it probably wouldn't come to
that.' Maureen took another deep breath. 'The upshot was
that Kate was offered a permanent position at the bank
working for a different team; same department, mind you,
but a different group. She was given a hefty salary and all
the perks: pension scheme, private health care, big annual
bonus, etc., etc. I'm sure you can see the attraction and sadly
so did she. In hindsight she should have just left but . . .'
Maureen shrugged. 'Anyone can have twenty-twenty vision
with hindsight, can't they? Anyway, Kate accepted the job,
moved teams but unfortunately that wasn't the end of the
problem. This young man became a real nuisance. It was
as if he couldn't have a proper relationship, he had to have
control. He became almost obsessive about Kate, would
corner her in quiet corridors, touch her up, he started to
ring her at home, follow her to lunch, all sorts of things.
And then one night, quite late, he turned up at her home.
He said he needed to talk to her because he was in love

with her. Kate let him in and he—' Maureen Parks broke off and stared down at her hands. She didn't look up for several minutes.

Daniel said, 'He did what, Mrs Parks?'

She clasped her hands together to stop them shaking. 'It was never reported, you see, she was too ashamed, too distressed and he offered her money, a great deal of it to keep quiet . . .'

'What did he do, Mrs Parks?'

Maureen looked up. 'He raped her.'

It was mid afternoon and Cora had sat outside Premier Bank all day. She had seen Jason Wakes arrive for work at eight-forty-five, go out to lunch at one and return to the office a couple of hours later. It was now five-fifteen p.m. and she knew she was half-way through the wait. She returned to her book, her leg jiggling up and down, and she stared, unseeing, down at the words.

Detective Constable Pete Dowe walked into the reception of the College of Arms in Queen Victoria Street and gave his name to the receptionist.

'The Officer-in-waiting will be with you in a few minutes,' she said. 'Would you like to wait in the waiting room?'

'No, I'm fine here, thank you.' He stood and looked up at banners hung around the room emblazoned with the coats of arms of the realm and felt momentarily overawed by it all. Then he turned as the Officer-in-waiting approached him, all thoughts except the job in hand gone, and said, 'DC Dowe, we spoke earlier on the phone.'

'Yes, hello, Detective Constable. I think I've got exactly

what you want. Wakes was the name, was it? A Mr Jason Wakes?'

DC Dowe felt like punching the air. 'Yes, d'you have a record of him?'

'As I told you earlier, Detective Constable, once a search for a particular coat of arms is commissioned and a fee paid over, we open a file. According to my records, Mr Jason Wakes commissioned such a search in January this year. See, here, I have a note of all his details, the details you gave me over the phone.' The Officer held out a ledger and a file.

'Would it be possible to photocopy these?'

'Of course.'

'And people who commission these searches, what do they do with their family crest once they find it?'

'A number of things. Some have it put on notepaper, business stationery, that sort of thing, others have it put on a signet ring, some just keep it as part of their family history.'

DC Dowe took the ledger and file. 'What's the most likely use?'

The Officer thought for a moment. 'In my opinion, it seems to be signet rings.'

DC Dowe smiled. 'Thank you,' he said, tapping the ledger under his arm. 'Thank you very much indeed.'

Daniel Ellis had stayed a great deal longer than his allotted forty minutes with Maureen Parks. Once the story was out, the words seemed to fall like dominoes and before she knew it, she had said far, far more than she had ever intended to. What, she asked, do I do, with this on my conscience? And

Daniel told her only what she already knew: that she must convince Kate to go to the police.

From the moment he took Cath's call early that morning, DS Lawrence knew that this was his lucky day. By lunchtime they had the garage security surveillance tape in police custody and several copies of it made for evidence and by mid afternoon he knew that he was really flying. He'd had a call from DC Dowe outside the College of Arms and Louis Judd had located Lockhart, Corinne White's ex-boyfriend, holed up in a bed and breakfast in Tooting Bec, not five minutes from where he lived.

'It was a stroke of luck, boss,' DC Judd called in over his radio. 'I was hanging round the betting shop, asking if anyone knew him and the bugger walks in. He made a run for it but I got him.' Judd, standing by his car, the radio in his hand, grinned at Ewert Lockhart in the back with his colleague. 'I got him,' he said again and, back at Crawley nick, Lawrence threw his fist in the air.

An hour and a half later Judd brought Lockhart into the station. 'Where d'you want him, boss?'

'Let's put him in interview room two. Has he said anything on the way in?'

'Just that he hasn't done anything, which we know.'

'Then why'd he disappear?' Lawrence lit a cigarette. 'Let's charge him.'

'Charge him?'

'Yes, for the violent assault on Corinne White.'

'You're joking?'

'No I'm not. He assaulted Corinne when she came to boast of her sexual conquest of Wakes. That's what the defence are alleging so let's charge him for it and let him worm his way out of it.'

Judd looked at Lawrence. There were times when he thought Lawrence was a genius and others when he came close to insanity.

'Charge him,' Lawrence said. 'Trust me, Louis! I know what I'm doing.'

Another hour on, Lockhart was in the interview room protesting his innocence for all he was worth. He'd been in there for thirty minutes and was already beginning to crack.

'You can't charge me 'cause I ain't done nothing wrong!' he snapped. He looked at his brief. 'They can't do this to me, they fucking can't! I ain't done nothing!'

His brief said, 'Let's just answer the questions, Mr Lockhart.'

'Where were you then?' Lawrence continued. 'On the morning of May the fourteenth between the hours of three a.m. and five a.m.?'

'I told you, I was at home in bed!'

'Do you have anyone to verify this statement?'

'No of course I don't! I was asleep!'

Lawrence sighed. 'No you weren't Ewert, you were watching telly, a film on Sky, and Cora Whitby arrived at your place to interrupt that film about three o'clock. She was full of herself, boasting that she'd just been laid, taunting you, and you were furious. You were insanely jealous, you'd been drinking and you lost it. You lost it big time, Ewert, and you laid into her. You beat her about the face and thighs and then kicked her out. Only she didn't take it this time, she drove to her friend who insisted that she go to the police.'

'Jesus Christ! This is bullshit! It isn't true!'

'The next morning, you sober up and ring her to apologise, but she tells you it's too late, she's already gone to the police. That's why you disappeared, isn't it? You did a runner, scared shitless that—'

'That isn't true!' Lockhart cried. 'Christ, man, where'd you get all this shit?'

'Why have you been hiding, Ewert?'

Lockhart said nothing.

'How come you disappear the day after Cora gets assaulted?' Still he said nothing, but as he reached for a cigarette Lawrence saw that his hands were shaking. 'You disappeared because you violently assaulted Cora!' Lawrence snapped. 'You laid into her and knocked her for six! What did she say to rile you, Ewert? That he had a bigger dick than you? Is that what she said? That he was better at it? Did he—'

'No! No, none of it! She never said nothing like that!'

'No? Then what did she say? What did she say that made you beat the hell—'

'She never said nothing!' Ewert suddenly shouted. 'She never said nothing because I wasn't even there!' He stopped, looked at Lawrence, then dropped his head in his hands. After a minute or so, he said, 'I was with a woman, at her place. She's called Julie, she works for Cora, a stripper.' He looked up. 'I was there all night, she can back me up.'

Lawrence looked at Judd, then said, 'DC Judd is leaving the room at . . .' He glanced at his watch. '. . . six-fifteen p.m. Check it out, Louis. Where does she live, this Julie of yours?'

Lockhart gave the address.

'Right then, if you weren't even there, then why did you go into hiding? You have been hiding, haven't you, Ewert?'

Lockhart nodded his head.

'For the benefit of the tape, Mr Lockhart is nodding his head. Why, Ewert? Tell me, I don't understand it.'

'This bloke came round Sunday morning, about eight o'clock. I was home, Julie kicked me out early because her old man was due back off his shift. He offered me seven grand to keep my mouth shut, told me that he'd pay for a bed and breakfast, plus expenses, and all I had to do was disappear, lay very low for three to four months, six at the most.'

'But you couldn't disappear, could you, Ewert, you liked the gee-gees too much.' Lawrence shook his head. 'What else did he tell you?'

'He told me it involved Corinne, that's Cora, and that I'd be in big shit with the police if I cocked up. That's all.'

'Did he say who he was?'

'Nah.'

'He never gave you a name?'

'No.'

'Not even for emergencies?'

'No.'

'What about these expenses?'

Lockhart went silent.

'The expenses, Ewert?'

'I collected them from reception at the hotel. They were delivered by a courier, I saw him once.'

'What, a motorbike courier?'

'Yeah.'

Lawrence let out a long, tense breath, then he leant forward and offered Lockhart a cigarette, lighting one of his own at the same time. Got him, he thought, this time we've really got him.

Daniel got off the train at Gatwick and drove straight to Thea's cottage. He called Petula from the car and told her that he'd be out for the evening, then he called Thea and told her he was on his way.

'I think I've cracked it,' he said. 'I'll explain when I see you.' But to his surprise Thea said very little in reply.

It was nearly seven by the time Daniel made it to Tanbry Cottage. He had spent the afternoon getting Maureen Parks's tape copied, then transcribed, and placing both in a safe-deposit box at his bank in Thea's name. As he drove up to the house, the door opened and Thea came out.

'You all right?' Daniel climbed out of the car.

'No, no I'm not. I've had a call from my mother, this afternoon. She said that Cora left her the night before, that she'd been really strange recently, very withdrawn, preoccupied – just strange, and that she . . .' Thea stopped and put her hands up to her face.

'Thea, what is it?' Daniel moved across and embraced her. Despite the worry, her obvious distress, it felt better than anything had done for weeks.

She pulled back. 'Hedda rang because she found this afternoon that her boyfriend's gun is missing and she thinks it might be Cora.'

'What? Why on earth does she think it's Cora?'

'Cora knew where the house key was apparently, he keeps a spare one in a terracotta pot in the garden and there was no sign of a break-in. Plus she had gone, left a note and gone.' Thea's voice rose again in panic. 'She kept talking about justice apparently, justice and retribution! And she left a note saying she was coming home! Oh God, Daniel, I hope she isn't going to do anything stupid! I—'

'Have you called the police?'

'I've rung Dave.'

'Dave?'

'DS Lawrence. He's interviewing a suspect and I can't get hold of him.'

'Won't anyone else do?'

Thea shook her head and Daniel felt a shot of envy that almost took his breath away. 'Ring again.'

'I just have.'

'What about Cora's apartment?'

'I've tried. No reply.'

'Right, get in. Let's go over there and see if she's been back. Have you got a key?'

'Yes.'

'What about Tom?'

'Betty's here.'

'Right, get the key and let's get going.' Thea headed for the house. 'You really think this is serious, do you?' Daniel called. She looked over her shoulder and her face had the answer. Daniel shook his head; this was all he bloody needed! The things you do for love, he thought grimly, and he got back in the car and started the engine.

Cora stood in the phone box across the road from the Higson Wine Bar on the King's Road and watched the party in the window. The party with Jason Wakes in it.

It was Friday night, eight o'clock, and, having been there since opening time, a few of Wakes's group had started to drift away. Wakes had been outside to use his mobile, Cora presumed to call a taxi, so she had her car double-parked, ready, her bag and her golden treasure in the boot.

At eight-fifteen a black cab drew up and Wakes emerged from the bar, unsteady on his feet and helped by a mate. Cora moved out of the phone box and crossed the road. The mate gave her the eye as she passed. She stopped for a moment, supposedly to look for a tissue in her handbag, and heard the friend giving directions to Wakes's weekend place in Horsham.

Cora smiled.

'He's a bit pissed, I'm afraid,' the friend said, 'but here, take his wallet and help yourself to whatever he owes you. He should sober up by the time you get there.'

The driver took the wallet and got out to help Wakes into the cab. Then he got back in and indicated to pull out with Wakes slumped on the back seat.

'Stupid prat,' the friend said to Cora as she turned to recross the road to her car. She smiled at him. Yeah, she thought, stupid prat. She climbed into her car, started the engine and headed off towards Putney and the A3. Stupid dead prat, she thought and then, for the first time in months, she laughed.

Cora's flat in Chichester was as deserted as the last time Thea had been there. Thea took a brief look round, then went back down to Daniel in the car.

'Nothing. She's not been there. Any luck with DS Lawrence?'

'He's still unavailable.'

Thea climbed in and looked at Daniel. 'Crawley police station?' he asked. She nodded and he shifted the car into reverse and turned it round. 'I don't know why I'm doing this,' he said, making a half-hearted attempt to lighten the atmosphere.

Thea put her hand on his arm. 'Yes you do,' she said. At that moment he would have driven her to the moon and back if she'd asked.

DS Lawrence was on the phone when he got the message from the duty sergeant. He glanced at it, carried on with his call, then on replacing the receiver, stood to go downstairs.

'Any luck, Cath?'

'No, but I'm only half-way through.' She was ringing round every courier company in London.

'Good girl, keep at it.'

He stepped out into the corridor.

'Ah, Louis! You there yet with Lockhart?'

'Not yet, boss.' He was working with a police artist to come up with a photofit of the man who'd approached him.

'OK. Look, I'm downstairs with Mrs Marshall, she wants to see me apparently. Let me know when you've got it, OK?'

'Right.'

Lawrence carried on down to reception. He saw Thea through the glass doors and felt that immediate attraction again. She was on her own; Daniel had thought it safer to stay in his car.

'Hello, Thea.'

She turned and he was caught by the distress on her face. 'My God, Thea, are you all right?'

She shook her head. 'Cora left France yesterday and we think she left with a shotgun. There's one missing from the place she was—'

'Boss?'

Lawrence turned. It was Louis Judd. 'Dave, we've had an emergency call come in, the CAD room passed it straight on to me, it's from Wakes's place in Horsham . . .'

Thea gasped.

'He reported a break-in but the line was cut off.'

Lawrence didn't hesitate. 'Have we answered the call?'

'Yes, they're on their way now, we—'

'Armed back-up,' Lawrence said. 'Get it organised, Louis, we might need it. Thea, you stay—'

'No!' Thea interrupted. 'No, I can't stay, I've got to come with you. Cora might be distressed, she might need me.'

Lawrence looked briefly at her and made a snap decision; something he was famous for. 'OK. Let's go. Louis, we'll meet you outside in a couple of minutes, yeah?'

DC Judd nodded and disappeared back into the station. Moments later they were out of the door.

Chapter Twenty-Six

Jason Wakes was slumped on the floor. He cowered, sweating and shaking, hugging his knees and murmuring something Cora couldn't hear. He was pathetic; Cora despised him. Behind him she had blown a hole in the plasterboard wall the size of a dinner plate, surprised at the force of the shotgun. She could see through to the next room and she thought: One shot and I'll plaster his brains all over the wall. Wakes began to whimper.

'Shut up!' Cora snapped. She was sorting through his ties, choosing the best and the most expensive. She had three already, she just needed a fourth and then she was ready. She found it, a red and blue silk Hermès, and smiled.

'Get up,' she said.

Wakes scrambled to his feet, holding on to the wall for support. He'd wet himself when she'd fired the gun and his hand-made Prince of Wales check suit had a damp stain around the crotch.

'Get on to the bed,' Cora ordered, 'and lie down.'

Wakes stared at her. 'What're you going to do?'

Cora bent to pick up the ties. She fingered them lightly in her hands, then looked at him. 'Kill you,' she said. Wakes began to cry. 'Get on the bed!' Cora shouted. Wakes jerked forward and climbed on, his body shaking so much that he had little control over his limbs. 'Lie down,' Cora said. He did, and she watched the water-filled mattress move under the weight of his body.

She moved to his legs, took hold of one ankle and tied it with the silk tie to the corner of the bed frame. She did the same to the other one, then moved up to his head and took one wrist, tying that and twisting the tie so that it hurt. Wakes cried out and Cora smiled again. Moments later he was secure.

Cora walked across to the window and looked out. She held the gun close to her chest, almost caressing it, and saw the flashing blue light from some distance as it moved towards the house. It comforted her, brought her closer to what she had to do. She hadn't ever thought she'd get away with it but she had always known that she'd do it.

'Please,' Wakes cried out. 'Please, Corinne, I'll do anything, anything, please . . .'

He had totally lost control and Cora's anger was so sudden and violent that she wanted to turn and smack him across the face with the gun. She moved forward, gun raised high and stopped herself within seconds. 'Shut up!' she shouted. 'Just shut up or I'll kill you now!'

Wakes clamped his mouth shut and closed his eyes. Cora turned away from the window and began to pace the floor.

Lawrence's car arrived minutes after the patrol car. The two uniformed officers were already in the process of cordoning off the area having been radioed to wait for armed back-up.

'Any sign of movement?' Lawrence asked, climbing out of the car.

'No, nothing. The front door's been forced, it's still open but there's no noise, no movement.'

'Right. Once you've blocked off the area move this vehicle out of here and stay behind the lines, OK?'

Thea had also climbed out of the car and was looking up at the house. Her whole body ached with fear but she knew what she had to do. If Cora was going to stand any sort of chance, she knew exactly what she had to do.

Daniel drove like a maniac. Sitting outside Crawley station, he'd watched a patrol car leave, lights flashing, and then seen Thea get into an unmarked car with Lawrence and follow it. He hadn't given it another thought. He'd shifted into gear and set off in pursuit. Driving at eighty m.p.h., he'd broken every traffic law in the book keeping up with Lawrence, but somehow that just didn't enter his head. Wherever Thea was going he was going too; whatever danger she was going into, she wasn't going into it without him.

Thea waited for her chance. She was back behind the lines listening to Lawrence talking to Cora with the megaphone when she saw Daniel's car. He came haring up the road, his hazard lights flashing, and screeched to a halt behind the patrol car. Lawrence turned, as did both the uniformed officers. 'What the fuck?' Thea ran for it.

Daniel was the only one to see her go. Flinging the door of the car open, he jumped out and ran after her.

'What the fucking hell are you doing?' Lawrence shouted.

'Get the fuck out of—' He broke off and slammed the mega-phone to the floor. 'Jesus Christ!' One of the uniformed officers ran forward but Lawrence stopped him. 'Leave it!' he snapped. He turned to the officer. 'We've got to wait for back-up!' And saying that, he slumped against the car.

'Cora?' Thea was inside the house when Daniel caught her from behind. She let out a short cry and then, seeing it was him, fell against him for a moment and he held her, as tight as he could. She pulled back.

'What the hell are you—'

'I'm the only one she's got,' Thea said quickly. 'I had to.'

'But she's unbalanced, God knows what she might do.'

'Not to me, she won't do anything to me. She trusts me.' Thea turned and headed on through the house. 'Cora?' she called as she went. 'Cora!'

She stopped as they heard a muffled scream.

'Upstairs,' Daniel said. 'She's in the bedroom.' He ran towards the stairs and Thea ran after him.

'Cora!' They both stood by the door of the main bedroom – the only one shut – and Thea put her face up against the highly glossed wood. 'Cora, it's me. Open the door, please. Open the door and talk to me.'

There was a silence but they could hear whimpering and Thea found herself silently praying that they weren't too late.

'Cora, please, open the door, I want to talk to you.'

Again there was a silence, then from the other side of the door, Cora said, 'What's the point?'

Thea let out a breath. An answer, and she'd moved to the door.

'Listen to me, Cora,' Thea said. 'You mustn't do anything. Please, you must stay calm. Something's already happened, there've been developments with your case and . . .' Thea suddenly found herself faltering. She was scared, her nerve was failing her and she just wanted to weep. 'Cora?' she whispered, 'Cora, please don't . . .'

'Cora?' Daniel put his mouth close to the door. 'My name is Daniel Ellis, Cora, I'm a barrister and I've been looking into your case. I've found a few things out, I've found out that Jason Wakes has done this before, he raped another girl, her name was Kate, only no one has ever found out about it, Cora, because Kate has been too frightened to come forward. She was terrified, Cora, just like you've been, but not any more. She's going to the police, Cora, she's been encouraged by you, by your story and your bravery and she's going to the police. He won't get away with it, Cora, not with your rape or—'

'It's a lie!' Wakes suddenly screamed out. 'It's a fucking lie, Ellis, and you know it!'

'Shut up!' Cora shouted.

Thea closed her eyes and murmured a prayer over and over, under her breath.

'It's not a lie, Cora,' Daniel said gently, 'and I can tell you something else: he's been bribing people, or at least his father has, to keep quiet about it, he's been—'

'I never!' Wakes cried out. 'I never did anything, I never touched . . .'

Cora raised the gun. Wakes began to sob as she walked away from the door, the gun aimed at his groin.

'Oh God no, please God, don't, oh God, please God, oh God, dear God . . . NO!'

She fired.

There was the massive sound of a gunshot, it seemed to explode out of the room and Daniel hurled himself at the door. He fell through it and ran at Cora, knocking her to the ground. As he hit it a torrent of water washed over him and he had to struggle to breathe. 'Jesus . . . Cora, are you . . .'

Thea ran into the room and gallons of water poured over her feet, knocking her off balance and flooding down towards the stairs. She grabbed the wall and stared down, momentarily confused, then she turned to the bed. She saw Wakes. A huge hole had been blown out of the water bed between his legs and he was crying, straining at the arms and legs to get free.

'Are you—?' She stopped; he was intact and she turned away. 'Cora?' Cora was with Daniel, he was cradling her like a child and she was crying, great noisy sobs racking her body. Thea knelt by them and gently Daniel eased Cora towards her friend, freeing himself and getting to his feet. He headed towards the door with no time to waste.

'You won't get away with this, Ellis!' Wakes shouted from the bed. 'I'll have you disbarred, you bastard! And I'll get that bitch, I'll—'

Daniel knew the police were on their way in, but he couldn't leave it. He darted back to Wakes and put his face an inch from Jason's. 'That is the last threat you will ever make, Mr Wakes,' he said coolly. 'You will not "get" Cora because she has got you. It's over, Jason, she'll get a suspended sentence for an illegal firearm and you'll get fifteen years, possibly more if I know the judge. And as for me, you won't get me disbarred, young man, because I wasn't here.' He stood up. 'Was I, Thea? Cora?'

Thea glanced up and shook her head. And as footsteps came running into the hall, he turned and walked away.

'Daniel?' Thea called. 'Daniel, wait!' She left Cora for a moment and ran after him. 'Daniel, can I see you, I mean, tonight, in the drive? Will you call for me, throw stones up at the window . . .'

'No,' he said. There was no going back for him. Thea looked at his face and saw that. She closed her eyes and in that moment she felt as if she'd lost everything.

'But you can come to the beach,' he said, 'with me and Petula and the boys and you can bring Tom and Cora, if she's up to it. Tomorrow, at eleven, beach hut number twenty-seven at West Wittering.'

She had opened her eyes and the tears in them spilt out and ran down her face.

'I love you,' he said. 'It's time to move on, Thea.' And with that, he walked out, past Lawrence and his armed back-up, down the stairs and out of the house. There was a move to stop him but Lawrence intervened. He had a hunch about that man, he didn't know what it was but something told Lawrence that it was best to let him go. Perhaps it was a bad decision but he doubted it.

After all, today was his lucky day.